Gold Strike

TIGER AND I WORKED midway along the bank. We heard Gentle Annie scream and we looked quick to see a big chunk of the bank—about a wheelbarrow load—break loose and cascade around her. Still shrieking in surprise, she jumped back and narrowly missed being hit by the slide.

She fell and Tiger and I sprinted to help her. She was sitting up when we got there, staring at the bank like she was in a trance. I thought maybe she'd got walloped in the head. "You okay, Annie?" I yelled.

She just sat there, eyes upturned at the bank above her. "Yeah. Yeah. I'm all right. But, Sweet Jesus, would you look at that!"

Tiger and I tore our eyes from her to the bank and what held her attention; the slide had exposed a vein of almost pure gold running several yards long and a half to three-quarters of an inch thick and imbedded in the crumbly granite probably deeper than we could imagine. It was the strike I had a hunch was there all along. My breath jammed in my throat. That pure gold would come out of there like slabs of peanut brittle.

Tiger looked at me. "We got to talk this over."

—from "We'll Kill the Old Red Rooster
When She Comes"
by R. C. House

New Trails

Twenty-three Original Stories
of the West from Western
Writers of America

EDITED BY JOHN JAKES AND
MARTIN H. GREENBERG

Introduction by John Jakes

BANTAM BOOKS
New York   Toronto   London   Sydney   Auckland

This edition contains the complete text of the original hardcover edition.
NOT ONE WORD HAS BEEN OMITTED.

NEW TRAILS

A Bantam Book / published by arrangement with Doubleday

PUBLISHING HISTORY
Doubleday edition published November 1994
Bantam edition / December 1995

Page 355 constitutes an extension of this copyright page.

ISBN 0-553-57316-0

Published simultaneously in the United States and Canada

Bantam Books are published by Bantam Books, a division of Bantam Doubleday Dell Publishing Group, Inc. Its trademark, consisting of the words "Bantam Books" and the portrayal of a rooster, is Registered in U.S. Patent and Trademark Office and in other countries. Marca Registrada. Bantam Books, 1540 Broadway, New York, New York 10036.

PRINTED IN THE UNITED STATES OF AMERICA

RAD   0   9   8   7   6   5   4   3   2   1

Contents

Introduction

You are about to set out on a journey into virgin territory. This is a collection of new, never-before-published short stories by members of Western Writers of America. Each story comes from a certified professional, because only pros are eligible to join the national organization. There hasn't been an anthology like this one in twenty or thirty years (that I know about, anyway).

But there's something even more exciting. This book not only presents writers whose successful careers span several decades—Elmore Leonard and Elmer Kelton are notable examples—but also presents stories from a new generation of writers taking the western in new directions.

The work of these strong, fresh voices frankly came as something of a revelation to me, and to my co-editor and friend, Dr. Martin H. Greenberg, after we issued a call for material over a year ago.

Yes, we received, and chose, any number of traditional westerns—stories that descend directly from masters such as Zane Grey and Louis L'Amour. But there were fewer of this kind than we expected, and fewer utilizing the historic West, though these are represented. Among the history-based submissions, several involved Custer and events central or peripheral to the Little Big Horn massacre—an interesting comment on what still fascinates writers.

Along with traditional stories—the kind Marty and I have enjoyed for years—a great many came in that made us blink. Strong and interesting trends became apparent.

First, more women are writing westerns—and writing them from a woman's perspective. No more hiding behind initials, as Dorothy Johnson did when she was "D. M. Johnson." Understandably, this was her defense against a backlash of male chauvinism from readers and editors. To this new wave of feminine subjects and perceptions in the western, we say hurrah.

Next, more stories are being written about Native American characters. No longer are Indians the stereotypical bad guys. Another turn for the better.

Finally, we received a large number of stories set in the contemporary West. This kind of tale has already whipped up a tempest within WWA; some members insist that "real" western stories can only be set in the years from 1865 to about 1900. Marty and I have a more inclusive view; we have included several contemporary pieces.

But why this kind of collection at all?

For some years, the West as a subject for short stories, novels, feature films, TV movies-of-the-week, drifted into a sort of limbo. In Hollywood, where the western was once a staple, it was all at once taboo; killed off, some say, by the special effects and razzle-dazzle novelty of films such as *Star Wars*.

The perception that westerns were passé was suddenly challenged by the extraordinary ratings of the *Lonesome*

Dove miniseries. To this was added a huge box office and crossover audience (people from many age groups) for *Dances with Wolves*.

Then came the watershed summer of 1992: Michael Mann's spellbinding visualization of *The Last of the Mohicans*, plus Clint Eastwood's *Unforgiven*, immediately labeled a classic. Both pictures were hits. As a result, there are presently twenty-five or thirty theater and TV westerns ready for air, in production, or in development.

Which only proves what a lot of us knew all along: on the page or the screen, the western never really lost its appeal. Some people just thought it did.

Dale Walker, current president of WWA, put it this way in a column in the *Rocky Mountain News:*

> The West is *not* dead, my friends—though there seems to be a small cottage industry, centered mostly among academic critics of American literature, dedicated to pronouncing, with a suspicious level of glee, the death of the western. These premature burial notices, cropping up with regularity in books, popular magazines and scholarly journals, are written by western history reconstructionists, political correctness drones and certain other scholar-morticians who seek to embalm western fiction without first checking its pulse.

Dale wrote that in the fateful summer of '92.

Through the lean times, a few publishers such as Doubleday and Bantam Books continued to believe there was an audience for the well-done western novel. Bantam author Louis L'Amour demonstrated it resoundingly during the later years of his long career.

Because I'd like to see the western short story make a comeback too, I proposed doing this book. Markets for shorts are almost nonexistent today, save for the new *Louis L'Amour Western Magazine*.

Doubleday and Bantam backed the idea; Marty Greenberg, who has edited something over five hundred anthologies as of this date, enthusiastically signed on as co-editor; and we issued our invitation to members of WWA to send us their best.

You're holding the result. It mixes traditional stories by old hands with westerns by newer authors who have responded to a changing world with changing creative approaches.

So if you've been hankering for some western tales in shorter lengths, you've come to the right book.

Read on!

—JOHN JAKES
October 1993

"Hurrah for Capt. Early"

Elmore Leonard

THE SECOND BANNER said "HERO OF SAN JUAN HILL." Both were tied to the upstairs balcony of the Congress Hotel and looked down on La Salle Street in Sweetmary, a town named for a copper mine. The banners read across the building as a single statement. This day that Captain Early was expected home from the war in Cuba, over now these two months, was October 10, 1898.

The manager of the hotel and one of his desk clerks were the first to observe the colored man who entered the lobby and dropped his bedroll on the red velvet settee where it seemed he was about to sit down. Bold as brass. A tall, well-built colored man wearing a suit of clothes that looked new and appeared to fit him as though it might possibly be his own and not one handed down to him. He wore the suit, a stiff collar and a necktie. With the manager nearby but not yet aware of the intruder, the young desk clerk spoke up, raised his voice to tell the person, "You can't sit down there."

The colored man turned his attention to the desk, taking a moment before he said, "Why is that?"

His quiet tone caused the desk clerk to hesitate and look over at the manager, who stood holding the day's mail, letters that had arrived on the El Paso & Southwestern morning run along with several guests now registered at the hotel and, apparently, this colored person. It was hard to tell his age, other than to say he was no longer a young man. He did seem clean and his bedroll was done up in bleached canvas.

"A hotel lobby," the desk clerk said, "is not a public place anyone can make theirself at home in. What is it you want here?"

At least he was uncovered, standing there now hat in hand. But then he said, "I'm waiting on Bren Early."

"*Bren* is it," the desk clerk said. "Captain Early's an acquaintance of yours?"

"We go way back a ways."

"You worked for him?"

"Some."

At this point the manager said, "We're all waiting for Captain Early. Why don't you go out front and watch for him?" Ending the conversation.

The desk clerk—his name was Monty—followed the colored man to the front entrance and stepped out on the porch to watch him, bedroll over his shoulder, walking south on La Salle the two short blocks to Fourth Street. Monty returned to the desk, where he said to the manager, "He walked right in the Gold Dollar."

The manager didn't look up from his mail.

Two riders from the Circle-Eye, a spread on the San Pedro that delivered beef to the mine company, were at a table with their glasses of beer: a rider named Macon and a rider named Wayman, young men who wore sweat-stained hats down on their eyes as they stared at the Negro. Right there, the bartender speaking to him as he poured a whiskey, still speaking as the colored man drank it and the bartender poured him another one. Macon asked Wayman if he had ever seen a nigger wearing a suit of clothes and a necktie. Wayman said he couldn't recall. When they finished drinking their beer and walked up to the bar, the colored man gone now, Macon asked the bartender who in the hell that smoke thought he was coming in here. "You would think," Macon said, "he'd go to one of the places where the miners drink."

The bartender appeared to smile, for some reason finding humor in Macon's remark. He said, "Boys, that was Bo Catlett. I imagine Bo drinks just about wherever he feels like drinking."

"Why?" Macon asked it, surprised. "He suppose to be somebody?"

"Bo lives up at White Tanks," the bartender told him, "at the Indin agency. Went to war and now he's home."

Macon squinted beneath the hat brim funneled low on his eyes. He said, "Nobody told me they was niggers in the war." Sounding as though it was the bartender's fault he hadn't been informed. When the bartender didn't add anything to help him out, Macon said, "Wayman's brother Wyatt was in the war, with Teddy Roosevelt's Rough Riders. Only Wyatt didn't come home like the nigger."

Wayman, about eighteen years old, was nodding his head now.

Because nothing about this made sense to Macon, it was becoming an irritation. Again he said to Wayman, "You ever see a smoke wearing a suit of clothes like that?" He said, "Je-sus Christ."

Bo Catlett walked up La Salle Street favoring his left leg some, though the limp, caused by a Mauser bullet or by the regimental surgeon who cut it out of his hip, was barely noticeable. He stared at the sight of the mine works against the sky, ugly, but something monumental about it: straight ahead up the grade, the main shaft scaffolding and company buildings, the crushing mill lower down, ore tailings that humped this way in ridges on down the slope to run out at the edge of town. A sorry place, dark and forlorn; men walked up the grade from boardinghouses on Mill Street to spend half their life underneath the ground, buried before they were dead. Three whiskeys in him, Catlett returned to the hotel on the corner of Second Street, looked up at the sign that said "HURRAH FOR CAPT. EARLY" and had to grin. "THE HERO OF SAN JUAN HILL" my ass.

Catlett mounted the steps to the porch, where he dropped his bedroll and took one of the rocking chairs all in a row, the porch empty, close on noon but nobody sitting out here, no drummers calling on La Salle Mining of New Jersey, the company still digging and scraping but running low on payload copper, operating only the day shift now. The rocking chairs, all dark green, needed painting. Man, but made of cane and comfortable with that nice squeak back and forth, back and forth . . . Bo Catlett watched two riders coming this way up the street, couple of cowboys . . . Catlett wondering how many times he had sat down in a real chair since April twenty-fifth when war was declared and he left Arizona to go looking for his old regiment, trailed them to Fort Assinniboine in the Department of the Dakotas, then clear across the country to Camp Chickamauga in Georgia and on down to Tampa where he caught up with them and Lt. John Pershing looked at his twenty-four years of service and put him up for squadron sergeant major. It didn't seem like any twenty-four years . . .

Going back to when he joined the First Kansas Colored Volunteers in '63, age fifteen. Wounded at Honey Springs the same year. Guarded Rebel prisoners at Rock Island, took part in the occupation of Galveston. Then after the war got sent out here to join the all-Negro 10th Cavalry on frontier station, Arizona Territory, and deal with hostile Apaches. In '87 went to Mexico with Lt. Brendan Early out of Fort Huachuca—Bren and a contract guide named Dana Moon, now the agent at the White Tanks reservation—brought back a one-eyed Mimbreño named Loco, brought back a white woman the renegade Apache had run off with—and Dana Moon later married—and they all got their pictures in some newspapers. Mustered out that same year, '87 . . . Drove a wagon for Capt. Early Hunting Expeditions Incorporated before going to work for Dana at White Tanks. He'd be sitting on Dana's porch this evening with a glass of mescal and Dana would say, "Well, now you've seen the elephant I don't imagine you'll want to stay around here." He'd tell Dana he saw the elephant a long time ago and wasn't too impressed. Just then another voice, not Dana's, said out loud to him:

"So you was in the war, huh?"

It was one of the cowboys. He sat his mount, a little claybank quarter horse, close to the porch rail, sat leaning on the pommel to show he was at ease, his hat low on his eyes staring directly at Catlett in his rocking chair. The other one sat his mount, a bay, more out in the street, maybe holding back. This boy was not at ease but fidgety. Catlett remembered them in the Gold Dollar.

Now the one close said, "What was it you did over there in Cuba?"

Meaning a colored man. What did a colored man do. Like most people the boy not knowing anything about Negro soldiers in the war. This one squinting at him had size and maybe got his way enough he believed he could say whatever he pleased, or use a tone of voice that would irritate the person addressed. As he did just now.

"What did I do over there?" Catlett said. "What everybody did, I was in the war."

"You wrangle stock for the Rough Riders?"

"Where'd you get that idea?"

"I asked you a question. Is that what you did, tend their stock?"

Once Catlett decided to remain civil and maybe this boy would go away, he said, "There wasn't no stock. The Rough Riders, *even* the Rough Riders, were afoot. The only people had horses were artillery, pulling caissons with their Hotchkiss guns and the coffee grinders, what they called the Gatling guns. Lemme see," Catlett said, "they had some mules, too, but I didn't tend anybody's stock."

"His brother was a Rough Rider," Macon said, raising one hand to hook his thumb at Wayman. "Served with Colonel Teddy Roosevelt and got killed in an ambush—the only way greasers know how to fight. I like to hear what you people were doing while his brother Wyatt was getting killed."

You people. Look at him trying to start a fight.

"You believe it was my fault he got killed?"

"I asked you what you were doing."

It wasn't even this kid's business. Catlett thinking, Well, see if you can educate him, and said, "Las Guásimas. You ever hear of it?"

The kid stared with his eyes half shut. Suspicious, or letting you know he's serious, Catlett thought. Keen-eyed and mean; you're not gonna put anything past him.

"What's it, a place over there?"

"That's right, Las Guásimas, the place where it happened. On the way to Santiago de Coo-ba. Sixteen men killed that day, mostly by rifle fire, and something like fifty wounded. Except it wasn't what you said, the dons pulling an ambush. It was more the Rough Riders walking along not looking where they was going."

The cowboy, Macon, said, "Je-sus Christ, you saying the Rough Riders didn't know what they were *do*ing?" Like this was something impossible to believe.

"They mighta had an idea *what* they was doing," Catlett said, "only thing it wasn't what they *shoulda* been doing." He said, "You understand the difference?" And thought, What're you explaining it to him for? The boy giving him that mean look again, ready to defend the Rough Riders.

All right, he was so proud of Teddy's people, why hadn't he been over there with them?

"Look," Catlett said, using a quiet tone now, "the way it was, the dons had sharpshooters in these trees, a thicket of mangoes and palm trees growing wild you couldn't see into. You understand? Had men hidden in there were expert with the rifle, these Mausers they used with smokeless powder. Teddy's people come along a ridge was all covered with these trees and run into the dons, see, the dons letting some of the Rough Riders pass and then closing in on 'em. So, yeah, it was an ambush in a way." Catlett paused. "We was down on the road, once we caught up, moving in the same direction." He paused again, remembering something the cowboy said that bothered him. "There's nothing wrong with an ambush—like say you think it ain't *fair?* If you can set it up and keep your people behind cover, do it. There was a captain with the Rough Riders said he believed an officer should never take cover, should stand out there and be an example to his men. The captain said, 'There ain't a Spanish bullet made that can kill me.' Stepped out in the open and got shot in the head."

A couple of cowboys looking like the two who were mounted had come out of the Chinaman's picking their teeth and now stood by to see what was going on. Some people who had come out of the hotel were standing along the steps.

Catlett took all this in as he paused again, getting the words straight in his mind to tell how they left the road, some companies of the Tenth and the First, all regular Army, went up the slope laying down fire and run off the dons before the Rough Riders got cut to pieces, the Rough Riders volunteers and not experienced in all kind of situations—the reason they didn't know shit about advancing through hostile country or, get right down to it, what they were doing in Cuba, these people that come looking for glory and got served sharpshooters with Mausers and mosquitos carrying yellow fever. Tell these cowboys the true story. General Wheeler, "Fightin' Joe" from the Confederate side in the Civil War now thirty-three years later an old man with a white beard; sees the Spanish pulling back at Las Guásimas and says, "Boys, we got the Yankees on the run." Man like that directing a battle . . .

Tell the *whole* story if you gonna tell it, go back to sitting in the hold of the ship in Port Tampa a month, not allowed to go ashore for fear of causing incidents with white people who didn't want the men of the Tenth coming in their stores and cafés, running off their customers. Tell them—so we land in Cuba at a place called Daiquiri . . . saying in his mind then, Listen to me now. Was the Tenth at Daiquiri, the Ninth at Siboney. Experienced cavalry regiments that come off frontier station after thirty years dealing with hostile renegades, cutthroat horse thieves, reservation jumpers, land in Cuba and they put us to work unloading the ships while Teddy's people march off to meet the enemy and win some medals, yeah, and would've been wiped out at El Caney and on San Juan Hill if the colored boys hadn't come along and saved Colonel Teddy's ass and all his Rough Rider asses, showed them how to go up a hill and take a blockhouse. Saved them so the Rough Riders could become America's heroes.

All this in Bo Catlett's head and the banners welcoming Capt. Early hanging over him.

One of the cowboys from the Chinaman's must've asked what was going on, because now the smart aleck one brought his claybank around and began talking to them, glancing back at the porch now and again with his mean look. The two from the Chinaman's stood with their thumbs in their belts, while the mounted cowboy had his hooked around his suspenders now. None of them wore a gunbelt or appeared to be armed. Now the two riders stepped down from their mounts and followed the other two along the street to a place called the Belle Alliance, a miners' saloon, and went inside.

Bo Catlett was used to mean dirty looks and looks of indifference, a man staring at him as though he wasn't even there. Now the thing with white people, they had a hard time believing colored men fought in the war. You never saw a colored man on a U.S. Army recruiting poster or a picture of colored soldiers in newspapers. White people believed colored people could not be relied on in war. But why? There were some colored people that went out and killed wild animals, even lions, with a spear. No gun, a spear. And made hats out of the manes. See a colored man standing there in front of a lion coming at him fast as a train running down grade, stands there with his spear, doesn't move, and they say colored men can't be relied on?

There was a story in newspapers how when Teddy Roosevelt was at the Hill, strutting around in the open, he saw colored troopers going back to the rear and he drew his revolver and threatened to shoot them—till he found out they were going after ammunition. His own Rough Riders were pinned down in the guinea grass, the Spanish sharpshooters picking at them from up in the blockhouses. So the Tenth showed the white boys how to go up the hill angry, firing and yelling, making noise, set on driving the garlics clean from the hill . . .

Found Bren Early and his company lying in the weeds, the scrub—that's all it was up that hill, scrub and sand, hard to get a footing in places; nobody ran all the way up, it was get-up a ways and stop to fire, covering each other. Found Bren Early with a whistle in his mouth. He got up and started blowing it and waving his sword—come on, boys, to glory—and a Mauser bullet smacked him in the butt, on account of the way he was turned to his people, and Bren Early grunted, dropped his sword and went down in the scrub to lay there cursing his luck, no doubt mortified to look like he got shot going the wrong way. Bo Catlett didn't believe Bren saw him pick up the sword. Picked it up, waved it at the Rough Riders and his Tenth Cav troopers, and they all went up that hill together, his troopers yelling, some of them singing, actually singing "They'll Be a Hot Time in the Old Town Tonight." Singing and shooting, honest to God, scaring the dons right out of their blockhouse. It was up on the crest Catlett got shot in his right hip and was taken to the Third Cav dressing station. It was set up on the Aguadores River at a place called "bloody ford" being it was under fire till the Hill was captured. Catlett remembered holding on to the sword, tight, while the regimental surgeon dug the bullet out of him and he tried hard not to scream, biting his mouth till it bled. After, he was sent home and spent a month at Camp Wikoff, near Montauk out on Long Island, with a touch of yellow fever. Saw President McKinley when he came by September third and made a speech, the President saying what they did over there in Cuba "commanded the unstinted praise of all your countrymen." Till he walked away from Montauk and came back into the world Sgt. Major Catlett actually did believe he and the other members of the Tenth would be recognized as war heroes.

He wished Bren would hurry up and get here. He'd ask the hero of San Juan Hill how his heinie was and if he was getting much unstinted praise. If Bren didn't come pretty soon, Catlett decided he'd see him another time. Get a horse out of the livery and ride it up to White Tanks.

The four Circle-Eye riders sat at a front table in the Belle Alliance with a bottle of Green River whiskey, Macon staring out the window. The hotel was across the street and up the block a ways, but Macon could see it, the colored man in the suit of clothes still sitting on the porch, if he tilted his chair back and held on to the window sill. He said, "No sir, nobody told me they was niggers in the war."

Wayman said to the other two Circle-Eye riders, "Macon can't get over it."

Macon's gaze came away from the window. "It was *your* brother got killed."

Wayman said, "I know he did."

Macon said, "You don't care?"

The Circle-Eye riders watched him let his chair come down to hit the floor hard. They watched him get up without another word and walk out.

"I never thought much of coloreds," one of the Circle-Eye riders said, "but you never hear me take on about 'em like Macon. What's his trouble?"

"I guess he wants to shoot somebody," Wayman said. "The time he shot that chilipicker in Nogales? Macon worked hisself up to it the same way."

Catlett watched the one that was looking for a fight come out through the doors and go to the claybank, the reins looped once around the tie rail. He didn't touch the reins though. What he did was reach into a saddle bag and bring out what Catlett judged to be a Colt .44 pistol. Right then he heard:

"Only guests of the hotel are allowed to sit out here."

Catlett watched the cowboy checking his loads now, turning the cylinder of his six-shooter, the metal catching a glint of light from the sun, though the look of the pistol was dull and appeared to be an old model.

Monty the desk clerk, standing there looking at Catlett without getting too close, said, "You'll have to leave . . . right now."

The cowboy was looking this way.

Making up his mind, Catlett believed. All right, now, yeah, he's made it up.

"Did you hear what I said?"

Catlett took time to look at Monty and then pointed off down the street. He said, "You see that young fella coming this way with the pistol? He think he like to shoot me. Say you don't allow people to sit here aren't staying at the hotel. How about, you allow them to get shot if they not a guest?"

He watched the desk clerk, who didn't seem to know whether to shit or go blind, eyes wide open, turn and run back in the lobby.

The cowboy, Macon, stood in the middle of the street now holding the six-shooter against his leg.

—————

Catlett, still seated in the rocker, said, "You a mean rascal, ain't you? Don't take no sass, huh?"

The cowboy said something agreeing that Catlett didn't catch, the cowboy looking over to see his friends coming up the street now from the barroom. When he looked at the hotel porch again, Catlett was standing at the railing, his bedroll upright next to him leaning against it.

"I can be a mean rascal, too," Catlett said, unbuttoning his suitcoat. "I want you to know that before you take this too far. You understand?"

"You insulted Colonel Roosevelt and his Rough Riders," the cowboy said, "and you insulted Wayman's brother, killed in action over there in Cuba."

"How come," Catlett said, "you weren't there?"

"I was ready, don't worry, when the war ended. But we're talking about *you*. I say you're a dirty lying nigger and have no respect for people better'n you are. I want you to apologize to the Colonel and his men and to Wayman's dead brother . . ."

"Or what?" Catlett said.

"Answer to me," the cowboy said. "Are you armed? You aren't, you better get yourself a pistol."

"You want to shoot me," Catlett said, " 'cause I went to Cuba and you didn't."

The cowboy was shaking his head. " 'Cause you lied. Have you got a pistol or not?"

Catlett said, "You calling me out, huh? You want us to fight a duel?"

"Less you apologize. Else get a pistol."

"But if I'm the one being called out, I have my choice of weapons, don't I? That's how I seen it work, twenty-four years in the U.S. Army in two wars. You hear what I'm saying?"

The cowboy was frowning now beneath his hat brim, squinting up at Bo Catlett. He said, "Pistols, it's what you use."

Catlett nodded. "If I say so."

"Well, what else is there?"

Confused and getting a mean look.

Catlett slipped his hand into the upright end of his bedroll and began to tug at something inside—the cowboy watching, the Circle-Eye riders in the street watching, the desk clerk and manager in the doorway and several hotel guests near them who had come out to the porch, all watching as Catlett drew a sword from the bedroll, a cavalry saber, the curved blade flashing as it caught the sunlight. He came past the people watching and down off the porch toward the cowboy in his hat and boots fixed with spurs that chinged as he turned to face Catlett, shorter than Catlett, appearing confused again holding the six-shooter at his side.

"If I choose to use sabers," Catlett said, "is that agreeable with you?"

"I don't have no *saber.*"

Meanness showing now in his eyes.

"Well, you best get one."

"I never even had a sword in my hand."

Irritated. Drunk, too, his eyes not focusing as they should. Now he was looking over his shoulder at the Circle-Eye riders, maybe wanting them to tell him what to do.

One of them, not Wayman but one of the others, called out, "You got your .44 in your hand, ain't you? What're you waiting on?"

Catlett raised the saber to lay the tip against Macon's breastbone, saying to him, "You use your pistol and I use steel? All right, if that's how you want it. See if you can shoot me 'fore this blade is sticking out your back. You game? . . . Speak up, boy."

In the hotel dining room having a cup of coffee, Catlett heard the noise outside, the cheering that meant Capt. Early had arrived. Catlett waited. He wished one of the waitresses would refill his cup, but they weren't around now, nobody was. A half hour passed before Capt. Early entered the dining room and came over to the table, leaving the people he was with. Catlett rose and they embraced, the hotel people and guests watching. It was while they stood this way that Bren saw, over Catlett's shoulder, the saber lying on the table, the curved steel on white linen. Catlett sat down. Bren looked closely at the saber's hilt. He picked it up and there was applause from the people watching. The captain bowed to them and sat down with the sergeant major.

"You went up the hill with this?"

"Somebody had to."

"I'm being recommended for a medal. 'For courage and pluck in continuing to advance under fire on the Spanish fortified position at the battle of Las Guásimas, Cuba, June 24, 1898.'"

Catlett nodded. After a moment he said, "Will you tell me something? What was that war about?"

"You mean why'd we fight the dons?"

"Yeah, tell me."

"To free the oppressed Cuban people. Relieve them of Spanish domination."

"That's what I thought."

"You didn't know why you went to war?"

"I guess I knew," Catlett said. "I just wasn't sure."

To Challenge
a Legend

ALBERT BUTLER

THE NOSE OF THE BULLET had flattened against the bone. I took it from the shelf, holding the misshapen .45 slug in the palm of my hand, thinking of the pain it had caused all these years. And I had been the cause of it.

Tears came to my eyes even now as my thoughts went back to that time, waiting with my mother on the depot platform, for the 12:15 train . . .

Whoooo . . . oooo came the distant sound. Soon the engine burst into view, around the curve by the river, smoke puffing from its stack, streaming back over the mail and baggage and passenger cars. With a flare of steam, the whistle pounded my ears and the platform vibrated, and when the last note faded, I could hear the rhythmic clanging of the engine's bell, the screeching of brakes.

I felt a hand on my shoulder and I looked up and my father was standing beside me looking so handsome in his station agent uniform. He smiled at me and I thought for sure I'd be a railroad man when I grew up. But the train had stopped and two women got off the first passenger car and then I saw Grandpa Hawke and I knew I wanted to be just like him.

Someone shouted something from a car two or three back and my grandfather stopped and looked that way. I couldn't see who it was because of the baggage cart on the platform and then Grandpa saw us and waved and hurried toward us.

I remember he hugged my mother and kissed her on the cheek and said, "You're beautiful as ever, Prissy Powell." He tousled my hair. "How are you, Billy?" He shook hands with my father and I swelled with pride when he turned back to me and said, "My—you're getting to be a big young man."

Since we lived only three blocks away, we walked home. Grandfather carried his heavy carpetbag; he let me carry a small but quite heavy leather bag. Father said he'd bring a large package wrapped in heavy brown paper when he came home.

I had seen my grandfather only once before and I didn't remember him very well. He and Mother talked a long time to "catch up" as she called it. My grandmother Hawke had died when Mother was born, so she grew up living with the Fields, her grandparents.

"Well, young man, we need to get acquainted," Grandfather said at last. "Come on up while I unpack."

"Yes, sir," I said. "I'll be right there."

I ran to my room and got *the* book. I stopped a moment at the top of the stairs to catch my breath. Grandfather heard me and called, "Come on in, Billy."

He'd put his derby hat on the bureau along with his tie. "Making myself comfortable," he said, taking off his coat and vest. "Can you reach high enough to hang these up?"

"Yes, sir."

The room only got used when someone came to stay and I looked around for a place to put *the* book. A big old trunk sat in one corner so I laid the book there.

After we got his clothes put away, he sat in a chair next to the bed and patted the cover. "Come sit here and tell me about school—about yourself."

"Yes, sir."

I couldn't wait any longer. I didn't want to talk about me. I got *the* book from the trunk and came and sat down on the bed. "Grandpa—I've read these stories so many times I know them almost word-for-word."

The wrinkled cover showed a drawing of my grandfather with a gun in each hand belching flames. It didn't look much like him because in the drawing his mustache was bigger and he wore a big broad-brimmed hat and a vest with a star pinned on it. The title said *The Exploits of Ross Hawke: Frontier Marshal* by Ned Buntline.

He took the book from me and held it at arm's length and said, "I didn't think any of these were still around."

"Yes, sir. I got it last year when we lived in Omaha. A kid in my school had it and he didn't believe it was about my grandfather. I traded him a mouth organ for it."

Grandpa Hawke reached for a pair of glasses on the bureau and put them on. He looked at the book's cover, thumbed through a few pages before giving it back to me. "Billy—these are mostly just stories. Made-up stories."

I remember that I felt shocked when he said that. "But you—you were a marshal like it says."

Grandpa nodded. "I only met Ned Buntline once. Talked maybe an hour. Not even his real name. Judson. Something like that."

"He says you were a marshal in Ellsworth and Abilene and Wichita. And a U.S. deputy marshal for Judge Parker."

Grandpa took his glasses off. "Buntline was right about that. Now all those things he said I did—well, they're pretty farfetched. I guess folks get some pleasure from reading them."

Grandpa put his glasses back on the bureau. "You take

Bill Cody—he's quite a man, but Ned Buntline's stories made him into a myth. Now I'm just *me*. Walking the streets, waiting around to head off trouble before it starts; riding long miles through the Nations isn't very exciting, Billy. If someone wrote about those things, no one would read it."

"What about that time in Abilene? When you faced those seven Texas men all alone?" I found the chapter headed OUTDRAWS SEVEN DESPERADOES. "It says Marshal Hawke drew both guns before any of those 'seven murderous desperadoes' hands touched the butts of their weapons.'"

"First, Billy, there were five men, not seven. Second, I never carried two guns. Third, those men were trail hands. One, Adam Schmitz, owned the herd they'd driven up from Texas. The City Council passed an ordinance making it illegal to carry a gun in town and they didn't like it. The year before, the men had pretty much had their way, hurrahing the town—riding up and down the streets firing their guns. I told them we wanted them to have a good time, but they'd have to check their guns in the marshal's office until they were ready to leave for their camp outside of town, or home.

"Well, one of the hands said, 'Marshal, you care to count, you see five of us and one of you, so what's it going to be?' I simply told him whatever happened I figured I could get off one shot and they'd have to bury their boss, Adam Schmitz, or pack his body all the way back to Texas. So Schmitz said to his men he thought it best they comply and they all went in the office and left their guns and we didn't have any trouble."

I remember sitting there on the bed, wide-eyed, and I said, "Weren't you scared, Grandpa?"

"You bet. I don't think those men were feeling all that good right at the moment either. They were hard-working ranch hands, not desperadoes, and they knew I meant what I said."

"What about that time in the Indian Nations when you

rode into that camp where there were a dozen outlaws and you told them they were under arrest and they pulled their guns and you shot four of them and the rest surrendered?"

Grandpa didn't say anything for a moment. "A dozen?" He glanced at the Ned Buntline book on the bed beside me. "I never did read all of that nonsense. A dozen men? Well, Billy, to show you how smart I was, I didn't even see that camp. In fact, I would have ridden on past if those men hadn't taken a shot at me. I didn't have any place to hide and I turned my horse and rode in and they were shooting and I shot back." He shook his head. "A *dozen* men! Two. There were two, Billy. One was only seventeen. I always felt bad about that."

I hopped off the bed. "Grandpa! I'll be right back."

I ran downstairs to my room and reached under the pillow for the wooden revolver my father had made for me. Now as I remember it was only a flat piece of wood cut with a grip and a hole for the trigger guard, the barrel partly rounded. Proudly, I ran back upstairs and handed it to Grandpa Hawke. "Well, Billy," he said, "this is a good-looking revolver. A Colt?"

"Yes, sir. Just like yours."

When he gave it back, I said, "Grandpa, can I see your revolver?"

"Mine? Where would it be?"

I pointed to the leather bag I'd carried from the train depot.

Grandpa Hawke just looked at me without saying anything. Finally he got up and unstrapped the bag that he'd left on top of the bureau. He held up his razor and a box of cigars. "Looks like that's about all that's in here, Billy."

"Please, Grandpa."

Grandpa Hawke carefully lifted his revolver out of the bag, the barrel resting against the palm of his left hand. It was a Colt single-action army model.

"Can I hold it, Grandpa?"

"No, Billy. It's loaded. Five cartridges. You always leave

the chamber under the hammer empty to avoid accidents. You already knew that, didn't you?"

"Yes, sir . . . Can I see the notches?"

"Notches?" He shook his head. Gripping the barrel tightly with his left hand, he let me see the smooth walnut grip. "It makes a good story, I guess. I never knew anyone who did it."

"Wes Croy does. He has three of 'em."

"This Croy—you know him?"

"Talked to him once. He doesn't really live here, but he comes here some and he's my friend Jay Mason's cousin."

Grandpa Hawke put his revolver away and said, "Billy, your mother says your teacher tells her you are the best pupil she has."

I remember that I sort of shrugged.

"So what would you like to be when you grow up?"

"A marshal just like you."

"Well, I'm not a marshal anymore, Billy. That was quite a few years back."

"I could still be one—like you, Grandpa." I pointed my wooden revolver at the window and said, "Bang! Bang! Got 'em both."

I remember Grandpa Hawke looked at me and sat down. "A man has to fit his time, and change when times change. The country is growing up, just like you, Billy. We'll always need lawmen, but mostly we're going to need people who can think and learn to do new things. Why, last week I read in a Kansas City newspaper about this inventor, Edison. He's built some kind of machine that makes pictures that move. Besides, you can never be like someone else. You have to be *you;* do the things your mind and hands let you do best."

That night after supper, Grandpa Hawke asked me to open the paper-wrapped package my father had carried home. When I started untying the string and the paper loosened, I could smell leather. Inside was a beautiful handbag for Mother, a belt and gloves for my father, and a short deerskin coat for me with fringes and some silver decorations. I went and hugged Grandpa, then I put the coat on and it was a bit too big. Grandpa laughed and said, "Had to guess some at your size, Billy. You wait—come winter, you'll be filling it out and another year or two you won't be able to get it on."

All of the gifts were made by Grandpa Hawke in his Kansas City leather works and I knew I'd keep my coat even when I could no longer wear it.

If ever there was a time in your life you'd like to take back, the next few days would haunt me for years. Often I'd wake up with a start and see every detail and feel the hurt.

Grandpa Hawke had walked downtown to talk to Asa Gordon at the tannery about some leather he wanted to buy. It was almost summer and I went barefooted, the dirt soft and warm, over to Jay Mason's place, my wooden revolver tucked in the waistband of my trousers. Jay was sitting on the porch and I sat down beside him and told him how my Grandpa Hawke had come to visit and how he'd shown me his Colt revolver. Jay had heard me talk about him a million times and borrowed my Ned Buntline book and read all the stories about Grandpa.

I remember the screen door opening behind us but I didn't look around because I thought it was Jay's mother or his sister, Nan. "Boy," someone said, "you tell that old windbag grandpa of yours I'm lookin' for him, and when I find him . . ."

I looked over my shoulder and Jay's cousin Wes Croy was standing there. Quick as a wink his hand flashed to the revolver at his hip and whipped it out of the holster and the hammer clicked back and the barrel was pointed right at me.

"Wes! Don't you be scaring that boy!" Jay's mother called.

He grinned and tilted the barrel up and let the hammer down and holstered his revolver. "Come on, Hank. My whistle is gettin' dry."

Wes Croy stepped down off the porch followed by

Hank Dixon and Hank stumbled like he'd already been drinking too much. He used to help out some at the depot until my father said he let him go because he caught him going through some passengers' bags. Hank had a revolver, too, but there were a lot of ranches in the area and most of the hands wore guns and carried rifles in saddle boots when they came to town.

Everything had happened so fast the fear didn't catch up with me for a minute. Then I started to shake and I said something to Jay about having to get home.

I remember I hardly ate any dinner and I could hardly look at Grandpa Hawke. I wanted to tell him about Wes Croy and I didn't know quite how.

"Billy," my mother said, "you don't look like you feel very good. Why don't you go take a nap? Your grandfather and I haven't had a chance to really talk since he got here."

"You get to feeling better," Grandpa said. "I'll take all of you to the Palace Theater tonight."

I went to my room and I knew I couldn't sleep. I fluffed up my pillow and sat on my bed and thumbed through the Ned Buntline book, looking at the illustrations. I wanted to keep believing every word despite what my Grandpa Hawke said. I finally closed my eyes and I could see my grandpa out in the middle of the street, walking toward Wes Croy and Hank Dixon, and both of them reaching for their guns and Grandpa's Colt revolver appearing like magic, bucking, smoking, and Wes and Hank lying in the dirt . . .

I didn't know how long Grandpa planned to stay, but at supper he said he was going to leave the next day on the 12:15 train.

I had to put on shoes and wear my Sunday clothes, and we walked to the Palace Theater. There were a lot of people and it got hot inside and I sat next to Grandpa Hawke and felt very proud. A traveling troupe put on a play and there was a lot of shouting, the women in the play crying; finally a man shot the one making the women cry and when the gun went off Grandpa's arm bumped me.

When we started outside, Grandpa held on to my hand. People were crowded around in front of the theater and I saw Wes Croy and Hank Dixon, and Wes yelled something at Grandpa Hawke.

"This way," I heard my father say. Grandpa's hand gripped mine tightly as we squeezed past people, out of the light, and down a narrow alley between the theater and Brock's Mercantile.

My father and mother were ahead of us, and when we reached the end of the alley, they hurried along the back of Brock's and no one said anything until we were on the street that led to our house.

With a sigh, Father said, "I feel better now."

"Is he still angry with you?" my mother asked.

"I don't think so. He isn't very bright," and I knew he was referring to Hank Dixon. "That Croy—he's the bad one."

Grandpa said, "Sorry to cause so much trouble."

Nothing more was really said when we reached home and I was sent off to bed soon after. I could hear them talking in the parlor for a long time before I went to sleep.

I suppose the muffled voices woke me. Father had always got up early; he had to be at the station when the 6:10 morning train came through, but I seldom ever heard him. He'd fix some coffee and let Mother sleep, then come home for his breakfast at eight.

I got out of bed and crept to the door and listened and I could hear Mother, Father, and Grandpa Hawke talking in the kitchen. Then I heard the front door open and close. Pretty soon the crack of light under the door went out. The soft steps I knew were those of my mother going back to bed. Why didn't I hear Grandpa Hawke go back upstairs? No matter how quiet you tried to be, the stairsteps always creaked.

Dawn light spilled around the edges of my bedroom window shade as I pulled on my shirt and trousers. Quietly, I slipped out of my room, tiptoed across the cold linoleum kitchen floor, past the warm cookstove, to the front door. We never locked the door and in a minute I was outside.

The town was still asleep; a rooster crowed, the only sound until I neared the depot. One of the men pulled a cart loaded with mail sacks and boxes across the platform. Then I saw Grandpa Hawke standing at the end of the platform smoking a cigar. "Grandpa!" I called, running through the cindery dirt, up the slope to the level of the platform.

"Billy! What are you doing here?"

"Are you leaving, Grandpa? You didn't say good-by."

I stood looking up at him and he didn't say anything for a moment. Then he touched a hand to my shoulder, pulled me close, and I could feel the revolver under his coat.

"You said you were going home on the twelve-fifteen."

"Sorry, Billy. I decided to leave earlier—after you were in bed."

"Why?"

"Well—there are some things I'd forgotten about I have to do." His hand tightened on my shoulder. "Billy—you better run on home."

Grandpa had glanced over his shoulder, and when I looked, I saw two men coming along the dusty street to the depot. The sun wasn't quite up but I could see it was Wes Croy and Hank Dixon.

"Billy!"

Grandpa Hawke sounded gruff and he gave me a little push and I knew there was going to be some kind of trouble. Instead of going home I ran along the tracks to the water tank about a hundred feet from the station and ducked behind one of the big wooden tower legs.

"Hawke!" Wes Croy called, when he and Hank stopped walking. "You tryin' to run away?"

I remember when he said that I suddenly felt sick. Was my grandpa scared? Was that why he hadn't said good-by to me last night—why he'd decided to take the morning train? Then I saw his cigar go sailing and he slowly lowered his arm to his side. "I don't want any trouble with you."

"Old man—I do believe you're a coward! I see that grandson of yours hidin' under the water tank over there. He thinks you are some kind of hero and now he's gonna be disappointed, you tryin' to sneak outta town."

"There's no need for you to do this, Croy. So you are good with a gun. I accept that. You don't have to prove it to anyone."

"I do for a fact. I beat a man like Ross Hawke with all the stories they tell like in that book Billy Boy's so proud, ever'body'll know I'm the best."

Grandpa Hawke said, "I'm not going to fight you," and turned his back. In a second or two splinters flew from the platform by Grandpa's feet, the boom of Wes Croy's gun reverberating across town. Grandpa Hawke slowly turned and the sun, now peeking over the horizon, outlined him against the sky. This time I saw flames shoot from Wes Croy's revolver and Grandpa staggered and two shots sounded almost simultaneously and Wes—facing slightly uphill—seemed to stand on his toes then go over backward like he'd been hit with a sledgehammer.

By the time I saw Grandpa Hawke's Colt, it was pointed at Hank Dixon. Hank whirled around, stumbled to one knee, got up and ran as fast as he could go back down the street.

"Grandpa!" I ran to him. When I reached him, his revolver was poked behind the waistband of his suit and he was getting his coat off.

My father and the baggagemen were there in another minute. My father took one look, said, "Billy—go get Doc Waters!"

The rest remains somewhat a blur. Grandpa Hawke had been hit in the left shoulder and Doc Waters put on a big bandage to stop the blood. "You'll have to come down to my office," Doc said. "All right," Grandpa told him.

By that time Marshal Turner and one of his deputies were there. Grandpa Hawke said, "I didn't intend to kill him. My eyes aren't what they used to be."

Grandpa Hawke had to stay over two days for an inquest. No one could find Hank Dixon, but several people testified that Wes Croy had been talking about killing Grandpa Hawke and the coroner's jury brought in a verdict of justified self-defense.

I could hardly look at my Grandpa those two days without feeling that none of it would have happened except for me. I hid the Ned Buntline book away. And the day Grandpa Hawke went home, I burned my wooden revolver in the kitchen cookstove . . .

Memories. They came flooding back. Grandpa Hawke buttoned his shirt collar, put his coat on, and reached for his cane. "I don't need to come back?"

"No. Everything looks fine." I held out the .45 slug. "Do you want it?"

He shook his head.

I dropped the old slug in a waste container, walked to the door, held it open, then followed Grandpa Hawke out on the covered entrance. The sun was shining. A beautiful day. He turned and ran his fingers over the raised lettering of the nameplate beside the door: W. Ross Powell M.D.

"Grandfather . . ." I began. For the first time in all the years I brought myself to tell him about that day at Jay Mason's house. "You see, it would never have happened if I hadn't been bragging and Wes Croy learned that you were at our place."

"No, no. He was on the train I came on. Someone pointed me out and he challenged me. He'd been drinking and I thought at first he'd forget about it when the liquor quit talking."

Another piece of memory fell in place. That day at the depot—someone had called to Grandpa Hawke when he got off the train.

He took his glasses from his coat and put them on. Once more he ran his fingers over the nameplate. "I'm glad that boy, Billy, decided to be himself. After all these years it's a great relief to be rid of the pain."

"Yes," I said. "It certainly is."

Wildfire

MARIANNE WILLMAN

MONTGOMERYVILLE, TEXAS: 1860

"LOOKING MIGHTY PURTY today, Miss Parmenter."

Annie looked up from her baking chores. Seth Begley stood just inside the lean-to that was her summer kitchen, idly chewing on the butt of his cigar. Annie read derision in his voice. She had no illusions as to her beauty. She was homely and she'd known it all her twenty-four years. Thread-thin and freckled as a wild bird's egg. Mama had told her that often enough.

She fixed Seth with a wide blue stare. "I am not going to sell you my land, Mr. Begley. No matter how many hollow compliments you may pay me. And I'll thank you not to come sneaking around my place again."

"Wasn't sneaking . . . Ma'am. My horse is down at the creek. Thought it'd be a nice morning for a little walk.

And some neighborly talk." His thin face hardened. "I like to do business in a right friendly fashion. When folks'll let me."

Annie didn't challenge the implied threat but she didn't intend to sell her land to him or anyone. The land was all she had left, the only thing that was really hers. She punched the heavy dough down with her knuckles, pretending it was Seth Begley's face. Childish, she knew, but immensely satisfying.

"Ain't you gonna offer me anything to drink? Cold buttermilk or hot coffee, either one'll do. I'm not hard to please."

She slapped the floured dough into a mound and punched it down so hard she lost a hairpin and a wisp of hair tumbled loose at her nape. Begley noticed the color then, red-gold and fine as floss. It was the only pretty thing about her. He came a little closer.

"Is it true what they say about redheads? Being fiery and passionate and all?"

She was too mortified and angry to answer his impertinence in the way that he deserved. Face flaming, she buried her floury hands in the bread dough when she really wanted to box his ears soundly. It wouldn't do to antagonize him right now while they were still negotiating for her rights to the creek. Pounding and punching the dough instead of Seth Begley, she struggled with her temper. It was her greatest flaw and Ma had warned her time after time to mend her hotheaded ways.

Seth watched her with growing interest. With the high color in her face and her hair coming loose in wisps, Miz Annabel Parmenter was looking better and better. There might be other ways to bring her round his thumb than his original plan. He reached out and fingered one of her curls. Annie jerked away with an angry exclamation but Seth grinned more widely.

"Right pretty hair. Bright as a new penny and a might softer. Better watch out, Miz Parmenter, or one of them Comanche braves'll have your scalp dangling from his belt." He lit the cigar and puffed a cloud in her direction. "They're raiding again hereabouts. Winged one yestidy. Damn savage tried to steal my horse."

Annie had never liked Seth Begley, but she'd never been afraid of him, either. Something had changed. Her skin crawled. Not knowing the best way to react, she did what she'd done in the past when he'd pestered her: She ignored him so thoroughly he grew tired of needling her.

He blew out a blue cloud of cigar smoke. "Play your little games, Miz Parmenter. You're gonna have to talk to me sooner or later. You can't keep a spread going alone, even with them two Whistler boys helping out when they can." He shambled into a patch of strong morning sun. "I'll be back. You can count on it."

There was no response except for the angry flush staining Annie's face and throat. Begley frowned in aggravation. Compliments and intimidation hadn't worked. So far. But he'd be back. He certainly would.

Leaning past Annie, he dumped the long gray ash of his cigar over the tops of two loaves of dough already rising on her worktable. Annie's arm swung round to slap him. Seth caught her wrist and their eyes locked. "Let go of me, at once!" She'd meant her voice to sound strong and steady. It came out in a hoarse squawk. Seth laughed, held her arms long enough that the fear showed in her eyes, then shoved her against the table and sauntered out.

A woman alone had to be careful whom she antagonized, but Annie was suddenly terrified beyond caution. She grabbed her always-loaded rifle and racked the shell into the chamber as she followed him to the door. He didn't see her raise the rifle to her shoulder and aim, but the whine and zing that followed got his immediate attention. Whirling around he saw her aiming again. The explosion of dirt and gravel was too close to his heels for comfort.

Annie faced him coolly. "The next one will be a lot closer, Mr. Begley. I'd advise you to get on your horse and *git*!"

He got. But as he wheeled his sorrel, he called back to her. "And I'd advise you to light out of here within the week, Miz Parmenter. 'Cause your creek is gonna be drier than dirt—and if any of your cattle stray onto my propity, they's gonna die of lead poisoning."

"Vulture! Jackal!" she called out to his retreating form, and dashed a sting of angry tears from her eyes. Mama would have been upset to know that Annie had threatened a man with a rifle—but a lady could only hold so much in. She would never give up this land her parents had fought and died for. Not for a dozen Seth Begleys.

She had regained her equilibrium by afternoon when the new bread was baked and the little house was filled with its warm, yeasty flavor. Annie enjoyed baking. There was something rewarding about seeing quick results from her labor. Less frustrating than wresting crops from the Texas soil.

Her Pa had worked hard to plant and harvest their land and she'd worked right along beside him. Mama had always been too delicate. As her hopes of a fine estate and an elegant, eligible daughter had faded beneath the harsh sun, so had she.

After Mama's death everything had begun to fall apart, beginning with Pa. "I never should have brought her out to this godforsaken place," he said every evening, after a long day's work. "But we've still got the land, Annie. We've still got the land. That's the only thing a man can hold on to in this world."

She looked up from the cooling loaves of bread and out the open window. Now the only things left of Pa and Mama's dreams were a few worn buildings, a section of land slowly blowing away as dust—and two graves up on the hill behind the house.

And herself, Annie amended. Well, that would have to be enough. She'd promised to hang on to the land and to make the ranch productive. The greater the odds grew, the more important it became to succeed. No matter what the

Seth Begleys of the world did, she would fight for this land. It meant everything to her.

The bread was still too warm to slice, so Annie tore off a corner of one loaf and daubed it generously with cool butter. It melted on the tongue, crusty outside, light as air inside and fragrant with yeast. She smiled with pride. This was her one small vanity: She might not be much to look at but, by God, she could cook and bake. It just wasn't much fun to do it just for herself. Maybe she'd take the buggy over to the Whistlers' place, with a few loaves and some of that quince jam.

She was still trying to make up her mind when she heard squawking from the henhouse. Some varmint in there after the chickens. Annie hurried there, pushed the door open and stamped her feet. "Shoo! Get out. Shoo!"

She didn't see the blood until she stepped in it, just inside the door. It was sticky and already darkening, but she knew blood when she saw it. She'd done enough nursing and birthing in her twenty-four years: Always a midwife, never a wife.

The hens were all safe and settled their feathers, complaining sharply among themselves. Most likely an animal predator, yet Annie didn't discount Seth's story of a wounded Comanche. The Potterville massacre of '48 was still very much alive in people's minds. Annie's Mama had told her she would be better off taking her own life than to be captured by the evil Comanche. The things they did to captives were told only in whispers. The things they did to women were never spoken of at all.

Annie checked things out and breathed a relieved sigh. Whatever—or *who*ever—was injured had not tarried here. She went outside and peered around. There was a spatter of bloody droplets and another splotch farther on, leading to an empty shed. After a moment's hesitation she went back to the house and fetched the rifle, and slipped her father's old Army Colt into her belt. These were unsettled times. Best to be prepared for anything.

She stood aside and threw open the shed door. "Come on out, you varmint."

There was no response. She waited. The wind blew softly, insistently, as it always did this time of year. A low sound, like a muffled groan, made the hairs on the back of her neck stand up. The marmalade cat that had littered in the shed came prancing out of the shadows and sat in the sun outside the doorway, washing her pink paws.

Annie relaxed. Ginger wouldn't have been so calm if there was anything dangerous lurking inside. Propping the rifle against the wall, she entered the shed. Rays of golden light sifted through the chinks in the dry wood and dust motes danced as Annie made her way past the jumble of odds and ends and gardening tools. She stepped around the wheelbarrow—and almost tripped on a body lying just beyond it.

She gasped and froze in place. An Indian was sprawled flat on his back on a pile of sacking, arms outflung as if he were crucified. There was dried blood down his chest and beneath it his ribs stuck out gaunt as the hoops of a broken barrel.

So this was one of the dreaded Comanche. This poor starving creature, matted with blood and dirt. But she slid the gun from her belt and held it ready. A wounded animal could prove the deadliest.

Beneath the filth and pallor the lines of his face were young. Why, he's not more than a boy, she thought, with a swift stab of pity. Then his eyelids flew up and she saw that she was wrong. No boy had eyes like this, bleak with knowledge of life's impartial cruelties. It pained her to look into them, yet she was unable to look away.

She was compelled to move closer. Annie knelt down beside him, forgetting that she held the gun. His right hand shot out and clamped around her wrist. It was strong and hard and had the heat of iron fresh from the forge. Fear constricted her throat but she knew she mustn't let him see it.

She laid her other hand firmly on his arm. "You needn't

be afraid," she said, defiant of her fright. "I won't hurt you." She was pleased to hear her voice so brisk and steady. "You need help. You are injured and feverish. Let me see where you are hurt."

He stared back at her, understanding the tone, if not the words. Weighing, judging. Then he released his grip, surprising them both.

Annie put the Colt out of reach and examined him with cool efficiency. Her calm tones and slow, deliberate actions soothed him, or perhaps he had merely resigned himself to the inevitable. She found a superficial wound some six inches long over the left shoulder. That had caused most of the bleeding. His other wound, on the outside of his right thigh, hadn't bled much because the shot was still lodged in it. The flesh was purple and puffy.

She prodded the edges. He tried to roll away and was stopped by a wall of solid pain. "This will have to come out, you know."

He didn't hear her. He'd passed out cold. Annie sat back on her heels and tried to think of what to do. First she'd have to remove the bullet and clean the wounds. She'd worry about the healing later. And she'd have to conceal him. With Seth Begley poking about, that was a prime necessity. Annie had no doubt of what he'd do to a Comanche. And she felt strangely protective of this one. After all, it had been her shed where he'd sought refuge.

The shed had very special ties for her. In the early days when Mama and Papa had first brought her to the ranch, this homely structure had been their first house. Then it had been her refuge from a hostile world, shielding the family from heat and cold, from rain and wind and hail. There was a partition at the back where her parents had slept. It would be a safer place for her uninvited guest. She stood and regarded the problem a moment, then bent and grabbed her patient by the ankles and began pulling.

What she lacked in strength she made up in determination. She didn't look up until he was completely hidden behind the flimsy wall. If he'd awakened and passed out again during the effort, she couldn't tell, and she didn't need to know. She felt a strange kinship with him. They were both alone.

Wiping her soiled hands on her apron, she retrieved the Colt and went back to the house, making a mental list of required supplies. Cloth for bandages, shears to cut it, ointment and alcohol. Canvas needle and waxed thread and Papa's knife with the thin steel blade and carved bone handle. And blankets and quilts, of course.

Without realizing it, Annie began humming a jaunty little tune under her breath.

When Buffalo Heart regained consciousness, the barn was shadowy as a cave and it took a moment to remember. If he strained his eyes, he could make out strips of dim lavender sky through chinks in the roof and walls. Someone had covered him with a woolen blanket. A white-eyes blanket.

He looked around. His left shoulder was bound with tight strips of torn sheeting, his leg with flowered calico, and his throat was as parched and cracked as a dry riverbed. A creak of wood came from beyond the inside wall and he lay still, preparing to fight for his life with all his remaining strength. There was no time to subdue his pain.

He smelled the woman before he saw or heard the rustling of her skirts. It was a pleasant scent, flowery and light, but alien. A moment later she rounded the partition with a shuttered lantern in one hand and a lidded basket in the other. She knelt beside him and opened the lantern. Her face was thin and bony and speckled like an owl's breast. There was nothing rounded or womanly about it. He wondered if all white women were so ugly.

But when she re-dressed his wounds, he forgot about her ugliness and knew only that her hands were strong and gentle. By the time she finished, he was weak, his flesh chill and clammy, and all the while Buffalo Heart wondered why she did this for him. He'd heard of white women who lived together and spent all their days aiding the ill and wounded, or kneeling in prayer before their little wooden gods. Perhaps it was their punishment for getting no husbands to provide for them.

Annie propped his head on her arm and gave him a spoonful of syrup so bitter that he spit it out immediately. "Pah!"

She was not pleased. "Don't do that again. It is very hard to come by." She poured out another and held the spoon to his mouth.

He swallowed it. Surely she would not bandage his wounds earlier, only to poison him now. But logic told him she had some ulterior reason for her aid. Perhaps she meant to keep him as a slave. It had happened to a Kiowa brave he'd known. His face was fierce as his namesake creature. No one would ever make a slave of him. He would die first. By his own hand, if necessary.

Annie stood up. Her patient was bathed, bandaged, fed, and dosed with poppy syrup. There was only one thing she'd forgotten. Until now. She rummaged through the shed and returned with a wide-mouthed brown bottle. Buffalo Heart watched her every move but his lids were drooping. When she set the bottle down within arm's reach, he picked it up and peered inside. It was empty. He flung it away. Annie retrieved it and hesitated, cheeks hot with embarrassment in the lantern light. Finally she held it somewhere in the region of her hips, then pointed at his loins.

Buffalo Heart understood and laughed aloud. Sliding his hand behind the flap in his breeches he sent a glittering stream of water arcing against the shed wall. Annie went stumbling back in dismay, but recovered herself quickly.

"Heathen!" She picked up the bottle and plunked it down beside him again. "You are to use the bottle from now on!"

He grinned at her discomfiture. When she turned and stormed out, he was still chuckling.

The next morning he had a raging fever and Annie had no time for further etiquette lessons. By the third day he was much improved, although she had to cauterize the edges of his leg wound once more. Her life took on a new rhythm. Now Annie's days were filled with purpose, and so busy she fell into bed and slept like a baby. She added extra meat to her beef broth, and when she stewed a chicken, she found herself checking and adjusting the taste: Did it need more salt? Parsley? Perhaps an extra bit of carrot? She realized how lonely she had been, and then forgot about her loneliness in this strange new life she was leading.

And on the sixth day Seth Begley came again. Annie had just opened the door of the shed.

"Afternoon, Miss Parmenter."

She let the door swing shut and started back toward the house. "I said I won't have you sneaking around here, Seth Begley. You've got no call to trespass on my property."

"That's no way to treat a visitor, now." Begley followed her onto the porch. "Right unfriendly for a woman living alone with no man to protect her." He stepped closer. "I think it's time you and me got to be friends. Good friends."

"What . . . !" Before Annie knew what he was about, Begley grabbed her by the shoulders and pushed her through the door. He backed her against the table and pawed at her and Annie walloped Begley along side of the head. He yelped, then cuffed her so soundly he split her lip. Annie's head struck the support table, dazing her. In an instant he had her down on the floor and her skirts up over her waist, tugging at her undergarments.

She realized he meant to rape her and fought as strongly as she could. The front of her dress was torn open with one swipe of Begley's big hand as Buffalo Heart burst through the door brandishing a hoe. There was a hollow smacking sound, like a pumpkin smashed against the ground, and Begley went limp atop her. Buffalo Heart took another solid swipe with the rusted hoe and then pulled the corpse off Annie. She scrambled out of the way while he kicked Begley's body over on its back. The hoe came down again, obliterating the face, then chopped at the torso. He was swift and methodical, like a hawk killing a rattler, and Annie watched unblinkingly.

When he was through, Buffalo Heart threw the hoe down and smiled at Annie. She should have been horrified. She wasn't in the least. But reaction made her sway dizzily. Buffalo Heart caught her before she hit the floor. When Annie came to, she was lying on her bed with the Comanche hovering anxiously over her. She tried to sit up but he pushed her back, quite gently. She was shaking violently.

"Stay," he commanded, as she had to him so many times.

She complied, finding it both novel and comforting to have someone else look out for her interests. He covered her with the blanket, then stretched out beside her so close she thought she could hear the beating of his heart. But maybe it was only her own, after all. She drifted into an uneasy slumber, and when she awakened, both Buffalo Heart and the body were gone.

She sat up. There was not so much as a bloodstain to tell what had happened earlier. The soft clanging that had awakened her was only the lid on the stew pot, bubbling away on the hearth. Annie rose and swung the pot off the fire, then went outside.

The Comanche was just coming up on the porch. He looked exhausted. His face was all hollows and sharp planes and the skin beneath his eyes looked bruised. She checked his bandages, but there was no fresh bleeding. How strong he was. How courageous. Later she'd ask what he did with the body. But not now.

"I set some stew to simmer earlier. I'll bring some out here for us."

They sat side by side on the porch, not talking. Neither knew the other's language. A fresh wind blew up from the northwest and cloud schooners scudded across the dark sky, fleeing the coming fury. A massive storm was brewing and the air crackled with its aura. Annie could feel the hairs prickle along the back of her arms and neck.

She jumped at the first flash of lightning and its echoing rumble of thunder. No rain followed the threat but ragged red and orange lights flared about the edges of the clouds until they seemed to be on fire. It was an awesome display, a wild celebration of the forces of life.

Annie rose. Buffalo Heart came to stand nearby. She felt small and insignificant beneath the flaming sky yet oddly exhilarated, and very glad of his protective bulk beside her. He searched the sky, wondering if this was a sign.

They watched together while the breeze picked up, blowing curtains of dust across the plains, like fine Spanish veils. The wind whipped Annie's hair loose from her neat bun until it twisted like satin ribbons behind her. Crimson flames licked the edges of the clouds. Buffalo Heart's fingers brushed her arm lightly and she turned. He gestured toward the sky.

"What is it?" she said. "I'm not sure."

He shook his head. *He* knew what it was. There was nothing in all of nature that his people did not know. It was the white-eyes name he wanted to learn. He pointed to himself and said his name in Comanche, then pointed at her and said her name, as she'd told it to him. "Ahnnie Parmenter."

The light flashed overhead and this time he spoke the Comanche word for the phenomenon and pointed from Annie back to the sky.

"Oh! What is it called? I'm not sure of the actual name. Wildfire. My papa called it wildfire."

"Wildfire." The word sounded strange but felt good on his tongue. Almost absently he caught a strand of Annie's hair and wound it through his strong fingers. "Wildfire," he murmured again. Their eyes met and held. Simultaneously they looked away. Neither of them spoke.

Annie was tense and uncomfortable. The air was charged with the coming storm. The fire-show ended abruptly and the rains came howling down. Buffalo Heart held the edge of his blanket out to shelter Annie. She shook herself free and ran into the house. He pulled the blanket up to keep the rain from his eyes and went back to the shed slowly.

Annie huddled in her rocker, with Mama's shawl around her shoulders. Thunder rattled the rafters and lightning lit the room for the next hour, seeming to race around the walls with every flash. When it ended, the sky was clear and cool starlight iced the landscape. She undressed and went to bed, but didn't sleep for some time. Hazy, half-formed plans floated through her mind. She tried not to think of "the Indian" but his image haunted her.

There was no avoiding it, so she tried to work around it. Perhaps he would stay on, help her work the ranch. After all, she had found him—a poor, half-starved, wounded creature—and saved his life. Even a Comanche could show gratitude. And the arrangement would be to his benefit as well. She could offer him good home-cooked meals, shelter from the elements. Even companionship of a sort. Why, with some decent clothing he wouldn't look so uncivilized. She could take in some of her father's old things. But try as she might, Annie couldn't picture him in a pair of trousers and lace-up boots.

She wondered what he thought of her . . . if he thought of her at all. It was nice having him around. Funny, she hadn't even realized that she was lonely until . . .

Annie let her hands fall idle, bemused. The one person she'd begun to count on, the one person whose company she enjoyed, was a Comanche. Mama would have been appalled.

She snuggled beneath the down comforter. A short time ago life had looked bleak. Now her entire outlook had changed. Irrelevantly, she wondered what the Comanche thought of her hair.

Wildfire.

Eventually her thoughts tangled up with one another

and she fell into a deep, confused sleep where the night sky was filled with the strong face of a Comanche warrior and his eyes shone like dark stars. Like wildfire.

When she woke in the morning, he was gone, taking her brindle horse with him.

Annie was outraged at the Comanche's ingratitude. She felt hurt. Abandoned. She told herself she was glad to be rid of him and the extra work he entailed. But to steal her horse! And after all she'd done for him!

She worked at her chores by day, and every night she cried herself to sleep without quite knowing why. And three weeks to the day he left, Buffalo Heart returned.

He rode up to the house early one morning on a fine gray gelding, with her brindle and six other horses in string behind it. They were fine animals. She wondered whose ranch he had stolen them from.

He tied them to the porch rail and waited. Annie walked slowly from the henhouse, noting that he seemed to be completely healed of his wounds. Only a thin scar traced the path of the bullet across his shoulder and his lean frame had filled out. Someone was feeding him well.

A wife, she thought, wondering why it hadn't occurred to her before. She bit her lip and kept on her beeline to the house.

Buffalo Heart saw the stubborn set of her shoulders. He mounted the gray and rode a short distance away with the rest, but Annie refused to look at him. She took the eggs into the house and made herself an omelet with three of them and the last of the winter onions. She realized that she didn't even know his name.

When she came out of the house an hour later, the horses were still there but the Comanche was gone. Were the horses a gift? Or payment for her care of him? Annie put her hands on her hipbones and stared at them. She had neither the time nor the energy to care for them. The land came first, would always come first.

And she wanted nothing from him, nothing at all.

She filled the trough and watered the horses, her hair sticking to the back of her sweaty neck. Hot as a stovelid, and not a hint of breeze to fan her cheeks. She went inside and stubbornly closed the door. The place was like an oven.

Near sundown he returned, remaining at a distance. Each time Annie looked out the window, he was still there. Watching. Waiting. For what? The sun set in an angry puddle of light, promising a fine day on the morrow. It was hot in the little house. Annie paced the room several times then stomped over to the door, red with anger and the heat. When she opened it, he was gone. No trace. Not even a puff of dust on the horizon.

Maybe she had imagined it. Didn't the heat cause hallucinations? But the horses were real enough. Annie tended to them and went to bed early.

She spent the night tossing and turning. A dozen times she got up to look out between the crack in the shutters, thinking she heard the pad of unshod hooves, the whisper of moccasined feet over the coarse ground. Her gown clung to her shoulders and breasts and thighs. It would be more sensible to sleep naked but she could not make herself strip down.

She fell into a disturbed slumber some time before dawn and dreamed she was withering away like a dried plum, all her vital juices evaporating in the deadly heat.

She should have been happy. No one had thought of a skinny spinster in regard to Seth Begley's mysterious disappearance. Mrs. Whistler blamed it on the Comanche, although someone suggested he'd been killed by a jealous rancher. He'd had a wandering eye, had Seth Begley.

With her enemy dead, Annie thought she might sell Mama's brooch and wedding ring. Hire some hands from town to help with the planting. Maybe get some cattle. But she was too restless to make plans. She knew what it was: that Comanche, coming around again. Well, he was gone now, and good riddance.

The next morning he was there again, waiting. And the morning after that. She continued to feed and water the horses, but refused to put them in her barn. On the fourth morning she almost tripped over a pack of pelts sitting just outside her door.

Buffalo Heart sat his patient gray a few yards away. Annie was exasperated beyond bearing. "What do you want? Leave me alone, damn you. Leave me alone!"

He held out his hand to her commandingly. Annie went back inside, slamming the door behind her. She leaned against it, shaking as if she had the ague. She knew what he wanted, had known from the beginning, in the shadowed recesses of her heart. It terrified her.

"I can't do it." Her voice echoed in the small house and she brushed away the tears that streaked her face. She had worked hard all her life, asking nothing in return; but carrying the deeply buried hope that some man would see beyond her plain features and freckled skin, so she might have a home, children. A simple measure of love and respect.

Two of those dreams had withered with the passing seasons. She did have a home of her own, though. This was her ranch now. Hers! Everything her parents had worked and died for belonged to her and it was her duty to somehow see that their hopes and dreams of a flourishing ranch were realized.

Wasn't it?

Buffalo Heart waited patiently. He had learned to wait silently as his quarry came into sight, then into the range of his arrows. A man who rushed out at the wrong time would send the shy doe bounding away in terror. This woman was no different. He sat his pony as the sun arced down the great bowl of sky to its western home.

On the tenth morning, just after sunrise, the cabin door opened suddenly. When she came out on the porch, Buffalo Heart saw that she'd been weeping. She stared at him for a long while, then went back inside. He heard the bolt slide shut. He waited.

It was almost sunset when she finally came out. She was dressed for traveling and her arms were filled with a wealth of nested pots and pans and thick wool blankets over her arm. She didn't look his way as she went to the henhouse and propped the door open, then went to the stable and opened the stall doors. Annie returned to the cabin and went inside.

A moment later she returned with a rifle in one hand and the Army Colt revolver in the other. A leather bag of cartridges was slung over her shoulder and a sheathed knife was tucked into the waistband of her divided skirt. She handed him the guns and waited for his reaction.

Buffalo Heart nodded in satisfaction. Ah, the other braves would envy him! A strong woman and practical, too. One whose heart was full of courage, yet as gentle as her hands had been, tending his wounds. His own seemed filled with light and warmth. He jumped down and secured the other horses, then strode back to Annie. He didn't touch her until her rapid breathing slowed.

Gently he untied the yellow ribbon that held her hair in its smooth plait, and shook the shiny tresses out so they covered her shoulders like a tawny shawl. He stared at her until she had to look away from the light in his eyes. Buffalo Heart wondered how had he ever thought her ugly. She was so beautiful, with her strange, pale eyes like a still lake, and her glorious, fiery hair. He caught a swath of it across his palm and carried it to his cheek. Soft as the inside of a milkweed pod.

"Wildfire," he said, and smiled.

She had never really seen him smile before. Her answering one was tremulous and brave.

Buffalo Heart wanted to claim her then and there, to make her truly his, but something held him back. The shadow of the house and outbuildings, of the two neat graves with their simple crosses. This was the past and must be left behind them both. The future lay ahead of them, west toward the setting sun.

He caught Annie by the waist and set her upon his

horse, then leaped up in front of her. She wrapped her arms loosely about his waist, then more tightly as he nudged his gray into a trot. She was trembling but it eased as the heat of his strong young body radiated through hers. As they rode away from the little house with its shabby outbuildings and worn soil, its forlorn hopes and memories, she did not look back, even once.

The sun sank lower, turning the dry earth to copper and umber and gilding the bellies of the high, vaporous clouds. Buffalo Heart rode proudly, his heart bursting with the fullness of life. Joyously the bridegroom sang aloud, as they rode across the open plain toward his distant lodge.

Annie smiled and rested her cheek against his naked back. He was young and brave and strong. He was life.

As they rode away, her unbound hair streamed out behind them, shimmering in the dying light like wildfire.

The Death(s) of Billy the Kid

ARTHUR WINFIELD KNIGHT

BILLY: HOME

FRIENDS TELL ME I ought to leave the territory. But what would I do in Mexico with no money? I can stay here awhile and get some money, then go to Mexico.

Fort Sumner's home. I love this country: the Valley of Fires, the Pecos River.

I'm not going to let Garrett scare me away.

Friends think I don't know what I'm doing when I ride around the country in circles, tracking myself; I know where I'm going because I've been there. I've been to Alamogordo, Tularosa, too.

I like the purple light on the mountains at twilight and the sound of guitars coming from the cantinas along with the laughter of the señoritas. Once, I fucked the earth, I loved it so.

I want *this* soil in my face when I die.

I know times are changing. There's a new law each day of the week. Men like Pat call it progress. I call it loss.

This is my home. Nobody's going to make me go.

GARRETT: APPLES

The Kid was eating an apple minutes before I shot him.

He and Paulita were in bed together, naked. She'd take a bite of the apple, then give it to Billy. They were laughing in the moonlight, passing the apple back and forth, the moon in their eyes, licking each other's lips. Some of the juice dribbled onto Paulita's dark breasts.

Billy kissed them and said, "I love apples," then he went into the kitchen. He was silhouetted against the light when I pulled the trigger. The juice was still running down his chin when he fell.

BILLY: THE PREMONITION

"Can you feel the baby moving?" Paulita asks, placing my hand on her stomach. I hold it there a long time, too tired to move, too tired to talk. But I feel the life within her.

We lie on the double bed. The windows are open, but it's July. The heat is trapped like a fly in the barrel of a pistol, and the moon seems blue.

"The baby should be here by the first frost," she says. "I know it will be a boy."

Sometimes my groin is numb, as if a cold wind blew across my body, but there is no wind.

When I shiver, Paulita puts her arms around me. "What are you thinking?" she asks.

I think Garrett must be getting close by now; I can almost imagine him coming through the peach orchard with some men, coming to kill me, but I don't tell Paulita that.

The baby kicks like a .45 beneath my hand. "See, see," she says, laughing.

Suddenly, I'm sad.

I won't be here to see our son.

PAULITA MAXWELL: PEACHES

He brought me a peach the first time he came. It was the Fourth of July, dusk, and some children were playing with fireworks.

Billy and I sat on my father's porch, sharing the peach he'd plucked from the orchard behind our house. He seemed embarrassed when I put his left hand on my breast, holding it there. The juice from the peach ran between my breasts and my breath came faster.

A rocket exploded, showering us with blue and green sparks, and Billy's eyes were blue and green.

I was surprised at how thin his wrist was. I looked at his right palm in the light from the doorway and knew he was going to die soon.

I said, "A dark woman will love you."

PETE MAXWELL: APPLE BRANDY

I come into the house and find them—Billy and Paulita— naked. I tell her she's disgraced herself, but she just laughs. "You're my brother, not my keeper."

(When we were small, I played with Paulita in the tub.)

It's tornado weather, hot and still, and the sky's electric.

Paulita grabs Billy's black sombrero, covering her breasts, her eyes huge in the soft light.

Billy's pud's tumescent.

Paulita says, "Billy brought me brandy so the afternoon wouldn't seem so long," and I can smell apples on her breath and death on his.

BILLY: HYMNS

I'm tired of singing. It seems like that's all we ever do on Sundays.

I want to dance, want to get drunk, and I'm tired of dressing like a country Jake. But Mr. Tunstall says it's good to get some religion, so we go to McSween's house every Sunday afternoon. When we're not singing, we listen to Dr. Ealy preach about Paul and Silas at Philippi, but I'd rather be at the Wortley Hotel. They have a nice bar and the beer's cold.

I don't even know where Philippi is and I don't want to know if I can't get there on my horse. Do they serve beer?

I want to sing "Turkey in the Straw" or "Sewanee River," something I can stomp my foot to.

Why do I have to listen to all these damn hymns?

I'm not going to heaven.

CELSA GUTIERREZ: ADULTERESS

Sometimes Billy comes to me when my husband's gone.

I know Billy has another woman and it hurts when I see Paulita. She's younger. Prettier.

I know what they call women like me: Whore. *Puta.* Adulteress. They are just words. When Billy touches me, they have no meaning.

Now I hear distant fiddles as I lie next to my sleeping husband. I imagine Billy whirling around and around, dizzy, in Paulita's arms, imagine his lips touching her cheek.

I know the things he says: Oh my love.

I touch the inside of my husband's thigh, touch his sex, rubbing it, until he awakens, hard. I keep my eyes shut. I say, "Make love to me."

GARRETT: MARRIAGE

When my wife died, I married her sister. I needed someone and she always cared for me. Even the priest approved. It was a church wedding. Most of my friends came for the reception.

When Billy arrived he asked, "How does it feel to fuck your dead wife's sister?" He was holding a bottle, drunk, but that didn't make it right. I hated him all that hot afternoon.

My wife asked, "How come you sweat so much?" My white suit turned dark under the arms.

A lot of people wondered how I could shoot Billy. We'd ridden together. We'd been friends. How could I do it? They thought I must have needed the money or that I was ambitious, but it's simple: Billy ruined my wedding.

ZAVAL GUTIERREZ: CUCKOLD

The men in Fort Sumner make clucking sounds when I walk past them, and I no longer go to the cantina. I drink alone.

I watch my wife hang the laundry, watch her breasts stretch against her blouse, and I want her even though I know she has a lover.

Once, I watched from a window as Billy and Celsa undressed each other. They were laughing and did not know I was there with a pistol. I aimed at Billy, my finger tightening on the trigger at the moment he came. I wanted to say, "I hope that fuck was worth dying for," but I ran clucking into the apple orchard.

I'm not even man enough to kill my wife's lover.

BILLY: THE WASP

One of the boys caught a wasp and brought it inside, trapped in a bottle. He said, "It's going to die anyway."

It was almost fall, but the days were still hot.

The boys began to bet how long the wasp would last.

It made it through the morning and the afternoon. By dusk it was barely moving, but it was still alive when we blew out the lantern. I thought I could hear it hitting the sides of the bottle.

The heat seemed suffocating.

There was a five-hundred-dollar reward for me, dead or alive.

In the moonlight I could see beads of sweat on my arm, could see the bottle with the wasp in it on the table.

As I got up, I felt my lungs constrict. By the time I got to the table, I was panting.

Outside, I let the wasp go.

GARRETT: THE JOB

They say I never gave the Kid a chance that night in Fort Sumner. They say he came toward me naked, unarmed, and they wonder how I could shoot a friend.

Let me tell you, Billy had a six-shooter in his right hand and a butcher knife in his left. I was just defending myself, doing a job; I had a warrant for his arrest, dead or alive.

I let the Mexican women carry his body across the yard to the carpenter shop, where they laid him out on a workbench and lit candles around his body, conducting a wake. You'd have thought he was Jesus the way they were all crying when I went to look at his body.

Some of the women spit at me and swore although I told them, "He was a dangerous man, a killer. I shot him mercifully through the heart, a clean shot. Look! I'm the sheriff. I was just doing my job." But they still spit at me and called me names.

BILLY: WHORES

They're always glad to see me when I go to the Doll House. Becky and Soap Suds Sal run toward me, Sal with her hands wet; she used to be a laundress and still loves hot water.

They both ask, "What did you bring us?" and I give them dried flowers and chocolate hearts because it's nice to be wanted for something besides the price on my head.

They tug at me, both wanting me to go upstairs.

Here, I'm not a killer. I'm kind. I give them money and they say, "Billy, you're such a man." Here, things are simple. There's no bickering. No jealousy. Just an exchange: love for money.

I shiver when Sal puts a wet hand into my pants. She says, "Come with me."

GARRETT: PISS-POT

They butchered a yearling the morning they knew Billy would be back because he'd want beefsteak and beer and Billy always got what Billy wanted.

When I saw the Kid, he was silhouetted against the light from Maxwell's kitchen, licking his fingers. I wondered why so many women loved him, then I pulled the trigger.

I heard his body hitting the table, heard dishes breaking as I ran outside. An Indian woman cursed me: "Sonofabitch. Piss-pot."

I think she'd imagined Billy a prodigal son come home. After he ate the fatted calf, he wasn't supposed to die.

BILLY: SHACKLED

They bring me in chains to the house of my girlfriend so we can say goodbye.

"It's a hell of a Christmas," I say, trying to smile.

It must be ten below outside and the snow's deep enough to hide the chains on my legs.

Paulita's mother asks my guard if he'll unlock the irons so Paulita and I can go into the bedroom for an "affectionate farewell," but he tells her, "I ain't Santa Claus," and laughs when I stumble toward Paulita, my chains clanking. They put them on me when I was captured at Stinking Springs yesterday.

Paulita's face is soft in the light from the candles.

She cries, hugging me, and says, "Merry Christmas."

Bob Olinger: Deputy

"You little bastard. You twerp. I'm goin' to enjoy watchin' you hang. The great Billy the Kid will kick his feet and crap in his pants just like anyone else at the end of a rope.

"You better get straight with Jesus, boy. Get straight now.

"One prisoner they hung had his head ripped off. It was bruised, kind of purple lookin'. Someone put it in a bottle of alcohol and charged people to see it.

"Maybe I could pickle your head if it rips off. Huh? Or if it don't, maybe some other part.

"They say you get a hell of a hard-on when that rope tightens around your neck. It sends all your blood rushin' down below, boy. You'll have the biggest boner of your life."

Billy: Revenge

They hung me by my thumbs when I tried to escape from the jail in Santa Fe. The jailer would jab me in the stomach with his shotgun and hum, "Rock-a-bye, Billy," as he watched me swing.

"This'll prepare you for the hangin'," he said, and laughed until he shook.

I spit in his face, but he put his weight on me, hard, and I thought my thumbs would rip off.

When they cut me down, I couldn't move my hands or legs for hours. All I could think was, I'll get you, I'll get you.

Later, I stuck my pistol into his mouth and said, "Suck on this, you bastard." I could hear his teeth chattering on the barrel and his eyes were bloodshot between my sights.

I pulled the hammer back and asked, "How come you're not laughing now?"

SISTER BLANDINA: NAILS

When I heard they brought Billy to town, I went to see him.

The shackles around his hands and feet were nailed to the floor so he couldn't sit or stand.

He said, "I wish I could offer you a chair, Sister." That was all.

I wanted to say, "Forgive us," but I just stood there. He must have thought I was dumb.

Then I ran out of the room into the dark streets. A March wind blew.

In my dreams that night I kept seeing our Lord, His hands and feet bloody, nailed to the Cross, but He had the Kid's face and He kept saying, "I'll kill them before I let them take me again."

BILLY: SNOW BIRDS

"Suppose Pat Garrett was a pretty little bird and suppose that pretty little bird in the street was him," I say, pointing at a snow bird in front of the saloon. "If I was to shoot that little bird and hit him anywhere except in the head, it would be murder."

We've been drinking all morning.

I shoot from the hip and a headless snow bird floats in the bloody air.

I say, "No murder," then fire again and another bird runs in a bloody circle, its head missing.

Acquitted again.

The boys laugh and cheer.

The third time I fire feathers fly and the bird has a red bib where its breast used to be.

"Boys," I say, "I've murdered Pat."

GARRETT: NEW YEAR'S EVE 1900

Men shy away from me since I shot the Kid. I even had to hire an attorney to get the five hundred dollars I'd been promised for killing him.

I had a wife and seven kids to support, but no one cared about that.

When I go into a bar, the conversation stops and, these days, I always drink alone.

When the Kid was alive, we'd ride out into the country together, playing cards, drinking, dancing. Even my kids ask why I did it. I've tried to explain; I even wrote a book about me and the Kid.

Since I shot him, I've tried ranching in Roswell and Fort Stanton. Tried breeding horses in Uvalde.

I failed.

Then I rode with the Home Rangers. Worked as a cattle boss.

Failed again.

Ran for sheriff in Chaves County.

Failed.

Now it's a new century, but everything ended the night I shot the Kid.

BILLY: LAST WORDS

In the other room, the girl I made love to is sleeping now.

I love these hot nights in New Mexico, love the desert air on my naked body. I'll never leave Fort Sumner.

Paulita says I can't stop laughing when I start. It's true I like to laugh and I've done it while I'm dancing or drinking or whoring, even when I've killed men. (They all deserved it.)

After I shot Deputy Olinger with his own shotgun, I danced on the balcony of the Lincoln jail for an hour, laughing.

Some of the boys asked why I didn't just ride away, but you don't get many moments like that.

Somebody's coming toward me, silhouetted against the moon. He has a familiar walk, but it's so dark I can't focus my eyes.

"¿Quién es? Garrett?"

I ask again, louder: "Who's that?"

SALLIE CHISUM: CANDY HEARTS

They say he was a bad man, that it was a good thing Garrett shot him, but that's a lie.

Billy brought me two candy hearts one hot afternoon in August. I remember how soft his hands seemed. It was like being touched by a cloud.

I was new at my uncle's ranch, lonely. Billy smiled and said, "Don't believe everything you hear about me."

I was thirteen and had never been kissed and the chocolate melted on my lips.

GARRETT: PALS

We drank double shots of bourbon back-to-back with beer. I told Billy's older brother it had to be the way it was, the

Kid would never surrender, and Joe said he understood. Billy was always wild.

I told Joe that the Kid and I rode together, played cards together, drank together, slept with the same women; we were pals.

Joe said, "Now we're pals," slurring his words, his arm on my unsteady shoulder, but it wasn't the same as when Billy touched me.

The Burial of

Letty Strayhorn

ELMER KELTON

GREENLEAF STRAYHORN frowned as he rode beyond the dense liveoak motte and got his first clear look at Prosperity. The dry west wind, which had been blowing almost unbroken for a week, picked up dust from the silent streets and lifted it over the frame buildings to lose it against a cloudless blue sky. He turned toward the brown packhorse that trailed the young sorrel he was riding. His feeling of distaste deepened the wrinkles which had resulted from long years of labor in the sun.

"Wasn't much of a town when we left here, Letty, and I can't see that it's got any better. But you wanted to come back."

Prosperity had a courthouse square but no courthouse. Even after voting some of its horses and dogs, it had lost

the county-seat election to rival Paradise Forks, a larger
town which could rustle up more horses and dogs. Greenleaf hoped the dramshop was still operating. He had
paused in Paradise Forks only long enough to buy a meal
cooked by someone other than himself, and that had been
yesterday. He was pleased to see the front door open. If
the sign out front had been repainted during his twelve-
year absence, he could not tell it.

"Finest in liquors, wines and bitters," he read aloud.
"Cold beer and billiards. Our kind of a place. Mine, anyway. You never was one for self-indulgence."

The sorrel's ears poked forward distrustfully as a yellow
dog sauntered out to inspect the procession. Greenleaf
tightened his knee grip, for the young horse was still prone
to regard with great suspicion such things as dogs, chickens and flying scraps of paper. It had pitched him off once
already on this trip. Greenleaf was getting to an age when
rodeoing was meant to be a spectator sport, not for personal participation. The dog quickly lost interest in rider
and horses and angled off toward the liveoak motte to try
and worry a rabbit or two.

Greenleaf tied up the horses in front of the saloon,
loosening the girth so his saddlehorse could breathe easier.
He checked the pack on the brown horse and found it still
snug. Seeing no others tied nearby, he knew the saloon
was enjoying another in a long succession of slow days.

He stepped up onto the board sidewalk, taking an
extra-long stride to skip over a spot where two planks had
been removed. Somebody had evidently fallen through in
the relatively distant past. The rest of the boards were
badly weathered, splintered and worn. It was only a matter
of time until they, too, caused someone embarrassment,
and probably skinned shins.

The whole place looked like the tag end of a hot, dry
summer. Whoever had named this town Prosperity was a
terrible prophet or had a wicked sense of humor, he
thought.

A black cat lay curled in the shade near the front door.

It opened one eye in response to Greenleaf's approach, then closed the eye with minimum compromise to its rest.

The bartender sat on a stool, his head upon his arms atop the bar. He stirred to the jingling of spurs and looked up sleepy-eyed.

"Beer," Greenleaf said. "A cold one if you've got it."

The man delivered it to him in a mug and gave him a squinting appraisal. "Ain't your name Greenleaf Shoehorn?"

"Strayhorn."

"A name like Greenleaf ain't easily forgot. The rest of it . . ." He shrugged. "Didn't you used to work on Old Man Hopkins' place?"

"And married his daughter Letty."

Memory made the bartender smile. "Anybody who ever met Letty would remember her. A mighty strong-willed woman. Where's she at?"

"Outside, on a horse."

The bartender frowned. "You'd leave her in the hot sun while you come in here for a cool drink?" He walked to the door. "All I see is two horses."

"She's under the tarp on the packhorse, in a lard can. Her ashes, I mean."

The bartender's face fell. "She's dead?"

"Took by a fever two weeks ago. Last thing she asked me was to bring her back here and bury her on the homeplace alongside her mama and papa. It was so far, the only way I could do it was to bring her ashes."

Soberly the bartender refilled the mug Greenleaf had drained. "Sorry about Letty. Everybody liked her. Everybody except Luther Quinton. He hated all the Hopkinses, and everybody that neighbored them."

"It always makes it easier when you hate the people you set out to rob. Less troublin' on the conscience."

"He still owns the old Hopkins place. He may not take it kindly, you buryin' Letty there. Asked him yet?"

"Wasn't figurin' on askin' him. Just figured on doin' it."

The bartender's attention was drawn to the front window. "If you *was* thinkin' about askin' him, this'd be the time. That's him comin' yonder."

Greenleaf carried his beer to the door, where he watched as the black cat raised up from its nap, stretched itself luxuriously, and meandered out into the windy street, crossing Quinton's path. Quinton stopped abruptly, turning back and taking a path that led him far around the cat. It stopped in the middle of the deserted street to lick itself.

The bartender remarked, "Superstitious, Luther is. Won't buy anything by the dozen because he's afraid they may throw in an extra one on him. They say he won't even keep a mirror in his house because he's afraid he might break it."

"He probably just doesn't like to look at himself. I never liked lookin' at him either." Quinton had long legs and a short neck. He had always reminded Greenleaf of a frog.

Quinton came to the door, looking back to be sure the cat had not moved. He demanded of the bartender, "How many more lives has that tomcat got? I've been hopin' a wagon might run over him in the street."

"She ain't a tomcat, and there ain't enough traffic. She's liable to live for twenty years."

"I'd haul her off and dump her, but I know she'd come back."

Quinton's attention shifted to Greenleaf, and his eyes narrowed with recognition. "Speakin' of comin' back . . ." He pointed a thick, hairy finger. "Ain't you the hired hand that married the Hopkins girl?"

"Letty. Yep, I'm the one."

"There's no accountin' for some people's judgment. Wonder she ain't killed and scalped you before now. Has Indian blood in her, don't she?"

"Her mama was half Choctaw."

"Probably some kind of a medicine woman. That Letty laid a curse on me the day I took over the Hopkins place. Cow market went to hell. Calf crop dropped to half. Rain quit and the springs dried up. I had nothin' but bad luck for over a year."

"Only a year? She must not've put her whole heart into it."

Dread was in Quinton's eyes. "She back to cause me more misery?"

"She died."

Relief washed over Quinton's round, furrowed face like sunshine breaking through a dark cloud. He was not one to smile easily, but he ventured dangerously near. "I'm mighty sorry to hear it." He gulped down a glass of whiskey in one long swallow. "Mighty sorry."

Greenleaf grunted. "I can see that." He turned to the bartender. "Old Brother Ratliff still doin' the preachin'?"

The bartender nodded. "You'll find him at the parsonage over by the church. My sympathies about Letty."

Greenleaf thanked him and walked out. He had not expected this to be a pleasant homecoming, and running into Luther Quinton had helped it live down to his expectations. Untying the two horses, he looked a moment at the pack on the second animal, and a catch came in his throat. He had worked his way through the darkest of his grief, but a lingering sadness still shadowed him. He wanted to fulfill his promise to Letty, then put this place behind him for once and all. His and Letty's leavetaking from here had created a residue of memories bitter to the taste.

Not all the fault had been Quinton's. Letty's father should have known he was dealing himself a busted flush when he tried farming on land where the average rainfall was only about fifteen inches a year, and half of that tended to come in one night if it came at all. Letty's stubborn nature was a natural heritage from both sides of her family. She had tried to keep on farming even though her father had accomplished four crop failures in a row. He had died of a seizure in the middle of a diatribe against the bank for letting him borrow himself so deeply into the hole and refusing to let him dig the hole any deeper.

All Quinton had done, really, was to buy the notes from the frustrated banker and foreclose on Letty. Quinton had acquired several other properties the same way. He was not a hawk that kills its prey but rather a buzzard which feeds on whatever has died a natural death.

Greenleaf had not considered Brother Ratliff an old man when he had lived here, but like the town, the minister had aged a lot in a dozen years. Greenleaf had to knock on the door a third time before it swung inward and a tall, slightly stooped gentleman peered down at him, cocking his head a little to one side to present his best ear. From Ratliff's gaunt appearance, Greenleaf judged that the Sunday offering plate had been coming back but little heavier than it went out.

"May I be of service to you, friend?"

"I'm Greenleaf Strayhorn. You may not remember, but you tied the knot for me and Letty Hopkins a long time ago."

The minister smiled broadly and made a gesture that invited him into the spare little house. "I do remember. Quite a beautiful bride, she was. Have you brought her with you?"

"In a manner of speakin', yes sir. I was wonderin' if you'd be kind enough to say some fittin' words over her so I can put her ashes in the ground?"

The minister's smile died. "The Lord calls all of us home eventually, but it would seem He has called her much too early. I hope she had a good life to compensate for its shortness."

"We did tolerable well. Got us a nice little ranch up north, though we wasn't blessed with kids. She just never could shake loose from her old family homeplace. The memory of it was always there, itchin' like a wool shirt. She wanted me to bring her back."

"It's a sad thing to preach a funeral, but part of my calling is to comfort the bereaved and commend the soul to a better land. When would you want me to perform the service?"

"Right now, if that's not too soon."

The minister put on his black coat and walked with Greenleaf to the church next door. "Would you mind pulling the bell rope for me, son? The devil has afflicted my shoulder with rheumatism."

Afterward, Greenleaf unwrapped the pack and fetched the lard can containing all that was left in the world of Letty Strayhorn. He placed it in front of the altar. A dozen or so citizens came, curious about the reason for the bell to ring in the middle of the week. Among them was the bartender, who knew. He had removed his apron and put on a coat, though the church was oppressively warm. Its doors and windows had been kept shut because the wind would have brought in too much dust.

The sermon was brief, for Brother Ratliff did not know all that much to say about Letty's past, just that she had been a hard-working, God-fearing woman who held strong opinions about right and wrong and did not easily abide compromise.

At the end of the closing prayer he said, "Now, if any of you would like to accompany the deceased to her final resting place, you are welcome to go with us to the old Hopkins farm."

A loud voice boomed from the rear of the church. "No, you ain't! The place is mine, and that woman ain't fixin' to be buried in any ground that belongs to me!"

The minister was first surprised, then dismayed. "Brother Quinton, surely you would not deny that good soul the right to be buried amongst her own."

"Good soul? A witch, I'd call her. A medicine woman, somethin' from the Indian blood in her."

"She has passed on to another life. She can do you no harm now."

"I'm takin' no chances. You want her buried, bury her here in town. You ain't bringin' her out to my place."

Apologetically the minister looked back to Greenleaf. "I am sorry, Brother Strayhorn. I may argue with Brother Quinton's logic, but I cannot argue with his legal rights."

Greenleaf stood up and studied Quinton's physical stature. He decided he could probably whip the man, if it came to a contest. But he would no doubt end up in jail, and he still would not be able to carry out Letty's final wish.

"She's goin' to be disappointed," he said.

The town cemetery was a depressing place, the site picked for convenience rather than for beauty. His sleeves rolled up, Greenleaf worked with a pair of posthole diggers that belonged to the minister. Brother Ratliff, looking too frail to help in this kind of labor, sat on a marble gravestone and watched as the hole approached three feet in depth. The length of the handles would limit Greenleaf's digging. The bartender had come to the cemetery but had left after a few minutes to reopen the saloon lest he miss out on any thirsty customers. Or perhaps he had feared he might be called upon to lend a hand with the diggers.

Ratliff said, "It matters not where the body lies."

"So the old song says," Greenleaf responded, turning into the wind. Though its breath was warm, it felt cool against his sweaty face and passing through his partially soaked shirt. "But I feel like I'm breakin' a promise. I never got to do everything I wanted to for Letty while she was livin', but at least I never broke a promise to her."

"You made your promise in good faith. Now for reasons beyond your control you cannot fulfill it. She would understand that. Anyway, you brought her back to her hometown. That's close."

"I remember a couple of times my stomach was growlin' awful loud at me, and I bore down on a whitetail deer for meat but missed. Close wasn't good enough. I was still hungry."

"You've done the best you could."

"No, I ain't." Greenleaf brought the diggers up out of the hole and leaned on their handles while he pondered. "Mind lendin' me these diggers a little longer, Preacher?"

Ratliff studied him quizzically. "You'd be welcome to keep them. Should I ask you what for?"

"A man in your profession ain't supposed to lie. If I don't tell you, you won't have to lie to anybody that might ask you."

Greenleaf used the diggers to rake dirt back into the hole and tamp it down. The lard can still sat where he had placed it beside a nearby gravestone. "We had a full moon last night. It ought to be just as bright tonight."

The minister looked up at the cloudless sky. "Unless it rains. I would say our chance for rain is about as remote as the chance of Luther Quinton donating money for a new church. Would you like for me to go with you?"

"You've got to live here afterward, Preacher. I don't." Greenleaf finished filling the hole. "If I was to leave you the money, would you see to it that a proper headstone is put up for her?"

"I would consider it a privilege."

"Thanks." Greenleaf extended his hand. "You don't just know the words, Preacher. You know the *Lord*."

Even if the moon had not been bright, Greenleaf could have found the old Hopkins place without difficulty. He had ridden the road a hundred times in daylight and in darkness. Nothing had changed in the dozen years since he had last traveled this way. He rode by the deserted house where the Hopkins family had lived while they struggled futilely to extract a good living from a soil that seemed always thirsty. He stopped a moment to study the frame structure. The porch roof was sagging, one of its posts buckled out of place. He suspected the rest of the house looked as desolate. The wind, which had abated but little with moonrise, moaned through broken windows.

"Probably just as well we've come at night, Letty. I doubt you'd like the looks of the place in the daytime."

Memories flooded his mind, memories of coming to work here as hired help, of first meeting Letty, of gradually falling in love with her. A tune ran through his brain, a tune she had taught him when they had first known one another and that they had often sung together. He dwelled at length upon the night he had brought her back here after their wedding in town. Life had seemed golden then . . . for a while. But reality had soon intruded. It always did, after so long. It intruded now.

"I'd best be gettin' about the business, Letty, just in case Luther Quinton is smarter than I think he is."

The small family cemetery lay halfway up a gentle hillside some three hundred yards above the house. Rocks which the plow had turned up in the field had been hauled to the site to build a small protective fence. Greenleaf dismounted beside the gate and tied the saddlehorse to the latchpost. He let the packhorse's rein drop. The brown would not stray away from the sorrel. He untied the rope that bound the diggers to the pack, then unwrapped the pack.

Carefully he lifted down the lard can. He had been amazed at how little it weighed. Letty had never been a large woman, but it had seemed to him that her ashes should represent more weight than this. Carrying the can under one arm and the diggers under the other, he started through the gate.

He had never been of a superstitious nature, but his heart almost stopped when he saw three dark figures rise up from behind the gravestones that marked the resting places of Letty's mother and father. He gasped for breath.

The voice was not that of a ghost. It belonged to Luther Quinton. "Ain't it strange how you can tell some people *no* and they don't put up an argument? Tell others and it seems like they can't even hear you."

The shock lingered, and Greenleaf had trouble getting his voice back. "I guess it's because *no* doesn't always make much sense."

"It don't have to. All that counts is that this place belongs to me, and I don't want you on it, you or that woman of yours either. Lucky for me I set a man to watchin' you in town. He seen you fill that hole back up without puttin' anything in it but dirt."

"Look, Luther, you hurt her enough when she was livin'. At least you could let her rest in peace now. Like the preacher said, she's in no shape to do you any harm. She just wanted to be buried next to her folks. That don't seem like much to ask."

"But it is. You heard her when she laid that curse on me after I took this place. She named a dozen awful things that was fixin' to happen to me, and most of them did. Anybody that strong ain't goin' to quit just because they're dead." Quinton shook his head violently. "I'm tellin' you, she's some kind of an Indian medicine woman. If I was to let you bury her here, I'd never be shed of her. She'd be risin' up out of that grave and hauntin' my every move."

"That's a crazy notion. She never was a medicine woman or anything like that. She wasn't but a quarter Indian in the first place. The rest was white."

"All I know is what she done to me before. I don't aim to let her put a hex on me again."

"You can't watch this place all the time. I can wait. Once she's in the ground, you wouldn't have the guts to dig her up."

"I could find twenty men who'd do it for whiskey money. I'd have them carry her over into the next county and throw her in the river, can and all."

Frustration began to gnaw at Greenleaf. Quinton had him blocked.

Quinton's voice brightened with a sense of victory. "So take her back to town, where you ought to've buried her in the first place. Since you seem to enjoy funerals, you can have another one for her."

"I hope they let me know when *your* funeral takes place, Luther. I'd ride bareback two hundred miles to be here."

Quinton spoke to the two men beside him. "I want you to ride to town with him and be sure he doesn't do anything with that can of ashes. I want him to carry it where you can watch it all the way."

One of the men tied up Greenleaf's pack and lashed

the diggers down tightly against it. The other held the can while Greenleaf mounted the sorrel horse, then handed it up to him.

Quinton said, "If I ever see you on my place again, I'm liable to mistake you for a coyote and shoot you. Now git!"

To underscore his order, he drew his pistol and fired a shot under the young sorrel's feet.

That was a bad mistake. The horse bawled in fright and jumped straight up, then alternated between a wild run-away and fits of frenzied pitching in a semicircle around the little cemetery. Greenleaf lost the reins at the second jump and grabbed at the saddlehorn with his left hand. He was handicapped by the lard can, which he tried to hold tightly under his right arm. He did not want to lose Letty.

It was a forlorn hope. The lid popped from the can, and the ashes began streaming out as the horse ran a few strides, then whipped about, pitched a few jumps and ran again. The west wind caught them and carried them away. At last Greenleaf felt himself losing his seat and his hold on the horn. He bumped the rim of the cantle and kicked his feet clear of the stirrups to keep from hanging up. He had the sensation of being suspended in midair for a second or two, then came down. His feet landed hard on the bare ground but did not stay beneath him. His rump hit next, and he went rolling, the can bending under his weight.

It took him a minute to regain his breath. In the moonlight he saw one of Quinton's men chasing after the sorrel horse. The packhorse stood where it had been all along, watching the show with only mild interest.

Quinton's second man came, finally, and helped Greenleaf to his feet. "You hurt?"

"Nothin' seems to be broke except my feelin's." Greenleaf bent down and picked up the can. Most of the ashes had spilled from it. He waited until Quinton approached, then poured out what remained. The wind carried part of them into Quinton's face.

The man sputtered and raged and tried desperately to brush away the ashes.

"Well, Luther," Greenleaf said, "you really done it now. If I'd buried her here, you'd've always known where she was. The way it is, you'll never know where she's at. The wind has scattered her all over the place."

Quinton seemed about to cry, still brushing wildly at his clothing. Greenleaf thrust the bent can into his hands. Quinton made some vague shrieking sound and hurled it away as if it were full of snakes.

The first Quinton man brought Greenleaf his horse. Greenleaf's hip hurt where he had fallen, and he knew it would be giving him unshirted hell tomorrow. But tonight it was almost a good pain. He felt strangely elated as he swung up into the saddle. He reached down for the pack-horse's rein.

"This isn't what Letty asked for, but I have a feelin' she wouldn't mind. She'd've liked knowin' that no matter where you go on this place, she'll be there ahead of you. And she won't let you forget it, not for a minute."

Riding away, he remembered the old tune Letty had taught him a long time ago. Oddly, he felt like whistling it, so he did.

The Day of
the Rain

TEDDY KELLER

DAVE KRAMER shouldered through the saloon's swinging doors and halted inside. The rain dripping off his slicker made little splashes at his feet. The usual sour saloon smells mingled with the scents of wet leather and soaked linsey-woolsey, of mud tracked in and warmth tracked out.

Of the half-dozen cowpokes bellied up to the bar, only Billy Holt didn't turn to eye the newcomer. But there was a tremor in Billy's raised hand, a tightening of slender shoulders beneath a faded jumper.

"There's only one gent that stomps in here like he owned the town," Billy said. "Mr. Dave Kramer came to tell me my cows ate a whole handful of his grass."

Beside Billy a puncher chuckled, another grinned.

Dave's hard gaze swept the men. The chuckle choked; the grin collapsed.

"Very funny." Dave jammed fists against hips, not bothering to flip his slicker clear of his gun. "You were warned for the last time a month ago, Billy. Your stock's fat off my grass. I figure half that meat is mine, and I aim to sell those critters and keep my share."

"You can't . . ." Billy wobbled when he turned.

"If you haven't sold your horse for booze, you'd better saddle up and ride clean outa this country."

"You can't do that." Billy's legs got tangled and he sloshed whiskey out of his glass. His eyes needed time and effort to focus. "That's stealing."

"You've been stealing my grass for a year," Dave said, "and I'm tired of it. You can pay up or clear out. If you want to make a fight of it, I'll still be in town come sundown."

"Big talk," Billy muttered. "Who's gonna know sundown on a day like this?" His feet shuffled and got him turned back to the bar.

Dave growled, "We can call it sundown right now."

"Oh, listen to the big, brave rancher." Doc Avery sat at a corner table, his half-eaten steak and beans before him. He was about as big as a banty rooster with a temper to match. His thin gray hair was mussed and his wet suit coat hung over the back of his chair.

Dave nodded and said, "This isn't your business, Doc."

"Of course it's my business. I couldn't patch up Billy's brother good enough. Remember? This town doesn't need any more cripples."

"I warned him, just like I warned Billy."

"Is a little bit of grass that important to you?"

Dave half turned, and a small splash of water cascaded off his hat brim. "We've got laws about that."

"Damn the laws," Doc shouted. He slapped the table and his plate and cup jumped. "Dave Kramer, I remember when you weren't much more'n a yearling and you started to show that ornery streak. Folks thought it was kinda cute, then. Now you're an overgrown bully with a streak of cuss-edness and—"

"You heard me, Doc." Dave faced the bar. "And so did you, Billy. You can fight or run, but you're done stealing my grass."

Dave spun on his heel and marched out of the saloon. Ann Maitland stood on the covered boardwalk directly in front of him.

Dave halted, startled, his mind shifting from the mild turmoil of the saloon to a totally pleasant mood. "Well." He smiled and moved to her. "This is nice."

"Not very," Ann snapped. The soft rain had woven a sparkling tiara in her black hair. But her dark eyes flashed and a frown slashed furrows between her brows. Her wide, full lips clamped in a grim line. "I was on my way to . . . well, I couldn't help hearing what you said to Billy and Doc."

"That was business."

"Dave, you promised to leave your neighbors alone."

He wanted to shout his dominance, but he took his time and said, "I leave them alone until they start pushing me."

"You've got square miles of pasture. Do Billy's cows eat that much?"

"They got fat on my grass."

"You're his neighbor." She removed her dark shawl and shook the rain out of it. "Neighbors help one another."

"Good neighbors don't take advantage of each other."

She flipped the shawl over her shoulders again. She sighed, but her jawline could've been forged. "I'm sorry, Dave."

"What does that mean?"

"It means I'm seeing a side of you I thought was gone. It means you didn't keep your word to me. It means . . ."

"What?" Dave swallowed against a rage for Billy Holt and a fear of what Ann was thinking.

"It means . . . I have some things to think about."

"What things?"

"The plans we've made."

Just then a sodden, mongrel dog limped past Ann and sagged against Dave's leg. Dave kicked sideways. The dog tumbled away, whimpering.

"Dave!" Ann cried. There was hurt in her dark eyes.

He glared at the wretched, knee-high dog, and he boiled over. "Do you expect me to back down on what I said to Billy?"

"Yes."

"I can't. I won't."

Ann made a choking sound. "Then maybe I can't." She tugged the end of the shawl over her face and turned away.

Dave wheeled around and his boot bumped against the mongrel dog. He lurched, fought for balance, and staggered for two steps. Now all his anger focused on the miserable dog. He spun around and cocked his right leg.

Too late he saw Ann plunge in front of the dog. His kick grazed her arm and his spur raked across the sleeve of her dress. She tumbled to the boards beside the soggy animal and she threw a protective arm across the dog. The dog's stub tail twitched wearily. He licked Ann's face.

Dave stepped around the dog. He bent and gripped Ann's shoulder. She shook him off and shoved to her feet. The dog, holding high its right front leg, limped to Dave.

"If you want to help somebody," Ann said, "help this poor dog."

Dave shook his head. "His leg's broken. I'll put him out of his misery."

Ann hunkered down beside the dog and put her arms around him. "You're not going to hurt anybody else."

Now the dog represented all of Dave's rage and frustration. He whirled away and stepped off the boardwalk and out from under the wooden awning. The rain settled upon his hat. Three days of heavy drizzle had turned the street into a squishy mass that would mire a wagon to its hubs. His boots were clots of mud when he swung into the saddle.

"No, no, doggie," Ann called. "Come back. Here, boy."

Dave hipped around and saw Ann, arm extended, as if reaching a helping hand. The dog limped along the boardwalk. With something like hope in its eyes, the dog peered at Dave. But it kept going.

"Dave," Ann called, "he wants you to follow him."

At the end of the boardwalk, the dog plunged into the street. He seemed to find the best footing, but even so he labored through the muck. The rain washed the matted hair of the brown back, and one shoulder was red where blood oozed from a wound at the neck. There was more blood on the short nose. A bullet was the merciful answer for the miserable animal.

Dave cursed under his breath, flicked back his slicker, and jerked the Colt from its holster. He flapped the reins. The horse came around sluggishly. Dave squeezed the trigger at the same moment the horse slipped in the mud. Dave's bullet kicked up a geyser of mud ten feet short of the dog.

"Dave Kramer!" Ann screamed. She tucked up her skirt and jumped from the boardwalk. Instantly her shoes knifed through the mud and she sank past her ankles. She called, "Here, boy," and struggled to take a step.

Doc Avery, his napkin in one hand, pushed the swinging doors and surveyed the street. "You shooting at people already?"

"All right, Ann," Dave said. "Get back to dry land. I'll follow the dog."

He left Ann and Doc to talk things over, and he wheeled his horse into the track made by three small feet. The dog was headed out of town, into a thickening curtain of rain. Dave wouldn't have to follow far before the sound of a gunshot would be muffled, and the death of a stray dog would go unnoticed.

Past the upper edge of town, the dog angled onto thick buffalo grass and found better footing. He quickened to a weary, three-legged trot. The road became more solid where it bent into the rocky earth of the canyon. But now the dog slowed. Its crippled leg dragged uselessly.

Dave touched rowels and the horse closed on the dog. The swaying brown back made an easy target. Dave pulled his gun again. He took casual aim.

The dog looked back and up into the rain, checking on Dave, and its good front leg stumbled over a small rock. The dog sprawled on its chest and uttered one small cry. Immediately he scrambled gamely to his feet and seemed more determined to guide Dave into the canyon.

The dog stumbled again. Dave holstered his gun. He swung to the ground, scooped up the dog and climbed aboard. With a small whimper, the dog clamped his teeth onto Dave's wrist.

Dave cocked his free hand to hit the dog. Then he shrugged and said, "Hurts, doesn't it, boy?"

The dog scraped a rough tongue across the wrist he had bitten. Dave grinned and urged the horse into motion. But the maneuver to retrieve the dog had shifted Dave's slicker. Cold rain began to dribble down inside his shirt.

The canyon walls squeezed closer and the road clung precariously to the near vertical cliff. The usually docile stream, gorged by rain and dirt, thundered through the gulch. The horse shied. A ragged rock, the size of a kitchen stove, slithered from above and pitched across the road to tumble down, down into the river.

Dave scanned the cliffs ahead. Three days of rain had washed Nature's mortar from around great boulders. They hung there now, ready at any moment to drop a landslide upon horse, dog and man.

Suddenly the dog squirmed from Dave's arm. He hit the ground on his feet and let out a howl. He stood a moment, swaying, then plunged down the steep slope toward the river. Only now did Dave see the wrecked wagon far below.

Dismounting, he knelt at the edge of the road for a quick survey. Through the rain he could see that a chunk of cliff had broken off and had dumped wagon and mules into the gulch. The wagon lay twisted and splintered upon the rocks. One mule hung dead in the traces. Another, cut and limping, grazed upstream from the wreckage.

The dog had reached the wagon. He paced beside it for a moment. Then he turned his face up into the rain and barked urgently.

Dave spoke words of quiet assurance to his horse while he stuffed his gunbelt into the saddlebag and tied his rope to the saddle horn. Wondering at his own intelligence, he gripped the rope and stood for a moment at the brink. Then, boots slipping at every move, he let himself down the steep slope a foot at a time. Each step threatened to dislodge a new landslide. And with each step the flooding river roared louder.

At the foot of the cliff Dave slipped and slid, found precarious footing and turned loose of the rope. The dog hobbled close, his tail wagging furiously. And Dave saw a man's body twisted across the shattered wagon seat.

Dave stepped into the lapping reaches of the brown water and dragged the man off the seat and onto the rocks. He was not past his mid-thirties, only a few years older than Dave. Now he was a pathetic rag doll, his neck and legs broken in the horrible plunge.

Dave's stomach knotted and he turned away. He found the woman lodged against a wheel, her head and shoulders under water. He pulled her out and gently placed her body beside her husband's.

An unfamiliar lump wedged in Dave's throat. Hot tears mingled with the rain on his face. He bent over the couple and straightened the man's head. Then he locked the man's arm through his wife's. Even in death, the man's courage seemed plain in his face. The woman had been almost pretty. Care had etched the beginnings of maturity around her eyes, but hers was a face that had laughed a lot.

The yipping of the dog brought Dave around. Above the roar of the river, he heard a thudding sound overhead. He glanced up to see an anvil-size boulder bounding down the slope. He leaped aside. The boulder smashed down close to the bodies, then bounced high over the wagon and splashed into the booming stream.

Dave moved toward the dangling end of his rope and called to the dog. This time his guide ignored him. The dog turned an imploring gaze to the man, then whined and pawed at the water's edge where the wagon's tailgate was just out of reach. Dave watched, puzzled, for a moment. Then he hurried to the dog.

It took him one more moment to discover the small hand protruding from under the wagon's torn canvas. He stepped into the water and floundered in a knee-deep flood. Another boulder plunged down the cliff and smashed into the river twenty yards upstream.

Grabbing the tailgate, Dave hauled himself close to the wagon. He flung ripped canvas aside. A small boy blinked at him.

Dave couldn't allow himself even seconds for shock or surprise, not with more rocks rattling down the cliff. He clambered aboard the tilted, pitching wagon box. The boy sat in shallow water, with spray breaking over him. He had a foot wedged under water, beneath a clutter of heavy boxes.

Dave wrestled one box aside. As he struggled with another, he caught the deep thudding sound. He threw himself across the boy and waited. There was another heavy thud and an eternity of waiting. Then the boulder plunged into the river directly beside the wagon.

Spray drenched Dave and the boy. The wave sent up by the boulder shook the wagon. Its shattered bulk shifted, and the riverbank seemed to lurch away.

Frantically, Dave flung boxes and crates aside, and the small foot came free. Dave cradled the boy in his arms. The wagon creaked, then groaned in its death throes and floated into the wild current. Dave leaped as far as he could and plunged into the water.

The current snatched at his billowing slicker and slapped his feet from under him. He drove his boots down and felt a rock. He kicked hard. Again the swirling water yanked his feet from under him. Again he stomped down onto a solid rock and drove himself toward shore. His free hand grasped a tree root.

He set the boy on the muddy bank, then heaved himself up. For a moment he lay there, sucking in great breaths of air. Then the dog licked his face. Downstream a section of rocks and mud thundered into the river.

Dave scrambled to his feet and glanced up. A small rock sang past him. Already the wrecked wagon had been swept out of sight. He remembered the dead mule that had gone with the wagon. The other mule had wandered upstream.

Another rock splashed into the river a few yards away. Dave didn't waste more time scanning the cliff. He bent the boy over his shoulder and floundered across to his rope. He checked the boy's balance, then gripped the rope and went up hand over hand.

Arms leaden, lungs bursting, Dave dragged himself onto the road. He pushed to his feet and placed the boy in the saddle. The horse shied as more rocks hurtled past. Dave quickly coiled his rope and climbed up behind the saddle. The horse twitched at the double load and peered back inquiringly. Apparently satisfied, he got into motion.

The boy stirred. His head twisted and his lips moved. At last he cried, "Toby! Where's Toby?"

"Whoa," Dave shouted.

He slid over the horse's rump and stepped to the edge of the road. Far below, the dog pawed weakly at the canyon wall. Then, tail drawn under, he turned and dragged himself to the bodies of the man and woman. He collapsed between them.

Small rocks clattered across the road and down to the river. Dave hesitated, staring at the dead couple, the valiant dog. He heard the boy choke out another cry.

Dave backed the horse to a point directly above the dead folks. Again he tied his rope to the saddle horn and stepped to the cliff's edge. Plunging down the slope again, he burned his hands on the rope and banged every part of him against the slick, jagged rocks.

The end of the rope sawed through his hands. He tumbled across more rocks and mud and slammed against a boulder. The wind gushed out of him.

Gasping for air, he rolled to his hands and knees. The dog stared at him through eyes that seemed half dead. The tail managed one feeble wag. Dave crawled to the man's body, reached across and picked up the dog. Toby only groaned, apparently too weak to cry with pain.

Dave fought to get himself upright. His feet heavy with fatigue, he stumbled and staggered to the end of the rope. Now he ducked his head and arched the dog across the back of his neck, as he might have carried a deer.

He ripped a strip from his torn slicker, tied the dog's back legs together and lashed them to the good front leg. With hands raw and bleeding, he grasped the rope and sucked in a deep breath.

Through the rope he felt the horse shy again, too near the cliff's edge. Rocks plummeted down. A small boulder hurtled past, inches from man and dog.

His hands were raw, his lungs bursting. His boots slipped on the wet rocks, the rope burned in his hands. Halfway up, he bumped over a protruding rock and paused to catch his breath. He glanced up through the rain to gauge the distance and his sapped strength.

At the very rim of the canyon, far above both horse and boy on the road, a torrent of mud flushed around a giant boulder. The huge rock oozed an inch, then another.

"Giddyap, boy!" Dave shouted. He twisted the rope around his wrist. "Hey! Run for home!"

The line snapped taut. The horse peered down the cliff. The big boulder sloughed on its ancient foundation.

"Giddyap, dammit!" Dave yelled.

The horse lunged. The rope cut into Dave's wrist and dragged him off his perch. He kicked against the cliff, swinging like a crazy pendulum. The boulder crashed onto the road where horse and boy had been, then plunged on down the cliff. It flung mud into Dave's face as it hurtled past.

"Whoa!" Dave called. "Whoa, boy. Steady now."

The horse halted obediently. Toby made a sound that might've been pain or relief. Dave hauled himself up, hand over trembling hand. He knew he was too exhausted to reach the road again, but he made one more effort. He wanted to cry out his hopelessness, but he clamped his mind around the image of boy and dog, and he clutched the rope with bleeding hands.

And then he was at the brink, then onto the road. He crawled a few feet and collapsed, the dog still across his neck. After a long moment, he raised his head and peered to horse and boy. Close by a towering rock tipped and plunged and tore away a section of the road.

Dave unlashed the dog. Then he turned and peered through the rain to the raging water below. The last landslide had buried the bodies of the man and woman.

"Mama?" the boy asked. "Papa?"

Dave coiled his rope. He carefully took the dog in his arms and heaved himself up behind the saddle. When he touched heels to the horse's belly, he realized that his spurs were gone. The horse moved ahead slowly. Dave reached around dog and boy to grip the saddle horn. He knew that he'd never been so wet and cold. But he was conscious only of the rain and his burning hands and the gentle sway of the horse.

When he opened his eyes, the rain-soaked false fronts and the ooze of the street looked like the Promised Land. Nobody stirred along the boardwalk. Dave guided his horse past the livery stable and beckoned to old Charlie there. Then he rode to directly in front of Doc Avery's office.

"Hey, Doc," he shouted. "Come on out here."

Old Charlie, head down and slicker flapping, plowed through mud to the boardwalk. He made grumbling noises.

Dave said, "Wait'll we unload. Then this guy deserves a good rubbing and plenty of oats."

Doc Avery jerked his door open and stomped onto the

walk. "Dave Kramer, what in blazes are you hollering . . ." He broke off when he got a look at the horse and its burdens. "What in the world?"

"Take the boy," Dave said. "Gently. No telling what may be busted."

"Yeah," Doc growled. "I've handled hurt kids before."

Doc eased the boy from the saddle and cradled him with professional ease. Charlie offered a hand as Dave slid onto the boardwalk with the dog in his arms. Doc gave Dave and the dog a long look. Then he hurried into his office. Charlie got the horse turned. Dave patted the horse's rump as Charlie led him toward the stable.

Inside the office, Dave felt a sense of ease. A potbellied stove radiated warmth, and Doc, secure in his sanctuary, exuded skill and knowledge. The low cots, the operating table, the cabinet of instruments and bottles, all were testimony to the medical miracles performed here. The doctor was already peeling off the boy's clothing, wrapping him in blankets, placing him carefully on a cot.

Dave watched for only a moment, then put the dog down on another cot. Over a washstand he found a stack of neatly folded towels. He grabbed an armload and began working over the dog. Mud, dirt and blood stained towel after towel. Many minutes later Dave had the long brown hair dry. He wrapped Toby in a blanket and petted the frowzy face. When Dave straightened, he met Doc's outraged gaze.

"What the hell do you think you're doing?" Doc demanded. "This is no dog hospital and I'm no damn' dog doctor. Now get that fleabag out of here."

"Toby?" the boy breathed. His eyes fluttered. "Where's Toby?"

Doc glanced to Dave and then to the dog. He leaned over the boy and murmured, "Everything's fine, son. Toby's right here."

The boy smiled weakly, and his eyes closed. Doc frowned at Dave, then bent over the boy, probing, feeling, listening. Dave slumped into a chair near the stove. He pulled off his boots and related all that had happened.

After long minutes, Doc straightened beside the boy's cot. He was thoughtful as he crossed the room and placed Dave's boots closer to the stove.

"It's a miracle," Doc said, "but there're no broken bones. The boy's had a terrible shock and he's suffering from exposure. But with luck, he'll be throwing conniption fits if we try to keep him in bed after tomorrow."

"Good," Dave said. He spread his hands to the stove. "Now how about Toby?"

"I thought his leg was broken."

"Looked like it to me."

"Then he'll have to be shot."

Dave shoved upright in the chair. "Like hell."

"Maybe amputation."

"That'd be worse."

Doc shuffled to his rolltop desk, opened a drawer and took out a revolver. Jamming it into his belt, he strode to Toby's cot. He gently lifted the dog. Without a glance to Dave, he headed for the back door.

Dave leaped past Doc to block the door. Doc halted in his tracks. Underneath the blanket, Toby's tail wiggled.

"That dog went through hell to save the boy." Dave hooked his thumbs in his gunbelt. "He deserves to live, and by gadfrey, Doc, you'll see that he makes it."

Doc calmly regarded Dave for long seconds. "Your socks are making wet spots on my floor. You've already got this office smelling like a Chinese laundry."

"What about Toby?" Dave demanded.

Doc carried the dog to the cot. He stood for more long seconds and shook his head. "I don't know what to do."

"If a man breaks his leg, do you shoot him?"

"No."

Dave peeled out of his soaked vest and shirt and hung them over the back of the chair. "Of course you don't. You set the bone and you rig a splint to hold the leg and you fix him up as good as new."

"Somehow I seem to remember that."

"Well, treat Toby like a man." Dave sat in the chair and pulled off his pants. "He's done a man's job today."

"There're dry long johns in that cupboard. I can't have my surgical assistant dripping on the patient."

"Assistant?"

"You're going to help. And that get-up of yours looks purty ridiculous."

Dave found the clean things. He got behind a curtained frame and changed into dry underwear and socks and pants and a raggedy shirt. Nothing fit, but it was all dry. By the time he came out, Doc had transferred Toby to the operating table.

Now both men hunched over the table. Doc touched the broken leg, and Toby cringed. Dave began petting Toby, talking to him. Toby looked at Dave and an understanding seemed to cross his face. He nuzzled Dave's hands. That's when Doc seized Dave's wrists and turned his hands over.

"What in blazes did you do to your hands?" When Dave winced, Doc released the wrists and inspected the rope burns. "I'll put something on those cuts."

"After Toby's in the clear," Dave said.

Doc shrugged and turned his attention back to Toby. His stethoscope probed across the small, brown chest and he peered into the sad, brown eyes. Then he straightened and looked long at the dog.

"Our friend's about done in. He's been going on heart too long." Doc shook his head. "Ether may kill him, but I don't think he could stand the pain without it. Can a dog take ether?"

"How would I know?" Dave grunted.

"How would anybody know?" Doc turned away to collect some instruments, then returned to the table. "Hold him."

Dave bent low over Toby again and began petting him, scratching his ears, murmuring to him. Doc's face was grim. His slender hands moved quickly and gently. When

Toby whimpered, Doc muttered under his breath. Perspiration glistened on his forehead. Then, after long minutes, the leg was straight. From somewhere Doc produced two rulers and fashioned a splint.

Toby exhaled slowly.

"I think he knows it's over," Dave said.

"He's a tough little guy." Doc had his stethoscope out again, and he checked Toby's heart beat. "He's a fighter, but he's got maybe one tail wag left."

Dave helped tuck the blanket around Toby, and then the boy stirred and groaned. The two men crowded over the cot. The boy blinked bright blue eyes. His white face against the dark blanket was ghostlike.

"What's the matter with Toby?" the boy asked.

"He has a broken leg," Doc said, "but he's going to be okay."

"Honest?"

Dave glanced to Doc and said, "Honest."

"What's your name, son?" Doc asked.

"Matt. Matthew Lonnergen."

"Can you tell us what happened?"

The boy's gaze flicked between the two men. Then his eyes clouded as he began to remember. "We were headed for . . . Papa told us about land that grows corn higher than you can see. Mama wanted to stop, but Papa said there was a town not very far. We needed hot food, he said. We needed a dry bed. And then . . . then the mountain fell on us."

"Do you know what happened after that?" Doc asked.

"It was awful dark." The boy's eyes brimmed. "I heard Mama crying, but I couldn't move my foot. She said Papa was . . . she said he didn't make it. And she said she couldn't move and the water was getting deeper." He choked on a sob and took a deep breath. "Pretty soon she didn't say anything more. That . . . that's when Toby went for help." He swallowed hard and his eyes were agonized. "Will Toby really be all right?"

"Sure," Doc said, his assurance sounding forced. He cleared his throat. "Sure, Matt."

Matt's solemn gaze fixed on Doc, then on Dave. Doubt clouded the blue eyes. The lids closed. He began to cry softly.

Doc's eyes filled and he muttered, "Damn."

"A child of the frontier." Dave dabbed at his own eyes. "He's seen death before." Now he turned and glanced at Toby. "You didn't convince the boy."

"It's out of our hands," Doc said with quiet resignation. He moved away from the table. "Toby's still alive, but I wouldn't say for how long."

Doc shambled to his desk and lighted another lamp. Somehow the illumination failed to drive out the deathly gloom that filled the office.

Dave stared at the lamp, then at the dog, then at the boy. He recalled what he had seen and what the boy had told, and he knew what Toby and Matt had been through.

Hot tears spilled down his cheeks. He spun around to face the wall. In the stillness he listened for the boy's breathing and the dog's. And suddenly he knew what was wrong.

For the first time he could remember, Dave Kramer wasn't in charge. He wasn't telling people what to do. He didn't command the town and half the county.

Right now he felt helpless. He couldn't remember ever feeling helpless before. He thought of the valiant dog and the brave boy, and there was nothing he could do to help. He had seen the dead couple in the canyon, and there was nothing he could do for them. The mighty Dave Kramer was powerless.

Doc made notes at his desk and checked on both his patients. Dave slumped into the hard chair and stared at the glowing stove. In a moment, Doc came to stand over Dave.

"Let's get some salve on those hands."

Dave barely heard. His mind spun like a cyclone and

he fought against the pictures that were taking shape. Half aloud, he muttered, "Is that the way Billy Holt feels?"

"Huh?" Doc grunted. "Billy doesn't have a broken leg."

Helpless. Was that why Billy clung to the bottle? Did he feel helpless and futile and frustrated? Dave remembered Ann's words, and he wondered if he really had become such an unpleasant person. Or maybe he always had been a bully.

How many times had he promised to control his foul moods? Today he had lashed out at Billy Holt. And he had kicked at Toby and at Ann. He had failed the boy by not following the dog soon enough. And now Toby was dying and there wasn't a thing Dave could do about it. In a little while the last of the boy's entire world would be taken from him.

Dave lurched up from the chair and grabbed for his ripped slicker. He jammed his feet into his wet boots. He had to get out of this place of his impotence.

The door swung open and Ann stood there, the rain still drumming down behind her, the droplets in her hair catching the lamplight. She glanced to Doc, to the two cots, to Dave, and she stepped into the room.

"Dave, what happened?" she asked. She halted, a fresh shawl wet, the hem of her skirt showing traces of mud. Again she looked at the boy, the dog, the doctor. Then her gaze held on Dave, appraising his ill-fitting clothing, his sodden boots.

"Hello, Ann," Doc said.

"It's all over town about Dave riding in with . . ." She peered at the boy. "Dave, what's wrong?" She studied him more closely. "What did you do to your hands?"

How could he explain anything to her that he couldn't explain to himself? He knew only that he couldn't stand to listen to Toby's final breaths. He muttered, "Doc'll tell you," and he rushed past her and out the door.

He halted at the edge of the boardwalk and steadied against an awning post. He barely knew where he was, and he had no idea where he was going. Surely when he lost his power, he lost his mind, maybe even his soul.

Dave stepped off the boardwalk into the mud. His legs moved him without volition. The rain curtain closed in around him, drowning his immediate memories, engulfing the town and the whole world. Sound scarcely penetrated the curtain. Then from far off he heard his name shouted. The call seemed to come from behind in a woman's voice, from ahead in a man's. Still he slogged on through the mud.

Then a voice hot with anger knifed through the rain curtain. Dave halted and stared at the boardwalk beside him. Billy Holt stood just outside the saloon's batwings.

"It's sundown, Dave," Billy shouted. "This's your idea."

"Billy?" Dave murmured.

"Let's get it over with." Billy reached for his gun.

"Dave!" Ann shouted from behind.

Dave pivoted sharply. His boots mired. He slipped and sprawled into the mud. Billy's gun roared. The bullet sprayed mud into Dave's face. From hands and knees, Dave peered around to Ann, to Billy. Doc ran along the boardwalk.

"Put your gun away, Billy," Dave said. He shoved to his feet. "I'm done fighting."

Billy stared through the rain, uncertain for a moment. Then he holstered his gun. Doc halted almost beside him.

"Dave," Doc called. "Toby's okay. He's going to pull through."

That's when Ann jumped off the boardwalk and plowed her dainty way toward Dave. Doc slapped Billy's shoulder. Ann's skirts dragged through mud as she rushed into Dave's arms. She was laughing and crying at the same time. She didn't seem to notice that Dave smeared more mud on her.

Doc helped tug the two of them up onto the boardwalk. He led them back to his office and opened the door. Matt was propped up on one elbow. There was color in his face now, and his eyes had the sparkle of a boy who had just found his strayed pup.

Toby's eyes rolled groggily. When his gaze caught Dave, the stump of a tail thumped the cot.

Ann slid an arm around Dave's muddy waist and snuggled against him. She said, "Matt can stay with me until . . . and Toby needs the run of a ranch. And the judge can draw up the adoption papers when . . ." Her face flamed, but her smile was loving and maternal.

And now Dave was warm where the cold rain would never reach. Everyone, he thought, needed to feel helpless once in a while.

"Make it soon," Doc pleaded. "If I keep this dog as a patient, folks'll start bringing me their sick cows."

Dave grinned. "I know where there's a mule that may be hurt."

"I'll refer that case," Doc said, "to my expert surgical assistant."

Sweet Revenge

JUDY ALTER

THE WOMAN in the bed next to me lies curled in a ball all day, moaning for her lost baby. The child, as I understand it, died at birth, and the mother went mad with grief. On the other side of me is a woman who calls out stridently, "Release me this minute! I do not belong here! If my daughter knew how you were treating me . . ." In truth, it was her daughter, unable to care for her any longer, who put her here, saw to it that she was tied each day in a rocking chair, untied only to take care of personal needs and, sometimes, for a brief walk around.

I've been here six months, and during that long, tedious time, I have made it a point to be very quiet, so I am neither tied nor confined. Not that I am free to come and go. No, indeed. I sit here each day, staring out the window at the Kansas prairie, plotting my quiet revenge against the husband who put me in the county poor farm, the only place able to care for the "dangerously insane."

That was what the judge said of me at the hearing, "dangerously insane." Howard Smith stood there with all his might and influence—the town's banker who holds the mortgages on every home and business for ten counties—and swore that I'd come after him with a butcher knife when he was sleeping. "Only the grace of God that I'm alive today, your honor," he said humbly. "The woman's dangerous. I tried, Lord knows, I tried to care for her, keep her at home"—here his voice broke a little with emotion—"keep the world from knowing my shame. . . ."

In spite of good old Brother Bacon, the preacher who protested strongly and who is still my champion, the judge ruled that I should be confined in the poor farm where, as he put it, "they have the facilities to care for someone like her."

I did take after him with a butcher knife once, but the story was different than he told it. I never wanted to marry Howard Smith. When I was seventeen, he was a widower of forty, wealthy beyond measure because he was mean as sin to those that owed his bank money. He approached my parents with a marriage proposal which they leapt to accept without consulting me.

Father was a farmer in southwestern Kansas and, it pains me to admit, a weak man, bent on doing the Lord's work but never sure which way the Lord wanted him to jump. He was a great deal surer which way my mother wanted him to jump, for she made it perfectly clear. She also made it perfectly clear that the Lord had not meant her to live the poverty-stricken life of a sod farmer's wife, and she blamed my father for not providing for her in a more fitting manner. That he was a farmer when she married him never seemed to occur to her.

"A perfect marriage," she had crowed, when she told me of Howard's proposal. "You will live a life of comfort, and perhaps your poor dear father and I will not have to scrimp so—"

"Did he offer a marriage settlement?" I asked coldly.

"Oh, now, dear Callie . . . how can you think such. . . ." She was off in a flutter of denials, but I had my answer.

I never pleaded nor cried hysterically, neither being my style, but I made it plain that I did not want to go through with this marriage, that I would do almost anything to avoid it. I considered, seriously, running away but reasoned that Mr. Smith, with his wealth and connections, would no doubt find me, even in Topeka. My logical arguments to him had met with bland confidence, "Once we are married, it will all work out."

Work out, my foot! We were married in the church at Liberal, with Brother Bacon performing the ceremony and me a reluctant bride in white, Howard a beaming groom in his best black suit, though I thought the knees and seat shiny from wear. For me, a kind of hell began with that ceremony. Howard was a randy old man, always pawing at me, sometimes waking me in the middle of the night with his insatiable passion. I learned to lie perfectly still, close my eyes, and take my mind to a faraway place during his rutting. When he rolled over, sated, and began to snore, I rose to clean myself, praying each time that no child had been conceived, for I don't know what I would have done to avoid bringing a child into that household.

Days, I was a servant, though he could well have afforded household help for me. He preferred, he said, to think that his own little wife was taking care of him. So I ran the house, fed him the hearty meals he expected three times a day, made my own clothes and most of his, and worked like a dog from dawn to dark. Howard was as demanding upright as he was in bed, expecting meals on time, whisky when he called for it, my undivided attention when he wanted to recount his latest triumph.

His temper, when aroused, was fearful, and he had his hates and his dislikes. In spite of the fact they had made him wealthy, he hated farmers, swore that they were out to cheat him, that the only honest men he'd ever met were those who refused to toil on the land—just the opposite of what most men believed. And he hated schools, thought young people should be put to work at the age of twelve instead of filling their heads with the foolishness called "higher education." When he'd yell and carry on about how the universities were ruining people, I cringed, for I wanted nothing more than to attend the state university in Wichita and become a teacher. "No school will ever get a penny of my money," he would rage, shaking his mighty fist in the air. He was the epitome of the man who would, as they say, take his fortune with him to the grave if he could.

By the time I'd been married five years, I was twenty-two years old, thin and gaunt, with dark circles under my eyes and, occasionally, a bruise on my cheekbone, a black eye, and once or twice, cracked ribs. Good Brother Bacon asked often how I was feeling, but I brushed his concern aside. What could he do?

I began to refuse Howard in the night, and then I took to sleeping in a separate bedroom. Twice, he kicked open a locked door to drag me back to his bed, and on those occasions he was rougher than usual. "I'll teach you," he'd mutter between clenched teeth.

The night I took the butcher knife after him, he was drunker than usual and more violent. He'd throttled me until I nearly lost consciousness, and then had forced me to the parlor floor, where he raped me and then fell asleep. I left him on the floor and would have left him all night, but he roused, and I could see from the murderous look in his eye that he was coming for me again. Hoarse and unable to cry out—as though anyone would have helped me—I ran for the kitchen and grabbed the first thing handy, the butcher knife.

He thought I was bluffing, that I was too soft to cut someone, even him, but when he got close enough I sliced at his ribs, opening a long, wide cut that bled so hard I was reminded of the proverbial stuck pig, an analogy that fit in more ways than one. Scared, he retreated to his bedroom, and I went to mine, building a barricade of furniture and sleeping with my hand on the knife handle.

Next morning, he was gone. Curious but unconcerned, I set about straightening the house and, unfortunately, had it all tidy and repaired—no sign of a struggle—by the time Howard arrived with the sheriff.

That was how I ended up in the poor farm. Howard said only one thing to me in private and that was, "A lot of women would love to have your chances. I'll find one won't come after me with a knife."

My only revenge is that it is against state law to divorce an insane person. Howard is saddled with me, and the next ladies in his life are condemned to illegitimacy. But that's cold comfort as I sit here, rocking away the endless days.

"Brother Bacon!" I fight the impulse to grin, to let my eyes light with happiness—bland is safer in this place—but I am glad beyond belief to see the old man.

"Callie, dear," he says, leaning to touch me on the shoulder, "come with me. You're leaving here."

It is almost too much to believe, too much to bear. "Leaving?" I echo.

"Take me away from here this instant!" the woman next to me demands. "I know you came to get me!"

Brother Bacon ignores her, speaking softly to me. "You're leaving. I've just gotten a court order."

"How . . ." I am almost unable to speak, and when I rise, my knees threaten to buckle under me.

"Finally had a traveling judge come through," he says, "one that didn't know Howard. I convinced him you weren't dangerous . . . said I'd take responsibility for you myself. Now we must go."

"Howard?"

"He doesn't know."

We go through the formalities, with a disapproving matron frowning all the while she signs the necessary papers, but Brother Bacon is his usual kind and patient self. I stifle the urge to scream at the woman. When we finally are in the buggy and driving away, I demand, "Take me to Howard."

"Now, Callie . . ."

"I want to see Howard," I say with steel in my voice, though I am not sure what I will say once I am in front of the devil who has engineered my misery.

He protests but finally agrees, and we ride in silence for a long time.

"You can't just go in there," he warns as we approach the house. "It . . . well, it might be dangerous for you."

"It might be dangerous for Howard," I reply, and see in his face the first sign of doubt. Maybe, he is thinking, she did go after him with a butcher knife for no reason, and maybe I've done the wrong thing. By then we are in front of the house, and he has stopped the horse.

"It will be all right," I tell him, heading boldly up the steps of the front stoop.

The door is locked, but I knock loudly, wait a minute, and then knock again. There is no answer, no sound within. After a long wait, I return down the steps, march around the house, and enter through the kitchen door. The kitchen is a mess—dirty dishes, food crumbs, all the signs that no one has been taking care. Howard has been too cheap to hire someone to replace me.

I walk through the dining room, parlor, up the stairs to the bedroom, and there is Howard, dead in his bed, his face beginning to mottle. For a moment, I am furious enough with him to go again for the butcher knife, furious that he has had the final laugh, robbed me of whatever revenge I sought. His empty eyes stare glassily at me, and I turn slowly and with deliberate, measured tread return to Brother Bacon.

"You best come," I say. "He's dead."

"Dead?" He is alarmed. How, he wonders, could I have killed him so soon.

"I didn't do it," I assure him. "I think his own cooking killed him. You should see the kitchen."

When Brother Bacon examines Howard, he suggests it was probably a heart attack. I long instead to see a butcher knife sticking out of his chest, but it's a longing I don't even whisper.

Brother Bacon goes for the sheriff, and I wait. To pass the time, I clean the kitchen, remembering ruefully that cleaning has once before gotten me into trouble. But this is now my house, I reason, and I cannot bear for anyone to see it so ill-kept.

The sheriff is not kind. "I won't offer you sympathy, Mrs. Smith," he says. "I 'spect you're rejoicin'."

"Not quite, Sheriff," I say, "I've been robbed."

He is puzzled but won't admit it. "If I could prove you did this. . . ." His threat dangles.

"Sheriff!" Brother Bacon is angry. "Mrs. Smith was at the home and then with me. There is no way she could have any involvement in her husband's death. Ate and drank himself to death, if you ask me."

"I didn't ask," the sheriff says rudely. He used to drink with Howard of a night, and they were friends, which means he has always been my enemy.

I am the nearest relation and so in charge of arrangements. Howard is buried in the town cemetery, with bank employees and a few townspeople in attendance—he was not popular—and Brother Bacon says a few words over the grave. The good man speaks nervously as he commends Howard's soul to God, and I throw a handful of dirt on the coffin and turn away. The sheriff, who has come uninvited, opines that it's a crime not to give a man a proper church burial.

"Not," I say, "a crime for which one can be tried."

Within a week, I have made the house my own, given away every trace of Howard's clothing and personal effects, opened the windows to sunshine and air, beaten the old dust out of the rugs, and put flowers in every room, even the cubicle Howard called his office. His papers have been packed and sent to the lawyer.

Said lawyer comes to call a week later. "Mrs. Smith, you're a wealthy woman," he says and proceeds to outline my wealth.

My instructions are direct: a certain amount to my parents, not generous but enough to ensure that I won't have to worry with them daily; another, larger amount to the county poor farm, with the stipulation that it be used for treatment of the "dangerously insane."

"That barely makes a dent," the lawyer says. "Any further plans?"

"Yes. I plan to attend the university in Wichita and get an education. And I'll build them . . . let's see, a library. Yes, a library. Howard hated books. We'll call it the Howard Smith Memorial Library." I envision Howard, spinning in frustration for all eternity.

The lawyer's face is blank.

After he leaves, I go to the kitchen for the butcher knife. Now it hangs framed, in a place of honor, over my desk in the private library I have built for myself. No one ever asks about the knife, but I find it a great comfort.

Yearlings

JIM MARION ETTER

IT WAS the most important cattle drive of J.T. McCoy's
life. That was partly because he knew in his heart it would
be his last, but mainly because his son, Jed, had come with
him and this was his last chance to make the boy into what
he ought to be.

McCoy, a weathered, stout man in his late fifties, felt a
strange contentment as he rode apart from the others,
aware of the smell of the sagebrush and the long shadows
of the yucca shoots in the freshness of early morning, a
hawk floating against the blue sky, the squeak of saddle
leather and the soft clop of his horse and the scuffle of the
cattle ahead, raising just shy of enough dust to spoil the
whole pretty picture.

Funny, he thought with a pang, how a man starts noticing life all around him when he's near the end of it.

That fact also was making him think—or worry—more about Jed.

Just then another horse galloped up and slowed beside his, and he glanced over to see his son, a skinny but friendly and somewhat handsome youth of twenty-one who was holding awkwardly onto the saddle horn until his pony came down out of its rough trot.

He flashed a boyish grin. "Pretty morning, isn't it? I'm sure glad I came with you, Papa."

J.T. felt a surge of warmth, but showed it with only a thin smile. "I am, too, Son." Then he turned his eyes straight ahead: "You gotta remember, though, it'll be hot before the day's over, and you can't let that keep you from stayin' close behind these calves. We can't let any get scattered and lost before we get 'em loaded.

"The way times are now, as dry as it's been and with some extra expenses I've had lately, we can't afford to lose a single one. Most of these are just yearlin' steers and heifers that I'd like to keep and graze out this summer, and use some of the females for breedin' stock, but right now we need every pound we can take to the market.

"And by heavens," he added, "despite all the hard luck I've had, I'm going to do whatever I have to do to keep ranchin' and not go to farmin'. Our land's always goin' to raise cattle, not crops—as long as I'm alive, anyway."

Not that this little drive was anything a ten-year-old boy couldn't handle by himself, J.T. thought. Here it was around the start of the twentieth century, and western Oklahoma Territory was not only seeing more cussed fences and farms but had gotten so civilized that he and Jed and their neighbor, Woodrow Cline, and his sons had to drive the two families' combined herd of about two-hundred mixed cattle for only three or four days to the railroad at Woodward.

It was nothing like the big drives from Texas to Kansas that as recent as five years or so ago were still coming right through this part of the country—and which took his father's life less than thirty years ago, he recalled in an instant, wishing again he could blot out the nightmarish picture he saw over and over of his father's drowning.

J.T. was one of the hands on the drive that was crossing the rain-swollen Red River, and he had watched in horror from a few yards away as his father, who was trail boss, was swept from his saddle by the currents and swallowed by the nasty-red swirls. J.T. had jumped from his horse to grab him, but failed—and himself had gotten his lungs nearly full of water and had to be dragged out by the others.

But it never had been easy for J.T. to keep his son's mind on business, and this little drive was his last chance to make the boy responsible enough to become a cowman—something J.T. was hoping very hard was even possible.

"Don't worry, Papa, we'll get all of them to market," the young man was saying, then he pointed to one of several bare, red hills up ahead. "See that big mound over there? When we're in camp tonight I'm gonna draw a picture of it and put you and your horse right on top of it. And have a few clouds overhead and . . ."

J.T. breathed out in a tired gesture. "Son, we just don't have time for scratchin' on paper and such as that. What you need to be doin' is keepin' count of these calves; we gotta make sure every now and then that we still have the eighty-five head that we started with.

"And there's no time to waste. I figure the sooner we get there, the better chance we'll have of gettin' a decent price. By heavens, I aim to cross the Canadian with 'em today and have 'em at the railroad by day after tomorrow.

"Besides," he added, "if we get as far as we oughta get today, you'll be too tired tonight to do any drawin', I'll guarantee ya that."

J.T.'s father had ranched in South Texas long before he began taking his herds north over the Great Western Trail, and had fought everything from renegade Indians and gun-toting cattle and horse thieves to spells so dry the cows choked on dust and lived on mesquite beans and prickly pear cactus.

Following his father's death, J.T. had begun making arrangements to graze cattle up in the usually lush grasslands of the Indian country. And finally, eight years ago, he and his small family had made the run and homesteaded in the Cheyenne and Arapaho lands—but to raise cattle, not farm like many settlers did.

It was fine country, overall, and after living in a dugout for a while he had built a decent house.

But during a hard winter a few years later, his wife, Edna Mae, the prettiest and kindest woman he had ever known, had died of pneumonia. It made life both lonely and difficult for him and Jed, neither of whom was good at housekeeping or cooking.

Then a few years after that came the dry spell, over much of Texas and the territory, too, and many cattlemen started reducing their herds, bringing down the price of beef.

Then about six months ago, J.T. got up one morning with an odd tightness in his lower back that came and went, making him feel like he had a cottonwood pole strapped to his backbone and was walking downhill and about to fall on his face.

He finally had seen a doctor in Cheyenne—the first physician he had ever gone to—who looked him over, then referred him to another doctor over in Canadian in the Texas Panhandle, who in turn sent him to another doctor out in Amarillo. He was finally told the trouble was with some kind of male gland and was what the medical men called a "terminal" condition. In short, they said, it would continue to worsen until the end—which could come within a year, maybe a little later.

J.T., who had always considered himself tough enough to handle about any kind of trouble, finally accepted the idea, but hadn't seen any reason to tell Jed until he had to.

And now, since ranching had always been his life as his

father's before him, his sole aim was to do a good job of passing his land, cattle, and all his knowledge down to his son—who was all he had.

But as another bit of hard luck, he had seen years ago that making the boy into a rancher wouldn't be easy. Jed, while always a decent, well-mannered boy who was eager to please, couldn't seem to do anything right. He couldn't stand to see calves burned with a branding iron and couldn't handle the best lariat rope without it twisting. And a horse fast enough to catch a calf, he usually couldn't stay on.

When he was little, he was always running off to go swimming in the Washita River when it had enough water, and when it didn't, in the first stock tank he came to.

And when he was older, he usually wasn't around for ranch work because he was off by himself reading books, or just wandering around looking at the country and drawing pictures.

Also, the boy had talked him into letting him go away to a school in Missouri. Even though Jed worked at some odd jobs to help out, the expense on J.T. was an extra burden—and then Jed came home a few weeks ago with the crazy idea that he could be a professional artist. He also had let on like he had met a girl, too, but talked more about his drawing.

And while J.T. didn't mind looking at the impressive images of events such as the Battle of the Washita, trail drives and roundups and the nearby red hills and his own cattle and horses hanging all over the house, he couldn't seem to convince the boy that he couldn't run a ranch, or feed the family that he'd have someday, by drawing pictures like a schoolboy.

Woodrow Cline trotted up on his horse, grinning in his big, happy bucktoothed way. J.T. and Jed had known him and his two fun-loving boys, Jeff and Andrew, both a little younger than Jed, ever since they had come to the territory, and often partnered with them when working their cattle and taking the animals to market. They were fine neighbors.

At that moment, one of the larger animals in the herd, a part longhorn steer owned by the Clines that had been balking and acting cantankerous in general since they started, stopped and slung his head, then bolted, heading off to the right toward the thick cover of some shinnery bushes.

"That ol' steer's the orneriest thing you ever saw when you try to drive 'im out of brush," Cline said. "One of these boys might oughta go rope 'im."

Jeff and Andrew both were bringing back a few strays to the left of the herd and were barely out of earshot—and it was obvious Jed felt the glances of the two men on him.

He hesitated a moment, then began shaking out his coiled rope as he spurred his pony into a lope.

Soon he was closing in on the steer with his loop swinging, and apparently was feeling and looking somewhat like a top hand.

"Git 'im, Jed!" Cline hollered, grinning bigger than ever.

J.T. stood up in his stirrups as he watched his son, feeling some pride but praying that it wasn't for nothing.

The steer wheeled just before reaching the shinnery, and about a second before Jed threw the lasso. Jed's loop dropped neatly over an idle tumbleweed about the time the long-legged critter was several jumps away and heading straight for a brushy canyon.

Jed's horse, meanwhile, had slid to a stop the moment Jed swung the rope, and thrown Jed plumb over the saddle's tall pommel and left him hanging by one arm around the pony's neck.

A chorus of laughter and good-natured shouts of derision arose from the Cline boys—who now were on their way over to get into the action—and even Jed, though red-faced as he eased himself to the ground, joined in with a joking excuse about how the steer was too dumb to know he was supposed to stick his head in the loop.

But J.T. wasn't having fun. He fixed Jed with a cold

stare he had often given him over the years, then reined his horse off in the other direction, knowing it was like a slap in his son's face.

"Sorry, Papa," Jed said, his face flushed in a different way this time and his eyes cast downward.

"I'll go drive him back," he then said quickly, picking up his hat and climbing back on his horse.

"Let 'im go," J.T. said tiredly, rolling his eyes toward the sky.

Then he called out to the Cline brothers. "Jeff! Andrew! You boys better go bring that wild hombre in. This ol' pony Jed's ridin' has got a bad leg"—the excuse, he knew, hurting Jed even worse than his earlier insult of silence.

"Sorry, Papa," Jed said again.

The Cline brothers then took off together, both their ropes whirring impressively and their horses in an eager gallop. They went out of sight over a rise and in moments returned, their ponies in a hard run and both only a few yards behind the steer.

"Yah-hooooo!" yelled Woodrow. "They're puttin' on a regular ropin' show, ain't they?"

Andrew then threw his loop, which grazed but failed to catch one of the horns as the cagey steer slung its head.

Jeff's loop shot out like a striking rattlesnake and tightened around the base of the steer's horns, and it seemed in the same instant his stocky dun jerked the animal around and to a twisting, snorting standstill.

"Ya see, Andrew, that's how ya do it. Want me to do it again so you can watch and learn how?" the youth hollered, grinning widely.

"Lucky, ain't ya? Too bad you're so bashful about talkin' about yourself, too," answered his brother, slightly ruffled.

"Remember now, Andrew," the senior Cline said, his bucktoothed grin at its best, "like they say over in Texas, 'If you can do it, it ain't braggin'.' "

"Let's turn 'im loose and try again," Andrew said to Jeff, gathering his rope. "I'll bet ya two bits I'll beat ya this time."

But Cline, while still laughing, called an end to the fun. "That's enough, boys. No use runnin' any more fat off these hides than we have to."

"They're right smart good hands, Woodrow," J.T. said with a smile, trying to keep the bitter disappointment in his own son out of his voice for Cline's benefit—and not caring much whether he failed to for Jed's benefit.

"Yeah, but I gotta keep a tight rein on 'em," Cline said, still grinning. "Them boys of mine are just yearlin's—that's what I call 'em. They don't know much, but maybe they'll grow up and learn somethin' one of these days."

The drive during most of the afternoon was slow, dull, hot, and dry—and the drought, which was beginning to seem as bad as those he had seen in South Texas, was more and more on J.T.'s mind and in what little conversation went on between him and Woodrow.

Big, fluffy clouds with dark undersides kept building to their west over the Texas Panhandle and gave the herders a little refreshing diversion—but little hope for rain, as such cloud banks this time of year didn't always mean moisture.

J.T. noticed Jed looking in his dreamy way at the heavenly display that J.T. had to admit was truly pretty—starkly white, billowy masses suspended against the clear blue sky—knowing his son was trying to memorize every detail of the wondrous sight to put in one of his paintings.

But to J.T. and the others, the clouds only meant what likely were false promises. And they were reminded of this when, as one of the clouds moved past the sun, its wide, blessed shadow spread over them—then in a moment or so, flowed across the prairie and was gone.

The hot afternoon dragged on, the time passing as slowly as the herd and the herders trudged.

Then, at nearly sundown, the cattle and horses smelled the Canadian River.

As the cattle revived and began moving a little faster, J.T., Jed and Woodrow Cline rode around the herd in order to get a look at the river and find a good crossing before the cattle got there. Jeff and Andrew stayed back and on either side of the cattle to keep them from scattering before they hit the stream.

"I might even take me a bath," said Cline as all three horsemen went at a long trot. J.T. and Jed both laughed. All three were excited about what was ahead.

But then they heard the roar—such an odd sound that at first they couldn't believe what they knew it was.

"Now don't tell me the river's rollin'!" said Cline, wearing one of his few serious looks. "If it is, it had to've rained a bunch out in the Panhandle in the last day or two."

Then all three men lifted their horses into a lope.

Sure enough, the river, while only slightly above normal level, was visibly rising, meaning that, like the clouds had indicated and Cline had said, it had rained upstream—but the roaring, now much louder, was coming from up the river.

Jed indicated he had heard stories about people actually hearing a river flood coming down the channel before it got there, but had never thought it possible. He obviously was amazed to witness such a thing.

J.T., though, wasn't entertained. He had been in a bruising saloon fistfight once, been thrown from a few bad horses, been bitten just below the knee by a rattler, and even had a tooth pulled without benefit of liquor—but had forgotten how he feared and hated the nasty, stinking, muddy river water with its horrifying whirlpools and scummy edges that often turned up bodies of drowned varmints and occasionally even calves.

Not only was he from a dry country and had never learned to swim, having always crossed streams when the water was no higher than his stirrups, but there was the terrifying memory of his father's river drowning that had long haunted him.

Maybe he had spouted off too soon when he promised Jed they'd cross the river this same day, he thought. He hadn't given a thought to the possibility of high water—rare in this country, especially during dry periods.

But he and the others didn't have much time to ponder, as the thirsty cattle were now circling them on their way to the water, some of the animals drinking from the edge of the muddy stream while others plunged into deeper holes of the swift, swirling waters.

"Think we can push 'em across before it gets too high?" asked Cline, his face even more serious than before.

For one of the few times in his life, J.T. didn't have a quick and definite answer. "Well, I don't know much about rivers. Do you . . . You don't think it's too high already to swim the cattle over, do you?"

"I think we can do it, Papa," Jed put in, to his father's surprise. "We'd have to hurry, though, since it's nearly sundown, and while the cattle are still thirsty and won't stop to think about it."

Cline agreed. "That's right, Jed. That way, we can git 'em across before dark and before the river's any higher. Come on, fellers, let's put 'em in." He gave a loud whoop and waved his coiled lariat.

J.T.'s tightness in his lower back suddenly worsened and he also felt his heart skip a beat or two, and for a moment he was certain he would die in the middle of the muddy torrent as his father had done—but he lifted his reins and spurred his horse, shutting his eyes as he felt the cool water rush above his boot tops.

Then, despite his will, his body actually revolted, and before realizing he was doing it, he was wheeling his horse around and plunging it through the water back toward the bank.

"I can't do it!" he said before he knew what he was saying, then as he slid from his saddle to the ground, said in lower tones, and in a shamefaced manner, to whoever was listening, "I don't know what happened—it was just like I couldn't help it."

It was Jed who spoke. "Well, the river *is* rising fast, and it's nearly dark. We might have a better chance in the morning, when it might be dropping by that time."

J.T. felt grateful to his son, and that made him feel odd.

They ate their beef jerky, raisins and other few items and drank coffee made from their canteen water, then rolled out their bedding and went quickly to sleep on the ground—except for J.T.

Here he was, he thought as he looked up at the stars and listened with dread to the rushing water. He had ridden herd on his son for years because of his weaknesses, and now he himself was as scared as a trapped coyote.

He knew already what he'd do when he entered the river again, since in his brief contact with it today he hadn't been able to keep from growing as crazy as a wild cow in a thunderstorm.

And even though he hated the prospect of dying a lingering death in bed, he knew he wanted to go any other way but drowning.

But his biggest predicament now was, he didn't know which would be worse—drowning in the muddy water or seeing his son embarrassed by his father.

Funny, he thought, for the first time since he learned of his illness, that didn't seem near as big a worry as this.

It was also funny, he thought—this time he gave himself a twisted smile—this was one time he wasn't worried about how *Jed* was going to perform.

Morning came quickly—J.T. wasn't sure if he dozed any or not—and in moments all were up, drinking the coffee Woodrow Cline had boiled over a fire, eating jerky and otherwise preparing for a big day.

And J.T. looked at the river, which was roaring like he had never seen one, rushing by dizzily in filthy, reddish foam that carried occasional floating logs and tree branches.

"We might as well try it, fellers," said Cline.

J.T. wondered how anyone so silly-looking could be so cussed brave.

While it was clear no one had his heart in it, no one wanted to back down, so in a few moments J.T. and Jed, who, since they had taken the lead yesterday and were expected to today, took the lead, wading their horses gently out into the water. If they crossed, the others would drive the herd behind them, then all would gather the cattle after they scattered some on the other bank.

J.T., determined not to turn back as he did the day before, even if it meant drowning, clinched his teeth and shut his eyes as he again felt the cold water, more chilling this time, rise to his knees—then in a breathtaking instant rush to his armpits as he sensed his horse's feet leave the bottom of the river and felt both himself and the animal floating. He then nearly passed out as the water rose to his chin and he felt his body float up off the saddle. He could see only the animal's head above the water and a few inches in front of his own.

"Jed! Where are you? Help me!" He wasn't sure those were his words, but he knew they had to be, as the river now was a speeding, dizzying monster that swept him in a blur past the trees and everything else he could see on the far bank. He bent his neck backward to keep his nose out of the water and prayed.

Then suddenly, apparently as the river's main current hit him, he felt his horse go sideways to the right and, as he thought he heard Jed yell for him to hold to his horse, felt the horse's reins and mane slip from his hand in spite of himself—and he lost sight of daylight and felt himself sink and become lost in the blurry, choking world below the water's surface.

In a spasm of panic and gagging and coughing, he was fighting and clawing at the water with all his might, feeling his head bob above the surface only for a second or two at a time, and he believed he was drowning—until his right hand caught a rope that jerked him half out of the water.

"Papa! Hang on to the rope. Keep your nose out of the water when you can—and remember, stay calm." It was Jed's voice. He was off his horse, too, but was in the water a few yards ahead of him, and was holding the other end of the lariat rope. The whole thing was confusing.

"Now, Papa, keep your nose up, and kick your feet, and breathe in every time your nose is out of the water—but when your face goes under, hold your breath," Jed was saying, and every time J.T. started sinking again, jerking the rope again to make him raise his nose out of the water.

"And try to stay calm—that's the most important thing in water," Jed was saying. "Water's nothing to be afraid of, unless you fight it. Nobody knows, but maybe that's what happened to my grandpa that time in the Red River."

The water seemed less terrifying now, maybe because J.T.'s eyes were less blurry, and because he could see the bank a little ways on the other side of Jed. Then, after they had reached a little bend where the current no longer hit them full blast, he felt his feet touch the muddy bottom. It was a miracle, J.T. told himself. Thank God!

"Son, I thought I was a goner," he said to Jed as soon as he could stop coughing and found his voice. "But it'd been just as well, I reckon. You see, I'm dyin'—chances are, I don't have many months left."

"I figured that, Papa. I knew something was funny when I heard you went to three doctors, and never before had been to one in your whole life. That's why I came home to help with the drive. But let's don't worry about that till we have to. In the meantime, I'm here with you."

Then, in another moment or two, J.T. slopped out of the water, still holding to the rope that Jed was holding several feet in front of him as they climbed up the grassy bank to safety and where Woodrow Cline and his two sons were standing.

The three Clines cheered. "You made it, fellers—and both of ya'll was way out in the middle!" yelled Woodrow, his bucktoothed grin now a welcome sight for J.T.

"Wait a minute!" J.T. said, still coughing a little and spitting out river water. "What are you and the horses all doing on this side? I thought we swam across."

"No, it was too swift, Papa," said Jed. "Our horses couldn't buck the worst part of the current. When I saw you come off your horse, I let mine go, too, and swam a little ahead of you. And I threw you my rope—if I'd let you grab my hand, you might have pulled me under and drowned us both."

"Soon as we hit the main current," he added, "I knew that even if we made it, chances are most of those yearling calves wouldn't."

"Besides," he said, "I figure this side of the river's the best place for us now, anyway."

J.T. wasn't sure what he meant, but was cut off by his son when he tried to ask.

"You did good, Papa. If you hadn't stayed calm and done exactly like I told you, I couldn't have pulled you out, as strong as that current was, and chances are you'd have drowned. You did good."

"That's right," said Woodrow, still grinning. "You two swum over halfway across, then back. Next high river we have to cross, I know which two fellers are goin' in first."

"No, that ain't right, by heavens," said J.T. "I wasn't worth two cents in that water—I'd be a drowned rat if it hadn't been for my son, Jed."

He looked down as he walked slowly, his boots squishing, toward where his horse was now grazing. Even if Jed did learn what he knew about water by running off and playing when he was a kid, he had shown he was a real man when he had to be, J.T. thought. And maybe his being a grown-up man, whether he was a cattleman or anything else, was all that was important.

Maybe, J.T. thought, the boy was a lot more grown up than his old papa—who, like Woodrow might say, was the one who was still a yearling, judging by the way he had acted.

"In fact, Jed," J.T. said, forcing the words out, "I done a lot of thinkin' last night and today. I've been a cussed fool. I guess you're man enough to be an artist or whatever you wanna be. I guess . . . I guess there's things I just didn't understand."

He turned away from Jed like he had done many times before, but this time it was because he didn't want his son to see the tears that were burning his eyes. He wanted to say more, but couldn't.

"Ah, say, now, Papa, you're getting way out ahead of yourself. I'm going to be an artist, all right, because that's what I'm good at. I didn't tell you, but I've sold some of my paintings already—that's been one of my part-time 'jobs' I told you about. So I'll always be drawing pictures. After all, ranching isn't going to take *all* my time."

"What's that? You mean you're—"

"That's right, Papa. I never said I wasn't going to help you run the ranch. In fact, I'd like to talk to you about planting some alfalfa, and winter wheat, too—that's something cows can eat like grass right in the middle of wintertime. Cattle can eat other things besides buffalo grass. You don't have to give up ranching, Papa, but it doesn't hurt to steal a few ideas from the farmers."

"And as for now," he added, turning and looking at the grazing cattle, "that river's not going to go down as soon as we thought, and maybe that's just as well. We haven't come but about a third of the way to the railroad anyway, so—providing Mister Cline agrees with this—why don't we drive the herd back? Maybe we all can sit down together and figure out a way to keep from selling right now.

"For one thing, I'd like to see some of these yearling steers get some more weight on them first, and some of these females kept as replacement heifers."

J.T. used his sleeve to wipe the mud and mucus from his face, then stood agape. "How do you know about things like that?"

"I studied a few things besides art in school, Papa," Jed said, smiling patiently, then went on. "Now, I know times are hard, but I believe that if we don't get in a hurry to sell and all get our heads together, both our outfits can survive. Since we've always worked together, maybe we can combine into one big outfit, under one brand, and do better. With what I've learned in school—and with your experience, Papa—and with expert cowmen like Mister Cline and Jeff and Andrew, I'll bet we can make it."

"I got a feelin' Jed's right, J.T.," Cline said, grinning bigger than he had during the whole trip.

"And look," Jed added, nodding toward the river, then the western sky, "it's raining in the Panhandle, and that should mean the drought's about to end for us, too—so the buffalo grass should be greening up good even before we plant the alfalfa and wheat."

"Could be, Son," J.T. said thoughtfully. "Maybe you can make the ranch last longer than I will, anyway."

"That's another thing, Papa. None of us knows for sure what will happen tomorrow. And as strong as you look, I'll bet you live to see the first of your grandkids."

"Grandkids?"

Jed went on. "You see, it's probably a good thing the river was too high to cross. That'll make us all go back and do something better than sell all our cattle when the price is down. Like Amy Lee always tells me, things sometime work out for the best."

"I don't know about all this, Jed. Besides, I . . . 'Amy Lee?' Who, by heavens, are you talking about?"

"Amy Lee's a girl I met at school, Papa. I've been planning to tell you about her when I caught you in a good mood, which is why I haven't done it until now. Amy and I were married two weeks ago. I was going to send for her after this drive, but now that we're postponing that, I'll send for her right away. She's up in Kansas with her folks.

"She grew up there, by the way, and she knows about as much about cattle and alfalfa and wheat—especially wheat—as I do. She's looking forward to living on the ranch. She can cook, too."

J.T. was overwhelmed. It was the craziest cattle drive he'd ever been on—but maybe the best, come to think of it, even if the cattle weren't going anywhere this time except back home.

That thought caused him to look again at the river, which was still roaring—but it didn't seem as loud as it did, and he didn't think he was so afraid of it anymore.

All of a sudden there wasn't even a hint of stiffness in

his lower back, and he felt better than he had in years. But even if he died tomorrow, he thought, he couldn't complain too much.

But he didn't plan on it, because this whole thing had given him a new aim.

During these two days he had learned that his son had grown up without his really getting to know the boy. And by heavens, he was going to live long enough to do something about that.

Bloody Badge,
Bloody Gun

ROBERT GLEASON

THE GRIZZLED OLD MAN stood in the thoroughfare of New York's Coney Island Amusement Park. One hundred feet overhead towered the ever-turning Ferris Wheel. The steam calliope oom-pahed "Stars and Stripes Forever," while the carousel down the strip rotated in time to the music, its horses and unicorns, inundated with children, pumping up and down, up and down.

But the old man was oblivious to it all—the screaming kids, the pounding music, mechanical marvels. Instead he stood still as a statue in the middle of the thoroughfare, his brooding eyes fixed on the cracking rifles and chiming bells of the Coney Island shooting gallery.

He was a strange old man. His deeply lined face was burned brown as a hide from too many years of staring into desert sun and wind and High Plains snowstorms. His was a face set hard as concrete, bitter as gall, a face that neither asked nor gave.

He wore a black Plainsman's hat, and on the lapel of his frock coat shone a U.S. Marshal's badge. His suit was black as any undertaker's, and from the looks of the sawed-edged notches on the ivory-handled butt of the Navy Colt protruding from his half-breed shoulder-holster, he had arranged a few cheap funerals.

Reaching into his inside coat pocket, he removed a hammered-silver whiskey flask with the initials *BM* lavishly engraved in Gothic script. He poured a large draught into the two-jigger cap and tossed it off.

His eyes remained fixed on the shooting gallery. Steel horse-borne Indians, mounted on brass hinges, trotted across the target range, where young boys in short pants shot them with pellet guns.

His thoughts drifted back to another place, another time, another horse-borne horde. . . .

There were a thousand Indians this time, charging the hide-hunters' camp out of the blazing dawn sun. The hunters' Sharps rifles were scoped-in, and they were having a field day. The grizzled old ramrod was nineteen, and dropping Comanche as fast as he could slam the trigger guard forward, eject a spent shell and shove another round into the smoking breech.

Toward the end, the man beside him—twenty-four-year-old Billy Dixon—let out a fair imitation of a Cheyenne war whoop.

"I smoked that one proper—at 1600 yards," he roared.

The young man later paced the distance off himself and confirmed the kill.

"I smoked him proper," he could still hear young Billy Dixon roar, "at 1600 yards."

The cocky young vender in corduroys and a sailor's cap, running the shooting gallery, caught his eye.

"Hey, mister, come and try your luck. Bet my take against your Navy Colt and that shiny badge you can't hit 'em all."

"Save your money," another man shouted from up the thoroughfare.

It was that new young sports writer, Damon Runyon.

"Don't you know who you're challenging?" Runyon said, falling in beside the old man. "This is Marshal Masterson."

"Bat Masterson?" the young man said. "Jesus, mister, I didn't recognize you. Please don't put me out of business. Here, I'll let you shoot for free. I know you can knock them down."

A murmur spread through the fairground. "Bat Masterson?" one man muttered. "No kidding. He killed more men than Bill Hickok and Coleman Younger put together."

He was twenty-four then and marshaling in Dodge. It was late at night and he was heading home after rounds. He almost made it when his brother Ed came stumbling out of the Lady Gay Saloon, clutching his gut, his mouth flooding with blood.

"Bat . . . Bat . . ." were his last words.

Jack Wagner and Alf Walker following him, their guns smoking, turning toward him.

But his Colt was already out, his arm extended, gun hand steady.

Two more scallops were carved on his gun.

Kids crowded around him now, waving Dime Dreadfuls by Ned Buntline in his face. Many of the covers bore his own picture. The boys pleaded for autographs and begged to touch his badge, the butt of his gun.

He brushed them off and headed up the thoroughfare,

away from the shouting kids. Runyon, the young reporter in a tweed suit and black bowler, fell beside him.

"Can *I* touch your gun-butt?" the reporter mocked.

"Fuck you," Masterson said.

"Bitter words," said Runyon, "from a man who's holed as many as you."

"I still say, fuck you."

He talked tough, but his bloody past was catching up with him.

"Jesus, honey," Diamond Lil had told him in Denver, before the good folks had run him out of that town too, "do you look old."

"Can't sleep," he explained.

She pulled her pink chemise tight around her shoulders and flung her long hennaed hair down over her back. Shuffling the cards, she recommenced dealing stud to him and his six associates seated at the octagonal, baize-covered poker table in the Light of Love Parlor House that November night, 1888.

"It's your conscience," Lil explained. "It's bothered by the ghosts of them you planted."

A tinhorn snickered.

"What's so funny?" Lil asked.

"Never heard no one suggest Bat had a conscience before."

"You planted as many men as him," Lil said, "yours'd ache too."

"Ease off, Lil," Bat said quietly.

"It ain't gonna get no better," Lil said. "This here's your third bottle of Sour Mash tonight, your fourth Soiled Dove, and you still can't shut your eyes."

"It's watching you deal seconds. Keeps me on edge."

"You ain't spotted me yet, honey. You'd've done something, you had."

"But I can hear you. I can hear that second tick."

"You ain't heard nuthin', Bat, 'cept the rattle of dead men's bones," Lil said.

"And the sound of that hacksaw carving scallops on your gun," the tinhorn said.

"I can still hear this," Masterson said.

The crack! *was the sound of his gun barrel laid across the man's head.*

"Jesus, honey, you do need some rest" was Lil's only remark.

"Bat," Runyon was saying as they strode cross the fairground. "You look like hell. You ought to head home, get some sleep."

"Heard that before from a lady in Denver."

"Probably ran a whorehouse, knowing you."

"That she did."

"It was good advice. You should try it."

"Maybe I will."

"Don't sound likely. Hear Theodore Roosevelt wants you for a third term. Says he won't take no for an answer. Says the Bowery is filled with desperate men. Wants you strapping on that gun and parading your badge. Gonna accept?"

He took out his notepad, indicating that his answer was for the record.

Masterson shook his head, no.

"What you going to do? You sure aren't planning on honest work."

"Thought maybe I'd take up sportswriting like yourself."

Runyon sneered. "At least, it ain't honest."

Masterson turned toward the gate.

"Where you going?" the reporter asked, putting down his pad, taking his arm. "Thought I might let you buy me a drink."

"Never happen. I'm heading home. Gonna get some rest."

"You know how?"

"Yeah, I know how. It's easy."

He unpinned his badge and unholstered his blued-steel Navy Colt. He laid them both in the reporter's hands.

"Let someone else keep the world safe for democracy. I'm done."

Runyon studied the hardware and let out an appreciative whistle. "I don't know, Bat. These are worth a lot of money. You know what you're doing?"

"I purely hope so."

"Tell you what: I'll hold them for you, 'case you want them back."

The old man fixed Runyon with a hard stare.

"You keep 'em, boy. There's blood enough on them already."

Head down, he turned and walked out the Coney Island gate without looking back.

Half a Day
from Water

GORDON D. SHIRREFFS

There's gold, and it's haunting and haunting;
It's luring me on as of old;
Yet it isn't the gold that I'm wanting
So much as just finding the gold. . . .
—ROBERT SERVICE
"The Spell of the Yukon"

THE SOLITARIO DESERT was a hell's delight, a great sink bottomed by a vast and barren *playa*. It was rimmed by low hills and the more distant mountains with their gunsight notches and silent, hidden canyons, veiled during the summer months in a perpetually shifting haze which gave the viewer the impression that the lead-colored mountains were moving slowly up and down and sideways in a clumsy rhythmic elephantine rigadoon. The terrain was quiet as a vacuum. It was barren of life and growths. It was a lonely

and brooding land, harsh and inviolate with an intense
solitude that was heavy enough to break the heart. It was a
vast and deadly area, merciless and sunbeaten, broiling in
the summer months with an average temperature of 120
degrees. It was hell with the hide burnt off.

There was no live water in the hills to the east. At
times there was water in the western hills located in the
tinajas, so called, which were hollows eroded in the granite
over many centuries by the raging, pounding "male" rains
which burst across that arid country during the summer
months. *Tinaja* translated from the Spanish into "large
earthen jar or pot." The gringos simply called them "tanks."
It did one no good to depend upon water being in the
tanks very long. There was, however, one set of tanks
called Solitario Tanks which could usually be depended
upon for a store of water most times but like everything
else in that deadly country it was always a gamble, a long
shot to depend upon them at all, especially in the summer
months.

There was always an eerie, frightening quality about
the Solitario Desert. The absolute minimum of water required to travel on it was at least one gallon a day. The
Mexicans said: "Even the ghosts of the Solitario Desert
stay underground during the summer."

It was midday on the Solitario Desert.

Something moved, almost imperceptibly on the vast
dun-colored surface of the *playa.* It was as though a mite
was slowly crawling westward through the hazy, shimmering waves of heat.

Azro Sutro was afoot crossing the very core of the
Solitario Desert—the *playa.* Once, millenniums past, the
playa had been a miles-wide primeval lake shimmering and
sparkling beneath the hot sun. Now it was bone dry and
billiard-table flat, an expanse composed of irregularly
shaped pieces of mud like a great natural jigsaw puzzle.
Underfoot it was stove-top hot. The country to the east
was malpais country, "bad underfoot." Boot soles could be
macerated and shredded within an hour's passage on it.

Azro winced now and again as the burning heat of the mud seared his bare calloused soles. There were drying bloody footprints stretching back all the way he had traveled since before daylight. When he opened his mouth to breathe in the hot, dry air, his swollen lips would crack anew. The cloth-covered canteen hanging at his right hip was empty—dry empty. It had been that way since the day before. Azro kept his head down shading his sun-reddened eyes with the wide brim of his sweat-darkened hat. He already had a hellroarer of a headache from the sun.

Azro glanced up now and again. Somewhere in the low hills ahead of him was water. He had filled his canteens there five or six days past. He wasn't quite sure. He wasn't quite sure about *anything*. "My name is Azro Samuel Sutro," he grunted. "*Ass. . . .*" he added softly.

Azro wasn't too bright; he *was* determined. As a boy and teenager he had lived on his stepgrandfather's farm in New Hampshire. The old man had inherited Azro when he had been orphaned. The old man had grinned. Here was a sturdy lad who would work for his keep alone. Azro had never known his parents. He had no sisters or brothers. "Not even a damned cousin," he thought. His stepgrandfather was a good man; a deacon of the church he was. He was fairly good to Azro but his hand was quick and downright heavy.

The Rebels fired on Fort Sumter. Azro was almost seventeen and big for his age. He wanted to enlist. His stepgrandfather tried to beat some sense into Azro. Azro hit him once and floored him. He thought he had killed the old man. He got out of the county that night and later enlisted in the Fifth New Hampshire Volunteer Infantry. Later he learned that his stepgrandfather had survived and was now proud of his grandson serving his country. "Daniel Webster, a native son of New Hampshire, said New Hampshire breeds men," so Grandpa Sutro had proudly said when he had heard about Azro enlisting.

Azro grinned at the thought. "And all New Hampshire women are double-breasted," he snorted.

As he limped on he thought of Carrie Smith, his first and *only* love. She was of the bovine type: broad of beam and big of breast. Of course Azro had truly enlisted because the Flag had been fired upon by those damned Rebels. Another reason had been that Carrie had told him she was pregnant and three months on the way. She hadn't said by *whom* but she wasn't particular and she did like Azro. The state motto of New Hampshire as quoted by John Stark, a New Hampshire man of the Revolution, was: *"Live free or die."* Azro had elected to live *free,* so he had enlisted.

Azro was a little more than five feet eight inches in height. He was thick of chest, wide of shoulder and lean muscled. His hair was reddish, as was his graying beard. His sun-tightened eyes were a steady gray and dark like a stormy sea. His face skin was a saddle brown, dry burnished and toughened by the winds and the sun of the Southwest. His large ears stood out from his hard block of a head like the handles on a jug. His big nose had been bent askew by a fist blow in his past. He never could quite remember where and in what barroom brawl he had taken that blow.

Azro had a rock of a jaw. It jutted out, granitelike and similar to that of The Old Man of the Mountains, the epitome of New Hampshire. A phenomenon of Nature's whim, it jutted out from a sheer cliff 1,400 feet high up the side of Cannon Mountain in Franconia Notch, a forty-foot-high depiction of a venerable human face. It was a real Yankee face, a resolute face with the jaw firmly set, while looking south. It embodied a spirit expressed in the words of Daniel Webster, orator and statesman: "Men hang out their signs indicative of their respective trades: Shoemakers hang out a gigantic shoe; jewelers, a monster watch and the dentist hangs out a gold tooth but up in the mountains of New Hampshire, God Almighty has hung out a sign to show where He makes men."

Azro closed his burning eyes. "Amen," he murmured.

Azro's limp had been caused by a spent Rebel minié

ball at bloody Antietam which had struck him just above the left knee. His regiment, the Fifth New Hampshire, had fought there across the blood-soaked Sunken Road.

The waning sun struck like a mailed fist at his eyes. Sweat ran down his burning face. On the right-hand side of his skull was a lump encrusted with dried blood. He wasn't quite sure how he had acquired it. Perhaps he had fallen in the dark and struck his head on rock. Perhaps (and here it was a disconcerting and eerie thought), someone, or *something*, perhaps not of this earth, had struck him from behind. He had heard nothing nor seen nothing and yet the persistent thought ranged through his weary mind—perhaps he *had* been struck from behind. . . .

There was burro blood dried in his mustache. He had gone into the malpais country with three burros. One of them had been loaded with small kegs of water which Azro had filled at Solitario Tanks. The burro had fallen over a low cliff and died in a welter of its own blood and water from the smashed kegs. *All* of the water. . . . One of the other burros had strayed and he had not seen it again. There was not quite enough water for the last remaining burro and Azro to get back to Solitario Tanks. "God help me," he had murmured as he cut the burro's throat. He had drunk all of the blood he could.

The left sleeve was missing from his flannel shirt. He had filled it and tied the ends together to keep that with which he had filled the sleeve contained therein. He could feel the weight of the sleeve within his shirt pressing against his lean belly.

"How much farther?" Azro queried aloud.

"Mas allá. On beyond . . . ," the soft voice seemed to whisper into Azro's right ear.

Azro whirled, dropping his right hand to draw and cock his Colt.

There was no one there. . . .

"I've been out here far too long," croaked Azro.

He plodded on. His thirst was a living torment. He was in the first stages of deep thirst. He had experienced it before. It was a thirst more of the bones than of the flesh. At least that is what it felt like. It was a common dryness— a cottony feeling in the mouth and throat accompanied by great thirst, a deep craving for water that could only be assuaged by drinking water, *lots* of water.

Azro had stretched out his limited supply of water by gargling it without swallowing it and then spitting it back into his canteen. He had added his dwindling supply of urine to the water. All that was now gone. . . .

He was beginning to experience the second stage of great thirst—functional derangement and the onset of pathological disturbances. His tongue clung to his teeth; his ears drummed annoyingly. The hallucinations were soon to come, followed by delirium.

"Before God," murmured Azro.

"Curse man and trust God," the voice seemed to say.

This time Azro did not look back. The voice was an illusion; a chimera of the mind and memory.

Supposing there was someone, or something, behind him dogging his faltering footsteps, moving quickly and silently out of sight when Azro turned, perhaps to vanish entirely, only to return when least expected to goad him again and again?

He felt he was in the first stages of delirium.

The sun was low over the western hills. It was dying in an exquisite agony of gold, salmon and tints of yellow.

His saliva would stop flowing altogether. His mucus would dry. His lips would retract and his eyelids would stiffen. He would not be able to articulate clearly. He grinned a little. Who was out there to whom he *could* articulate? There was nothing but that damned haunting, insinuating mind voice or *whatever* the hell it was.

The sun was suddenly gone as though a vast curtain had been drawn down. Soon the wind would creep down the heights toward the cooling desert. The furnace winds would then sweep across the *playa,* burning against the flesh almost as hot as the sun had been doing.

Numbness would come next to Azro, creeping over the

face, the hands and finally under the clothing against the skin, imparting a dry husklike sensation so nerve-trying that few, if any, suffering from it could resist the temptation to cast off their clothing in an automatic effort for relief.

His heart beat erratically, thumping and pounding within his chest. The desire to lie down came almost overwhelmingly. To lie down was to die. . . . He must keep on. . . . He closed his eyes as he limped on.

Azro opened his eyes. The sun was fully gone. Darkness enveloped the land. It was then he saw it, or *thought* he saw it—a quick, infinitesimal speck of light, coming and going so swiftly he could hardly believe he had seen it. It was dark again but he had noticed there was a notch in the dark mass of the hills and that he remembered the light had shown somewhere far below that notch. It was little enough to go on but he had nothing else. He plodded on through the darkness.

Azro kept on. After a long time he thought he felt loose sand beneath his blistered soles. He leaned backward, could not save himself from falling, and had an intense whirling sensation in his brain and then his thoughts left him and he knew no more.

Azro dreamt he was back lying on the snow-covered ground of the December Battle of Fredericksburg. It was night. His regiment had been one of those who had gotten close to the stone wall behind which the Rebels had mowed down like falling leaves many of the Yankee attackers. He was lying naked amid many of his dead comrades, all of whom, including himself, had been stripped of their warm uniforms during darkness by the Rebels, who lacked such clothing. During the attack the white, snow-covered ground had been fully colored blue with the bodies of the uniformed fallen. Now the ground was covered with the cold, freezing bluish bodies of the dead. Evidently Azro had been stripped while he was still unconscious.

The hands were rough and harsh against his skin. "For Christ's sake!" he croaked. "Take it easy!"

The rubbing stopped.

Azro opened his eyes. The sky to the east was faint with the coming of the gibbous moon. He was lying naked beside one of the tanks of Solitario Tanks. His thirst was still paramount. He leaned to one side to scoop water into his swollen mouth.

"¡Cuidado! Take care!" the dry voice warned in Spanish.

Azro slowly turned his head and looked up.

A small, gray-bearded old man sat on an *aparejo*, a packsaddle, about fifteen feet away. His craggy face had a wisp of gray beard. He wore a thin, ragged shirt and baggy white pantaloons. Dusty huaraches were on his brown feet. A threadbare serape hung from his right shoulder. A faint thread of tobacco smoke leaked from his nostrils. A firepit covered with a layer of ashes was at his feet. The wind swept the ashes aside to reveal glowing red embers like secretive eyes studying Azro. The sudden flareup of firelight illuminated the brown and wrinkled face of the old man like a hide left too long in the sun. His eyes were clear and dark brown; the eyes of a man old in years and in body but perhaps quite young in mind.

Azro looked about for his clothing. It was heaped to one side. His holster was empty. The loaded shirtsleeve was not visible. He got unsteadily to his feet and looked about himself.

The old man reached behind himself and brought forward the sleeve for which Azro was looking. "Here, hombre," he said quietly. He tossed it toward Azro. Azro missed it. It fell into the water. Azro plunged in after it and fell face downward in the water. He groped for the sleeve with his hands.

Azro's head was lifted from the water. He looked sideways and up into the wizened face of the old man. "Take care," warned the old man. "You've had too much water already."

"Let me alone," croaked Azro.

The old man shook his head. "No more water," he cautioned.

"I wasn't after the water," rasped Azro.

The dry-sounding click, clicking of a pistol being full cocked, sounded inordinately loud in the stillness.

Azro found himself looking into the muzzle of his own pistol. "Would you shoot me, you old bastard?" he demanded.

"Try me," replied the old man. "That damned stuff in your shirtsleeve has already almost caused your death. Would you die for it now? Can you eat it? Can you drink it?"

"*¿Quién sabe?*" asked Azro. "Shoot, you old sonofabitch!"

The old man shrugged. He let down the hammer of the pistol. He threw it into the pool. "Go get your damned treasure," he grunted. "After all, hombre, you already owe me your life."

"What do you want in return? That which is in the shirtsleeve?"

The old man shook his head. "You owe me nothing."

It was quiet except for the Aeolian hum of the night wind through the trees and brush of the *bosquecillo* on the reverse slope beyond the tanks. The desert lay like a great calm sea under the beautifully subdued illumination of the rising moon. Shadows moved gently in the wind. It was the ethereal quality of a moonlit night; a ghostly barren landscape frozen in silence.

"Beautiful, is it not, Azro Sutro? But a lizard would do well to live out there."

Azro turned. "How do you know my name?"

The old man handed Azro's wallet to him. "Your name is in here."

Azro nodded. "How are you called?"

The old man bowed a little. "Gregorio Sanchez, at your service. *Arriero* and woodcutter. Now retired."

Azro smiled. "A mule packer? A woodcutter? *Here?* On the Solitario?"

Gregorio shrugged. "I *said* I was retired."

"Why are you here?"

There was no answer from Gregorio.

Azro dressed with the exception of his soleless boots. He swung his pistol belt about his waist and buckled it with practiced ease. He settled the belt about his lean waist and hips.

Gregorio eyed him. "I could have let you die or kept your shirtsleeve and killed you with your own *pistola*." He paused. "Do you wonder why I did not?"

"How much do you want?" asked Azro shortly.

"I said: You owe me nothing."

Azro waded into the pool and retrieved the shirtsleeve and his Colt. He removed the cylinder of the six-gun. There were no cartridges in the six chambers. He looked back at Gregorio. "You said: Try me. You bastard!"

Gregorio shrugged. "Why should I kill a man whose life I had just saved?"

Azro looked away. There was much about this strange and eerie old man he did not understand. An old man living in a place, where as he had said: "A lizard would do well to live out there."

Gregorio lifted the lid from an olla buried in the embers and ashes. A delicious smell emanated from the olla. "Frijoles," he said. "The beans that have made Mexico the greatest country in the world."

Azro nodded. *"Verdad.* You have been across the Solitario yourself?"

"Long ago. Long, long ago. . . ." replied Gregorio.

"Why?"

Azro looked at the bulging shirtsleeve. "The same reason you were there."

"You found no gold?"

Gregorio spread out his hands, palms upward. "I found nothing. I lost everything. I saved my life by coming back here."

"A coward's way?" suggested Azro.

Gregorio shrugged. "Perhaps. But *I* am still alive. . . ."

Azro looked about himself at the barrenness. "Still with nothing. . . ."

"It is enough that I am still alive," Gregorio said quietly. "And hombre, that is all I ask of God. And if I had not been alive, and experienced in saving men who were about to die of thirst out on that desert of Hell itself, you would not still be alive."

"I could have made it," growled Azro.

"Of course," Gregorio agreed dryly. He paused. "You have been a soldier, perhaps?"

Azro nodded. "How did you know?"

"When I stripped you to the skin, I saw the scar above your left knee and the long scar along your right ribs. Where did you get them?"

"At the Battle of Antietam in our War Between the States. And in Mexico."

Gregorio was puzzled. "*Mexico?* You fought with the French to keep Maximilian on the throne of Mexico?"

Azro shook his head. "I fought with the Juaristas. The wound along my ribs was from a French Zouave in battle." He shrugged. "It was almost a death wound. I killed the Zouave. I lived."

There was respect in Gregorio's eyes. "Why did you take up the cause and fight for the liberty of the Juaristas?"

"I was in many battles in the War Between the States. I returned home after the war. I knew no one. I had no friends and no relatives. I had grown used to war and killing. Perhaps I was beginning to like it. I knew no other trade. You see, hombre, soldiering for some men is like whoring for some women. What else can they do? So, I looked for a war and found one in Mexico. So, I joined the Juaristas."

"But why Juarez and his cause?"

"I believed in his cause. The French had no business being there in Mexico. After that, I was still homeless. I had nothing. So, I looked for gold."

"That is all? You do not seem to know your own destiny."

Azro shrugged. "Who does?"

"*Verdad.* But some know more about it than others."

"And some, like myself, know nothing about it at all."

"I find that hard to believe in you."

"Believe what you will."

Gregorio studied him. "And what *do* you believe in?"

Azro picked up the plump shirtsleeve. He cut loose the thong that bound one end and poured the contents down on the ground. The firelight flickered on and reflected from the material lying there. "Strawberry quartz. Matted together with gold wire and coarse gold. *This* is what I believe in. . . ." he said quietly.

Gregorio stepped fearfully back from the quartz as though it were a venomous snake lying there ready to strike and kill. "Where did you find it?" he quietly asked, never taking his eyes from it.

"Easily removed from the loose earth on the side of a sloping hill. The side of the hill and the ground below it were covered with blow sand. I dug this out with my bare hands. There seems to be a vein of it rich with natural gold coursing up the hill and perhaps down the other side as well." He paused. "Rich, rich, *very* rich, hombre," he murmured.

"Why did you leave it?" Gregorio already knew the answer.

"I was almost out of water. In fact, I was looking for water when I found the gold. No matter how rich the strike was, it could not buy me one drop of water out there. Without water, there is no life. . . ."

Gregorio studied him. "Can you find your way back there?"

Azro slowly shook his head. "I don't know. Why are you so interested?" He looked suspiciously at Gregorio. "Do you plan to look for it yourself?"

Gregorio shook his head. "Satan himself and a horde of his demons could not drag me across that damned desert and the accursed hills beyond it."

"But why?" queried Azro.

Gregorio pointed down the rocky slope to where the blow sand merged with the flat surface of the *playa*. "What do you see?" he asked.

"Nothing but that damned desert," grunted Azro.

"Look closer. *There*. . . ."

Azro saw it then. It was a gray wooden weatherbeaten cross leaning away from the usual course of the wind. He looked at Gregorio.

Gregorio nodded. "My young wife, Lupita." His voice broke. "She died out there on the *playa*," he continued. "Many years ago. I was young and strong then as you are now. I was mad with gold fever as you are now. I could have left that place of hell but I stayed on in my lust for gold. Lupita was as fragile as smoke. She would not leave me. Where could she go? Only *I* knew that damned country or *thought* I did. I was wrong, as you are wrong. . . ." His voice died away.

"Did you find any trace of gold?" asked Azro.

"I did not," replied Gregorio.

"But you knew about the gold being somewhere in there?"

"All I knew about it or thought about it was that it was a legend, no more, hombre."

"Legends almost always have some basis in truth."

Gregorio shrugged but he did not speak.

Azro eyed Gregorio. "Tell me about your wife, Lupita."

"She was dying in those damned hills. I carried her in my arms across the *playa* to reach the water here. She died somewhere out on the *playa*. I did not know that she had died. I buried her here in the blow sand."

"Where the cross is now?"

Gregorio shook his head. Tears welled from his sad eyes. "I buried her and did not mark the grave. I was near death myself, you know, even as you had been. I left here and did not return for some years. When I did return, I could find no sign of her grave. The blowing sand, you know. All I knew was that she *was* buried somewhere in there. I carved the cross and placed it down there. You see, the whole area must be considered as her grave. I come here from time to time and try to find where she is buried. I have not been successful. But perhaps, someday. . . ."

"Why did you bring a woman out here with you?" asked Azro.

Gregorio did not reply. "The beans will be ready," he said. "Let us eat."

The beans did not last long. The two men sat on opposite sides of the dying fire, smoking two of the lean and crooked black Lobo Negro cigarillos.

"How did you get that lump on the side of your head?" Gregorio asked suddenly after a time.

"I must have fallen," replied Azro. "I have little recollection of what happened. Some of the events maybe occurred only in my imagination. I must have fallen." He paused and looked oddly at Gregorio. "I *might* have fallen," he continued quietly. "The lump might have come from the fall, or *perhaps someone I did not see struck me from behind*. The lump might have come from the fall, or the blow, or perhaps both. As I said, I have little recollection of what happened. The first thing I can truly recall was finding myself walking west on the *playa* after killing my last burro for its blood to drink. I do not clearly recall how I got hurt. I do not recall where I found the gold. All I know is that I had walked half a day from water, here at the Solitario Tanks, to the east and across the *playa* into the hills and canyons. The gold was in one of those canyons, but there are many canyons thereabouts and they all look alike."

"*Verdad,*" agreed Gregorio.

"Why did you bring a woman with you into that place of hell?" repeated Azro.

Gregorio shrugged. "I had not been married long. I could not leave her behind for fear of losing her. I wanted the gold for her, not so much for myself. I did not find the gold and lost her."

Azro studied him. "*Verdad?*" he quietly asked.

Gregorio nodded. "Why do you ask?"

"Because if you had not brought her with you, she might still be alive all these past years. In seeking that treasure you lost the one true treasure of your life, that which you already had—your young wife."

Gregorio was quiet. Whatever he was thinking he was keeping to himself.

"How did she die, Gregorio?" asked Azro. "Was it lack of water? Exposure? Perhaps she was injured in a fall?"

"Why do you want to know? It is enough that she died."

"There is something you are not telling me," Azro suggested.

Gregorio looked away from Azro's penetrating gaze. "What are you trying to say?" he asked.

"How did she die, Gregorio?" Azro persisted.

"I was not with her when she was injured. I was absorbed in my senseless search for gold. She was alone at our camp. I got back after nightfall. She was unconscious, lying on the ground, bleeding from a scalp wound on the back of her head. She had lost much blood. She was fragile." His voice died away.

"Go on," urged Azro.

"I went loco," continued Gregorio. "The burros were gone. There was no time to look for them. I carried her across the *playa* throughout the night. She had been still alive when I picked her up. She was dead when I got here. . . ."

"Who did it?" demanded Azro. "Indians? Mexicans? Gringos?"

"No Indian would go into those canyons. To them it is haunted. Mexicans mostly avoid that country. Gringos sometimes go in there. Usually they are never seen again. I found no tracks. No signs of anyone other than Lupita being at the camp. Nothing. . . ." He paused. He looked out across the *playa* frozen in bluish moonlight and utter silence. "The place is accursed. It is haunted by *something*; something that does not want men hunting in there for gold. There are old tales about such things. I was a fool to go in there. I was double a fool to bring her with me. She did not want to go, you understand?"

"But *you* have survived."

Gregorio's eyes were bright with tears as he turned to face Azro. "You say I have survived? I should have died instead of her. I lost the one thing for which I lived back then. I did not truly know it at the time; I know it now! I know that she lies somewhere down there in the blow sand but I do not know exactly where she is. Is that not punishment worse than death?"

There was nothing Azro could say.

"What will you do now?" asked Gregorio to change the subject. He could not talk longer about it, so painful it was to him.

Azro replaced the pile of strawberry quartz into the sleeve and tied the open end of the sleeve to close it.

"You will return to those accursed canyons," stated Gregorio.

"That is so," agreed Azro.

"You know how dangerous it is. Why will you go back?"

"I have nothing else. I have no one left to return to. No family, wife, children or friends."

Gregorio nodded. "If that is true, why do you want the gold? What good will it do you? What can you buy with it that will bring you happiness? There are men who will kill you for it. Dark-minded men. Killers . . ." warned Gregorio.

Azro looked at him. "Why, amigo, *I* can kill too. . . ."

"You are a blind fool!"

Azro shook his head. "It is you who is blind, sitting here on this damned hill mooning over the lost grave of a wife who died years ago!" He instantly regretted what he had just said. After all, the old fool had saved Azro's life.

"This is the life I have chosen," said Gregorio. "At that, hombre, it is a better life than you have chosen for yourself, a life that will likely lead to your death in some remote canyon where no one will bury you and weep over your grave. At least I have my memories and dreams. What do you plan to do now?"

Azro shrugged. "The only thing I can do—go into Yuma and cash in my gold to buy me supplies, a rifle and some burros—unless you will sell me yours."

Gregorio shook his head. "They are my family," he said quietly. "The instant you show up in Yuma, looking as you do with a shirtsleeve full of high-assay gold quartz, you will be recognized for what you are. You must come back here for your water. Men in Yuma will know that. You will be followed. They will follow you through the gates of Hell itself for gold such as your quartz indicates and much less for that matter."

"What do you suggest?" asked Azro.

"If you like, I will take your gold into Yuma. I have friends there. I will trade in the gold and buy your supplies and a pair of burros, perhaps. I will bring it all back here with me although I do not want to see you go back into those lost canyons."

"How do I know that you will return?"

"This is my home most of the time. I hope to die here someday. Perhaps some kind passerby will bury me and say a few words over my grave."

"What will you want from me if you go into Yuma for me with my gold?"

Gregorio smiled. "Only your friendship."

"How long will it take you to go to Yuma and return here?"

"Perhaps a week. What will you need?"

"Food. You will know what to get. A rifle. Caliber forty-four. Cartridges. Tobacco. Liquor."

"It is dangerous to drink on your quest. You will make mistakes."

Azro grinned. "For medicinal purposes only. Maybe snakebite."

"That doesn't work."

Azro nodded. "I know. But it is a comfort to know that it might. How will you get to Yuma?"

Gregorio placed two fingers in his mouth and whistled sharply.

There was a distant clattering of something on the rocky slope behind the *tinaja*. A moment later a burro poked its head beyond some scrub brush and eyed the two men with big, soft-looking eyes.

Gregorio smiled. "That's Theresa. She is the bold one."

Theresa trotted up to Gregorio. He stroked her head and fondled her big ears.

Another burro poked its head through the brush and eyed Azro suspiciously.

"That's Filomena," explained Gregorio. "She's the shy and cautious one. It's unusual for her to show up at all when a stranger is around here."

"When does a stranger ever show up around here?" asked Azro.

Gregorio shrugged. "You did."

"Will you ride one of the burros to Yuma?"

Gregorio shook his head. "Follow me." He walked down the slope toward a thick *bosquecillo* of scrub trees and brush followed by a wondering Azro and the two little burros.

A small iron-gray California mule trotted through the *bosquecillo* toward Gregorio.

"That is Solomon, my riding mule," explained Gregorio. "I will ride him into Yuma."

Gregorio led the way through part of the *bosquecillo* toward a sheer wall of rock rising above the top level of the trees. He approached the wall and pulled aside brush piled thickly against the base of it to reveal the narrow mouth of what appeared to be a cavern opening into the solid rock.

Gregorio led the way into the cavern and lighted a lantern. "My house is your house," he said with a broad smile.

A pallet lay on the floor. Stacked wooden boxes held cans and containers of food and condiments and a few cooking utensils. A miner's spade hung from a wall peg. Several packsaddles lay against one wall. There were small oval wooden kegs which were used to carry water on burro or mule backs. A saddle, bridle, saddle blanket and other horse furniture were lying on the floor. A heavy wooden box looked familiar to Azro. It was labeled in black ink: ARMY BREAD. UNION MECHANICAL BAKING COMPANY. BALTIMORE MD. It was a container for hardtack, the flinty square biscuits, usually aswarm with weevils, which had been standard army fare during the Civil War.

Azro looked about. "You have a rifle? A carbine?" he asked.

Gregorio handed Azro a carbine. Azro recognized it as one he had carried in Mexico for some time after the war. It was the Winchester Model 1866 saddle ring carbine with a brass frame nicknamed The Yellow Boy. It fired the .44 caliber rimfire cartridge with a 200-grain bullet using a 28-grain powder propelling charge. The firing pin was double-pronged, thus striking both sides of the cartridge rim. The tubular magazine beneath the barrel carried ten cartridges.

"You won't take it to Yuma with you?" asked Azro.

Gregorio shook his head. "I have no need of it. It is yours to use, amigo."

Azro nodded. *"Gracias.* You have cartridges for it?"

"The magazine is full. Ten cartridges. That is all I have."

Gregorio left that night after moonset.

After Gregorio was gone, Azro scouted around the *tinaja* area and removed all traces of Gregorio's and his own presence there. He returned to the cavern and cleaned the Winchester inside and out. He made coffee over the firepit within the cavern. While it was brewing, he poked about in the far reaches of the cavern and found a pair of what he recognized as Apache thigh-length moccasins, the *n'deh b'keh.* He wondered how the old man had come by them. It was something to think about. Maybe the old bastard was part Apache, or perhaps had been raised by them. It was not uncommon. Azro had known a few such men. They had been captured when children by the Apaches. They rarely kept adult men captives, considering them too dangerous. Their own numbers of warriors was always low owing to almost incessant warfare with Mexicans and gringos. A very young male Mexican could easily be raised and trained as an Apache warrior. Some of them liked the Apache way of life and would remain with the band rather than returning to their own people.

The moccasins were in good shape. Azro pulled them on and drew the tops of them high around his thighs then folded them neatly below his kneecaps and tied them in place. Apaches usually used the folds to carry small personal articles. The leg parts of the moccasins were made of soft deerskin while the soles were made of tough rawhide. There was no better mode of footwear for use in the desert and rough mountains. Azro grunted in satisfaction as he stomped about the cavern getting the feel of the moccasins.

The coffee boiled. Azro opened the case of hardtack and removed some of the biscuits from it. He poured some of the coffee into a big tin mug. He looked at one of the pieces of hardtack. It brought back memories to him. During the war he and his messmates used to soak their hardtack in water and then fry it in deep bacon grease. A little sprinkling of brown sugar atop the hardtack made it almost as palatable as pastry. He grinned. "Skiligalee," he murmured. That was what they had called it—*skiligalee*. There were many memories. One night his squad had been on outpost duty along the Rappahannock River with the Rebels on the other side of the river. Azro and his squad mates had been foolish enough to sit around a roaring campfire eating skiligalee. A Rebel musket across the river cracked once like a shingle being snapped over one's knee. Joe Calder had been hit in the head. He had fallen back from the fire. Azro and the others had sprinted for cover. Azro had glanced back. Joe lay on his back. His eyes were wide open staring sightlessly at the night sky. The piece of hardtack was still held in his mouth.

Azro dipped a piece of hardtack into the steaming coffee. Weevils came scrambling out of it and swam frantically about until they died. Azro casually skimmed them from the surface of the coffee and flicked them off. He ate the coffee-soaked hardtack. Some said the weevils had a distinctive taste, somewhat like weak vinegar. Azro had never noticed it. War was war and hardtack was hardtack. One endured both or one did not survive. It was as simple as that.

Azro finished eating and let the fire die down. He put out the lantern, took the Winchester and left the cavern. The moon was almost gone. It was tomb-quiet and windless. He worked his way through the *bosquecillo*. The two burros came to him. He stroked their ears and heads and spoke quietly to them. They looked up at him with their big, soft eyes. He knew how they must feel. Gregorio, their beloved master, was gone.

Azro softfooted up to the *tinaja* area. The desert was dark but there was still enough of the fading moonlight for him to be able to see fairly far out onto the *playa*. The darkness had softened the harsh effect of the ancient lake bed but it did not soften the effect that it had upon Azro.

"Why go back?" the mind voice said, or seemed to say out of the stillness.

Azro whirled, full cocking the Winchester as he did so. As before, *there was no one there*.

"I've been out here too long," murmured Azro. He knew well enough that a gun shot would have no effect on whoever or *whatever* it was that was speaking to him, providing he *could* see it.

What was *he* really looking for? He thought of the strange and lonely old man who had saved his life and who was now risking his own life to help Azro. He seemed happy enough at the prospect of spending the rest of his waning life here at Solitario Tanks in memory of the young wife whose grave he had not been able to locate, although he could never be very far from it. What was it he had said to Azro? *"Why do you want the gold? What good will it do you? What can you buy with it that will bring you happiness?"*

Azro shrugged. *"Nada,"* he murmured.

He must go back into those lost canyons to seek the gold. *He must go.* . . .

Azro limped down the reverse slope of the area behind the tanks. A faint wind had risen. It moaned through the *bosquecillo.*

Azro halted. He had heard something in the wind. It was not the bodiless voice, or possible presence, he had heard before or *thought* he had heard. He raised his head like a night-hunting wolf trying to detect by sight, sound or smell where his prey might be.

Nothing. . . .

He waited, straining to hear the sound again.

Nothing. . . .

He went on to the cavern. He paused again to listen. The burros were quiet. If there *had* been someone or anything alive hiding in the *bosquecillo,* the burros would have known about it. They would have warned Azro about it. That is, unless they were too frightened to bray. Perhaps they had not detected anything; anything *alive,* that is.

He entered the cavern and leaned the carbine against the rear wall. A faint musical sound came as the metal buttplate struck something. Azro lighted the lantern. He looked down at the butt of the Winchester. A quart bottle with a blue-and-white paper label lay sideways on the rock floor.

Azro picked up the bottle and read the label aloud: "The Abyssinian Desert Companion. Good for Wind Colic, Flatulent Colic, Botts, Diarhhea, Scouring, Dysentery, Inflammation of the Bowels, Bladder and Kidney trouble, Colds in the Head, Congestion, Fits, Mad Staggers, Looseness of the Bowels and Inflammation of the Brain. For Botts it has no equal."

Azro shook the bottle and watched the deep amber contents swirl seductively about. He twisted the cork out of the bottle. He sniffed the contents. He instantly jerked back his head. His eyes watered. "Jeeesuss Kerist!" he blurted. He suspiciously studied the contents.

Azro shrugged. "What the hell," he murmured. "Maybe I've got botts." He drank about three fingers of the powerful distillation. He jerked back. He could not get his breath. His eyes watered again. His face tightened as though enclosed in a huge and powerful hand. His teeth felt as though they'd suddenly been sharpened. Then came the silent implosion in his lean gut. After a few moments of thoughtful silence Azro nodded. "Wahoo," he murmured hoarsely. "Forty rod, at least," he added.

He lowered the lantern and lay down on the pallet with the Winchester on one side of him and his Colt on the other. He closed his eyes.

He heard the voice, calling softly, but he could not distinguish the words. He shook his head and rolled over.

The sound of the voice came again. It seemed as though it was a woman.

Azro sat up suddenly and closed his hand on his Colt. He sat there, breathing quietly, listening for the voice. After a time he got up, sheathed his Colt and took up the Winchester. He waited at the mouth of the cavern. It was quiet again. He waited. Minutes ticked past. The sound of the voice, if that was what it was, did not come again. Perhaps it had been the night wind. There *was* no wind.

Azro shrugged. "This damned place *is* haunted," he murmured. He grinned faintly. "Perhaps it was The Abyssinian Desert Companion." He lay down to sleep. He did not waken again.

It was just before dawn of the tenth day after Gregorio had left for Yuma. Azro awoke with an uneasy feeling growing within himself. The faintest of gray light showed at the cavern entrance. He stood up and took his Winchester and slung his field glasses case strap about his neck.

One of the burros brayed softly.

Azro walked softly to the cavern entrance and stood still just within it. He tilted his head forward, then turned it first to one side and then the other peering narrow-eyed into the grayness, sniffing the morning air and listening intently.

Nothing. . . .

The burro brayed again.

Azro catfooted through the *bosquecillo.* He stopped short when he saw a motionless and hatless mounted man seated on a mule just at the edge of the trees. It could be Gregorio mounted on Solomon. Why hadn't he called out? Perhaps he could not see the motionless shadowy figure of Azro within the *bosquecillo.*

A burro brayed again. There was an answering bray from the mule.

The mule entered the *bosquecillo* and moved toward Azro. The graying light struck the face of the mounted man. He was Gregorio, or at least there was some resemblance to Gregorio. Somehow the features were different. There was no doubt in Azro's mind that the mule was indeed Solomon.

Azro took a chance. He raised his carbine. "Gregorio?" he softly called out.

There was no answer to Azro's call.

The mule moved closer at the sound of Azro's voice. Gregorio's features became plainer to see in the growing light. His mouth gaped open. His eyes were wide and unblinking and they seemed to stare sightlessly toward Azro. Gregorio was obviously as dead as last night's liquor bottle. Gregorio had been lashed into his saddle. His left hand still held the reins in the cold grip of *rigor mortis.* The mule turned aside and Azro saw the haft of a knife sticking out between Gregorio's shoulder blades.

Azro moved swiftly, running softly through the *bosquecillo* until he could look out with his field glasses toward the faint trail to Yuma and the north that traversed the long slope of the land that lay stretching below the *bosquecillo.* The area was a static landscape. Nothing moved under the light of the rising sun. There was no sign of moving men and wreathing dust.

What was it Gregorio had said? *"The instant you show*

up in Yuma, looking as you do with a shirtsleeve full of high-assay quartz, you will be recognized for what you are. You must come back here for your water. Men in Yuma will know that. You will be followed. They will follow you through the gates of Hell itself for gold such as your quartz indicates and much less, for that matter."

Azro went back to Gregorio. He cut loose the lashings and pulled the knife from the old man's back. The old man had not been dead too long. Whoever had murdered him was likely somewhere along the trail waiting for their chance to deal with Azro.

Azro carried the body to the *tinaja*. He got the miner's spade and an old blanket from the cavern and returned to the old man. He carried the body down to the blow sand and dug a grave near the cross Gregorio had placed there in memory of Lupita. He closed Gregorio's eyelids and then wrapped Gregorio in the blanket. He lowered him into the grave and shoveled the loose sand back into the hole. He did not mound the grave but rather smoothed out the sand so that there was no indication that a grave was there. The cross would be marker enough.

Azro took off his hat and with bowed head recited the Twenty-third Psalm. He replaced his hat and looked down at the grave. *"Vaya con Dios, amigo,"* he murmured. "Go with God." He paused then spoke again: *"Vaya con Dios, amigo . . . acaso. . . .* Go with God, friend . . . perhaps. . . ."

Azro went back to observe the trail. It was the same as it had been before, with no sign of mounted men. He was sure they were out there, perhaps hidden in an arroyo waiting for their chance to surprise him, probably under cover of darkness.

To run would be against every fighting fiber in Azro's body.

"Run or fight? Which is it to be?" the mind voice seemed to say.

To fight on this ground would serve no purpose. His best course would be to leave the area as soon as possible and strike back across the *playa,* hoping to possibly evade whoever was out there and get into the hills and canyons beyond the *playa.* He'd need to carry as much water with himself as possible. He had the two burros to carry the water kegs and supplies. He could ride Solomon, if need be.

Azro went back to Solomon and instantly realized the mule was about done. He'd never last out on the *playa* and in the hills beyond. He looked through the saddlebags on the mule. There was no trace of his sleeve filled with strawberry quartz. He hadn't expected any. He did find two full bottles of Abyssinian Desert Companion, a supply of Lobo Negro cigarillos and some loose tobacco and a small sack of beans.

He hefted the bottles of Abyssinian Desert Companion. "Better than nothing." He grinned. "Maybe a helluva lot better."

Azro went to the cavern. He dumped what food he could find into a sack. The small oval water kegs seemed to be in fair shape. They had not thoroughly dried yet. He carried eight of them to the *tinaja* and immersed them, to soak them and swell the seams, weighting them down with rocks. They'd hardly carry enough water to get him beyond the canyons to the east. Yuma would be the closest and safest source of water within striking distance of Solitario Tanks, but of course he could not go there. In the other directions, south and east, there might be *some* water in a few isolated *tinajas* but he did not know quite where they were and most, if not all, of them were seasonal and it was now the driest part of the year. He would not have enough water in the kegs to support himself and the two burros for very long and perhaps not long enough to find any other water to the southeast, if there was any to be found. He *might* make it alone. . . .

It was midmorning. The sun blazed down. Azro checked the trail to Yuma. As before, there was no sign of life. The only movement he could see was that of a *zopilote,* the great buzzard of the Sonoran type of desert seemingly hanging almost motionless high in the sky like a scrap of charred paper carried highly upward from the draft of a bonfire. Azro *thought* he saw it. . . . It might be a portent of death lurking somewhere in the area. *Whose* death, he thought.

Solomon was still alive, but barely. There was no hope for him. "Sorry, Solomon," murmured Azro as he pulled the mule's head to one side and cut its throat. He let the blood drain onto the ground. Azro had spent some time with the Apaches, *friendly* ones, that is. Their usual canteen was the long gut or intestine of a horse or mule, sketchily cleaned, tied at one end and filled with water, then tied at the open end and looped about the neck of their horse. It was greasy, as was the water contained therein with an indescribable taste of its own, but it *was* water. Azro cut free the intestine and hung it from a tree branch while he cut some cooking meat, including the mule's upper lip from the body. Apaches liked the sweeter mule meat better than beef.

Azro carried the intestine to the *tinaja* and placed it in the water. He returned to the cavern and cooked the mule meat. The long, hot afternoon began. The dry, hot wind picked up. Wind devils appeared on the flat, dusty surface of the *playa*. Heat waves endlessly shimmered and postured: Distant objects were magnified while seemingly rising from the superheated ground into the shimmering heat waves.

Now and again Azro checked the Yuma trail. If there was anyone out there, they would likely be squatting in the hot shade of their horses waiting for nightfall. "Sweat, you bastards," he grunted. He grinned.

He'd have to leave the *tinaja* area before dusk. He'd have little chance against them if they closed in on him during the premoon darkness. He didn't know how many of them there might be. He was used to having the odds against him. He knew one thing for sure—he'd fight to the death before he let them take him alive. They would not try to kill, at first anyway. They would want to know the site of the gold lode. He grinned wryly. "I don't even know myself," he murmured.

He turned the mule intestine inside out and cleaned it as well as he could. He turned it inside out again, tied one end and filled the intestine by means of his coffee cup. When the intestine was full and bulging, he tied the open end closed. He took out the kegs he had placed in the water to soak. He got the packsaddles from the cavern and placed them on the two burros. He made sure the kegs were full and then placed the stoppers in them. He loaded each of the burros with four of the dripping kegs. He shook his head. Would they keep dripping? He hoped the seams would swell enough to hold the water within the kegs. If not . . . ? He shook his head. It was not good to think about it. He coiled the mule intestine and looped it about Filomena's neck.

The wind had increased. The wind devils traveled with the wind, appearing suddenly only to reappear again somewhere else to whirl and spiral, rising higher and higher as they moved along and then disappeared again. It would be sheer hell to cross the *playa* that day. Azro had no choice whatsoever. Cross the *playa* or die. It was that simple. Cross the *playa* and *then* die, he thought.

They would not be able to wring out of him the site of the gold lode. He didn't know himself, so how could he tell them? In reality he could not show them the location of the lode. They would not believe him. Either way he would be certain to die, either by their hands or by crossing the *playa* at the worst possible time of the year into a burning, waterless wasteland. He would be damned if he stayed and would be damned if he left.

He still planned to move at dusk, if they allowed him to do so. He stood at the *tinaja* and looked down at the lone cross there. He could still see the faint outline of the grave of Gregorio. In time the wind would level it off. The wind was shifting and fanning itself along the line of the blow sand, neatly sweeping up the higher levels of sand and then redistributing them to the lower levels to fill in the lower levels in its constant and never-ending task of tidying up the desert floor.

Both burros brayed loud and clear.

Azro whirled in the direction of the braying. A man was running crouched toward Azro, with a six-shooter in his right hand and a Winchester in his left hand. Azro fired his Winchester twice from his hip. The pair of slugs caught the man in the belly and slammed him backward. He fired his pistol into the air as he staggered sideways to the edge of the pool and then fell flat on his back, dropping the pistol into the water.

Something warned Azro to turn. As he did so he saw a man standing not far from himself with his clubbed rifle ready to strike. He evidently wanted Azro *alive*. He slammed the rifle down across the barrel of Azro's Winchester in an effort to turn it aside, then brought the butt upward to strike at Azro's jaw. Azro turned his head aside and caught the blow alongside his skull above his right ear. He staggered but he did not go down. He stood there swaying back and forth. It was a blow that might have felled an ox. Azro's attacker jumped back open-mouthed in astonishment that Azro had not gone down from such a blow.

Azro moved in swiftly with a crooked grin on his face. "That's New Hampshire granite you're hitting, you sonofabitch!" he rasped out. His hamlike left fist caught his attacker in the lower part of his belly. The man bent forward from the waist. His chin met Azro's upward driving right knee. He raised his head with the impact. Azro gave him the old one-two, a left to the belly and a hard right to the jaw. He staggered backward to the edge of the pool. Azro charged, butting the man in the chest with his hard head, and driving him flat on his back into the water. Azro was on top of him in an instant. His big hands closed about the man's throat. He forced his head under the water and squeezed his throat with all his strength. The man forced his body upward. Azro forced it back down. A reddish haze seemed to appear before Azro's eyes. Vivid memories of the violent and bloody hand-to-hand fighting at Antietam and Spotsylvania Court House poured through his tired mind. He squeezed his hands tighter and tighter.

Azro found himself standing on the edge of the pool looking down at the contorted face of the man he had just killed. It was just distinguishable under the water's surface. A few bubbles rose from his gaping mouth and burst on the surface.

It was very quiet. The air was dry and hot. The vagrant wind was beginning to beat its wings. Out on the surface of the *playa* there arose, here and there, the many ubiquitous wind devils, appearing and disappearing only to reappear again in the distance, whirling and spiraling upward.

Azro did not want to move. A lethargy had overcome him. He had had the same feeling after many of the battles during the Civil War and later while fighting in Mexico. It was difficult to shake off. Even the debauches with cheap liquor and drunken two-bit whores had never been able to erase the bloodshed from his tired mind. Still, he had always gone back into other battles when ordered to do so.

Azro picked up the Winchester '73 dropped by the second man he had killed. The magazine was full. He went to the first man he had killed. He removed all of the .44-40 cartridges from the man's pistol belt and fed as many as he could into the empty loops on his own pistol belt and then placed the remaining cartridges into his shirt pockets. He entered the pool next to the body of the second man he had killed and removed the pistol belt heavy with cartridges, holstered Colt and sheathed knife. He got out of the pool and emptied the cylinder chambers of the revolver and then shook it to get rid of the surplus water and then wiped it as dry as he could. He reloaded the cylinder and thrust the Colt under his belt.

Azro picketed Filomena and Theresa near the *tinaja*. "Stay here, you pretty little bitches," he said. "I'll be needing you soon."

Azro took up his station near the rock formation overlooking the Yuma Trail. He focused his field glasses on it. A thin thread of dust hung in the air but he did not see anyone on the trail itself. The dust was no wandering wind devil. It was moving slowly *against* the wind, instead of traveling with it as a wind devil was bound to do. Likely those who had been traveling toward Solitario Tanks had sent the two men he had killed to get Azro under control.

Azro scratched at his crotch. "Get *me* under control? The bastards!" He levered a round into the chamber of his Winchester. He grinned crookedly. "I'm a mean sonofabitch," he added quietly. "I'm a real cocked pistol man. I'm mean enough to hunt grizzly bears with a willow switch."

The trail wound up close to where Azro had stationed himself. He knew now they were too close for him to get safely away from the *tinaja* area. He'd have to make a stand where he was.

The dust thickened and then suddenly, as though like marionettes controlled by the strings of a master, five horsemen appeared on a rise in the trail seemingly coming up out of nowhere from the depths. They rode steadily onward with ready rifles across their thighs. The fine clear lenses of Azro's field glasses picked out their faces; hard faces with jaws set like closed wolf traps. They neared the bottom of the slope. They halted their mounts about 150 yards downslope from where Azro waited for them. The leader rode his dun horse closer, perhaps 100 yards from Azro.

Azro stepped out into the open. "That's far enough!" he shouted. His voice rolled echoing along the slopes: *"That's far enough. . . . That's far. . . . That's. . . ."* The sound slowly died away in the distance. It was quiet again except for the dry moaning of the wind through the *bosquecillo.*

The lead horseman reined in. "You're Sutro, eh!" he called out.

They must have gotten his name from Gregorio. That is, before they had murdered him.

"What do you want?" demanded Azro.

"Didn't Jim and Harry tell you?"

"They didn't have time."

"Where are they?"

"Dead," replied Azro. I killed them."

"Why?"

Azro shrugged. "They tried to kill me."

"That wasn't my orders."

"I didn't know that," said Azro. "When armed men attack me, I figure they kill *me* or *I* kill *them*." He paused. "I killed them."

The leader was quiet for a short time, as though he was sizing up the situation.

"What do you want?" asked Azro.

"I want to talk with you."

Azro shrugged again. "Talk," he said.

"We know you know where that strawberry quartz came from. You show us where you found it. We'll cut you in on the deal. Fair enough?"

"And if I don't?"

There was a pause. "You'll die," said the leader.

Azro grinned. "So, I show you where the quartz was found. You cut me in on the deal. What's my guarantee?"

"My word."

Azro laughed. "Is that the same deal you offered old Gregorio?"

"The old fool wouldn't talk."

"Because he himself didn't know where I found it. Did he tell you as well that I really didn't know?"

The leader shifted about in his saddle. "We need water," he said. "Let us come and get it. We can talk later."

"That so? You'll have to wait."

One of the men waiting behind the leader turned his horse as if to ride toward the far edge of the *bosquecillo*. Azro's Winchester cracked flatly. The horseman's hat was lifted from his head as if by magic. A second slug whined just over his head. He turned his mount and took cover in an arroyo. The double report echoed along the ridge into the distance. The powdersmoke drifted upward from Azro's position but he was no longer there. He had moved instantly after the second shot.

The leader had not moved. "You can't keep us much longer," he warned.

"I can try," said Azro. He moved again.

"We'll come after dusk."

Azro grinned. "You'll be damned thirsty by then."

It was quiet again.

"Damn you!" shouted the leader. He raised his Winchester and spurred his dun into a run toward Azro's position.

Azro fired. The dun went down with a .44-40 slug through its head. It was dead before it hit the ground. The horseman hit the ground running. A slug whispered just past his ear. He ran back toward his companions. One of them took him up behind himself on his horse and galloped his mount back toward the arroyo.

Azro trotted back to the *tinaja* area. He led the two burros down the slope to the blow sand. He took off his hat as he passed the lone cross. He struck off at a steady mile-eating pace across the *playa*. A half mile or so outward he looked back toward the *tinaja* site. He could see them walking about near the water. They would water up and start right out after him, he figured. He could put up a fight and maybe hold them off for a time but odds were they'd get him in the end. He'd die before he would tell them anything. He grinned. What *could* he tell them? "*Nada*," he said and turned to lead on the burros.

He was three miles out on the *playa* before he looked back again. He could see them on the edge of the *playa* moving toward him. They would be walking their horses.

The wind picked up. Here and there rose swirling, spiraling wind devils rising higher and higher hundreds of feet as the wind increased in velocity. Now and again one of them would pass between the line of vision of Azro and his pursuers, temporarily blotting them out from each other's sight. It would be a deadly game of hide-and-go-seek between them. Then, at irregular intervals the air between them would be clear again until the arrival of one or more of the sight-blocking wind devils.

Azro plodded on. He did not look back again. The drops of water leaking from the water kegs would vanish almost instantly as they fell and struck the hard, dry surface of the insatiable *playa*.

As the afternoon wore on, the wind velocity increased so that at times the masses of heated air within the wind devils was whirled spirally into a rising column of dust. There was nothing on the hot, dry surface of the *playa* to impede or obstruct the progress of the columns as they continued on hour after hour as the day wore on so that it became almost impossible to see beyond them across the miles wide surface of the *playa*. Sometimes the columns would remain almost stationary for hours at a time. The distant hills and the faraway mountains were almost completely lost to the sight of anyone on the surface of the *playa*. It had become a no-man's-land of hellfire heat and burning dust. In time nothing could be distinguished other than the wind devils themselves. After all, was it not their undisputed territory? Into this superheated nothingness plodded Azro Sutro leading his two burros. In time his pursuers turned back, realizing it was a hopeless chase into the deadly unknown after a man, who in reality, was probably not a man at all but rather a fleeting phantom.

EPILOGUE

Azro Samuel Sutro was never seen again, at least by anyone who could tell the tale about it. There were tales told by some who claimed to have seen him in the long following years after his disappearance—a dim figure seen through the dust and haze of the windswept *playa*—but it was never close enough to distinguish any true and particular features. Some claimed the phantom, or whatever it was, was that of a chunky, ragged-beard figure of a man with haunted eyes walking with a slight limp and always leading his two burros, but he was always traveling in the opposite direction from where he was first seen and always moving toward and into the remote hills and canyons east of the vast *playa*. The Apaches and Mexicans claimed he had turned into one of the wind devils which periodically swept clean the surface of the *playa*. The gringos said nothing. No true trace of Azro Sutro was ever found.

Somewhere in the tangled and isolated canyons and hills east of the Solitario Desert and its ominous *playa* there may yet be traces of Azro Sutro. Perhaps there is an empty sun-tinted bottle with a long-faded blue-and-white label of The Abyssinian Desert Companion. There may be only one distinguishable printed line left to identify its long-gone contents: "For Botts it has no equal." The delicate sun-bleached bones of a burro or two might be found as well. Perhaps there might be a grinning skull nearby. None of these relics have ever been reported. One *might* also find a vein of strawberry quartz of great potential value but who will dare enter that haunted land to find it?

Perhaps Azro Sutro *did* find the lost vein of strawberry quartz. *¿Quién sabe?*

We'll Kill the Old Red Rooster When She Comes

R. C. HOUSE

Tiger and I just about always stop in the bar at Reno's in Mojave and have a couple of what we call ditchwater highballs in celebration on our way home from Bakersfield and share a little bullshit with the boys who hang around there. We've come to know most of them by name or by sight. Kind of keeps us in touch with our fellow man, you might say. We live pretty far off the beaten track out in the Mojave Desert and don't see other people that often. We only get to Reno's about every couple of months.

After a while we go into the coffee shop and load up on a citified meal. The coffee shop of an evening is usually full of escapees from L.A., if it's around a weekend. They roar in there on their motorsickles or crunch in with their four-wheelers, or vans pull in with trailers loaded with those dirt bikes and such. Or they'll be retired folks passing through in their motor homes stopping off for burgers or grilled cheeses or a bowl of chili.

Wintertime, the place is a regular stop-off for L.A. skiers headed up to Mammoth or some such in the Sierra in their spiffy snowsuits and fancy brand-new sweaters and fashionable little sports cars outside with racks for his-and-hers skis. Lord, the number of times they must have to change clothes in a day to suit the occasion in those places, it's a wonder to me where they stow their duffle in those little motorized roller skates.

Stopping off at Reno's gets to be a tradition with just about anybody who goes through Mojave with any frequency. Being flush for a change after our occasional runs to Bakersfield, Tiger and I stoke up on steak and eggs, hashbrowns, good sourdough toast and a mess of coffee-shop coffee before heading on home. Home is a two-room cement-block shack up on the slopes of the El Paso Mountains near Garlock, of which there isn't much left these days, and a hop, skip and jump from Randsburg, perched up there over across the way on the slopes of the Rand Mountains.

Everything else is forty miles from nowhere, just the unending sprawl of rock and gravel and chaparral sweeping away to no place in particular. Randsburg's fabulous Yellow Aster Mine played out years ago, so there isn't much left around Randsburg and its neighbor town, Johannesburg, either, except over in Randsburg there's Olga Guyette's "The Joint," where Tiger and I pass the time when we go to town, the general store and soda fountain next to the post office, and a bunch of bottle shops. And all around are a few modest little houses and shacks and kind of dilapidated old house trailers scattered random as raindrops.

And up the hill above town the great mounds of jumbled tailings from the old Yellow Aster.

Tiger and I—they call me Ten High—have been partners out here for a lot of years. Both divorced, both living on Army retirement pensions; that's about all it took for us to become pals. We discovered that there's quite a bit of gold and a little silver in the El Pasos above our place, at least enough to whet a man's appetite. Oh, I had a hunch that a good-sized strike waited up there, but Tiger and I found enough on our claim to get by. For the hell of it, we took to calling it the Red Rooster Mine; never quite got around to filing any legal papers.

We spied the place about a mile above our shack; a long, high and steep crumbling granite wall of a wash where here and there a few flecks or a cluster of small bits of flake gold in a sort of vein showed themselves. Tiger and I got pretty good at spotting them quickly and breaking them out with our little pick-hammers.

In a couple of days of poking and pecking around up there, we can come down with all the small rocks we can carry in our knapsacks that'll run maybe three, four hundred dollars. Both of us were twenty-year Army men and we're getting small pension checks. So, between the two, we don't want for much. Beans and bacon and some ground beef and fresh eggs once in a while. A quart of Ten High bourbon does us for about a week. Well, sometimes maybe less; get a chilly evening with a fire glowing in the stove and the philosophy ricocheting like bullets off the walls, and the level in that Ten High quart will go down like the tank of a gas-guzzling Cadillac.

A man finds he doesn't need much more than that in this kind of country. Oh, there are times in the late summer when it burns like it's a hundred miles from water and only six inches from hell and lots of the time the wind'll rare up on its hind legs and paw the air fierce enough to sandblast the skin off a man's back and rattle his bones. Other times, it can get colder than the bejeebers a few winter weeks of the year.

But mostly the old Mojave Desert is kind to us, and that's all that matters. We've both about had our bellies full of women—been married, each of us, and badly—and our fellow man. Not that we're antisocial. It's just that conventional ways don't suit us much anymore.

If we get caught short of funds before the checks come in, we hike up to the Red Rooster and fill our knapsacks with promising rocks. Then we pile into Tiger's old International truck—we call it "The Binder," with its worn and fading paint and its butterfly collection on the radiator—and head out of Mojave on 58 for Bakersfield. We know a fellow there, a shifty kind of gent, if you ask me, who'll pay us fifty cents or so on the dollar for the gold in our rocks. We leave it up to him to deal with the proper authorities and go through the bureaucratic rigmarole and the dull baloney of officially selling it off into the gold market. He's a pretty good judge of what's in those rocks, and besides, Tiger and I aren't all that particular. Just looking to get by.

Tiger's a little whip of a fellow I got to know in and around Randsburg and Johannesburg—the place we call Joburg—after my wife and I called it quits and I was left with not much more than a pot to piss in and a pitifully small Army pension. We were still wearing parts of our old uniforms in those days and that got us talking around a nightfire of guys like us out on the desert and we've been partners ever since.

Tiger's lean and tough as jerky and not many shades lighter than the same color. Could be part Indian for all I know; black, straight hair without a hint of white at his age. In his room at the shack, he still keeps a mess of medals and engraved loving cups from his days of match shooting on Army teams and individual relays at the old Camp Perry shoots in Ohio. He keeps his trophies tucked away; that is to say, Tiger doesn't brag on them, though he was a crack shot with an issue .45 Colt automatic and an M1 Garand, or an oh-three Springfield, for that matter.

Still, neither of us keeps guns around. We've had enough of meanness and spite in our lives. If it comes to defense, and in this country it might, Tiger has an old pitchfork with the tines kept shiny and filed to points next to his bed. I've got a big old Bowie with a ten-inch blade in a scabbard that I keep handy and honed to a razor's edge and needle-tipped. I believe it's pretty old and came to this country with the first prospectors. Matter of fact, I traded an old guy out of it for about a half-quart of Ten High one night around a fire when we were drinking around camp and batting the breeze up there in the mining hills above Randsburg.

I spent my Army tour mostly as a company clerk and have my own share of trophies. But they are for what the Army considered whiz-bang typing skills. I guess I maybe still hold the Army record for error-free words-per-minute. Trouble is, these old knotty fingers probably couldn't so much as hunt-and-peck anymore.

Tiger and I drained the last drops of our ditchwater highballs in Reno's bar that night here sometime back. I looked at him and asked, "What say?" figuring it was time to get into the coffee shop for our steak and eggs before pointing The Binder for home. My stomach grumbled agreeably with the notion. It was a cold November night outside and our couple of jiggers apiece of well bourbon, light on the ditchwater, had kind of taken the chill-sting out of our toes and fingers. The heater in The Binder has been on the fritz for years, and neither of us really cares a damn. Minor annoyances we kind of take as a fact of life.

It was later, so only a few of the L.A. escapees were there—you can spot these characters a mile away—and only one old retired couple in for a late snack. I imagined they had a Win-a-Bagel motor home outside with their Good Sam Club sticker in the back window and "Min and Bill" or some such in glittery letters under the racked collapsible aluminum chairs on the chromed rear bumper.

A pretty good looking woman at the counter warmed herself with a cup of coffee, nothing more. She kind of looked Tiger and me up and down as we came in from the bar, but then went back to staring into her java. She was bundled up for the road, but not all that fancy bundled up either—hiker's boots, faded, stained Levi's and a thin, old windbreaker probably liberated from a Salvation Army store in L.A., over one or two sweatshirts. A thick wool scarf was tucked around the windbreaker's upturned collar, and wool knit gloves the same color as a Navy watch cap jammed over long blond hair that hadn't seen shampoo in a while. There was a strange kind of haunted hunger in her eyes. She had one of those pear-shaped blue knapsacks that are all the rage with the hikers and skiers bulging on the floor beside the stool. Probably everything she owned was in it. Tiger and I aren't strangers to down-and-out; there are earmarks and telltale signs. Tiger and I looked at each other as we walked past her and I'm sure we had the same thought. We would have bet she didn't have wheels out in the parking lot, and for one reason or another was bumming her way east out of L.A.

She was gone from the counter by the time we anted up for our grub. When Tiger fired up The Binder, backed out of the slot and The Binder's headlights swung on the highway, there she was at the curb watching the traffic outbound from L.A. on 14 through Mojave. There were precious few headlights eastbound, and practically none westbound but for a semi or two.

"That's the one, isn't it?" Tiger asked. "She's headed east all right."

"Or north to Bakersfield," I said. The junction is about a half-mile away where 58 splits away north and 14 continues sort of east by north.

It was Tiger's turn. "What say, Ten? Want to find out where's she's headed?"

"Don't get any big ideas, Tiger. Lord knows what she's carrying."

"Aw, hell, Ten, that wasn't on my mind at all. It's colder than a stepmother's breath out there, and she looks like she's pickin' in mighty poor cotton."

"Dammit, Tiger, we ain't taking her to Bakersfield, and that's final. I'm gettin' weary. If she's going out 14, that's fine. We can take her as far as the Randsburg cutoff."

"That'd be even a worse place to drop her, Ten." Tiger let The Binder idle in the lot while we debated.

"We ain't taking her up to the cabin," I protested. "Unless you want to give her your bed and you can sleep on the floor. The way you've been bitching about your bursitis lately, I wouldn't recommend it." I didn't approve of any of this.

"I ain't even thought that far ahead. Hell, Ten, you been down on your luck like that before. How many times have you stood out someplace like that in cold like this? And she's a woman. A pretty one at that. She's gonna be fair game for some perverted bastard or a carload."

I grunted. "I get your point."

"Last thing in the world I'd do is take advantage of her weakness."

I consented, but I didn't like it. "Okay, pull on out there. I'll ask her where she's going." Tiger eased The Binder along the curb next to her and I rolled down the window a crack to keep in what warmth we'd generated sitting there and banging our gums. "Which way you headed?" The wind had a hiss to it; a skosh this side of freezing.

She looked up at me, her pretty face scrunched up with the cold, and she had a tough time making her lips work. "Wherever the road's going, I guess." Her voice had the clear, tinkly quality of pieces of fine crystal clinking together—like the nice set my wife and I had before she hocked it for the hootch; between her and her binges, she went through my life savings and our nice things like a dose of salts.

"We're headed out 14 toward Ridgecrest. Want a lift that way?"

"Better'n standin' here."

I looked at Tiger. "Okay?"

"Yeah."

I opened the door and got out to let her in between us. "Believe I'd rather sit against the door," she said, and I caught a testy tone in her voice. I reacted.

"Look, you want a ride or don't ya? Don't read the cards wrong, little lady," I said. "Me and Tiger been in the same tight fixes a few times that you are in right this minute and we got no more notions about you than to help you out. Besides, we're both old enough to be your daddy and aren't likely to forget it."

Her face softened. "Okay," she said, and pushed past me to her place alongside Tiger. I hopped in and Tiger eased The Binder out into the road. We bounced over the Santa Fe spur track and past a couple more gas stations and hung a right on 14 where 58 swings up north past Tehachapi and then the long haul into Bakersfield. We were quickly headed out 14 across open desert as dense and as black as the inside of a boot. The only light was The Binder's yellow beams tracing the dips and occasional curves of the two-lane road that's mostly straight as a string.

Just the warmth of our three bodies took some of the chill out of the cab. We drove quite a while without saying a word. "You comin' from L.A.?" Tiger asked, breaking the silence. She'd been quiet, probably out of unfamiliarity with us two bozos.

"Yeah," she responded. "Had enough of that place and that's for sure."

"What'd you do there?"

"Huh!" she grunted. She mulled over an answer. "Nice girls don't say, but I haven't been what you'd call a nice girl and I guess that answers your question."

"Huh!" I grunted, astonished by her frankness, but I always respect people who don't beat around the bush.

She got a little talkative. "Maybe I'm older than you think. I've operated in L.A. about ten years. Came here from Omaha when I was twenty-three. That ought to give you an idea. What do you fellas do?"

"Not much," Tiger said. "We got a little place up in the hills on out here a ways. We're what you might call re-tarded."

"You mean retired," she said.

"He was making a joke," I said over the roar of The Binder's engine and transmission. "We're what they call desert rats."

"Married?" she asked.

"Used to be," Tiger answered. "Both of us."

"I get it. Taken to the cleaners. Like me, you're living pretty close to the bone these days."

"That's a polite way to put it," I said. "We don't want for much and we don't ask for much. Where you bound?"

"Any place but L.A. Nothing left for me there. And I couldn't hold my head up in Omaha, so that's out."

"You got any particular line of work? I mean other than . . ." I knew right there I'd put my foot in it. It didn't faze her.

She laughed a little and it was a nice kind of laugh; one that you'd like to hear more of. "Nope. Don't worry. I ain't sensitive about it. Was doing some little theater work before in Omaha. That's about all."

"I suppose that's what got you to L.A.," Tiger said.

"That and Crazy Charlie. Saw me in a show in Omaha and said he'd be my agent in Hollywood and get me into the movies. Stars in my eyes and all that good stuff, and I bit. Man, did I bite! Next thing I knew I was working American Legion conventions but from flat on my back. The bucks began rolling in, Crazy Charlie was getting fat off me, and from there it was downhill all the way. I was out of there yesterday morning about two jumps ahead of Skid Row."

"It seems to me I've heard that song before . . ." I sang.

She laughed again and then I knew I wanted to hear more of that laughter and sensed that in recent times it hadn't come often. I wanted to do something to bring more of that laughter back into her life. I didn't really have a fatherly interest in her, but at the same time, I didn't feel any urges about getting into her knickers.

"Look at it this way," she said. "At first they sent limousines around to my door. I finally wound up taking the bus to my dates. You figure it out. A few days ago, Crazy Charlie found a way into my bank account, him being my business manager and such, and looted it without my knowing it. When I was away, he came over to my place and stole everything worth hocking. To top it off, so I'd have no place to turn, he moved out of his apartment with no forwarding address. Probably found some younger chick to feed off of. I cried for two days and I came out of it saying, well, the same to you, L.A. and C.C."

"C.C.?" I asked.

"Crazy Charlie."

"Only C.C. I ever heard about," I said, "was the nickname for the compound cathartic we got from the Army medics on sick call when we were bound up."

She was damned quick on the uptake. "Same thing," she said. "Crazy Charlie could give you the shits, too." The Binder's lights picked up the road sign announcing the Randsburg cutoff coming up in two miles.

"This is it, Tiger," I said. "It's one o'clock in the gawdam morning and about 40 degrees in a raw wind out there, and it's halfway between nothin' and no place."

"Uh-huh," Tiger grunted. "What did you say your name was, lady?"

"Didn't. But it's Ann. Not my real name but the one I went under in L.A. That's still good enough. I'm used to it."

"Gentle Annie," Tiger said.

"What's that mean?" I asked.

"Gentle Annie. Something my mother used to say in place of swear words when I was a kid."

"Well, Gentle Annie," I said to her, "I figure about now I speak for Tiger and me. Ain't nothing out of the ordinary going to happen, but we'll take you on to our place for tonight. We'll get you back to the road here in the morning. We ain't got much but for now what we got is yours."

"I accept with gratitude, kind sir," she said with a Shakespearian theatrical tone. "He's Tiger. What's your handle?"

"Ten High. I've got another name, too. For now Ten High's good enough."

"Tell her, Ten. Tell her how you got your name!"

I tried to affect a Shakespearian theatrical tone. "I'll

fight any ten men in the Tenth Battalion at ten o'clock tonight for ten quarts of Ten High and a ten-dollar bill!"

"He was drunk as a Lord one night when a gang of us lived at a place called Ballarat—ghost town—up around the Panamint Mountains. I heard him say that and I hung the name Ten High on him," Tiger said.

I heard Gentle Annie's delightfully tinkly laughter again. "So how'd you get the name 'Tiger'?"

I spoke up. "He used to be quite the man with the ladies."

"Used to be," Tiger said, and let it go at that as he swung The Binder into the long, rolling ribbon of asphalt that was the way to Garlock and the road running over to Randsburg. Our place is about three miles this side of where the Randsburg road splits off, partway up on the slopes of the El Pasos.

"I've got a confession to make," she said. "Remember, I was in the business for ten years. You didn't scare me back there. If you were to get pushy, I know ways to put both of you out of action. It's just that I didn't want to have to do it in a car. A girl stands to get herself killed that way."

"Well then, you ain't got a lot to worry about," Tiger said dryly. "Pain and me ain't on the best of terms."

We built a fire in the stove when we got home and fixed her something to eat. We brewed up some coffee and added a dollop of Ten High in our cups and sat up the rest of the night talking. At daylight, we put Gentle Annie up in Tiger's room. I let Tiger have my bed because of his bursitis. I pumped up an old air mattress, and with what blankets there were left over, I had myself a pretty good day's sleep. We talked a lot more that next evening before it was too late to drop Annie off up at the highway.

We took her up to the Red Rooster the next day, figuring we didn't have too many worries about her as a claim jumper; even let her peck out some rocks with a few flakes of color in them. She got quite a kick out of it.

"Red Rooster?" she asked. "You guys sure come up with some quaint names. How'd you come by that one?"

I sang from "She'll Be Comin' 'Round the Mountain": "We'll kill the old red rooster when she comes . . ."

Gentle Annie's openness surfaced again. "I guess I did quite a lot of that in my time."

"How's that?" Tiger asked.

"Killed a few red roosters."

Tiger and I looked at each other with raised eyebrows; we'd caught her drift.

"Only when I got through with them, they had the reverse of rigor mortis," she added with kind of a philosophical tone. Tiger and I stayed silent. "It wasn't really all that bad a life, in spite of what the sob-sisters and the do-gooders try to make it out to be. You learn how to handle the pushy ones and the sadists. After what I've been through I believe that, if it came to a knock-down-drag-out, I could hold my own with any man. On the other hand, you get to meet some really nice people who treat you right, feed you in swell places, take you to shows once in a while, things like that. Been to Vegas any number of times, never gambled, but always came home money ahead. About all that's missing is that you don't have much of a place to anchor your emotions, your true feelings. To get over that one, you've got to get yourself strong—no, tough—inside. If you don't, you're dead. That's what's been so nice about getting to know you two characters. You've let me be myself. No passes. And I'm here to tell you, I appreciate it."

Tiger and I looked at each other. In a lot of ways, she was also talking about him and me when it came to our feelings toward our "fellow man." At that moment, she became one of us; cut from the same leather. We both knew that, as long as Annie wanted to stay with us, she'd have a place. In our shack, and in our hearts.

The next day we three went over to Randsburg and had a few drinks and a couple of hilarious games of three-way rotation on the beat-up pool table at "The Joint." We also took in the little Kern County Museum about Randsburg across the alley from "The Joint." Gentle Annie appeared to enjoy every minute of her visit and soaked up the information like a sponge.

Another day, we rode into Ridgecrest and got a cheap cut of meat and some beef heart and chili fixin's. Back at the shack, Gentle Annie used my old dutch oven to whomp up one of the finest chilis I ever sat down to. Lord, that woman can cook!

Annie stayed on and did everything she could to justify her keep.

Next thing we knew, a month had gone by and Tiger and I were low on funds again. We made another hike up to the Red Rooster for some serious pecking. In the morning, we all rode in The Binder to Bakersfield.

When we left old Sam Tolliver's place—the guy we have our gold dealings with—we drove Annie over to one of the better thrift stores and turned her loose with fifteen bucks. While Tiger and I had a couple of ditchwater highballs in a place across the street, she managed to fill up two grocery sacks with the kind of duds she'd need for the desert or the road, and a few things to get herself dolled up once in a while.

Both of us got a peck on the cheek by way of gratitude. Tiger and I registered proper embarrassment over her show of affection. Naturally we stopped off at Reno's on the way back for a couple more bourbons-and-branchwater before wrapping ourselves around heaping portions of our beloved steak and eggs.

Over the next few days, we got to playing Hearts with an old deck Tiger had in his duffle. When we got tired of cards, we sat around relaxing and philosophized and talked about our views about God and the Congress into the early hours. Annie took over most of the cooking and tidied up a bit here and there, but not so much as to get on the nerves of two old jaspers who didn't care much about having things too fancy.

We got to accepting her as part of our routine and she made no moves about leaving. Tiger and I were just as happy with her being around and becoming damned important to our lives.

I got to thinking how rough it was going to be again when Annie decided she had to go. I knew I would miss her—to beat hell. With three mouths to feed now, our gold takes and our pension checks didn't go as far as before. Our hikes up to the Red Rooster and cranking up The Binder—its windows specked with bug guts and smelling inside of crankcase oil—for the Bakersfield run became more frequent.

Tiger and I didn't care; the woman had brought a new dimension and a fresh attitude and new outlooks to our lives. We were content to have her stay as long as that was what made her happy. Spring in the desert had burst forth in all its glory when we hit the big strike at the Red Rooster. Rather, Gentle Annie hit the big strike. We'd gotten her a pick-hammer in Bakersfield and that day she was far up at the head end of the wash bank filling her little blue haversack with chunks of rock that showed plenty of good color.

It had rained pretty heavy—a common spring occurrence in the desert—for about three days and we'd stayed inside with the stove glowing and playing cards and drinking our coffee laced with Ten High. All that rain had loosened the crumbly rock along the bank. When we pecked out promising chunks of fractured granite, a lot of stuff around it would shear off and tumble to our feet.

Tiger and I worked midway along the bank. We heard Gentle Annie scream and we looked quick to see a big chunk of the bank—about a wheelbarrow load—break loose and cascade around her. Still shrieking in surprise, she jumped back and narrowly missed being hit by the slide.

She fell and Tiger and I sprinted to help her. She was sitting up when we got there, staring at the bank like she was in a trance. I thought maybe she'd got walloped in the head. "You okay, Annie?" I yelled.

She just sat there, eyes upturned at the bank above

her. "Yeah. Yeah. I'm all right. But, Sweet Jesus, would you look at that!"

Tiger and I tore our eyes from her to the bank and what held her attention; the slide had exposed a vein of almost pure gold running several yards long and a half to three-quarters of an inch thick and imbedded in the crumbly granite probably deeper than we could imagine. It was the strike I had a hunch was there all along. It looked like we could liberate chunks worth tens of thousands. My breath jammed in my throat. That pure gold would come out of there like slabs of peanut brittle.

Tiger and I stared at the rich strike, incapable of words. Tiger looked at me, and from that look, I knew his words before he said them. "We got to talk this over." You could build a lot of meanings into the way he said it.

"We're rich, Tiger!" I yelled. "Look at that! That's just the start! That vein probably goes back into that hill to where hell wouldn't have it." It seemed to be the thickest where it disappeared into the hillside.

"We got to talk this over," Tiger repeated, now with more emphasis. "Down at the camp."

"We can't leave it just like that, Tiger, all open and everything! What if somebody comes by? We'll be shit out of luck."

"Who's going to come by here, Ten? The only easy way in here is past our shack. Last Chance Canyon is miles west with the old road washed out, and the Mesquite Canyon road is about as far the other way. Nobody's going to come up here, Ten."

Annie stood by and listened, favoring one leg as she looked at the fabulous vein. "Think I pulled something," she said. "Like a cramp. I'll be all right. Don't you fellas have a claim or something on this?"

"Annie," Tiger said. "Ten and me don't own title to doodly-squat. We're just occupying our shack till somebody comes along with the right papers and tells us to get the hell out."

"Can't you file a claim?"

"Could," Tiger said, "but Ten and me figure we had enough of that bureaucracy bullshit. Let's get on down the hill. This stuff'll keep."

We were silent on the hike down, each busy with his own thoughts. You'd have thought we'd be screaming and shouting and running in circles. But there was more at stake here than just gold, an undercurrent of pretty serious things to think about, something Tiger and I hadn't done much of in recent times.

Tiger didn't speak again until we were back in the shack. "Annie, brew us up a pot of coffee. Ten, break out your bottle. Let's loosen up a little. I'm tighter than a violin string."

I could easily see why Tiger was discharged as a master sergeant and I never made it past buck sergeant; he knew how to take command. When the coffee was ready, he poured a stiff dollop of booze into his and downed it pretty fast and went to the stove for a refill. On the way back to his chair, he laced it stout with Ten High.

"Okay, folks," he said. "Let's lay it out. All the cards face up. Annie, this afternoon you went from being a guest in this place to full partner. You've got a say in this now, just as much as Ten and I have."

"But I don't—" she started.

"Put a lid on it, sister," Tiger said with emphasis. "Your say is asked, and it's needed. You been around long enough now. Like us, you been over life's road. Your vote counts."

"What's to vote on?" I asked. I was never gifted with seeing the forest for the trees.

Tiger's look bore straight into me. "You ready to turn your life around, Ten? You got any idea what's involved?"

"All I know is we're rich!"

"Think past the end of your nose, friend. With this stuff, there'll be no more pussyfootin' around with Sam Tolliver. We've hit the big time, and from here on out, we'll deal with the big guys by ourselves. Besides, old Tolliver's mixed up in a lot more sleazy stuff that just laundering our ill-gotten gains. All this could get a little sticky trying to deal with Sam Tolliver."

"Damned if you don't talk like a college perfesser, Tiger," I said.

"Okay. Let's look at both sides of the coin. One side is all bright and shiny; what we see right now, today, after Annie's discovery. The other side is darkened and dull; that represents the days ahead."

Gentle Annie intruded. "I don't see anything dark, Tiger. With what you've probably got up there, you and Ten could buy your own mountain to live on."

"We," Tiger said, emphasizing that she was part of the action. "I don't deny that, Annie. That might be part of the bright side. Again, it might be the dark side. But for now, leave it on the bright side. Money to do about what we please."

"What do you think it's worth, Tiger?" Annie asked.

"Who can say? But for figuring purposes, let's say we file a claim and then take the easy route and get an assay and get some engineers or geologists up here to look at it. Then let's say we offer the claim for sale and after everybody takes his cut—and there'll be a dozen or so show up with proper papers and their hands out—we clear a half million. I'm only guessing at that. I got no real idea what's at stake here."

Annie gasped. "That's a lot of money. Almost scary."

"Yeah. Scary for certain," Tiger went on. "I guess that's what I'm getting at. That's about all that's left on the bright side. Oh, you could do a lot of thinking about how and where to spend it. Me and Ten buy that mountain you talked about, Annie, and go live on it. You could take your share and go back to Omaha with your head high and open your own gawdam theater, to hell with the Crazy Charlies of this world."

"But I don't deserve—" she started.

Again Tiger cut her short. "We're just talkin' here. Speculatin'. But about a hundred and seventy thousand apiece sure begins to sound good in this place." Tiger looked wistfully around at our digs.

"Sounds mighty good, Tiger," I said.

Tiger looked at both of us a long time, thinking. "Yeah," he said finally. "But how is it going to change us? A couple of booze-ridden, broken-down old bums and a has-been whore!"

The shock of Tiger's outburst spread around us like a sullen gray cloud. Annie and I looked at each other with our mouths open; there was no denying in the looks that passed between us that we both knew that Tiger spoke the truth.

Before anybody said anything, Tiger got up and refilled his cup and went for his splash of Ten High to reinforce it. He came back and sat down. "I'm sorry," he said. "Didn't mean that to sound unkindly. It just struck me up there on the hill that we got to face facts, who we are, and what that stuff up there will make of us. By civilized standards we're losers, society's rubbish, all three of us."

Annie and I let him ramble; didn't say a word.

"If we go ahead and try to make something of that find, we'll have to start dealing with the big shots, get thick with the government, go through lots of red-tape bullshit, filling out forms, going for interviews. We'll have to hire accountants and high-priced attorneys and financial consultants and all such as that. In the process—and mark my words—it'll destroy who we are and what we've got here." He tapped his chest. "In our hearts and in our heads. In this shack, between us, together. Us three. That's what will be destroyed. How long do you think it would be before we'd be at one another's throats?"

"Never," I said.

"Come on, Ten. Grow up. Put it this way: Are you willing to stake your third of the Red Rooster against the chance that six months from now we won't be speaking to each other? I wouldn't."

"Since you put it that way, Tiger," I said, "I see why you

said what you said up at the Red Rooster. You saw it clearer than me or Annie."

"What's that?"

"That we had to talk about it. You saw the reality right away."

"Yeah," Tiger said, watching my eyes. "Let me ask you something, Ten."

"Uh-huh."

"These last eleven, twelve years. Most of that time we've been pardners. Haven't they been rich enough for you? They sure as hell have been for me. Like you told Annie the night we drove her out from Mojave. We don't want for much."

Annie piped up. "And I don't really want to go back to Omaha—or anyplace else—with or without money." Somehow she was talking to Tiger. "You and Ten have been decent with me, even beyond decent. I've come to think of us as a little family. You've made me feel that way and to feel wanted. All my life, the only things about me anybody wanted was my body and my twat. But not you guys. As long as you want me, I'll stay. When I've worn out my welcome, well, I'll be on my way . . . and happily. And I hope you'll both be man enough to tell me when."

"That'll never happen, Annie," I assured her. "I guess it's time for a vote. Me, I don't want any more gawdam gold than we're able to pick out of the hillside up there like before and pass along to Sam Tolliver. The way we've been doing all along. I don't want to change a thing."

"Annie?" Tiger asked.

"I already spoke my piece. I vote with Ten."

"Agreed," Tiger said. "I got an idea what we can do. We'll take enough of the gold to hammer out some little lumps that we can put on chains to wear around our necks. That'll always remind us of this day and our decision. And what we mean to each other. Be our talismans. And that way we'll none of us ever be totally broke again."

Annie laughed that delightfully tinkly laugh. "You sure know how to put things in their proper perspective, Tiger."

Tiger went on with his thoughts. "We'll set a dynamite charge in the hill above that vein. That should drop enough real estate over it to hide it for good and all. We'll always know that it's there, but tough as hell to get at and go on as though it wasn't there. Agreed?"

"Agreed," I said.

Annie looked at both of us. "Uh-huh," she said without a shred of regret or reluctance in her tone.

Tiger straightened in his chair. "Annie, we need something to eat. But I'm going to have another of Ten's 'coffee royales' to celebrate three people, including my two best friends in this world, coming to their senses."

He walked over to the coffeepot, still spouting a little vapor on the stove.

"I like cooking for you two birds," Annie said happily, heading for the stove behind him. "Even though you ain't got a pot to piss in."

Tiger stepped back with his filled cup, looked at the two of us and grinned. "Gentle Annie," he said. "God love ya."

"Who's for a game of Hearts after supper?" I asked, getting up to root around for the cards. As I did, something deep inside made me want to whistle. It came out as the tune of "She'll Be Comin' 'Round the Mountain." Annie started to sing as she banged around with the pots and pans. Tiger and I joined in.

". . . We'll kill the old red rooster when she comes; oh, we'll kill the old red rooster when she comes; yes, we'll kill the old red rooster; we will kill the old red rooster; we will kill the old red rooster when she comes!"

Suddenly Annie stopped and Tiger and I stopped, too.

"Great idea," she said. "What say on Sunday I whomp us up a big mess of chicken and dumplings?"

"Now, I vote in favor of that one," Tiger said.

"Me, too," I said. "Like everything around here, it's unanimous. Tiger, is there any of that coffee left? Tomorrow, we'd better crank up The Binder and hike over to Ridgecrest and get us a fresh jug of Ten High!"

From Our Special Correspondent

DALE L. WALKER

[New York Herald, July 4, 1877]:

IN CAMP, ABOVE THE LITTLE BIG HORN RIVER,
MONTANA TERR.

——ONE YEAR AND NINE DAYS have passed since Lt. Col. G. A. Custer and over 200 officers and men of the Seventh U.S. Cavalry perished here and the artifacts of that appalling fight are still everywhere in evidence.

I arrived here yesterday with Capt. Michael V. Sheridan, U.S.A., commanding a detail of soldiers, Crow and Arikara scouts, civilian guides, and teamsters with four ox-wagons. My party journeyed from Bismarck, Dakota Terr., on the steamer *John Fletcher* to Cantonment Tongue River and thence to the mouth of the Little Big Horn River.

There we rendezvoused on 28 June with Company I, Seventh Cavalry, consisting of eighty-eight men and two officers (Capt. Nowlan and Lt. Scott), which had traveled overland from Bismarck.

During our bivouac at the mouth of the Little Big Horn on the 29th, a dozen pine coffins were knocked together by a civilian carpenter in Capt. Nowlan's party and placed on the ox-wagons.

The mission of this forlorn force is to reclaim the remains of Col. Custer and the fifteen other officers who fell here.

[London Daily News, July 14, 1879]
In Camp, Field of Isandhlwana, Zululand

—It was the Portuguese under Bartholomew Diaz who sailed around Cape Horn in February, 1488, landing at Mossel Bay to fill their water casks, who first encountered the black denizens of this savage country. When the Hottentots showered the white interlopers with stones, Diaz, or so legend has it, aimed a crossbow and drove a shaft through the heart of the nearest native.

No doubt it is too much to say, but to one schooled in history, and steeped in the ironies of history, that first white incursion in South Africa may be said to have come full circle here on this brutal and eerie field where we have now come to pick among the bones.

On this rock-strewn plain on 22 January last, a mere six months save thirteen days ago, a Zulu "impi," a fighting force of perhaps 20,000 warriors, poured across the veldt from their kraals around Ulundi in a pitiless black tidal wave and onto this camp beneath the shadow of an ugly spur of the Nqutu range called Isandhlwana. By mid-day Europe had paid fifteen hundred-fold for Diaz's quarrel four centuries ago. King Cetshwayo's Zulus, armed only with spears and clubs, annihilated fifty-eight British officers, eight hundred British soldiers and an estimated six hundred native levies.

Six companies of an illustrious British regiment, the 24th Foot, died here, and at least a thousand Zulus, a free people who the British High Commissioner of South Africa said were little more than "drunkards and wild beasts," and whose presence in their own lands was termed "an incubus" to imperial designs, died here.

CAMP, LITTLE BIG HORN RIVER, JULY 4

. . . When Col. Custer and five companies of the Seventh U.S. Cavalry died here last summer, this valley was a vast carpet of dust. So says Tom LeForge, one of Capt. Nowlan's scouts, who has visited this field several times. Now the noisome breath of death, which a Sioux warrior named Pretty Shield said endured the whole of last summer, has dissipated, replaced by the glorious perfume of wild flowers and the sweet scent of grass, which is as high as our stirrups as we pick our way from one cairn of bones to another.

God's creatures and His elements have done their work. In a year of wind, rain and snow, the vultures, ravens and wolves have come foraging, gnawing the human and horse remains, and even the identifying stakes on the pitiful graves scratched in this sanguinary hillside by Capt. Frederick Benteen's men.

There is too little remaining here to really depict this unthinkable debacle. Most of the horror of it, in any event, has been reported in the months since it occurred from testimony of those in Col. John Gibbon's Montana Column (who relieved Capt. Marcus Reno's surviving force), and from the members of Capt. Benteen's detachment who, on 27 June last year, were the first to see this place after the battle.

We know that the corpse of Col. Custer was not mutilated. We know that Capt. Tom Custer had to be identified by a tattoo on his arm: his head was smashed flat to the ground by the war clubs of the Red savages; he was scalped and disemboweled. We know that Mark Kellogg, correspondent of the *Bismarck Tribune* and *New York Herald*, a colleague I never met, was scalped and his ears cut off. His oilskin satchel, found later among the abandoned Indian lodges, contained but a pathetic diary, a sack of tobacco and a shirt. We know there were atrocities that begged description: all the wounded were killed and all the dead were stripped of their clothing. There were beheadings, limbs hacked off, disembowelings, blindings, scalpings, and other, unspeakable, mutilations.

The Indian attacking force, said to number upwards of three thousand warriors, killed all the horses save one, Capt. Keogh's buckskin, which was found with many wounds wandering the battlefield, and in their frenzy even punched holes with their axes and knives in all the tinware, ration and supply boxes that were strewn about the field, by then a vile porridge of dirt, blood, human and horse intestines.

All this and a multitude of other details we know as this fatigue detail, in which I am assisting under a remorseless Montana sun, works to rebury the enlisted dead and to collect what remains of the officers who died here.

CAMP, FIELD OF ISANDHLWANA, ZULULAND, JULY 14

. . . Every living thing here was killed: oxen, horses, mules, even pet dogs. Officers and men, and two drummer boys (who were hung by their chins on butcher's hooks), died hideously. They died singly, in clumps of two or three, in last-stand groups of fifty and more trying feebly to form the square, and a few died as far as two miles distant from the camp proper. They died largely in the open, but some died in their tents and in or under the waggons. They died when they ran out of bullets, died with hunting knives clasped in their fists, died shoulder-to-shoulder and back-to-back. They were stabbed to death by Zulu assegais, those short-hafted spears with an iron head honed and pointed to razor sharpness, then were cut open from sternum to groin, their bowels spilled on the ground. They were scalped, their noses, lower jaws, and private parts excised. Some were beheaded. They were stripped of their clothing, their red tunics an especial prize, it seems. The camp was looted and everything not carried off was punctured by assegai, including small tins of meat and sardines.

At least a thousand Zulus fell here, victims of the Martini-Henry rifle and its long bayonet, but there are few Zulu remains to count as most of the black corpses were carried off by their comrades, the wounded as well.

King Cetshwayo's nation of warriors has now, of course, been destroyed, his kraal and all the others in the vicinity of it burned to the ground. The King himself has fled to the north and his capture is imminent.

There will be mass graves dug here at the camp of Isandhlwana to cover over this dreadful massacre and in a few years all that will remain will be a scattering of stone cairns, each doubtlessly decorated with a bronze plaque presented in Her Majesty's name, markers which will fail utterly to say what happened here on 22 January last.

CAMP, LITTLE BIG HORN RIVER, JULY 4

. . . What happened here? How came this stupefying defeat of our Arms? Even crediting the highest estimate of three thousand Red savages, and their undoubted collective courage, how could this rabble, armed with bows and arrows, war clubs and a miscellany of old, stolen weapons, which they knew not how to use, defeat and kill to a man over two hundred of one of the keenest, best-trained fighting forces in the civilized world, a force armed with, and skilled in the use of, the Springfield breech-loader, the finest and deadliest weapon of the day?

The essentials of the making of this massacre are by now generally known though they will be debated for many years to come. Col. Custer's advent into this valley was but an extension of the Army's policy, since the close of the late War, to wage unceasing war against the recalcitrant Sioux Nation and its neighboring and like-minded tribes. It is known that Col. Custer's command of twelve companies of the Seventh U.S. Cavalry, something over six hundred officers and men in all, together with a contingent of Indian scouts, marched off from the mouth of the Rosebud on 22 June. It is known that Col. Custer refused the offer of an additional battalion of the Second Cavalry, and also the offer of three Gatling guns. (These, he said, would impede his progress over the rough terrain between the Rosebud and the Little Big Horn.) It is known that Col. Custer and his command arrived here on 25 June after a grueling four days' march.

It is also known that Col. Custer defied a principle of war by dividing his command. He sent Capts. Benteen and Reno out with three companies each; left Capt. McDougall with over a hundred men in care of the pack train in the rear; and himself, with about two hundred men, occupied this bald and untenable position.

CAMP, FIELD OF ISANDHLWANA, ZULULAND, JULY 14

. . . The officers and men killed here were part of what is being called Lt. Gen. Lord Chelmsford's "middle invasion force," which means there was another force to the north and another to the south, a three-pronged invasion, as it were, of Zululand. The middle force crossed the Buffalo River at Rorke's Drift on 11 January and, it being the rainy season, bogged down its supply train, getting no further than Isandhlwana, ten miles to the west of Rorke's Drift, on 22 January, in its march toward Ulundi.

There is a maxim of the great scourge of Europe, Napoleon I, fully seconded by his nemesis, our immortal Duke of Wellington, which says, "Nothing is so important in war as an undivided command." This tenet, a truth never assailed by any thinking commander in war, somehow escaped the notice of Lord Chelmsford in the preparations for this ill-fated expedition into this Godforsaken land. He not only split his command into three at the outset, but, taking command of the doomed "middle invasion column," split even that, on 22 January, by taking a sizable force away from Isandhlwana on reconnaissance, leaving behind only six hundred Imperial troops, reinforced by a contingent under command of Col. Anthony Durnford. That gallant officer's brutalized corpse is among those many being buried here today.

CAMP, LITTLE BIG HORN RIVER, JULY 4

. . . It might be said, perhaps ought to be said, that this blood-soaked ground is a dividend collected by our Red Brethren for the infamous Treaty of 1868 at Fort Laramie in which our White Brethren consigned to the Sioux the Black Hills "for as long as the grass was green and the sky was blue." This field of death might also be thought of as a second Red response to the late Capt. William T. Fetterman of the Eighteenth U.S. Cavalry who liked to boast that he could "take eighty men and ride through the whole Sioux Nation." The first answer to the valiant but wrongheaded Capt. Fetterman was delivered eleven years ago, on 21 December, if memory serves, when he and eighty of his men were killed by the Sioux at Fort Kearney.

And, of course, some have already viewed this abbatoir of a battlefield as a demonstration of the veracity of what Col. Custer wrote in his book just three short years ago. In that extraordinary work, Col. Custer expressed his belief that the Indian must give way to "civilizing influence" but that they would not do this on their own accord and would have to be forced by a "stern, arbitrary power." And in his book, Col. Custer "stripped the beautiful romance" from the Indians of Fenimore Cooper's novels and said the Red Man is anything but noble; is, in fact, "a savage in every sense of the word . . . one whose cruel and ferocious nature far exceeds that of any wild beast of the desert."

CAMP, FIELD OF ISANDHLWANA, ZULULAND, JULY 14

. . . The astounding debacle that occurred here on 22 January last is already being called "Durnford's Disaster," a calumny against a courageous officer with a splendid record of fighting in the Kaffir wars. If blame is to be apportioned, let a fair share be assigned to the High Commissioner, Sir Bartle Frere, whose misjudgment of the strength and resolve of the Zulu army infected all who came to fight it, Lord Chelmsford chief among them. It was the High Commissioner who assured all and sundry that the Zulus were scarcely more than drunkards and wild beasts who, "once cowed would not rally." It was the High Commissioner who viewed English suzerainty over Zululand as the only answer to the "black threats and resistence" these people allegedly posed to Natal and its neighbors.

The Zulus have faced white encroachment in their land since the 1830s when the first Boers trekked here from Cape Colony. The Boers, no friends of England or its Empire, have great respect for the might and resolve, if not for the territory, of their Zulu antagonists and tried to warn the British commanders that a march into Zululand would be no promenade.

If what happened here in the shadow of Isandhlwana is

Durnford's Disaster, it is in equal parts Chelmsford's Catastrophe, and Frere's Folly.

CAMP, LITTLE BIG HORN RIVER, JULY 4

. . . Our work here is nearly done and we will soon be moving on to Capt. Reno's battleground to exhume the remains buried there, and after that will return to the mouth of the Little Big Horn to rendezvous with the *John Fletcher* to remove these pathetic pine boxes and their grisly contents to places more convenient, if less hallowed, than this ground.

Here, as the day closes, I can almost hear the notes of the "Gary Owen," that merry yet melancholy, sad yet triumphant, old Irish drinking song which the Seventh played on the march and claimed as its own. And, I'm wondering if we will remember this place, two years, a decade, a hundred years and more from now, and, if we do remember it, how we will remember it.

Will we remember this place and what happened here as, to date at least, the only complete extermination of a United States military force in the field of battle? Or will we remember it as Col. Custer's Massacre, an unfortunate, minor and momentary embarrassment in the spectacle of the white American's eternal efforts to "civilize" his nonwhite, and therefore savage, brothers?

Or will we ask ourselves what we were doing here? Will we remember this place for the lessons it teaches about that march of civilization if we will only read the bones that are strewn in the line of march?

CAMP, FIELD OF ISANDHLWANA, ZULULAND, JULY 14

. . . History will no doubt place Isandhlwana beside such inglorious incidents of our glorious military past as the tragic retreat from Afghanistan in 1842, and the splendid blunder that cost our Light Brigade at Balaklava in the Crimea. But Isandhlwana is more than these. The Afghan catastrophe was not a battle but a slaughter, in the main, of civilian innocents, and Balaklava would never have found a paragraph in history were it not for Lord Tennyson's bombastic poem.

Isandhlwana is much more than these. This field ought to give all of England pause, from Our Gracious Majesty down to the lowliest subject in our far-flung Empire.

But Englishmen have a short memory, I fear. Who today remembers such bloody fields of our own century as Ciudad Rodrigo, Badajoz, and Salamanca in Spain; Mudki, Aliwal, Delhi, and Lucknow in India; the Alma, Inkermann, and Sebastopol, in the Crimea?

Who will remember this pathetic battleground?

If Isandhlwana is remembered at all a decade or century from now, I hope the future historians of our Empire will remember it by answering this simple question: Why were we here?

The Wedding Dress

WIN BLEVINS

HE CAME THE DAY AFTER the Nariya dance. Running Water was ready. Excited. She could hardly keep a decent demeanor. She kept wanting to look straight into his eyes, or even touch him.

Since she first saw Morgan, she had hoped for today.

He gave her father six good horses, which was a splendid gift for a second daughter. All her life she'd expected to end up married to Horn, her sister's husband, in the manner of her Shoshone people. That would have been all right, she guessed. That was until she saw Morgan and her thoughts said what her heart felt.

The world was changing. The old way was good. On it the people prospered, and she revered it. But there was a new way now, since the Tibos, the white people, came. Your rabbit might run a different path, she thought.

The Shoshones told a story. When you were born, the spirit of a rabbit came ahead of you and took off running. It ran some particular path on the earth, a path you would never know. But whatever path it ran, you would follow that.

Her grandmother had told her the rabbit path might twist and turn crazily, might double back on itself, might seem to make no sense, but you must follow it. It's your path. Even if you didn't want to, her grandmother said, even if you rebelled against the path, you would follow it.

Because of the Tibos, Running Water thought, the rabbit might run new paths now.

When her grandmother was young, the people had never seen a white man. Just before her mother was born, the fur trappers built Fort Wyeth, right in the middle of their homeland. In another ten winters the Mormons came and thousands of them built houses down by the big salty water. Another fifteen winters and the whites built a road straight through her people's country and all the way to the gold mines in the faraway place called Montana. You could trade for white-man things, pots and knives and guns and cloth, at trading posts right on that road.

Things were changing, and something in her dreams, she couldn't have said what, said she must change with them. Not change everything. She might learn about God and wear a cross, but remember what the blackrobes said to forget, Duma Apa, and the people's dances and prayers. She might learn to live in a cabin but not prefer it. She might start sitting in chairs. According to her sisters, she would have to learn to let Morgan act improperly with her. White men acted nasty when it came to sex, Shoshone women said. Sometimes they giggled about it, and sometimes they were serious. Either way, Running Water would have to get used to it.

Morgan instead of her sister's husband—that was the commitment to the new way, maybe her rabbit ran that way. It was what her heart wanted, if that was a clue. A new path.

Morgan did more than she hoped for, took her straight to the mission and made their marriage official, as he called it, in the eyes of the Tibo. The blackrobe said the sacred words and wrote their names in the book. Morgan Roberts Morgan (she found out then he had these three names) said that made them really married. She knew that Tibos often took Shoshone women and later abandoned them. None she knew of had made the marriage "official."

When the blackrobe was finished with the words, Morgan did something incredible. He took out a piece of *nappaus*, one of the gold pieces the Tibos were so crazy about, one hammered into a ring. He put it on the fourth finger of her left hand and said it made them really married.

She blinked back the tears. Now she was sure.

She asked the blackrobe to write her name in his book as Marian, the name Morgan called her. Her people's name for her was Running Water, but Marian was special to him, his grandmother's name, and now it was special to her.

Yes, this was the path her rabbit ran.

Morgan Roberts Morgan could have conked himself for what he let happen next.

He could see the real marriage ceremony thrilled her, and the ring. Her feeling touched his old heart. (He was twenty-nine, but had been in the mountains ten years, and so was known to compadres as "old Morgan.") Then they went down the Tibo road to Anderson Station to pick up the other horses he'd traded for, and his mail. Marian thought the mail was peculiar, all those books and magazines, but she said naught but to ask if there were letters from Wales. He told her kindly that there would be no letters ever from Wales. He had no family over there anymore, only memories of the slate quarries he never wanted to see again, and he would never ever go back. He saw on her face that she thought that was terrible, and determined to make it up to him.

Cor, but that was as he wanted it. When he first laid eyes on this girl, he fancied her, he did. Said to himself that very day in his native Welsh, *"Dwi am Broidi'r eneth ma cwtches,"* I'm going to marry that girl and have love and hugs and such like.

He wondered if her mind was on giving him the relatives he didn't have, her entire family. He wasn't so keen on that part of it. He'd run across an ocean and a continent to get away from relatives.

While he wasn't paying attention, Mrs. Anderson spoiled things. She showed Marian her wedding dress.

The Andersons were Mormons. Morgan brought Marian here to trade because Mormons treated Indians decently. For some reason Mrs. Anderson couldn't stick to flour and boots (neither of which would impress Marian a bit) or the wood stove that warmed the cabin and you could even cook on the top of it. All the grand stuff that came up the Salt Lake road headed for the Montana mining camps.

Morgan was proud of himself. He'd trapped enough fur over the winter not only to trade for horses for her father, but another, bigger string of horses, and all this flour and bacon and coffee and sugar and blankets and tobacco, enough to make Marian think she was marrying a rich man.

When Mrs. Anderson put her foot into it by mentioning the wedding dress, Marian begged to see it. Mrs. Anderson got it out of a box. She herself had gotten married in it five years ago, she explained. It was boughten goods, she said, from a catalog, and wasn't it a beauty? She showed Marian the bodice, which was beaded with seed pearls. The skirts were full, very full, and resplendent—the material was satin, said Mrs. Anderson. "See, the sleeves are belled," meaning tight on the arms with huge puffs around the shoulders. "And look at this lace!" Even Morgan had to admit the color was fine, what Mrs. Anderson called "candlelight," creamy, the color of a gorgeously tanned sheepskin with a special luster.

Marian was big-eyed as if she'd been struck by lightning. Morgan watched the changes in her face, and the thoughts behind them. She'd never seen anything so beautiful in her whole life. They were buying so much . . . She didn't dare ask . . . But they were so rich . . . Well, it was her wedding day.

But Morgan, still thinking like a white man, was taken blind side by what she said next. "Morgan, will you buy me this wedding dress?"

Cor, she would ask, for wasn't it her wedding day? She didn't know the offense.

"Oh!" cried Mrs. Anderson, and turned away to hide her face.

Morgan knew what would be on the face, that expression of a respectable white woman when the way you acted was just too, too sodding awful. Marian knew it too, from a different angle. Morgan saw the hot blood of humiliation rise in her, and she went outside so the white woman wouldn't see her embarrassment.

Morgan cursed himself and followed.

She felt drenched in shame. She'd resolved to learn the Tibo way, as she'd been learning the Tibo language, and make a good Tibo life for Morgan. On her very wedding day she'd made a blunder.

The worst of it was, she still yearned for the wedding dress. She had to bite back words. Why couldn't she have it?

They left the trading post in a hurry, which was the way Tibos behaved when they were embarrassed, to run away, and started home. As they rode east, the three Tetons in front of them for pilot knobs, her husband patiently explained her mistake. It was not for sale. It was Mrs. Anderson's wedding dress, and you never wore it but once, that was the rule, or maybe a second time to celebrate being married twenty-five winters, or maybe you gave it to your daughter to get married in. It would be bad medicine, he said, terrible medicine, he said, to sell it.

Besides, Marian couldn't wear it anymore. The wedding ceremony was over. If only Morgan had known, he would have bought her a wedding dress for the ceremony, but . . .

Her poor husband looked truly distraught.

Marian told herself she would make many mistakes following this new Tibo way, and she would just have to be forgiving of herself and others until she understood better how to act. But she didn't feel that way. Her blood was thick with shame, and she wanted to get back at Mrs. Anderson. She forced herself to tell Morgan it was fine, she didn't need a wedding dress, she was excited with all the wonderful *things* they had (half of which she couldn't guess the use of), and she was really looking forward to getting to her new home.

She touched her new yellow-metal ring, rotated it gently on her finger. It was wonderful. Morgan was wonderful.

She couldn't help thinking, as they rode, that she could wear such a dress at the shuffling dance next summer, and the Nariya dance, and her sisters would ooh and ah over it.

That night she felt better. The cabin was good, their place good. She fixed up the cabin and made supper outside, while he was setting up the stove. They spent their first night in the blankets together on the wood floor, on the pallet of dry grass and buffalo hides, and she thought this husband was everything she wanted. She hoped she could please him, with his funny Tibo ways. He didn't seem nasty in the blankets to her. Just the opposite.

When Morgan first rode up to her village, four years ago, on a big American horse with his red hair and red beard flying (why were Tibos so hairy?), she had the strangest feeling of her life. It was like she knew him from

that other world, the world whe
the spirits came to you, and you
and truly than in the waking wor
day half-frightened, not knowing
angel.

All she knew, then or now, w
feelings for him, feelings powerfu
river. Last summer he began to cou____, and she felt the
true downhill-water-flowing force of her life.

Wherever these feelings took her, wherever this new
rabbit path with Morgan went, she would gladly go.

Marian looked out the window at the blue shadows on the
snow. The sun was almost gone and the wind was running
through the coulees and rattling the cottonwood limbs and
she was scared and she was lonely.

What she wanted was for Morgan to get home. Now.

She shivered, either from the cold or the lonesome-
ness, both terrible.

Home. Funny word in the English she was still learning. He had a strong feeling about home. He used that
word a lot about this place. And home, or that feeling of
his, home was part of the trouble.

So she thought sometimes.

Where was he?

She got up and threw two chunks of wood into the
stove, but the heat wouldn't really help. The cabin wasn't
well enough chinked, and the wind blew through the
cracks between the logs. If you stood near the stove, you
blistered on one side and froze on the other. If you didn't,
you just froze.

The stove, the precious stove that he had freighted
clear up from Salt Lake. It was a big deal to him, not only
because it cost so many of the important dollars, but because it was her wedding present, as he called it, and because this thing *home* was a big deal.

Where was he? Why didn't he come to her?

...bered his pride when he showed her the
...built, one room of stout cottonwood timbers.
...e in the wood stove, which you cooked on top of.
...his real feeling, she could see, wasn't for the little
...ucture there in the cottonwood bottom between the
creek and the river. It was for what he called their place,
the meadows along the creek bottom that had good grass,
the little lake that drew winged creatures, the good water
in the creek, and the beaver and fish there. Their place.

Place meant something different to Marian, something
wider. She'd lived in this country all her seventeen years,
most of them before the reservation. Her Shoshone people, whom the whites mistakenly called the Snakes, had
lived on this land since before the memories of the grandfathers of the oldest grandfathers. She loved the four-
leggeds, the rooteds, all the wingeds, all the swimmers—all
that lives, all the relatives of human beings. It was the
same as loving the earth and life and yourself.

It was home, all of it. The people moved around the
whole big place—up to the mountains, out onto the lava,
over to the hot springs, down into the grassy, sheltered
bottoms along the river, west to the falls. One place they
got the best grass for the horses, another place beaver and
otter skins, another salmon to eat, another good lodge-
poles, another the camas. On the lava flow they trapped
rockchucks to cook in a pit.

This man her new husband saw home differently. To
him their place was this land you could walk around in less
than a day, their home this cabin. A glory of a place, as he
called it, yes. But small. And not the family's place, or the
clan's, or the people's, but his personally, theirs personally.

She saw he loved it, and was glad. A Welshman from so
far away, with a language and ways born of another place,
come to her homeland and in love with it.

But it was a little strange to her, this cramped notion of
home. At night, when he read to her out of all the books he
had, especially that Shakespeare, she listened for that
word "home" and tried to feel what it meant.

She hadn't told him on their wedding day that she didn't like the cabin. She'd heard that a cabin let in more winter wind than a lodge, and she could see it was darker. It was the wrong shape, for there was something in the circle of a lodge that was like the earth when a square wasn't. But mainly it didn't move. The cabin was stuck in one place, so you couldn't go to the camas easily, or out onto the lava to find the ice that stayed hidden in the caves all summer, or go high with the elk in the summer and low in the winter. She didn't tell him because she knew the cabin was home to him, and she had a special, heart-held feeling, itself like a dream.

Besides, she had to keep in mind, this was the new Tibo path.

He banged the door back hard and loud, without intending to. He dropped the armload of firewood behind the stove, and saw from her face that he had his dark look on. Again. Everything was sour, yes, he was truly making a cock of his marriage. He was in a fug about it.

Yes, she was lonely, yes, she was cold, yes, she missed her family. But what could he sodding do about it? Didn't she see?

In silence he took off his blanket coat and sat on a box. She dipped from the stew pot on the stove and handed him a full bowl, and some bread.

He traded for the horses because they could make a living from them. He'd guided that government outfit around the Jackson Hole country. He'd taken a dude party into the Yellowstone country, and they'd liked his work, he said. There would be more guiding in the future. Yellowstone was a sodding national park now, whatever that meant. Well, it meant lots of white folks would come to see it, and need his horses.

If they didn't lose the horses. Some of her people burned the nearby hills off in the fall, sod them, and he wouldn't have good grass for another spring or two. That burning made Morgan curse. It was a demon of a winter—deep snow, more than a month of unbroken cold, sharp winds. Here it was the beginning of March, and Marian said she couldn't remember a winter colder or with deeper snow.

Yes, sod all, he had to be out all day feeding the horses bark of the sweet cottonwood, or driving them a few miles away onto better grass, grass they could paw down to. When he moved the herd onto better graze, he would be gone for several days, even a week, yes. Couldn't she see?

The other day he saw fear on her face. She was afraid of his dark looks, he knew, afraid of her own husband.

She said the other night that at home, among her people, she would have her mother and aunts and sisters to talk to. They would have projects to do together—not only cooking but making winter moccasins, sewing blankets into warm coats and hats, making parfleches to store their belongings, beading and quilling special dresses for the dances next summer. While they worked, they would talk and laugh and be a family. But bugger all, wasn't this her home now? Wasn't he her family?

Maybe not. She wouldn't give herself to him in the blankets anymore. He knew the Shoshones thought whites were odd in bed. Maybe she was disgusted by him. Not that he had any peculiar tastes, but you never knew what she might not like. Why did she shut him out? It was driving him bedlam for a truth, not so much the lack of sex as the wondering.

And she kept talking about home, meaning the village near Fort Wyeth. Home. Bloody hell, did anybody have a home anymore? Weren't they creating a home?

Maybe new paths were always scary, she told herself. Or maybe, if the new path meant being alone all the time, it wasn't for her.

"The Appaloosas are gone," he finally said. "North."

Meaning the two mares in foal. Meaning that their

tracks went toward the hills, where the wind had blown some of the ridges nearly clear of snow and the animals had hope of grass. Meaning that he would go after them, for otherwise anyone might drop a rope on them, or they might wander farther away and simply disappear, or they would not find enough grass and would spend their spirit hunting for it and come spring Morgan would find the skeletons.

When he went after them, he might be gone for days and days.

She sat next to him and touched his hand. "Come to bed," she said. Bed where she could get him to hold her, where she could feel close to him.

She knew he wasn't so keen on bed anymore. She was pregnant, and she couldn't make love with him—decent people didn't do that. She wondered, and then decided even Tibos knew that. She'd told him plain as could be: I can't eat meat with fat for a while. She wouldn't mention it, act like she thought he was stupid. *Everybody* knew you didn't have sex when you were pregnant.

So he must know she was making life grow within. But he said nothing about it. Why not? Wasn't he glad?

Tibos were very strange. She would wait patiently.

And he was nasty about sex sometimes. Until she pushed him away one day, he actually touched her out of doors. Took her hand, touched her hip with his hand, even tried to touch her breasts.

When she pushed him away, he looked hurt and mumbled something about no one being within ten miles. She supposed that made some difference, and tried to make it up to him, but right out in the sun was still right out in the sun.

Also, once he wanted to make love with the candle lantern burning. Said he wanted to see her.

She wouldn't even giggle with her sisters about that. That was *too* nasty.

"Come to bed," she said again. She wanted his closeness.

"Got to get started before they get too far," he answered, and stood up.

She grabbed him and put her head on his chest. He was very tall, this man of her new path, and her head didn't come to his chin. She put her arms around him. Though she couldn't see his face, she knew he had a hard look, a faraway look, the look of a man who was fighting and losing and despised himself for it.

Before she thought the words, they were out. "Let me come with you." She heard the pathos in her own voice, but she went on, "I can help. Please let me come with you."

He held her a little away and looked into her eyes, at least he did that much, truly look at her, and she wondered what was inside his head. Then he turned off and said in a remote way, "I've got to move fast."

And with his blanket coat and gloves and wolfskin hat was out the door into the dark, howling night.

She didn't say a word, that would have been improper, but it hurt, hurt in a big lump behind her breastbone. She had offered to help, she wanted to help, she could help. She had said so and he hadn't answered. Instead he drove them farther apart, made them both more alone, he in the fierce weather, she in the blankets that were not as thick and warm as buffalo robes.

She touched her belly. Yes, the child sometime next summer. But would she still have a man? New path or old? Which way had her rabbit run?

Right now she would give anything for her mother, her sisters, her father and brothers and nephews and nieces, the warm lodge, the talk, the sense of family.

She went to bed and shivered. She was pretty sure these Tibos didn't know how to live.

In the middle of the night she heard it, the wind. She went to the door and looked out. It was whipping even here in the bottom by the creek. She looked up toward the ridges of the hills.

It was mad, she knew. She also knew she was going to do it. Quickly she got into Morgan's funny long underwear, an elkskin dress, knee leggings, winter moccasins, her blanket coat, and rabbit mittens. As an afterthought she took a blanket to wrap over her head and around her chest.

It was mad. Why was she going?

Out the door, into the driving wind. Its force took her breath away. It was like the current of a fast river—you didn't realize until you were in it. She leaned into the wind and started for the hills to the north. She would pick up his tracks on the way.

Probably she had in mind standing on top of the first hill, or the bigger one beyond, and saying a prayer for him. A moment of vigil, a wife's devotion.

It wasn't like that. As soon as she cleared the trees, she saw that his tracks were drifting in. Before long the blowing snow would fill them, and even the tracks she herself was leaving. As she rose above the creek bottom, the wind picked up. It arrowed at her, whipped, blustered, and slashed. It buffeted her, and near the top of the first hill it clubbed her. She staggered and turned her back. Though she shouldn't have been surprised, she gasped. And sucked in cold that hurt her chest.

This was a full-scale ground blizzard, howling, flinging ice crystals in your face, blinding you, whipping away your body's heat like driven leaves. She wondered if Morgan had a chance in this blizzard.

"Hear me, Father," she murmured softly in her own language—*Numee Nahgai Ook, Duma Apa*. She realized she hadn't heard her own voice. She said it again, *"Numee Nahgai Ook, Duma Apa,"* belting it out this time, almost in anger, not a way to speak to the spirits. Then she whispered, *"Numee shone deah,"* Have mercy on us.

She turned her back to the wind and ran down the hillside in big, clumsy steps, sinking to her knees on every step.

Halfway down she had a thought like an icicle shafting into her chest: She was running to her death. Or was it Morgan's death she felt inside?

She smothered the thought and kept running. Her tracks were not quite filled in, still dimples on the snow. She didn't slow down till she got to the trees, or even until she saw the dark shape of the cabin.

She stoked the stove and undressed fast by its heat. She was shivering so hard her fingers fumbled at her clothes. She slid the pallet and blankets next to the stove, through all the clothes on top, and got in. Morgan would be all right, she told herself. He would know what to do. He would get himself and the pony into the lee of some rock and build a fire. Wouldn't he?

Before dawn she heard the change. Or felt it. Or somehow . . .

She burst out the door. She knew . . .

Yes, the wind was still blowing, a stiff breeze now instead of a howling monster, and it was warm. Warm. A black wind. The whites called it a chinook.

Black winds were gifts. Even in the middle of winter they would melt the snow, and it would be balmy for a few days, and all the four-leggeds could graze and get better. Then maybe winter again. But now, so near spring, the horses would survive.

And surely Morgan was alive, and he would come in sometime today. And his dark look would be gone, and he would hold her again, and love her.

She was so confident she made the batter for the flapjacks he liked for breakfast.

He banged the door again. He saw on her face again that she hated the noise, and the dark look was still on his face. Oh, a fine cock-up, this marriage. Well, maybe she was cocking it up. Wasn't she the one who wouldn't give herself?

"Didn't catch up with them Appaloosas," he said. "Have a look at my cheeks, will you? Fingers too."

She checked the frosted places, and said it was not serious.

He ate like a bear in the spring, devouring the flapjacks. Bears would eat carrion that time of year. He smiled sardonically. Like them, he was dangerous now.

"I've got to go after the horses," he said when he finished the third plateful. "They went off toward Sanders's. Look here, though." He got one of his books from the stack in the corner.

Morgan was crazy for these books. Sometimes Marian hated them, and sometimes she wanted to get him to teach her to read.

This was one of the books they called a catalog, full of Tibo things to buy. It was slow. You gave Mr. Anderson some hides and he wrote them down as dollars, and he sent papers in the important Tibo mail, and months later from the Mormon village at the big salt water, the village the people called Many Houses Close Together, whatever you ordered would come. She could make everything they needed, and that was her job, but the Tibos acted like these things that came in the mail were very special, like they had a feeling of . . . well, surely it wasn't a sacred feeling . . . about them.

"You want to go over to Anderson's next month?" he asked. "Do some trading? Get the mail?"

She nodded. She'd never be pleased to see Mrs. Anderson again, not after the embarrassment over the wedding dress, but she liked to trade for a few things, and seeing someone, anyone, would feel good after being cooped up for the winter. Well, the truth was, she was afraid to be away from Morgan.

He opened the book to the page he had marked. Pictures of panniers. He'd made new packsaddles during the fall, not as nice as the ready-made ones, he admitted, but sturdy. She'd made him panniers of rawhide, like big parfleches that her people stored their belongings in. He said he liked them, though they weren't as good as canvas panniers because they were stiff and didn't really fit the mules.

"We've got a pack of beaver," he said, "and the others. I think we can afford these." The panniers on the page were ones of heavy canvas like he wanted. The dudes would like them, he always said. "Dudes" was a new word, according to Morgan, and he pronounced it with a certain relish. Dudes were Tibos who didn't know how to live in this country, he said, who only could get along in cities like his books showed. Marian was shocked to think that there were Tibos even more helpless than most of those who came through here, who couldn't find game to eat or water to drink most of the time, and would get lost without a road.

The panniers were important to him. So was the glass he wanted, to replace the thin-scraped hide that covered their window. With glass this cabin wouldn't be so dark, and she'd like that.

"You want to order some clothes?" He showed her cloth dresses. She loved cloth, loved the soft feel of it, the way it clung to your skin. But it cost so many of the dollars, while deerskin cost just one ball of lead and some time. It would be irresponsible of her to order cloth for a dress.

"We need panniers more, and the glass," she said. "We could trade for more blankets." He nodded and turned the catalog pages.

One day she would have a cloth dress, though, and she would wear it in the shuffling dance.

He just gave her a look and a hint of lopsided smile on the way out. She wanted him to touch her, but he didn't.

In a fury she threw her awl against a wall. She was supposed to get to go!

Sanders had stopped by and brought the Appaloosas. He was on his way to the mountains, he said, he was starved for meat. She didn't ask him in because she didn't like him and Morgan told her not to invite anyone in when she was alone. Sanders's cabin was on Henry's Fork, one sleep west and north, and she hoped he stayed over there. He always called her "the squaw woman," and Shoshones hated that word.

Now he said Morgan was gone to Anderson's to get the mail and asked Sanders to tell Marian he would be back in a few days.

It wasn't true! Not a few days! A week, seven sleeps he would be gone! And he'd promised her she could go!

The precious mail, those goddamn books. "Goddamn" was a Tibo word she was really getting used to. Morgan said it was a bad-medicine curse, but the Tibos didn't seem to take that seriously and just said it about anything they didn't like. There was plenty she didn't like.

Later that night, when she thought about it, she understood. It was wrong, everything was wrong. One winter, that's all it took for her and Morgan to discover they weren't for each other. He had grown to dislike her, that was obvious—he preferred being away from her. Even now, when the grass would be coming green in a couple of weeks, when all the rooted and four-legged and winged and all creatures were coming back to life, he didn't want to be near her. He avoided touching her, but kept his back to her under the blankets.

And he didn't understand about her being with child but fretted because she wouldn't make love to him. And he made them live far away from her family. And, and, and!

She'd wondered once or twice if he knew she was with child. She'd let him know in all the little ways, changing her customs, and he must have felt the changes in her belly even if they didn't show. She thought about bringing it straight up to him, but that would be rude. Rude to say the obvious, and rude to talk openly about what must be unspoken.

Besides, if he didn't know, if he was that careless, that ignorant, maybe she didn't want to tell him. Maybe . . .

She slept fitfully and had strange dreams. In the morning she couldn't remember what the dreams were, but was left only with a feeling, the sense of them, like the sense of what a song says even when you don't hear the words. This meaning was clear. Go home. You are not a Tibo. The Tibo way is not for you, is not your rabbit path. Go home.

She felt a gush of relief. How could she ever have thought otherwise? What a strange way the Tibos lived, out alone, far from each other. No village, no family close, no company. No ceremonies either, as if Duma Apa didn't deserve honor. No lodge for the women's moon house. No sweat lodge, no medicine dreams, no prayers or dances to invoke the blessings of the spirits. It was a bad way, not for her, probably not for any Shoshone. A new way, yes, maybe the way of the future, but a bad way.

The future. It would be hard. Maybe her father could help, maybe she wouldn't have to become the wife of Horn, her older sister's husband. Three Bucks Dancing was an influential man, and could help his daughter. It would be worse for her child, to be half Tibo. *Numa-Tibo,* the people would call her child, half Shoshone, half Tibo. Bad. No one liked *Numa-Tibos,* and some people shunned them. The child would have no family on the father's side. But she couldn't help that, and there would still be family, always. Somehow she would make things work.

In an hour she had caught two horses, packed one and saddled the other. Her heart twisted a little. It wanted to stay with Morgan. But maybe her heart was wayward. Her mother always told her it was wayward.

She clucked at her mount and was on the way to her village, her real home.

Morgan came to the village after only two days. He must have gotten home early from Anderson's with the mail, or maybe he saw Sanders on the way and his friend told him the cabin was empty, the "squaw woman" was gone. Also, she heard, Morgan wore out his horses getting here fast.

She refused to see him. Her father talked to him. All Morgan would say to Three Bucks Dancing was, "I want to talk to Marian."

"I told him I have no daughter by that name," her father reported to her, "only one named Running Water who doesn't want to talk to him." He smiled at his daughter. "I also told him he's not welcome in our lodge right now, or with any of our people living here." Her father gave one of his satisfied looks.

Good. Morgan would know the village wasn't safe for him, and would go home. To his home, not hers. She felt relieved.

"Marian."

The word was soft, but she jumped.

Morgan, standing next to the willow he must have hidden behind. She was surprised. She was carrying a shiny brass bucket to the river for water because she was sure he'd left. It had been four days since he found out his scalp was in danger here.

What a fool he was, skulking around! He must have been sleeping in that dirty horse blanket he had over his shoulders.

She sat near him on a boulder by the bank, with a decent space between. She felt jittery. She was afraid to say someone from the village might see them, maybe her father, or worse, Horn. But she had to tell him the truth.

She took a deep breath. "Tomorrow I will to move into Horn's lodge," she said. "I'm lucky he'll take me."

She watched the pain wash across his face, and regretted there was nothing she could do about it.

"Lucky because of the child?"

So he did know.

"I'm sorry," he said. "I didn't know until Sanders asked me are you . . ." He touched his own belly. "I'm sorry."

What was he sorry about? That she was making life within? That he hadn't known? That it was her duty to refuse him? That he didn't know how to act like a human being?

He reached out and took her hand. It felt good. Instead of pulling it away, she turned hers on top, and looked at the two colors, her dark brown-red and his pale, underside-of-the-arm white. She looked into his face and saw that he understood what she was showing him. Too different. Impossible.

True, we have conceived a child. True, no Shoshone wants to be father to a *Numa-Tibo*. What difference did that make?

She felt tremulous, but she reminded herself, My rabbit path is not his.

"I been to Anderson's," he said.

Yes, you ran off to Anderson's to get mail and left me alone.

"I'm sorry I went by myself," he said. "I wanted to sort things out . . . about you and me. I done it." He let the words sit there, which was his way. "Things came real clear."

He reached inside his blanket coat and pulled out something, a deerskin hide folded around something, and handed it to her.

She unfolded the hide, quaking, telling herself it didn't matter what was in it.

She held some cloth and let it fall out full length.

Mrs. Anderson's wedding dress.

"I sent a note to Anderson's last fall," he said simply.

Oh, Marian would bet Mrs. Anderson had acted miffed about this order. She laughed.

Then she hugged the dress to herself, and felt the silky smoothness. It was so beautiful.

"It's just like Mrs. Anderson's," he said, "only new.

"I want you to wear it at the round dance this summer,"

he went on. "I wrote my dudes not to come till after that. Said I couldn't guide before then. Baby in the moon when the rivers are full," he plunged on, "then the Nariya dance. Us together."

He looked at her, and she saw the understanding in his eye.

"Thought you might like to stay with your folks after that, while I'm gone to Yellowstone. That way you'd have all summer with them. You could wear that dress out."

She couldn't speak. There was a hot stone in her throat. Besides, she was looking down the new path, and it was still scary.

He put an arm around her shoulders and drew her to him. She actually started to kiss him before she realized. They were out in plain daylight!

She pulled away but smiled at him with her eyes and her lips. Would he understand now?

He hesitated. Then he held out his blanket stretched across his shoulders and one arm, an invitation.

She stepped in. He closed it around both of them.

Where no one could see, she did a brazen thing, took his hand and squeezed it.

They walked back toward the tipis together. She looked around the lodges, the circle of lodges, and saw her people looking back.

Morgan's eyes were happy. So he knew this was her declaration in front of everyone.

Rabbit paths are funny things, she thought happily. They twist around and go off at crazy angles and double back and don't seem to make sense, but they take you where you need to go.

More Silent than the Male

RILEY FROH

The female of the species is more deadly than the male.
—*Rudyard Kipling*

SHE LOOKED AWAY from the May 1953 page of the Ace Reid calendar advertising the local cattleman's bank where they kept their tiny checking account a dollar or two above the red. As usual, Ace made her think of herself and her husband, for the comic illustrations of cowboys and their hard-used wives were all too painfully accurate for many Texas ranch couples. These marginal families lived out Reid's cartoons by taking as part of their pay living quarters on the ranch where they worked the long hours required to keep a place going for the owner.

"We don't look that bad yet," she thought as she turned to the window. "Another day like today and I will though," she added. In fact, at the Saturday night dance at Watterson they would soon attend as their only social life other than church, she knew that she and her husband would cut one of the handsomest figures on the floor. He still kept the reckless boyish good looks he had sported in high school, and the strenuous ranch work over the years had only served to keep her figure trim. If you didn't look too closely at the lines in their faces, they didn't look much different from the same two seventeen-year-olds who married right out of high school twenty years earlier in the first half of the Great Depression.

With these thoughts in her mind he rode into the picture the window framed, and by the way he sat his horse with a casual ease after such a long day in the saddle she sensed he had some ropin' 'n' ridin' tale to tell while they got the dirt off for the dance. When he sauntered in as tired as his horse, she always knew that he had doctored screwworm cases all day with no excitement. Then she saw he'd picked up a pretty good scratch on his face.

She lit the butane flame under the coffeepot while he unsaddled and turned his mare into the small horse pasture with his gelding, threw his chaps over the saddle tree back of his horse blanket, and clomped and jangled toward the back door, talking to the dogs that squirmed in the excitement of someone to communicate with. (He said he wore only one spur because if one side of the horse went at the speed he wanted he was sure that the other side would go along.) He kicked off his boots right inside the kitchen before easing himself into his place behind the table.

She saw that the scratch was worse than she thought but not as bad as she feared. She went on over it as though it were a grave matter as she had for two decades to keep the little boy in her precious husband happy. Mainly she saw his eye was all right as the gash went up the cheek and across the eyebrow into the forehead. The black screwworm medicine he had dabbed on would kill the infection, although she doubted any doctor would recommend it for humans.

"You know that ol' half-bramer cow that's so big and

always looking for a fight," he explained. "Well, she'd hid her calf in the weeds over by the river and had grazed up out of the bottom. I caught the calf and sure enough the screwworms had plum eat his navel out but I no more'n got the medicine on then here she come like a freight train. Tried to hook my head off as I fell backards and she just went right over me with my hat on her horn. Time she turned around I was on Penny and you know how she can dodge them horns while I was having to get the calf rope off my saddle horn and grab my other rope from behind me. I couldn't see out of one eye 'cause of the blood and I done good to catch that old bramer by the hind legs on the third try. Penny busted 'er good and kept backin' and trippin' her up while I got back off Penny and turned that blamed calf loose. I let the old killer step out of the loop and she still made one more run at me and Penny 'fore she went back to her calf. I ought to have tied her down and hauled her off and sold her while I had her."

She nodded approval, but she knew full well that the last thing her husband would do would be to sell the old renegade. She provided too much fun and excitement for her wild husband. And besides, she fought coyotes the same way she fought men and probably saved enough calves to make her worth keeping. Mother cows were all bad when their calves were small and the danger went with doctoring them. She was married to a cowboy known by old-time cowmen as the best man with a horse, a dog, or a cow in the county. He was just like her father, and she knew it when she married him.

Her husband's reputation and her capacity for hard work had got them this good job. Their small house had indoor plumbing the day they had moved in a decade earlier. She got the pick of the feed sacks with the best prints for sewing his shirts and her dresses. The ranch owner's wife had taken a liking to her and now and then gave her a piece of expensive furniture or a stylish dress from Neiman-Marcus she was going to discard. At their own lovely ranch house closer to town the old couple sometimes invited them to their parties, particularly when local politicians were entertained. Every two years the land owner bought a new Chevrolet pickup and passed the old one on to them for ranch work, but it was understood that they could drive it for personal use on their free time. They were allowed to run up to ten of their own cows with the rancher's herd as an added fringe benefit and the ranch bull worked for nothing, making no distinction as to brands. What chickens she wanted to keep and the garden space were her own business. Even with their tiny monthly salary they made do, and more importantly her husband was happy.

Her own father and mother still made their living the same way on a neighboring ranch and it was all she had ever known before marrying. But as a girl she had been exposed to the cutting blasts of Texas northers, driving a team of mules while her mother and father threw the hay out to the cold and surging cattle from the back of a wagon. Now she sat in the comfort of a nice heated pickup cab while her husband tossed out the regular winter feed. She knew her mother now drove a pickup for her father's feeding chores, and she realized deep-down that her own ways would never change, but she was also content with her life. Their hours were their own. She never tired of watching the fascinating habits of wild and domesticated birds and animals. She could keep all the pets she ever wanted, and her husband was always bringing her a baby squirrel that fell from a nest or an orphan fawn to cuddle until it grew up and ran back to the wild. She never penned any of her pets up, not even the brown thrasher that was her favorite. Brownie had flitted and hopped about her home for a year before flashing away to his own kind one spring, never to return. There was a quiet and a peace and a contentment in ranch life that could only be theirs with the job they did. Her own happiness exceeded that of her husband's, although his boyish exuberance reflected it much more openly.

But he was finishing his deer sausage and purple hull

peas and fried potatoes and she knew from his dancing
eyes that he was about to share another experience from
his day's adventures. She got him another cup of coffee
and pretended to give him full attention while she did the
dishes.

"You know that ol' sharp drop-off by the high ridge over
by the river bend," he started. "That old crazy muley cow
hides her calf out there every year and I figured that's
where she was at this mornin'. But Penny wouldn't go up
the cattle trail even with me spurrin' her good and when I
finally seen what was botherin' her I understood what she
smelled when I started up the ridge. There, right at the
top, coiled an' waitin' to bite the first cottontail to come by
was the biggest rattlesnake in the state. I know he's the
one bit that old Hereford bull last year that barely made it
back up here to the house, you remember."

Indeed, she did remember. They had found the fang
marks in the neck where the swelling was already getting
out of control. The bull lay out under the oldest mesquite
tree on the place behind the barn and heaved and wheezed
and whistled all night long trying to suck air through his
constricted windpipe. Finally she had got the deer rifle to
put him out of his misery, but he had stopped her, saying
the bull had as much right to try to live as anyone else.
And survive he did, no worse for the experience. Her father had come over to see him right before dark and had
said only an uncommonly big snake could have pumped
that much poison into the bull's brisket to cause such a
swelling.

Her husband fished around under a battered package
of Camel cigarettes in his shirt pocket, extracted the
lengthy string of rattles, and shook them ever so tantaliz-
ingly over his empty coffee cup. She took them, and after
mussing around the clutter of her sewing machine, she
dropped them into a faded cigar box with the other smaller
rattles and the growing collection of Indian arrowheads
they found together in their Sunday afternoon prowlings of

the ranch property. She planned to frame them all and hang them up one of these days.

"Well, I got off Penny and tied her to a elm tree," her husband continued. "And you know how it is when you find a snake needs killin' an' you can't find no big rocks layin' around to chunk always seems like. But there was this piece of cedar fence post that had broke off but hadn't rotted much and I grabbed it and waded into that snake. He shore wasn't fixing to run. Just stood his ground, coiled up weavin' that head back an' forth tryin' to get a shot at me. I throwed him over that high bob war fence over by the gulley yonder an' he drags the ground on both sides."

Her husband was content to smoke over his third cup of coffee while she quickly finished up the kitchen. She was in a hurry, for she wanted to get a good table around the dance floor before every one was taken. Here their group would settle in, her husband would repeat his stories while she caught up on the news from the same friends she had been talking to in the Watterson dance hall since high school. She felt thankful to be going to the dance after the battles she had fought that day.

First had been her fight with the water moccasin. Now that the drought had thinned out the frogs down at the creek, she had been seeing moccasins ever closer to the house, and this one had entered the barn in search of a meal where she was hunting the ever-elusive hen eggs. The snake had hit her thigh, burying and catching its curved fangs deep in the folds of her pleated denim skirt, shooting a spew of venom between her skirt and slip. Instinctively she had thrown up her hands, whirling automatically like a ballerina while the snake flopped and writhed sickeningly against her shuddering form.

"Get him," she shouted at the nervous terrier who had been busy ratting around the feedsacks. "Snake, snake, sic him," she rasped. With the timing of the best circus dog in a juggling act, Fibber, in one graceful leap, ripped the thick, black horror from her clothes by its neck, hitting the ground already shaking his prize with a fury long bred into the breed. Gasping for breath, she waited until her own legs quit their trembling before throwing the battered remains of Fibber's kill over the fence with a hoe.

She sat on the edge of the horse trough, bathing her face with her hands and thanking the Lord for deliverance from harm. Her goldfish rose from the green depths and peered at her with goggle eyes, waiting for the oatmeal she sometimes threw them before going back to nibbling the thick algae when no handout was forthcoming. Watching them calmed her and she remembered to call Fibber from his busy search of other dragons to slay and rub his ears and praise him highly, especially mentioning his high intelligence. Fibber seemed to nod his head in agreement and took on his look and pose of importance that such comments always brought out in him. Old Dorothy, the pit-bull and cur-dog cross, trained to get bad cattle out of thick brush, nosed her way in, jealous for a share of the attention.

A red-tailed hawk sailed the fence line in the distance, eventually resting on a corner post. Barnyard sounds began to reach her ears again as she got her complacency back. Snorts and grunts from a nearby pen told her the shoats needed their feed. She stepped into the pen with her half sack of Purina hog chow, tripping over the end of the hog trough as the five animals crowded around. Suddenly, the boar went for her ankle, got a mouthful of blue jean skirt and slip which he rent with a passion as he moved up her prostrate form for her face, gnashing and rooting horribly. All the gruesome but true stories of hogs eating children surged in her brain. Screaming for Dorothy she kicked at the filthy beast between her legs, a mouthful of denim under his snout with his little intelligent pig's eyes piercing hers from his grotesque position. Dorothy hit the swine with her usual ferocity, ripping the right ear before bloodying the hog's nostrils. As the pig's left ear was being shredded, the attacker released the skirt to run to the far end of the pen to squeal in pain and disillusionment as Dorothy kept up the vicious assault, nipping pieces of tender hide from leg and tail. In the meantime, Fibber had entered the fray with much noise and yapping and some more tooth work on the enemy's battered ears.

It was all she could do to call Dorothy off, who would stop and raise a foreleg, growling deep in her throat and threatening to return to battle as she reluctantly left the pen. The boar sulled in the corner, its face a bloody mess but its little malignant eyes shining with the thought of a new menu.

She cleaned her face in the horse trough, while Fibber looked on quizzically, head turned sideways at such theatrics. Now it was Fibber's turn to try to horn in on the kind words and caresses aimed at old Dorothy.

Clearly it was time to go to the house, but a casual glance through the bars of the horse corral showed her a guinea egg, lying in the sand by the snubbing post. She ought not to go home without anything for her troubles, she reasoned, and absentmindedly she slipped the latch and passed through the gate. As she bent over and grasped the egg, the stallion went for her, seizing her belt, skirt waist, and slip from behind in its powerful teeth. She instinctively realized that she had been too addled to think. Ranch-raised and the daughter of a noted bronc stomper, she knew better than to go around a stud horse during her period. She had helped her father with the horses all her early life, but he had always kept her away from the stallions at certain times of the month after she reached puberty. Menstruating women sometimes drove them to do strange things.

Now in spite of her training she was being spun in a circle, unable to breathe but certainly able to pray. She was about to promise never to attend a Saturday night dance again when her belt broke off in the teeth of the horse and her skirt and slip ripped off with it. The force of the release rolled her under the bottom bar of the pen where she lay for a while. When she became conscious that the guinea egg was clutched unbroken in her hand, she began to laugh. As the tears of laughter and release coursed her face, old Dorothy whimpered for some sort of consolation. Trained since a pup to leave horses and deer alone, she had been torn between loyalty and guidance during the final episode, and the old dog knew somehow that she should have helped. "It's all right, baby," she crooned to the ugly face as Dorothy's powerful halitosis almost overwhelmed her.

She started for the house in her panties and blouse. A bath and a cold Coca-Cola were in order even if the rest of the chores never got done. Too late she heard the crunch of tires as the local Watkins' Products salesman and the oldest Baptist deacon in their church coaxed his ancient, creaking Plymouth around his usual U-turn by the horse pens. This time both his window and his whole face were hanging open, though he was speechless as he gaped in startled amazement.

"I don't need nothing today, Deacon," she said with uncharacteristic coldness as she passed the car looking straight ahead.

"You may not want nothing but you sure need something," the Deacon said to himself as he shook his head in wonder and risked one eye for a last glimpse at the receding firm cheeks of a half-nude ascending a staircase.

As she put the day's workload out of her mind with the last dish she was washing, the scrape of her husband's chair brought her back to the present. "You don't want no more pie?" she asked as he started to leave.

"I don't reckon," he answered. "Let's go dancin'."

"Say," he said, "you think after we get bathed off and 'fore we get ready we could—"

"You know we can't now," she interrupted tenderly. "Maybe tomorrow."

"Oh, yeah," he said, reminded. And he added as an afterthought, "What went on around here today?"

"Oh, nothing much," she answered. "Just the usual."

The Leave-taking

RUTH WILLETT LANZA

BENNETTIE STOOD ON THE HILL, a short distance from their tent, alone. She felt more alone than she'd felt in all her fifteen years, as the hot prairie breeze blew the bluestem grasses around her ankles, catching her cotton stockings and bunching the hem of her calico skirt.

She stood, leaning her spare body into the wind, and held her hand to the brim of her sunbonnet to shade her eyes; eyes that were an unforgettable gray-blue.

Heaving a deep sigh, she stood motionless, gazing across the endless plain of knee-high grasses swaying in the wind, at the western horizon of Oklahoma Territory, and a lump constricted her throat.

Holding back tears, she strained after the wagon train snaking across the flat expanse that yawned before her. It carried with it all she'd known of love and security—her mamma and papa, and her two younger sisters, Sophia and Sephrina.

When the wagons had first started out on the trail to California that morning, she'd heard the creaking and grinding of the massive wooden wheels, and above the clamor, she'd taken comfort in the sound of her father's voice calling out to the six-span of oxen. Then from their wagon, which was the last in the line of white-canvassed prairie schooners, she'd heard the voices of Sophie and Sephrina drifting across the waving sea of grass as they called out to her.

"Bye, Bennie, bye," they'd called over and over again, their sweet voices sounding like a meadowlark on the wing, until she could no longer hear them, and could see only the faint outline of the two children as they waved from the back of the wagon. Soon they, too, faded from view, as the wagons lumbered along, tilting from side to side, gradually growing smaller and dimmer, like a line of white ants.

Even so, her ears strained for one more sound, only to hear the sighing of the wind. Finally, as she gazed across the open space, unblotched by tree or cloud, the wagons disappeared over the edge of the earth.

"Oh, Mamma," she whispered under her breath, as she brushed away a hot tear with the back of her hand, "how could you have left me here, all alone?" Alone in this wild, unsettled land they'd all just come to. Alone, amid the roaming bands of Chickasaw Indians, those fearful, red-skinned savages, whose land they'd confiscated in the Run and where she and Henry would make their home?

Alone—except for Henry. *Why did you have to go? When will I ever see your dear faces again? Probably not in my lifetime.* All these thoughts swirled through her brain, and she felt the hot winds closing in around her until she couldn't breathe. Then the tears she'd been holding back for the last several days squeezed out from behind her tightly closed lids, burning the fair, freckled skin of her cheeks.

Furiously, she wiped them away with the hem of her skirt, streaking her sunburned face with the red dust of the Oklahoma plain. Impatiently, she tore off the sunbonnet to wipe the perspiration from her forehead as the noontime sun beat down relentlessly, and setting her chin, she promised herself she'd not cry again.

Henry had said, "Your eyes are like the evening light, shot through with stars." She smiled, for she knew she was plain-looking—except for her eyes.

Mamma had told her she was strong, and smarter than most. That should be enough, thought Bennettie. But how she longed to be pretty, like the small-waisted, buxom girls with hair the color of goldenrod whom she envied.

"Whoa, whoa there, now." His voice rose deep and strong, breaking the silence that surrounded her. She turned to see him yanking the team of horses to a standstill, his sturdy body straining against their pull; watched as he hopped down lightly and secured the reins, tying them to the handle of the plow.

Then, raising his arm, he waved to her, a smile creasing his broad face, which was the color of a walnut. *Almost as dark as the braves who belong to this land,* she thought.

His black curly locks—inherited from his little French mother, back in Missouri—fell across his forehead, and his shoulders strained against the muslin of his shirt.

The sight of him made a warm, mushy feeling rise up inside her. Gulping back her grief, she waved at him. Then she tied on her bonnet, even though the hot winds felt good as they dried the strands of hair dampened by sweat. For she remembered her Gram's words: "Always keep your hat on, Ben, to protect your skin from freckling." She laughed when she remembered, for her skin was freckled like nutmeg on a cup of eggnog.

She watched as Henry strode across the field with his boots sinking in the earth, his stocky, compact frame bent into the wind. He strode up the slope to where she stood so straight and still, with her small, high bosom heaving with emotion, and perspiration trickling down her neck onto the edge of her dimity collar.

Henry reached out his arms, tanned and muscular, covered with fine black hairs, as he said, "Come, Bennie, you can't stand here all day. You'll get sunstroke for sure, and all the watching won't bring them back. You'll just make yourself sick, strainin' to see what isn't there."

She nodded that she knew he was right, but no words came.

"They've gone now, darlin' Bennie, for sure. They're well on their way to California by now, but you'll see them again someday. I *promise* you that!"

He wiped her tearstained face with his fingers, calloused by the plow handles, ax, and saw—tools of settling in this "Promised Land"—and wrapped his arms around her slender waist.

She, who stood nearly as tall as he, *hard and straight, like a tree,* she thought, leaned her head onto his shoulder, and her voice trembled when she finally spoke.

"Oh, Henry. What will I do without Mamma and Phenie and little Sophie? Without Papa?" She sighed, brushing a wisp of sparrow-brown hair back under the edge of her sunbonnet brim, and remembered.

"Have to go West," Papa had said to Mamma. She could still see the big white house with its peeling paint, and the airy rooms of her grandmother's plantation, the sleek race horses, and the rolling green hills of Kentucky.

"It's been a shambles since the Rebellion. It'll never come back, Melinda," he'd said. "Our only chance is out West."

"With Indians and *desperados*? Oh . . . Benjamin," Melinda had wailed.

Bennettie had never forgotten the look of terror in her mamma's eyes. *Mamma was brave,* she thought. But it was her father who'd suffered most, seeing himself as a Kentucky gentleman, he'd never been able to adjust to life as a pioneer. *Poor Papa,* she thought. And now her parents were off again, following another of her father's dreams.

When he'd heard that the government planned to open up the Indian Territory to settlement, in the spring of 1889, he decided to make the "Run" for free land.

"Oklahoma! I've heard that that means land of the redman," said Melinda, her voice trembling at the thought of going into that strange, wild country.

But when Bennettie looked at her father, new hope surged in her. His eyes were bright with anticipation at the thought of a new beginning. Benjamin loved beginnings. It was the staying and finishing of things he couldn't face. She knew that, now.

Bennettie guessed her father didn't see the look of fear in her mother's eyes, because he just laughed.

"It'll be an adventure, Melinda," he'd said. "And it's our chance to get a piece of the Promised Land."

So they'd set out in their wagon for Indian Territory.

Benjamin rode alongside on his Kentucky mare, which was his most cherished possession, the only thing of value they'd brought from the plantation. Except, of course, the silver castor set, with its cut glass condiment bottles, that Melinda had wrapped carefully in an old blanket to keep from breaking.

As their wagon rolled along behind the wagon train with Melinda driving the oxen, Bennettie sat up on the seat beside her, since she was the oldest. Sophie and Phenie rode in the back of the wagon, hanging their legs over the edge, watching Kentucky, Illinois, and finally Missouri, disappear from sight.

The first day on the open prairie seemed endless, with the sun beating down like a trip-hammer and the wind blowing against their faces like a blast from a hot oven. But at the sight of a dark, undulating mass of brown monsters grazing some distance away and hundreds of wild horses streaking across the prairie, Bennettie felt goosebumps rise on her arms, and she shivered with excitement.

She'd never seen buffalo, and she wished with all her might she could lasso a wild pony to have for her very own, for like her father, she loved horses.

She decided that she must have inherited a little of his spirit of adventure, too. After all, she was his namesake, even though she hated her name, given to her because she was supposed to be a boy. *How could anyone ever like a girl called Ben?* she asked herself, *and one as plain as me?*

When the western sky turned a rosy pink with shades of lavender, they looked for a place to camp. Benjamin rode up ahead to consult with the wagon master. Then, pointing to a fringe of green, he'd called back to Melinda.

"Over there, by those trees. That means there's water, they say, first we've seen and most we're likely to. We'll pull up there for the night."

Melinda heaved a sigh of relief, and stretching her neck and twisting her back, she turned the oxen toward the small clump of trees, pulling the wagon to a halt by the tallest cottonwood.

The children were down and out of the wagon in an instant, running to the river, splashing water on each other and squealing with delight. Bennettie wanted to join them, but before she could move, her father started giving directions.

"Ben, you gather some buffalo chips, should be plenty around here, so we can make a fire. And go get Flossie's bucket, so your mamma can get started makin' the corn bread."

Bennettie untied the bucket from behind the wagon, where Flossie's cream had jiggled all day until it had turned into butter. Her mouth watered as she thought of Mamma's hot corn bread spread thick with butter and sorghum molasses, and she was thankful that Papa hadn't asked her to milk Flossie, too.

That night she slept out under the stars on her bedroll, glad to give the wagon over to the little ones, because she liked to be alone to look up at the spreading canopy of stars that blinked overhead, to listen to the coyotes yipping, and to hear the soft hooting of the great horned owl she'd noticed sitting on the limb of a cottonwood tree.

She thought of Kentucky, with the rolling blue-green hills, her grandmother's white-pillared house, and for an instant, she wished to be back there, safe and secure. But there was something about the wildness and freedom of this land they were crossing, something that put joy in her heart.

In the days that followed, she could tell they were approaching an Indian village by the spotted ponies grazing on a hill. Then the white, deerskin tipis loomed on the horizon, with curls of smoke rising from the smoke-holes and campfires. She felt worried when the barking dogs warned the Indians of their approaching wagons.

One day, three warriors, with their bare, coppery-skinned chests glistening in the sun, holding their lances high, rode out to meet them.

Bennettie drew in her breath with anticipation and a tinge of fear, but when the Indians held up their arms, muscular and ringed with silver, to greet them in peace, she let out a sigh of relief and looked over at her mother.

Melinda, green eyes filled with apprehension, smiled a tight little smile. Then she grasped Bennettie's hand and glanced in the back of the wagon at the children.

"Hush, Phenie, keep Sophie quiet . . . Indians!"

But it turned out that they were friendlies. When the wagons drew to a stop, Indian women wrapped in blankets and brown-skinned children, half-naked, came out to mill around the wagons and peer inside, pointing to the copper pots and lamps and other treasures hanging from the side of the wagons.

The men traded whiskey and tools to the warriors for fox and bear furs. Melinda bargained with a sober-faced Indian woman, trading her a blue glass oil lamp for a willow basket.

Bennettie accepted a pair of soft, beaded moccasins from an Indian maiden named Morning Star, in exchange for *Little Women* (one of her favorite books, since she'd always imagined herself as Jo).

"Can you read?" Bennettie asked, surprised.

Morning Star looked at Bennettie, her black eyes sparkling with humor, and nodded, somberly.

"Go to Mission School," she said, "Nuns teach me to read good."

Bennettie admired Morning Star's smooth brown skin and large dark eyes. She was so lovely to look at. And she had such a pretty name. *Even Indian girls are beautiful,* she thought. *Oh, how I wish I was pretty, too.* And she wished that she and Morning Star could truly be friends. As they rode away from the village, she waved at the Indian maiden and Morning Star waved back. *Maybe someday we'll meet again,* thought Bennettie.

Benjamin explained to the children that the tribes were all different and that they were divided into nations.

"The Cherokees, the ones we just passed, are the most educated ones. But the Pawnees, they say, are wild and fierce."

So, they all hugged close together when they drew near the Pawnee nation. Bennettie noticed that her mamma clenched the reins so tightly she wore blisters on her hand and bit her lower lip until the blood came. She didn't look to right or left, as though she was fearful of what she might see. But if the Pawnees saw them, they let them be.

After weeks of traveling, they finally made camp by the South Canadian River, smack in the middle of the Chickasaw Nation, and there they waited for the big day—to make the Run.

Tents dotted the prairie as far as they could see, for hundreds of people from everywhere had gotten there before them. They'd come in wagons, buckboards, buggies, and even on the train. Gamblers had set up fortune wheels, so that the men could bet on which day the Run would be held and on who had the fastest horse to carry them to their free 160 acres.

Melinda wouldn't let Benjamin gamble on the fortune wheels, so to keep peace, he spent his days playing cards or pitching horseshoes with the other men. At night he sat in the tent and poured over his maps by the light of an oil lamp, trying to select the best site for their homestead.

The women washed clothes in the river, cooked meals over the open campfires, and tried to keep track of the children.

Bennettie wandered down to the river when her chores were done, and sitting on the riverbank, she unlaced her high-top shoes and dipped her bare feet in the cool water.

She took a tablet and stub of pencil out of her apron pocket, and as she watched a hawk soar across the blue sky, she tried to think of a poem. Licking the lead point, she wrote a few words:

> Far away from Kentucky
> I sit on a table of grass
> Wondering and waiting
> For my tomorrow . . .

Will I ever get more schooling? she wondered. How would she ever get more learning out here in this new country? There weren't any schools, or churches, not even roads or anything. She envied Morning Star, who was not only pretty as a newborn colt—with her glossy black braids— but was able to attend a Mission School.

Glancing back toward the camp, she saw her mother and noticed how frazzled she looked. *Gram should see her daughter now,* thought Bennettie. *Mamma's boots all caked with red mud, and her beautiful auburn hair, so dull and sticky with dust and sweat.*

And although Mamma kept wearing her sunbonnet most days to keep the sun off her skin, the sunbonnet was all limp and bedraggled and her skin was burnt red as a tomato.

Bennettie had heard her crying some nights after Papa was asleep, and it made her feel sad and confused. *Mamma's just tired of movin', I guess,* she thought. *It ain't been easy for her.*

The rains began just before the big day. At first everybody all along the river let out a yell of elation, because rain in this dry country was a blessing, for sure. It would cool down everything, making it all easier to bear.

Bennettie watched the little kids run through the rain, splashing in the puddles, letting it soak through to their skins, because it felt so good. She wished she was little enough to do it, too. But she stood by to help her mamma clean them up when they came back to the tent, dripping wet and grinning.

The rain didn't stop, but poured down in buckets, drenching them for three days. Everybody finally hunkered down in their tents and wagons to wait it out. Then the river began to rise, and they all forgot about getting wet and just stood around watching with horror as the river rose to the edge of the bank.

The menfolk stood all night, holding their lanterns high, watching the river and talking about what would happen if "she" overflowed the banks.

Benjamin stalked into the tent, his boots caked with sticky red mud, and throwing off his slicker, he spoke to Melinda softly, so the kids wouldn't hear. But Bennettie heard.

"Better, say some prayers, Melinda. If that river doesn't stop rising soon, don't know how we'll get across on the Big Day to make the Run."

Melinda nodded her head, numb-like, and grasped Benjamin's hand, squeezing it. Bennettie knew her mother had been praying all along.

The rain must have stopped in the middle of the night, because Bennettie was awakened one morning with everybody hollering and yelling bloody murder.

"She's goin' back! The river's goin' back! Praise the Lord!"

She and Phenie ran out in their nightclothes to see what all the excitement was about. The men were already pulling their rafts close to the riverbank to get across for the Run. People were taking down their tents and loading their wagons, making ready to take off when the gun was shot, giving them the signal. For the Big Day was here.

At noon—suntime— the government men stood on the line across the river, holding their guns in readiness and checking their watches. Then slowly they raised their arms, as a great silence spread over the camp and up and down the riverbank. The creaking of the wagons, and the pawing of horses hoofs against the muddy bank and an occasional whinny, were the only sounds.

Men on horseback and in buggies, buckboards, covered wagons, even men on foot, stood in readiness, holding their breath, waiting to hear the shot.

Her father would ride *alone* on Prancer, his chestnut mare, " 'Cause a man alone can ride faster and go further," he said. "You and the youngins can wait here in camp until I stake my claim and come back for you," he told Melinda.

So, her mamma and the children sat breathlessly in the wagon, waiting to hear the shot that would signal the start of the race.

Bennettie stood, so she could see her father take off. He looked so handsome, dressed in his best Prince Albert coat, his wide-brimmed white hat, and his new string tie.

Finally, the government men fired the shots into the air! Everyone took off with whoops and hollers, splashing across the river and up the other bank.

Benjamin was one of the first to reach the other side, and Bennettie watched him and Prancer race across the prairie, until they faded from sight.

For the next week, they waited and watched in the nearly abandoned camp for Benjamin's return.

Bennettie spent hours standing on a high rise a ways

down the river, looking through field glasses, straining for sight of her father.

Had he met up with uncouth people?

"There's lots of rough characters, jumpin' claims and stealin' horses, what'd just a soon shoot you as look at you," she confided to Phenie. "Then there's them Sooners what crept into the territory before the gun was shot—some long before—taking their piece of land before it was time." And they both wondered if Papa, with his Southern gentlemanly ways, could stand up to the likes of them.

One day, they saw dust whorls spinning over the plain, like a tumbleweed. As the horse and rider drew closer, they could see that it was Prancer. Her glossy body glistened with sweat, and Benjamin was grinning and waving his big white hat.

"Praise the Lord!" she heard Melinda whisper under her breath. And they all let out a yell, "It's Papa. Look, he's coming. Papa's coming."

Her mamma hugged her and little Sophie to her breast in thankfulness. And Phenie ran up and down the riverbank, jumping up and down with joy.

When her papa got across the river, Melinda hugged him, and Phenie and Sophie clung to the tails of his Prince Albert coat.

"It's done," he said. "We're landowners. Got a dandy claim, just ten miles south of Edmond Station on Bluff Creek."

They all hollered with joy, and Bennettie saw her mother wipe her eyes with the hem of her apron.

"We've got to get goin'," said Benjamin, "because I left a friend guarding my claim, until we get back."

Once again they set out across the prairie, and on the third evening they crossed Bluff Creek with the aid of lanterns, and an air of apprehension settled over them.

Was their claim safe? Bennettie saw the strained look on her mamma's face, and she held her breath while her papa fired three shots into the air with his rifle.

After an endless moment of silence, they heard from way over a hill an answering shot.

"Thank God," said Benjamin, "our claim is safe."

The next morning, when they reached their land, Bennettie walked away from the tent to see what they'd come to.

It is so beautiful, she thought, as she stood in the waist-high grass and marveled at the wildflowers spread across the prairie like a patchwork quilt of purple, white, and yellow. A majestic eagle sailed and dipped overhead, its wings spread wide, and a flock of prairie chickens strutted nearby, puffing orange ruffs all around their little faces.

I know Mamma hates it, she thought, *but I love it all: the wide-open space, the soft, hot wind in my face, the sky arching overhead till it touches the edge of the earth, like a pale blue tent. I love the newness of it all. It's like a piece of blank paper, still to be wrote on. Papa says it's a young land, settled by young people. It's my land, for sure.*

And then she met Henry. She smiled when she remembered how Henry had ridden across the prairie on his fine black stallion from his own claim to greet them, since they were neighbors. He owned a team of horses, and Papa said that horses were more valuable than gold in this new land—horses and a wife.

Bennettie liked Henry from the very first; the way his brown eyes sparkled with fun-lovin' and the softness that shone in them when he looked at her.

Then one day he came striding up the hill, his black boots newly polished, carrying a bouquet of wildflowers: blue larkspur, wild roses, and black-eyed Susans. He tipped his hat to her and asked if she'd like to ride into town with him the next day for a sarsaparilla.

She couldn't speak, but just nodded, as she felt the blush creep up her neck and onto her face, while her heart did somersaults.

Later, he talked of his dreams.

"I can see a town with churches and schools and a white house on a hill. We'll be leaders in this new land, because we're young and strong, and because we both love this prairie with its waving sea of grasses that grow as high as a horse's belly."

That night when she lay out under the stars, beneath the pale light of the moon, away from the others, wide awake, listening to the distant howl of a wolf, Bennettie thought of Henry.

Slowly, she smoothed her flannel gown with her hand, down the length of her long body, feeling the flatness of her stomach, the sharpness of her hipbones, then back up again until her hand cupped the small mound of her breast. She was no longer a child, she knew. But was she woman enough for a man like Henry? she wondered. She shivered with the thought of it.

The wagon train carrying her loved ones had disappeared over the edge of the horizon, and as Bennettie and Henry stood together on their hill, he tilted her chin up to make her look at him.

"Darlin' Bennie, my precious wife, you have *me*. I'll always take care of you, just as I promised. Have you forgotten all our plans and dreams? It's you and me for it, Bennie."

Suddenly, forgetting Mamma and Papa, Sophie and Phenie, she ripped off her bonnet, and with a smile creasing her face and a twinkle in her eyes, she said, "I'll race you to the tent." Then, lifting her calico skirt and her petticoats, so she wouldn't trip, she dashed with long-legged strides down the hill, laughing and panting for breath.

When he finally caught up with her, he grabbed her around the waist, whirling her to a stop, and they both fell to the ground, their laughter riding the wind across the prairie. Encircled in each other's arms, they rolled together in the tall grasses, which closed over and above them.

Henry placed a kiss on her freckled nose and said softly, "I love you, Bennie. I love you, my darlin' girl."

Bennettie closed her eyes and sighed, with a deep feeling of contentment, as she told herself, *Henry likes my name. He thinks I'm beautiful, and that my eyes are like an evening star. And someday I'll get more learning. I know for sure—that for me and Henry—this Oklahoma Territory is truly the Promised Land.*

A Two-Gun Man

JOYCE ROACH

THE WAY FUDGE HAD IT FIGURED, he was about ready and himself was the only obstacle standing in his way. "A man's got to do what's right"—that's what his daddy said and Fudge had never known his daddy to lie or to shirk his job as a cowboy on the great Crosswinds ranch, so named because the wind blew across the ranch nearly all of the time. Buck, his daddy's friend, said only the wind knew the way across so many acres but that wherever they were the wind found them. Buck was not a man to tell a lie, but he laughed a lot when he told the truth. Fudge aimed to be a cowboy himself, and that's why he had to do what he had to do, which was to become a crack shot with a pistola in either hand, a two-gun man.

For several reasons, an uneasiness, a tightness, was

building in Fudge, and he was thinking about guns morning, noon and night. Not that Fudge had ever seen his daddy shoot with both hands, but he had seen it done with one hand, and at a rattlesnake at that when he nearly put his own little hand right on the rattler. His daddy had put a bullet in that old snake's head not inches away from where he reached down to pick up a rock. His daddy fired, was off his big Cinnamon horse with his arms around him, and laughing before Fudge had time to be scared. Daddy pulled out a knife from his belt, handed it to Fudge and showed him how to whack the rattler off the snake. Then he scooped him up into the big saddle on Cinnamon and rode for the bunkhouse hollering, "Look here what my Fudge done. He ain't afraid of no rattler. No, sir. He whacked off his tale, and I'm proud of 'im." And the men cheered. But the boss man's wife came running out from the house, gathered Fudge up in her arms, squeezed him nearly to death and yelled at his daddy all in the same breath about how snakes, or horns or careless men were going to be the death of Fudge before he was six years old. The gun was the fault of all the hullabaloo, he thought. And he had seen the other men, his daddy's friends and his, target practice for fun at old tin cans that Mr. Richards' wife let them have. They joked about tin cans instead of the real thing. Fudge knew the real thing to be game for the table—turkey, quail, antelope, deer and sometimes beef. The men seemed to imply more in their teasing with one another, and sometimes they drew their guns on each other, but they just made bang, bang noises with their mouths. Fudge knew they were playing a game of some kind. He used his finger and thumb for such games, and then the men put their guns away and played finger-thumb guns back with him.

Sometimes the cowboys would take their ease about the bunkhouse late in the evenings when they returned from chores done for Mr. Richards, things such as building fence or moving cattle from one place to another, or doctoring stock. After supper around the big table in Mrs.

Richards' backyard, the men would take their plates and utensils to a big washtub of soapy water, wash them out in one bucket, rinse them in another and stack them in yet another. Then they were free to lollygag—that's what Mrs. Richards called it—but she laughed and Fudge knew that what they did was approved. Fudge did the same, sharing the good food, observing the table manners of the men practiced under Mrs. Richards' watchful eye, only he had to empty the water buckets and tidy up, as Mrs. Richards called it, after the men finished. It was the one time of the day they were under the stern hand of a high-toned woman, but to be able to get such eats on a ranch, to have canned peaches at every meal and a feast on Sunday was worth enduring prayer, napkins, two utensils, table etiquette and dish washing. That's what the boys all said, although Fudge had never known life to be any other way. Seldom were all of the men together at one time anyway since at any given day many were scattered clear to the Mexican border or camping and working in pastures twenty miles from the home place. They kept to a schedule, however, and rotation to the big house place was an event to be looked forward to rather than dreaded, except for Fudge, who rotated only from the henhouse where the rooster chased him, to the barn where the peacocks acted like they were going to, to the bunkhouse where the cowboys razzed him, to the big white house where Ma'am worried him, to the table where nobody noticed him and where he got his name, Fudge—roly, poly, brown and sweet—that's what the cowboys said.

About the farthermost he got away from the ranch grounds was to the outhouse situated a far distance out from everything else. That, he guessed, was why they called it an outhouse, but then Fudge had to guess about a lot of things. Trips out there beyond the chicken yard might turn up snakes, horned toads, scorpions and grandaddy longlegs spiders. Yes, Fudge's days were filled with tension and sometimes terror, although nobody guessed it. Too much time, he thought, was spent pouring the dishwater on the garden, checking for eggs in the henhouse or reporting the theft of eggs by animals too terrible to imagine, even planting and hoeing and gathering. "There sure is a lot of farming to be done on this ranch," Mrs. Richards said at least once a day as she worked beside Fudge or directed his chores. "They damn sure is," Fudge had replied once, but only once. Damn and guns were two items denied the youngest cowboy at Crosswinds.

Until recently when Fudge decided to become a two-gun man just as quick as he mastered being a one-gun man, the outhouse held no interest. Now, the place was beginning to look like just the right spot to do a little practicing. Fudge, however, had some hard times coming and difficult days ahead just to figure out how to get his hands on a gun of any kind, let alone shoot it. Now, with roundup and driving and shipping to be done, there wouldn't hardly be time to go to the outhouse for any reason, let alone to study on how to be a two-gun man.

Fudge knew a secret about guns at Crosswinds that nobody else knew. At least he thought no one knew but him. Mrs. Richards sometimes carried a gun—a rifle—and she could use it. She could do a lot of things that the men did such as ride a horse and even throw a rope, but the gun business surprised him some. The boy knew nothing of women except what he saw, and he once saw Mrs. Richards, whom he called Ma'am as did everyone else, away off from the house emptying cartridges into a target of some kind. It must have been okay since Mr. Richards was standing behind her pointing and motioning this way and that.

What really had Fudge determined to handle and shoot guns, however, was a recent event, one that burned in his memory during the day and brought him awake at night. One morning Ma'am called him from the bunkhouse before he started chores and said that he was going to town with her, maybe. She didn't explain why he was going since he had never in all his six years gone to a town, whatever and wherever that was. Never. Ma'am was upset, kind of mad like. His daddy was off down close to the border, so there was no way he could ask him. The other men were off doing what they always did and he couldn't ask them. Nobody was at the big house or on the grounds that morning except him and Mr. Richards and Ma'am. After Ma'am left the bunkhouse, Fudge became aware that not all was right at the big house. He could hear strong words, loud words, and then crying. Fudge was startled only by the crying. Sometimes he used to cry when he was a baby, but Ma'am or his daddy or Mr. Richards talked to him about it and said he shouldn't. He had to be a man, they said. And Fudge wanted more than anything to be a man and do such things as ride and rope and shoot a gun, two guns. So he cried as little as he could. Never in his life had he heard anyone else cry. He was in the loft of the barn trying to escape the rooster who was below flashing his spurs and flying up as far as he could when he heard the sound. It was Ma'am crying and she had to be carrying on loudly for Fudge to have heard. Her piercing sobs struck a chord deep inside Fudge. He knew not to bother Mr. Richards and Ma'am, but he ran as fast as his fat legs could carry him as far as the front porch steps, then up to the front window. They were in the hallway, which ran the whole width of the house. Mr. Richards was the one doing the talking now. "Ruth, the boy's not yours. You can't just up and take him and be gone two weeks What's got the bit in your teeth? Have I done something to you? Have any of the men hurt your feelings or been disrespectful?"

"Cater, you stop that! You know that isn't so. You're just wishing it was something you could do something about. I just want to go to town. It's been two years. I want to go to church, find out what the women are wearing, buy some, some . . . things, do-dads."

None of what she was saying made any sense at all. Town? Fudge had been to a line camp or two, but not town. Church he knew. He went up to the big house along with any cowboy who was about to hear the pump organ play and sing "Shall We Gather at the River." That would be the Pecos. Then Mr. Richards would say, "Shall we pray?" Nobody ever really decided whether to or not, so Mr. Richards did. "Dear Lord, hold us in the palm of your mighty hand. Give us what we need and a little of what we want. Amen." It was always the same prayer. It was just something to say to somebody named Lord, but Fudge liked the part about giving a little of what he wanted. He wanted a gun, two guns, and he had been filling in with words of his own lately and telling more than asking Lord because he was getting more and more worried. Then Ma'am read from the Bible. He surely knew about that book. He had to read from it himself every day in front of her. He even liked the time he spent in the house since it gave him a little relief from roosters, peacocks, spiders and rattlers. He read just from the first part and there were stories about men who moved their cattle here and there and got into arguments about land and who was going to get it. Ma'am explained a lot of what he didn't understand. The words were so funny and hard, but life sounded pretty much the same in the book as it did where he lived. Camels, asses and sheep were in some of the stories, but nothing about guns. David whipped a lion pretty bad with the jawbone of an ass and killed a giant with a rock, but none of the folks in the book seemed to be able to get hold of a pistola either.

All these thoughts flashed through Fudge's head as he listened to the pair in the hall. What were do-dads? Mr. Richards was saying, "Now, Ruth. . . . I can't do without you this time of year and I can't let you go alone knowing you'd be two hard days riding before you could meet up with the train to get you to Toad. And what good would Fudge be to you? He's got a good father and he's better off here away from people for a while. Darrell Lee Barclay is the best man in the world and he's my best man here at Crosswinds. I don't know what I'd do without him. And Fudge is better off here with him now."

Ma'am's voice was low in the beginning, "Cater, you

know we must do something for Fudge. I'm raising him and there are things he needs even if he sleeps in the bunkhouse with his daddy and the men. For starters, he needs clothes and boots. . . ." Fudge lost a lot of other things Ma'am said at the mention of boots. He looked down at his feet on which were sandals like the Mexicans wore. He got a new pair every few months when Old Manuel came through in his peddler's wagon. Manuel wore guns and ammunition strapped crisscross on his chest, two guns. That's how Fudge knew about some who carried two guns all the time. The cowboys at Crosswinds wore only one gun most of the time. In Manuel's wagon were more things, pots and pans and cloth, but Fudge knew Manuel carried shells for the cowboys in the wagon because he had seen. And Manuel had The News; that's what the men said, "Manuel, amigo, what's The News?" Even Ma'am wanted to know, but he never got to hear what it was that was The News.

". . . and I'm thirty-five years old and you know we aren't ever going to have . . . a . . ." Ma'am never finished the sentence but began to cry so badly she couldn't talk. Mr. Richards reached out his hand and touched Ma'am, patted her on the shoulder just like he did the men now and then, only softer. So, Ma'am was a real old woman, and there were some things she wanted and going to town would get part of them. And what was she doing to him, this raising word? Whatever it was, he liked most of it, but if she cried so then maybe she was going to quit. Would the do-dads fix everything? Another wispy thought crossed Fudge's mind, but it was gone too before he could make it take form. Were there other people, other Ma'ams somewhere out there who? Who what?

Fudge had no way to ask the whole questions in his mind and part of the trouble in thinking was that he had always to keep his mind on whatever was after him. From the corner of his eye, he caught the movement of the rooster moving in. If the rooster got up on the porch and came after Fudge, then the Mister and Ma'am would know he was there listening.

". . . think what will happen to Fudge, Ruth. Everyone in town will ask questions, questions we have never asked of his daddy when he rode up here four years ago with that baby boy. We just took 'em in and never been sorry. Nobody in town will understand." Mr. Richards said more and so did Ma'am, but Fudge never heard more because he had to do something about El Gallo, another of his daddy's words for rooster.

Fudge climbed over the porch rail and fell to the ground just as El Gallo jumped up the last step and came after him. What the boy did was an act of courage. Instead of retreating from the rooster, the child charged back up the steps after the bird, hollering at the same time. "Git out of Ma'am's yard. Git!" The noise brought the couple outside immediately and in time to see the rooster fly in Fudge's face, spurs up, and a spurt of blood appear near the boy's right eye. It was Mr. Richards who grabbed Fudge, separating him from the bird. It was Ma'am who grabbed a broom and, with both hands on the stick, swung at the rooster. Fudge looked on out of his one good eye at the bird as he arched high in the air and landed far from the porch, flopping around and around on the ground. Fudge looked clearly for the first time in his life at Ma'am. He saw that she was tall, noticeably taller than Mr. Richards. Before the rooster could gain his feet, Ma'am ran to the flopping desperado. He could see the soles of her boots as she hiked her skirts and gathered the apron she always wore. A broad-brimmed sombrero such as old Manuel wore bounced on a leather string behind her back. When she got to the object of her anger, she began to kick the bird. Then she kicked him again. Step, kick. Step, kick and crying, sobbing, with every kick. Ma'am kicked the bird until she was a long way off. Then she stopped, took one hand to fuss with her blond hair, which had come undone in the midst of battle, and with the other reached into her apron pocket, took out something small and began to shoot at the rooster as he ran crazily away. Almost all of the scene flashed before Fudge's eyes like the pictures he saw in the stereoptican he looked at in the front room of the big house, but the detail of what Ma'am held in her hand lodged in Fudge's mind while everything was forgotten. Ma'am looked like she was playing thumb-and-finger guns, but the rooster was running from the noise in her hand.

When she finally returned, Fudge was still beside Mr. Richards as he squatted down by the boy, blood running all over both of them, and both still immobile at the scene they had just witnessed. "Cater, can't you see the boy is hurt, maybe blind. And I could have killed the monster, but then what would we do without a rooster?" Even in his pain and fright, the thought flashed through Fudge's mind that the bird wasn't going to be in any shape to help her much for a while. Ma'am kept on talking without stopping for breath, "and he may have blinded Fudge," as she wrenched him from inside Mr. Richards' protective arm and marched into the house, still talking. "You see . . . see . . . don't you, what life is like. I'm lonesome and I'm scared and I just hate you, Cater, and I'm going to town because Fudge needs to real bad and . . . and you get me some more ammunition for the little gun because I shot it all up . . . and yes, some for the rifle, for the shotgun . . . and some for your pistolas too . . . and make sure the men's guns have plenty . . . 'cause I'm going to town and all of you will need every cartridge you can get your hands on while I'm gone. Yes, I know I've got this fine woodboard house, and trees growing and flowers too, and a windmill and I even got a Sears catalog to order the rest of the things I need, but now I want a little of what I want, not what I got, and I'm going to town and that's that!"

Of all the words Ma'am had spoken, only one word, ammunition, stuck in Fudge's feverish mind the next few days and nothing else of what Ma'am had said. She was talking big people's talk and he didn't understand much of anything he overheard that wasn't said directly to him. The rooster's spurs had indeed come almost too close to the little boy's right eye. Ma'am had washed his face, gently but over and over. She poured something on the rag which made his cheek burn, but not nearly as much as when she covered up his left eye too and began to push the skin under his right eye. Then he felt every prick of the needle as she sewed the skin in place. Fudge knew without being told what she was doing. Not more than a few months ago, he watched her do the same thing to one of Buck's horses. Buck had come to the back door of the house, called "Ma'am, Ma'am? Could you come to the corral and look at Jack? Mr. Richards says I was to ast you first before I put a bullet in 'im. Jack's cut hisself awful bad, Ma'am." Ma'am put down the Sears and Roebuck catalog, which was the other book Fudge read from, and went to see to Jack, taking with her the sewing basket and talking as she went out the back door, "Oh yes, I'll come, Buck, and sew up your horse, Buck, that has a man's name while you, Buck, have a horse's name." And sew she did, a great gaping tear on Jack's shoulder.

Ma'am said stuff all the time that didn't make any sense, but the hands seemed to think a lot of it was funny and a lot of it didn't make any sense to them either, so they said in the bunkhouse when Fudge asked for explanations.

Now, Fudge stayed as still as Jack when Ma'am stitched up the big horse. After the woman sewed up Fudge's cheek, she made him swallow something bitter. Then he went to sleep, and when he woke up, his face was throbbing and burning and he dreamed between the waking and hurting about guns and bullets, roosters, rattlers, scorpions, and phantoms with no names to call them and Ma'am taking something from her pocket that made a rooster get up and run.

Ma'am woke Fudge up when he didn't want to wake up and spooned warm liquid down him. He tried to swallow it, but most of it ran down his chin. Fever raged along with the infection and swelling on the right side of his face. His daddy and Buck, Rowdy, Skeeter, Fuzz and all the rest drifted dimly above him from time to time. Ma'am he knew by cool touch and her singing "Shall we gather at the river that flows by the throne of God."

Fudge had no idea how long he'd been coming and going from shadow to light mainly because of what Ma'am made him swallow, but one morning before daylight, he knew that he was waking up all the way. Pain like a thousand sharp knives was in his eye. He felt gently near the spot where the rooster got him and the skin was fat and puffy and he couldn't see at all on the right side of him. He lay awhile looking around out of the left eye. Shapes became objects in those moments just before dawn, and he recognized parts of his own body, then the bed and the covers of quilts, a chest of wood at the end of the bed, the slop jar, a chair with rockers on it and something shiny on the wall along with pictures of some people. Fudge was drawn to the shiny thing. He had seen items like those in the room before in other places in the house or bunkhouse, but never anything so bright and getting brighter as the sun was on the verge of rising. Fudge got up quietly and battled the pain in his face and eye. It was only a few steps to the shining on the wall, but when he got there, he was below the framed light, and his whole head throbbed with every beat of his heart. Seeing the chair as a solution, although a moving one, Fudge quietly moved the piece underneath the wall and climbed up. After he steadied the swaying motion, Fudge peered into a mirror and saw reflected back a brown face, black hair and one blue eye. The other he guessed was buried in the folds and puffs of blue-brown skin on the right side of his face. The reflection was not a sight to make a body feel all right about itself, especially if the body had never known that such an apparatus as a mirror existed in the world. Since the face heretofore had nothing with which to compare itself, however, the shock was not as bad as it might have been. And after Fudge had taken the measure of himself, both face and upper body, and after his heart had quieted some and along with it his face, the boy caught the glimpse of something behind him hanging on the right side of his bed. Draped over the high post was a holster and two guns, pistolas! The guns were smaller than the ones Old Manuel and the cowboys carried.

Fudge got down out of the chair and replaced it. Then he climbed back in bed and stood up beside the belt full of ammunition with the double holsters. Then he took out one of the guns, but only one, and without a minute's hesitation went back to the rocking chair, replaced it in front of the mirror, all the while holding the gun in his right hand. Then he climbed up on the swaying chair and, between coming closer and farther away, looked at himself as he held the gun in the front of him. Then he heard Ma'am coming.

By the time Ma'am entered the door, everything was exactly where she'd left it the night before except that the rocking chair was moving a little and Fudge was awake. "Why, Fudge, you're awake and you've even been up to the rocking chair. How do you feel?" and by the time she said it, the woman was touching and probing Fudge's distended cheek. "It does look better this morning, and I'll just bet in a few more days you can maybe even see. I'll get the stitches out. Oh, I hope you can see as good as new," but she didn't dwell on the words and went right on chatting about how some of the men were coming in from near and far . . . would be at Crosswinds for a week or more . . . were bringing a new bull, one without horns . . . talk, talk, talk . . . new kind of cattle soon . . . folks using some kind of wire they called bob war, which was really barbed wire, to fence places so they wouldn't have to ride so far. Manuel came by and brought her some plants from the border country called Spanish Dagger to put with the Prickly Pear Cactus and the thorny Ocotillo called Devil's Whip. She laughed shrilly, not at all like Ma'am, and finished with, "Everything goes armed here, Fudge. Even the rooster and the plants. Now the fences got points, spurs and thorns." Then she said some more things and added right before she left the room that they'd be going to town for sure in just a few days, at the most.

Fudge had never heard Ma'am talk so much. It amounted to jabbering, like they said Manuel did. But Fudge liked Manuel's jabbering. He did not like Ma'am's. Maybe it was because he did not understand much of anything she said. She even told him once he was like the little slate she used to teach him letters and figures. He was just being written on. Then everything was erased and something new put on it. All he had to do, she said, was let himself be written on. Ma'am was jabbering again when she said those words. He knew it wasn't supposed to make sense.

After Ma'am left, Fudge knew he wasn't going to be a slate to be written on any longer. He was going to do something, something good, something right, something that would make the whole ranch proud of him, especially Ma'am. Every man on the place including Mr. Richards and Ma'am told him all the time they were proud of him. "Fudge," they'd say at roundup, "I'm proud you brought me the iron." Or, "I'd be proud if you'd hand me a dipper of water." Or, "Stand up there proud, Fudge." Well, he was fixing to make them all prouder because he was going to learn to use two guns and he was going to do it in private and surprise them all. He didn't know if the secret part would make them proud, but they'd forget it just as soon as they saw what he could do. He knew if he could shoot the guns, then everything would come right for Ma'am and everyone else.

Then Fudge heard the rooster crow and it sent a shiver through him.

Once a thing is decided on, sometimes life just helps out. Fudge thought such a thought during the next few days after he made the decision to actively become a two-gun man. The men did gather from all directions. For a while every time Fudge looked for Ma'am, he found her standing on the perimeters of the ranch, one hand on her waist and one hand shading her eyes against the sun looking for something or someone. She counted everyone who came and spoke with sincere concern about the yellow-haired boy, Pete, or the black man, Mose, who hadn't shown up yet. Two men, she said, lived with their families on places nearer the border. She hoped they would bring their folks, but they didn't. Seldom had he seen them all together at one time even at roundup, but now they came in to Crosswinds by twos and threes and sometimes alone. Their coming had something to do with the new bull and bob war and stringing it out and something to do with getting ready for trouble ahead. As the men came in, they were doing a lot of talking. Some were in the bunkhouse and some camped close by, but all came to Ma'am's table in the backyard to eat in two shifts of ten. Ma'am was busy laughing, cooking and having Fudge tote and fetch for her the things she needed in the house, but she wouldn't let him go back to his place in the bunkhouse. Somebody else was in his bed anyhow, and anyhow, he had business in the house in front of the mirror, anyhow. That's the way Fudge looked at it. The men paid little attention to Fudge, not even his daddy. Old Manuel rolled in and at the sight of him the men cheered, and the man stood up, drew back on the reins of the mules, threw back his head and hollered "Ay-yi-yi-yi-yi" at the top of his lungs. Fudge had never seen the peddler act in such a way before. Everybody was sure glad to see everybody else, probably. However they were behaving left Fudge time to do what he had to do.

Three times a day, before daylight, in the afternoon and after dark, Fudge went upstairs, took off his leather sandals, climbed up on the bed and got a pistola out of the holster, moved the rocking chair in front of the mirror and, swaying back and forth, put his finger on the trigger and aimed. "Bang, bang," he whispered. Then he would perform the ritual backward and scoot for downstairs. Nobody missed him even once.

After two days of practice, Fudge grew tired of what he was doing upstairs. Nothing was coming of it anyway. It was, he thought, time to make a bold move. Since nobody paid any attention to him at all, morning, noon or night, because they were all wrapped up in wire and the stuff Manuel had in the wagon, Fudge grew bolder. He was going to take the mirror and the guns outside. That's what he would do—in the dark, of course, but by all means, outside. Outside, that's where guns belonged and that's where Fudge belonged too.

The lay of the ranch consisted of a group of buildings with the house in the center front; then miles and miles of open country in every direction. Fudge studied the layout from the inside out and realized that the place was perfect for his plan. If you were riding in from the south, that's what a person saw first, the house. A big corral and smaller pens, a barn, garden plot, chicken yard, home of El Gallo and henhouse where the *gallinas* laid their eggs, were behind the big house and fanned out on either side. The outhouse was beyond the chicken yard, and as he knew well, a person had to go around or through the chicken yard to get to it. The outhouse was really for Ma'am. He couldn't tell that anybody else made much use of it. And that, Fudge knew, was the perfect place to take the guns and the mirror.

After dark, but before the men turned in, they gathered around a big fire pit drinking coffee, told wild tales and made Ma'am laugh. "Angus, why didn't you bring Margaret Nell and the girls? We could have done some sewing or something," Ma'am was saying to one of the men. He answered, "Now, Mrs. Richards, I took her to a funeral in town not two years ago." From the sound of it Fudge knew Angus had cracked a funny by the way they all laughed, but he knew too that there was an uneasiness, a tension, in everyone, but he didn't have time to understand why. He was strung tighter than a wire himself.

It was during the campfire time that the gunman made his move. Fudge scooted for the house. On the way he heard the chickens squawking softly in the henhouse, knew the rooster was likewise settled in. Everything was bedding down, and he could tell not by the silence but by the noises everything made—the horses snuffling and stomping, the night birds asking, the chirping of crickets, the scratching of mice, even the soft meowing of Ma'am's beloved and pampered cat, as if they were all signaling their presence to each other in the dark. The noises were as comforting to Fudge at night as many of them were terrifying by day.

The child entered the dark house by the front door since everyone else was out back. He lighted no lamps, but rather felt his way upstairs. Fudge went immediately to the bed, climbed up, but this time he took not just one gun but removed the entire belt holding the cartridges, holsters and guns. The items were much heavier than Fudge had imagined, and try as he did, the boy couldn't carry the load without dragging the guns on the ground. When he got to the stairs, he moved with the confidence of one who knows he is not being watched and who is so scared that caution is thrown to the winds. He forged ahead and dragged the weapons behind him, bouncing them down the stairs. The term "gunslinger" took on new dimensions under Fudge's command. He continued the dragging procedure out the front door and down the porch steps, past the corral, the barn, the chicken yard and finally behind the outhouse. His destination reached with nothing but open land ahead, Fudge collapsed in a terrified heap behind the building at the same time he wet his pants. It was a problem he had not counted on when he thought he had calculated every other single detail. Fudge cried then. He may as well, he concluded, since he'd done everything else wrong. In the midst of the tears it dawned on him that he had forgotten to bring the mirror.

After a few minutes of crying, Fudge realized that what he'd come to do was ruined, his first practice with two guns ruined. Nobody heard anything at all, except for the creatures at Crosswinds. The cat heard the dragging in the dirt and thought it might be mice. One of the horses nickered to another to ask whether or not to nicker again. The chickens were always alert for whatever might invade the henhouse and clucking was coming close to squawking.

Fudge got up at the noises which he himself had caused, but he didn't know that. He started to get gathered up and start back for the house, but listening. His heart was beginning to pound again. Talk at the campfire stopped and one of the men said, "What's that?" Another said, "Nothing but the horses moving, I think. Buck, you're mighty jumpy." The group returned to their talk, but with one ear to the world outside their safe circle.

Fudge had just turned the corner from behind the outhouse when he saw it, saw something. Something was moving through the chicken yard. The boy felt his cheek sting and his eye begin to burn at the same instant he guessed at what the shape was. It might be El Gallo and making straight for him, he reasoned. Fudge returned to his hiding place behind the outhouse dragging the guns with him. At the same instant he knew that he was not hidden from the monster which, no doubt, was coming around the corner any minute. What to do? He would get in the outhouse. That was it! But too late. The phantom form rounded one corner just as Fudge went around the other.

Quicker than greased lightning, the child dropped the gun belt on the ground and pulled one of the guns free. While in the very act of saying bang, bang, his finger went to the trigger and pulled. Ma'am's calico cat which had come to hunt for mice yowled. Whatever Fudge had done was not stopping the creature. He closed his eyes and pulled the trigger again. Then again and again aiming high and low, deep and wide, and in whatever direction the gun, with a will of its own, wanted to fire.

While Fudge was putting down one gun and pulling out the other, the men around the fire were running toward the noise in an instant. Buck grabbed the rifle, went down on his belly, slid through the chicken yard and opened fire on the henhouse. Not knowing the source of the gunfire, but only the direction, other cowboys pulled guns and fired too. Like good men and true, their guns were aimed mostly in the air until they divined the source and shape of the trouble. Fudge just kept pulling the trigger on the other gun until it clicked as Fudge continued to say, "bang, bang."

Horses were running in the corral. The force of their weight knocked down one rail and the whole bunch broke for Mexico. The new bull in the barn began to bellow. He had been hit. The chickens moved from their roosts and fell squawking as they were shot. Glass shattered.

No one knew how long the battle raged before someone realized that only the cowboys of Crosswinds ranch were doing the shooting. Fudge's daddy was the first one who said, "Hey, hold up. Hey!" Buck was next: "Hold off. Stop. Darrell, is that you? You okay?" Fudge's daddy yelled, "Yeah. I'm okay." With the action over, the other men came up from behind troughs and from behind buildings. Before anybody had time to determine what had happened, Ma'am screamed, "Oh my Lord! Where is Fudge?" And with her own rifle spent in her hands, she ran toward the outhouse.

Finding out where Fudge was and just what had happened took some time, angry words, a whipping with the back of Darrell's hand, more tears, hysterics from Ma'am and decisions about Fudge's future which included a horse, boots and a trip to town. Gathering back the horses, digging bullets out of the bull, mending the corral, scalding dead chickens for plucking and cooking, repairing Manuel's wagon, cleaning the chicken yard off of Buck, ordering more glass for the house windows and scraping what was left of the cat off the outhouse wall took even more time.

Only one issue was clear and that was that Fudge was not going to pursue a career as a two-gun man. His daddy started him on a big old shotgun which knocked him down every time he fired it. "When the gun don't knock you down no more, Fudge, then Ma'am says you can get on with the rifle, and then the pistola business," his daddy said grimly. "And Mrs. Richards says we ain't gonna call you Fudge no more. We're gonna call you by your right name, which is Darrell Lee Barclay. But we'll call you Lee for short."

Lee's daddy was good to his word, every last word. And Old Manuel and the rooster in the chicken yard who lost not a feather heard it all.

News travels slowly, not fast, in the vast expanses of the West. An event might be translated, rearranged and filtered through the eyes and minds of many. So it was with the reputation of Lee Barclay, alias Fudge.

The law travels slowly in the West too. When Marshal Barclay was sworn in as one of the first along the Rio Grande border, he wore two guns and carried a rifle in the boot of his saddle, plain for all to see. As to his appearance, a deep scar on his right cheek close to his eye was visible. Any who cared to look closely noticed the clear blue eyes, the dark hair under a broad-brimmed Mexican-style hat which was secured with a leather string, and the bronzed skin from more than just a lifetime in the sun. For twenty years, the man dispensed justice fairly. *Mexicano y Tejano* claimed him, and called him friend. After all, they said, he carries two guns, one for each side of the border.

A newspaper reporter roaming the border country collecting fabulous stories to send back East once asked the marshal where he learned to shoot two guns.

"From a woman," the marshal replied without the slightest trace of a smile. The newspaperman responded with a sarcastic "Yeah, yeah, I'll bet," as he folded up his notebook and put it in his shirt pocket. Some stories were too preposterous to repeat, even for a newspaperman.

Reunion

LENORE CARROLL

NOTES TO TOURISTS.—The uniform railroad fare in the Territory averages ten cents per mile. Stage routes run all through
the mountains, fare from ten to twenty cents per mile. The
uniform rate of board is four dollars per day, and almost
every-where can be found excellent living; the nicest of beef
steak, bread and biscuit. In many of the mountain resorts
plenty of good fishing can be found, and delicate trout are
common viands of the hotel tables. The best season of the
year for a visit to Colorado is in July and August. As then
the snow has nearly disappeared from the mountains, and all
the beautiful parks and valleys are easily approachable.
—WILLIAMS, *The Pacific Tourist and
guide across the continent,* 1878

KATE'S KNEES ACHED when she stepped down out of the
stagecoach. The slope of the mountain tipped the seats

forward and she had been standing on the brake, it seemed, since Leadville. The road dust penetrated all the layers of fabric, all the folds of her skin. She felt pounded sore from days of riding, not like the old days when they left town on a moment's notice and never counted the effort. At least the air was cool here in Glenwood Springs and the high-altitude sun bright and the clouds soft.

She looked down the main street from the hotel to the steaming hot springs trickling into the foaming Colorado River. She would have to take the ferry across the river for a hot soak, get the stiffness out. She was only thirty-five, but she felt time's touch in the joints of her sturdy hands, and while her homely Hungarian face was still smooth, silver hairs twined in the knot on top of her head.

Later, she lay immersed in a concrete tub, the chemical-smelling water steaming. The sound of running water made her feel she were floating in a warm river. Was this what an unborn child felt floating in the sac of the womb, what her child had felt? Was this some internal refuge in the Earth, where she could draw strength?

She couldn't face him yet.

He had sent for her once again. The letter came the day they were breaking horses, when she heard the men's cries from the corral, and the dust hung thick in the air around the ranch house kitchen. She sat at the table in her room, the shade pulled against the heat, and held the letter, written in his perfect hand, for a long time, waiting for her heart to slow its ricochet around her chest. She'd have sworn her feeling for him was as dried and forgotten as a flower pressed in a book, but the envelope trembled in her hand. Memories came back, as real as the Arizona heat. She propped the envelope on her dresser and left it for four days.

When she read it, she packed and got on a train, then rode the stages over the mountains. She always came when he asked.

— — — —

"Where may I find Mr. Holliday?" she asked the desk clerk.

She knew the man saw a stout, middle-aged woman, probably never pretty, the week's travel in her face. He checked her signature on the register.

"Are you a friend of his?" asked the clerk.

"He sent word he wanted to see me," she answered. "If you'll tell him I'm here."

She waited in her room. Her traveling outfit went to be cleaned and she changed into fresh clothes. She sat with her feet up and watched out the tall, narrow window as a late afternoon shower moved down the mountain through the sun, and she felt the breeze stir the curtains. Fragments from the old days came back—the wild times. Drinking. His gambling. Loving. Scarred-over places she had ignored for years ached.

Did her arms remember his delicate touch or only the bruises? Did her eyes swell shut or did they remember his lips tasting her tears? Could she feel his fevered body in her arms? Did her blood race inside skin that burned from caresses, skin that took the print of his rage? Did the hate he spoke bruise the heart inside sore ribs?

Eventually, a man knocked and asked would she please to follow.

She hesitated outside the door, afraid to look at the once-familiar face, feel something give way inside, launch herself again into his sphere.

"You look mighty bad, Doc," she said. The servant, who seemed to be something between a valet and a nurse, pushed a chair near the bed where the wasted man with TB lay propped on pillows. She sat and took his white hand. She wanted his scent, individual, like his voice, but the stuffy sickroom smell was all she could catch.

"It was good of you to come," he said. His blue eyes were too bright. Morphine? The spotless nightshirt was buttoned. His thin, graying hair had been brushed straight back, obviously by someone else. His mustache needed trimming. Someone had cut his nails, but not filed them smooth.

"I always came," she said.

"But it has been a long time. I wasn't sure."

The cough she remembered took him and he pulled his hand away from hers to hold a blue handkerchief to his mouth. It came away streaked with red. She took a glass of water from the table and held his head while he drank a little. It made her shaky to touch him, remember the soft hair, the fine skull beneath, the warm flesh she met.

"Why now?" she asked. He always had such nice manners, like all Southern men, when they chose, and she was always too abrupt.

"I've been dying for years," he said with a glint of humor. "This time I think I shall succeed."

"You're too mean." She tried to sound jolly but failed.

"You're the one who's tough. You look mighty fat and sassy," he countered. "What are you doing these days?"

She thought of her days cooking for the ranch hands. That wouldn't sound good enough. "Last time I got a stake, I bought a cattle ranch instead of another whorehouse. I thought the cows would be smarter than the girls."

"Are they?"

"No, but they make me a living." It was like walking a razor to talk as though nothing were the matter.

"You survive, Kate." He made it a benediction.

She bowed her head. A headache drummed behind her eyes. She never cried in front of him, not when he beat her, swore at her, forced her to lie for him. She never gave him the satisfaction.

"I treated you badly," he whispered.

"What's a few broken ribs between friends?" she said, false and hearty.

"I wanted to say I was sorry, before I'm gone."

"I didn't have to come here for that. I knew you were sorry. Afterward."

"I could have sent another letter, I suppose."

"You were always a great one for letters."

The writing desk in his room held only medicine bottles and glass tumblers. Brush and comb on the dresser, handkerchiefs and water glass on the nightstand. Where were the sheets of spidery copperplate, finger-smudged rough drafts and flawless fair copies, that she remembered?

"Do you still write to your cousin?" she asked.

"She died."

"I'm sorry. Her prayers probably kept you alive all these years." And Kate was sorry she said that.

His hands shook and he coughed again. After the spasm passed, he closed his eyes. She waited for him to look at her again so she could apologize for what she said, but he slept, exhausted.

She got up and turned to the manservant who stood near the door. "I want to talk to him again."

The man shook his head.

She grabbed his arm above the elbow and steered him into the hall.

"I have traveled a week to get here." She spoke softly, but with force. "Don't shake your head at me."

The man looked mulish.

"How does he pay you?" she asked.

"I won't tell you."

"He doesn't pay you, is that it?"

The man looked startled.

"How long are you going to look after him? What do you live on?"

"People in town pay his bill, pay me a little. Sometimes."

"Is he alert when he is awake?"

"Pretty much."

"He doped up to talk to me."

The man shrugged.

"I want to talk to him again." She chewed her thumb a moment. "I'm going to the dining room for supper, then I will be in my room. If he wakes up within a few hours, fetch me."

The man's eyebrows went up.

She ignored him. "Tomorrow I will be available after ten." She thought again. "If I don't see him within twenty-four hours, I'll assume he died and hire an undertaker. Does a doctor see him?"

The man said yes.

"I want to talk to him, too." She studied the servant, who looked too stubborn to take orders from her. "If you want to get paid, you'll do as I say."

She walked down the steps to the lobby, across the wide plank floor and into the dining room, golden in lamplight as summer night settled in.

"He came for the vapors," said the banker. "One-way ticket. And the sulfur ate what was left of his lungs." The banker's watch fob gleamed against his waistcoat. "He is well liked. He tried to practice dentistry at first, but he was too ill to stand for hours. Don't know how he drank all night and kept a clear head for cards."

He could always keep a clear head, she thought, and remember the cards.

"Of course, everyone expected him to use his sidearm, but as far as I know he never drew it."

Only if some yahoo challenged his honor. Only if he intended to kill. Kate told the banker what she wanted. "If he needs more, let me know. Telegraph. I want a complete accounting when it's over. Tell him you took up a collection."

She signed some papers and walked back to the hotel.

Glenwood Springs looked prosperous. New buildings lined the streets that tilted down the mountainside, houses with gingerbread and fences, stores with wide windows. She noted the number of saloons and wondered how many miners' silver dollars Doc had won playing cards. He'd chosen a beautiful place to die. She looked up from the storefronts and drank in the valley of the Colorado, the

green and golden mountains, perfect, picturesque—ready
for the stereopticon.

"I fell asleep," he said. He had again been brushed and
propped up. She sat beside the bed.

"Don't overdo," she said, and felt stupid.

"I wanted to beg your forgiveness," he said.

"You have it."

"I saw a priest."

"Cousin Mattie's deathbed request?"

"Don't mock me."

"I hated her," Kate said. She pressed her palms into the
bunched fabric over her heavy thighs. "You would write to
her—long letters. Educated letters. She wrote you back.
We'd stay together for a while, high times. You were reckless because you knew you were dying. I was wild because
I didn't have anything more to lose. Men liked that. You'd
take me down, and when you were satisfied, you'd knock
me around and throw me out."

"How many times?"

"Ten? A dozen? I don't remember. I'd leave. Then you'd
take sick and write to me. I just always came back."

"Forgive me."

"I was the same person I'd been the day before you
beat me. You knew what I was when we started together."

"When was that?"

"Fort Griffin, maybe. Texas, then Kansas? I liked you
because you were clean and you treated me nice, at first.
My husband was a dentist, too, in Atlanta."

"He died."

"And my little boy."

"Poor Kate."

"Nobody pities me."

"Of course." His bloodless hands plucked at the blanket. Only his eyes were alive. "We had some times, didn't
we?"

"Always."

She must say it, make him hear it before he faded away again. "It took me all these years before I understood it all. Why we came together. Why you hated me, treated me bad. Why I always came back."

"I couldn't help it."

"I thought about it a lot, nursing split lips and black eyes. One time I had headaches for a month. Then I remembered it always happened after one of her letters. Your cousin Mattie, your first cousin who became Sister Melanie in the convent. I bet they wouldn't let you get married."

He started and one waxen hand lifted from the blanket for a moment. "No!"

"You got in some trouble, and came West. She went into the convent in Savannah. But she was the one you loved and she was pure, and when you couldn't have her, you took the lowest, dirtiest, wildest woman you could find."

The pale hand trembled and he frowned. "No," he said. "I loved you."

"Like a dog." She rubbed her thick nose with a linen handkerchief. "You wanted her and couldn't have her, so you took me and we did the wild things. And you hated yourself and you hated me. Because I loved that wicked part of you."

His delicate hand scratched the blanket. "Forgive me," he said again. "Kate." His voice faded to dry husks whispering.

"Yes." She leaned closer. She smelled death on him.

"I had to see you one more time."

And finally, after all those years, stinging like a slap, sharp as cheap whiskey, came her tears.

Spring Comes to the Widow

JOHN D. NESBITT

Sam Fontaine was riding south when he found the death camp. The breeze was blowing north from a small stand of junipers, and he caught his first whiff nearly a quarter of a mile away.

He had ridden north all spring and summer, eating dust and fighting flies, to deliver a trail herd in Montana. When the boss paid them off, Sam bought his favorite horse out of the remuda before the string was sold. Rather than go on a spree with the boys, Sam turned the good horse Sandy straight back south and rode alone, a season's wages in his pocket, a lightness in his heart, and a song on his lips.

The lightness and the song ended when he smelled death. It was never a good smell, but if a fellow saw what it was before he smelled it, things went a little easier. When the smell came first, the thing to do was to give it a wide flank, come at it upwind, and get the story before moving on.

Sam was nearly even with the trees when he heard a cry, the small cry of a small thing, like a lamb, but it wasn't a lamb. It was a baby. He touched his spurs to Sandy and got to the trees on a lope.

Four buzzards lifted from the camp as Sandy settled to a halt and Sam slid from the saddle, fighting the heaves that pounded in his stomach. He yanked on the reins to keep the horse from backstepping, and then he looked at the camp.

It was a camp of Mexican folk who had come to the end of their luck. Two oxen slumped dead in the harness of a wooden-wheeled cart. Next to a mounded grave with a wooden cross lay the body of a man with its mouth open. Sam looked away. The baby's cry came again from the off side of the cart, where the last of the morning shade still lingered. Tugging on the reins, he stepped around the end of the cart. There was a young woman sitting blank-eyed against the wheel, rocking the baby vacantly. She didn't seem to have the strength or the focus to care for the baby beyond that automatic movement.

Sam knelt by the woman. "*¿Qué pasó?*" he asked. What happened?

She licked her lips. "*Muertos. Todos muertos.*" Dead. All dead.

Sam nodded. "*Sí. Hombre muerto. Vacas muertas. ¿Qué pasó?*" Yes. Dead man. Dead cows. What happened?

The woman rolled her eyes. "*Agua.*" Water.

"*¿Quiere agua?*" You want water?

"*No. No agua. Agua mala.*" No. No water. Bad water.

"*¿Mala?*" Bad?

"*Veneno.*" Poison.

"*¿Quiere agua? ¿Agua buena, fresca?*" Do you want water? Good water? Fresh?

The woman nodded. Sam unslung one of his canteens

and held it to her lips. She drank and nodded again. *"Gracias."*

He dribbled a little water on the baby's mouth, but the baby just sputtered and coughed and cried. Sam settled onto his heels, still squatting, and asked again what had happened.

The woman spoke rapidly in a voice somewhere between crying and heavy sighing, a voice full of agony and sadness, a voice that seemed far too old for a young mother. From her rambling, Sam pieced together the story. They had all drunk from a poisoned spring, all but the baby. Her husband and son had died first, and then her brother-in-law, who presumably had lived long enough to bury the other two in a common grave. The woman seemed certain that she, too, was going to die.

Sam offered her more water and she took it, but it oozed out of her mouth and down her chin, sprinkling a few drops on the baby. She moved her mouth as if trying to speak, but no words came. Relaxing her hold on the baby to let it lie on her lap, she closed her eyes and leaned her head back against the hub of the wheel. She was on the way out, he could see that. He patted her hand and said the only thing he could think of, *"Vaya con Dios."* God be with you. The hand fluttered, and that was it.

In less than an hour, Sam had buried the brother-in-law, cut loose the oxen, and with Sandy straining, dragged the dead animals a hundred yards distant. All the while, the baby cried. When Sam returned to the cart, where he had stretched the woman out in the shade, the baby had crawled onto the mother's abdomen and was kneading at the dead left breast. That was the hardest moment, and it stayed with him through the burying, the mumbled words to God and the dead mother, and the long ride through daylight and darkness until he reached the town of Socorro.

— — — — —

La señora Ramos ground the dry oatmeal to a finer grain in her stone *metate* before cooking it for the baby. Fontaine sat at the table by candlelight, rolling a cigarette and then smoking it as the woman went about her work. When the gruel was cooked, she set it aside to cool, then went about the task of changing the baby's diapers. Sam looked away, studying a crucifix that seemed to move on the wall as the candle flickered.

La señora Ramos spoke good English. "I cannot keep this baby, you know, not forever," she said as she spooned mush into the infant. She looked at Sam, and he nodded. "When I was younger and my house was full of children, I never counted them. Everybody's children went to everybody's house. What was one more? I had eight myself. And four dead ones." She crossed herself. Then she resumed feeding the baby. "But my children are gone now, to their own families, and I am an old widow. I have to wash clothes and clean houses. The time is past for me." She shook her head and then smiled as she looked into the baby's eyes.

Sam took out the makings and rolled another cigarette. He lit it with the candle and blew out a cloud of smoke. "What do you think we should do? Could we ask around and maybe find a home for it?"

She shrugged. "We could."

"You don't seem to like that idea."

"There are two problems. A family might take the baby in a sense of obligation. Or a family could get jealous who did not get the baby."

"Uh-huh." Fontaine ashed his cigarette in his palm and rubbed the ashes into his pant leg. "You must have another idea."

She raised her eyebrows. "We could offer the baby through the Church."

"What's the problem there?"

"There is a couple, the Reyes, who have money but no children."

"And you wouldn't want them to get the baby."

"I would not prefer it."

Sam looked at the ceiling and then back at the woman. He shook his head. "What do we do, then?"

"You could keep the baby. You found the baby and saved its life. It would not be wrong. Perhaps it is God's gift to you."

Sam nodded. The thought of keeping it had occurred to him as he had cradled the baby in his right arm on the long ride into Socorro. "I can think on it," he said. "But I don't know how I could take care of it. I've got to work, too."

La señora Ramos had apparently been doing some thinking herself. "Get yourself a young widow," she said.

Having told the señora he would study on it, and having gotten her to agree to keep the baby for a week, Sam rode to Albuquerque with no more definite plan than to study on it.

Always before, when he had thought about marriage, Sam Fontaine had imagined a blue-eyed girl with light-colored hair, an innocent, untouched girl who, through his guidance, would step into adult life. There would be marriage and then children.

Now, life presented a different possible order. He had a child if he wanted it. The memory of the baby pushing against the dead mother's breast, together with the memory of it squirming against his own body as he cradled it on horseback, gave rise to a strong feeling he could not brush aside. Yes, he had a child if he wanted it, and he could find a marriage to match.

There was plenty for Sam to study in Albuquerque. He saw the blue-eyed girls, apparently untouched, and he saw their dark-eyed, dark-haired counterparts. He saw young mothers with their children, older mothers with older children, women without children but with the look of motherhood about them. As he studied, the girls moved him less and less, while the women interested him more and more. He did not covet these women, but in the mature presence of a woman who had had a child, there was a definite power or pull.

It was absurd to think of shopping for a woman as a man might look for a cow pony or a draft horse, but he did need to form a clear idea of what he was looking for. The señora, in her practical wisdom, had started him thinking that way. A young widow would not be rushed from girl-hood into motherhood. She would have matured some, and she might already have a child or two. At any rate she would have her own baggage, as Sam would have his. There would be an equality of sorts. And a young widow, Sam thought for the first time, with a widening smile, would be fit to have more. That would be a nice mix, he thought—mine, hers, and ours.

The young widow began to take on a definite image. She was a woman, not a girl—a young mother with one or possibly two at her side. She had dark eyes, dark hair, and skin the color of dark honey. Working backward, from child to marriage, had defined that for him—the baby should be raised in the language and customs of its mother.

"*Señora,*" he said as he laid his hat on the table, "I have decided to keep the baby." Then he winked. "But I have one question."

"Yes?"

"Is it a boy or a girl?"

La señora Ramos smiled. "He's a little boy. And we don't know his name, or whether he's been baptized, or—"

"Hold on," Sam interjected. "I've got to find the young widow first, and then we'll take care of the rest."

When he had sketched out the lines of his recent thinking, the señora nodded in agreement. "Well, we can look around," she said. "I know of one woman, in my town of Palomas."

"Down on the border?"

"Yes." At Sam's hesitation she added, "You could go take a look. You don't have to take the first one you see."

"It's a start," he said. Then, thinking, he asked, "What's the word for widow?"

"*Viuda.*"

"Beeyutha."

"That's close."

"Will she be dressed in black?"

"I think he has more than one year dead."

"How do you say, 'What does that mean?'"

"You'll need that one. *¿Qué quiere decir?*"

He practiced it a few times.

"And how do you say 'it doesn't matter'?"

"*No le hace.*"

"Nolayossay."

"That's close. What doesn't matter?"

"Whether it was a boy or a girl. And there'll be other things." He thought for another minute and then said, "I think I'd feel funny ridin' down there and knockin' on her door."

"It would be her father's door. She lives at his house."

"All the more reason. Hmmm. Does she have children?"

"I think she has one girl."

"Do you think you could get her to come here for a visit? Do you know her that well?"

"I barely know her, but I know her family. I can try."

The young widow María and the niña Ramona came to Socorro for a stay. Mother and daughter were dark, darker than the niño (who still went by the name of Niño) or his late mother, darker than the dark honey of Sam's imagination. Not that the darkness mattered—*no le hace*—but he had to adjust the qualifications he had projected. He admired the woman's fine features and shapely body, but more than that, he felt readily comfortable with her presence. She seemed to take a liking to him—probably would not have come if she had not been prepared to.

María was twenty-one and Sam was twenty-eight.

Ramona was three and Niño was not yet a year old, the women agreed. María took a mother's interest in Niño, and Sam was instantly fond of Ramona, who, in turn, took a liking to both Sam and Sandy, as well as a natural interest in the baby. It looked to Sam as if everything was going to fit together.

After a month of round-robin acquaintance, Sam asked María to marry him, and she said *"Sí."*

They did not marry in the church or from her father's house, but with the justice of the peace in Socorro. Theirs was not a boisterous celebration, and María seemed pleased. That night, when she took him to her, she said, *"Te quiero mucho, Sem."*

He repeated the pledge in English. "I love you, María."

In the morning sunlight he sat on the edge of the bed and held her at arm's length, standing before him, his hands on her hips. It was a beautiful being he had joined himself with, this even-toned, full-bodied woman who in her presence meant togetherness and family. That was where it began, for them, the fitting together of a family, and now they could fill in with the daily confidences and agreements that had already begun to develop. He pulled her toward him and kissed her on the stomach. "My wife. *Mi mujer."*

She held his head against her, the fingers of her left hand in his hair, the palm of her right hand against his cheek. *"Mi hombre."*

As the cool weather set in, Sam looked around for work to help them through the winter. There wasn't much work, but he did find two horses to break and train for pleasure riding. He spent the afternoons at that, and so he brought in a few dollars in November.

One evening la señora Ramos came to visit. After the preliminaries she made it clear she had come with a purpose. She spoke in the pattern she had developed for speaking with María and Sam: first in Spanish, then backing up to repeat or clarify in English, as Sam's expressions made the need clear. And so she launched into this evening's business.

This was a beautiful thing, this life and this love between two people, the joining of a family, a full life for them all, a life of pride for Ramona and Roberto (as Niño had come to be called). Everybody could see it. But you know how people can be. Some people can have everything yet wish to have something that belonged to someone else. There was no need to tell names, but there was a couple in the town who thought that perhaps not enough care had been taken to discover Roberto's true family. These people thought perhaps Roberto's future had been determined too quickly, perhaps the matter needed reconsideration.

These people had spoken with the priest and with the judge, and it was hoped by this couple that Roberto might be placed with a family who had no interest in the matter, until a satisfactory inquiry could be made. It was thought that if Roberto proved to be indeed without a family, then he could be eligible for legal adoption, with lawyers and the court and all of that.

Sam and María sat side by side in their chairs, their hand grip growing tighter. But Roberto has a family, María said.

Yes, and nobody can deny that. But his place is not secure. It is clear that there are some people who want a baby enough to take it.

Sam and María looked at each other. He said, in broken Spanish, this is not a good town for us. There is not much work. I don't like to run, but this is not a good town for us.

I think you are right, resumed la señora Ramos. You do not have relatives here, or a business. You are my friends, and I do not like to see my friends leave, especially at my age, but I agree with you.

Sam took María's hand in both of his. We could go south, he said.

She shook her head, not violently, but to show there was no strain in that direction.

We could go north. To a place I saw on the cow trip. It is cold there, very cold in the winter.

At what distance does it lie? asked María.

In good weather, three weeks. In bad weather, who knows? Maybe not until spring.

Three weeks in good weather, said la señora Ramos. That seems to me to be a good place.

Sam looked at María. It is a good place, she said, even if it should be cold. What is it called?

Wyoming. On the other side of Colorado. Much wind and very cold. Nobody wants to go there. A good place.

They all laughed. It was seeming easier already.

Every night on the trip north, when they were bedded down in the wagon, María cried. Sometimes they made love when the children were asleep and sometimes they didn't, but every night she cried. Sam held her and hugged her and patted her, brushed the damp strands of hair from her face and kissed her. He came to understand that it was the distance from home, growing longer each day, that weighed on her. Even though her family seemed agreeable to letting her go from the very first, and even though she showed no strong desire to make a home near them, the separation was being felt sharply.

Sam wondered if it was anything else. Your friends?

No. My father and my mother.

Your country?

No. Just my parents.

Your brothers and your sisters?

Yes, them, too.

Sam took a skate on thin ice. Your dead husband?

No, no. My father and my mother.

"Te quiero mucho, María." I love you very much, María.

"Te quiero, Sem. Para siempre." I love you, Sam. Forever.

— — — — —

They rested a week in Denver and another four days in Cheyenne. It was an open winter so far, as folks said in Cheyenne. Trails were open north; trains were running east and west. There was plenty of time yet to get snowed in, but it was an open winter so far.

In mid-January the Fontaines filed on a quarter section of land, rolling plains country a few miles off the Platte. They rented a small house in town, a drafty clapboard shack that had been vacated by a Texas family who went back south for the weather. Sam and María patched cracks, kept a fire going in the sheet-iron stove, and waited for the thaw.

The family lived on deer meat all that winter. María, who'd been raised on tough beef, took to it fine, as did the children. Sam liked all food.

Will we be able to grow chiles here?

I think so. The summers are hot. They grow wheat. And I've seen apple trees.

This is good meat, but I will want to cook it with chiles.

We'll see. I think we can grow chiles.

María did not cry every night now, just once in a while. Things had come together again. For a while it had seemed as if they were four people, from different places, not living in any of them, speaking a mish-mash. Now it was seeming to flow together again, the ebb and flow of their common life, the melting of boundaries, the mingling of selves, the overflow and overlap of words. Sam could look back and hope that the worst was behind them, strung out in the cold trek north, left on the frozen plains, part of the waste-land between the place they left and the place they came to.

Spring came on slowly, starting in late March with the first green shoots of grass in the snowmelt, then freezing up solid again before the gradual teasing of warmer weather. In early May they took the wagon to their parcel, to camp out and get a view of things.

They set camp at a clump of chokecherry trees, where two draws came together. Sam and María spread a canvas for the children and then went to look at the greening branches.

A close look at the branches startled him. The branches were bristling with the furry green tips of leaves, and the smooth bark was freckled with white dots. The trees seemed to be bursting with life, eager for the new season.

"*Una fruta,*" he said. A fruit.

"*¿Buena?*" Good?

"*Sí. No muy dulce. Chica.*" Yes. Not very sweet. Small. He pressed his left thumbnail against the tip of the little finger. "*Así de grande.*" This big.

She nodded. "*Está bueno.*" That's good.

They walked, hand in hand, to a rise in the ground where they could see their land slope away to the north.

"*¿Te gusta?*" he asked. It was important that she like the place.

"*Sí, me gusta.*" Yes, I like it.

"*¿Te gusta casa aquí?*" You like the house here? He pointed down at the place where he thought to build a house.

"*Sí.*"

Still, that night, she cried again, after they made love in the wagon.

Maybe it's the wagon, he thought.

In the morning she was sick, and when she returned from beyond the chokecherry trees, he looked up from the fire he was fanning with his hat. "*¿Estás enferma?*" Are you sick?

She took his hand, and he stood up.

"*¿Qué pasa?*" What's going on?

She looked at the wagon, where the children still slept. "*Estoy embarazada.*"

He looked at her questioningly. *"¿Qué quiere decir?"* What does that mean?

She placed his hand on her stomach. *"Bebé. Voy a tener un bebé."* Child. I'm going to have a child

Sam looked at his wife through watery eyes. *"¿Niño?"* Then his joy faded as he saw she was crying. *"¿Qué pasa?"*

"I sorry," she said. "I lie."

Her speaking in English alarmed him. She was confessing a lie and was coming over halfway to tell him. "Lie? *¿Mentira? ¿No niño?"*

"Sí, niño," she said, using his word and smiling through her tears.

"¿Qué mentira?" What lie?

She looked downward. *"Yo no era viuda."* I wasn't a widow.

"¿No viuda, tú?" No widow, you?

"No, no viuda." No, no widow.

"¿No esposo, no hombre? ¿No hombre muerto?" No husband, no man? No dead man?

"No, no esposo. Nunca." No, no husband. Never.

Sam smiled at her and kissed her on the forehead. He knelt and kissed her on the stomach, then stood up and held her hands as he looked her in the eyes. *"No le hace. No importa."* It doesn't matter. It's not important.

"¿Está bien?" It's all right?

"Sí. Tú eres mi mujer. Te quiero." Yes. You are my wife. I love you.

"Yo te quiero a ti, Sem. Para siempre. ¿Está bien, yo no viuda?" I love you, Sam. Forever. It's all right, I'm no widow?

"Está bien." It's all right. He loosened his right hand and made a triangular, circular motion to take in her, the baby that would be, and himself. Then he made a wider motion to take in themselves and the two children sleeping in the wagon. *"Familia."*

"Sí. Familia."

Iron Heart's Story

LOREN D. ESTLEMAN

PORCUPINE WOMAN and Sees Water were concerned about Iron Heart.

"He speaks of nothing but things dead," Sees Water declared. "He is a great hero of our people, but he grows older with each story."

Porcupine Woman, mother to Sees Water and Iron Heart's mate these past forty winters, continued to drag the strip of hide in her hands back and forth across the stone resting in her lap. Those hands now were as coarse as the stone was smooth, worn so from long use, as if the two surfaces had traded places. "It is the way of the People to say these things many times to our young, that they will remember and speak of them to their children, and they to theirs. In this way the deeds of our heroes do not drift away like the dry snow that comes in the Moon of Dead Trees."

"I understand this. Still, my father has lost interest in everything but the old stories. I think that he is waiting to die."

Porcupine Woman considered. It was a custom of her people, called the Cut Arms by their friends the Sioux, and the Cheyenne by the white long knives such as those who had followed the Yellow Hair chief to attack the People at the Washita the winter before, to listen betimes to the counsel of the young, who saw things differently and sometimes more clearly than their wiser elders. And Sees Water, whose breasts were high and whose face knew no creases, was uncommonly grave and thoughtful for one of her small years.

"Iron Heart is a great warrior," Porcupine Woman said. "He has stolen many horses from our enemies the Crow and counted many coup, and so has earned the right to speak of these things. It is just as true that he remembers the color of the feathers in the headdress of Spotted Calf, dead these twenty summers, at the cost of forgetting whether he broke his own fast this morning. This is bad, for he is not as old as old Broken Lodge, who has seen seventy winters and rides and shoots as well as a brave half his age. Yet he seems older."

"What shall we do, Mother?"

"In old times I would suggest that he go to the buffalo, or steal horses from the Crow. But the buffalo grow smaller in numbers each winter, and we have given our word to the great white chief of the long knives that we will live in peace with the Crow if they will do the same with us."

"Then he will die surely. The Wise One Above does not grant the gift of life to those who are not thankful."

During Porcupine Woman's silence the sun moved. The hide grew softer with each motion across the stone. At length she spoke.

"Be of good heart, child. Your mother is old, but she

has not forgotten those things that set a man's heart afire. We shall go to Iron Heart and ask him to tell us one of the old stories."

The face of Sees Water fell. "Mother, you have not heard me. It is the old stories that are killing him."

"This one will save him."

They went to Iron Heart, who sat cross-legged in a patch of sun holding up a tooth that had fallen from his head, staring at it as if it contained some great truth. His long hair had gone as gray as his name and the skin had begun to hang from his bones, but in the old face Porcupine Woman always saw the handsome brave who had taken her to his lodge when her summers were but sixteen. They sat facing him.

"The Powder River will freeze this winter," said he without greeting. "The beaver plew will be as thick as the grass that comes after the planting rain."

Porcupine Woman said, "The beaver are gone, my husband. The last one left before Sees Water first saw the sun."

"Sam Tyree said he will trade two bolts of gingham for each good plew."

The women exchanged glances.

"Sam Tyree was killed by the Pawnee the year the snow forgot to fall," Porcupine Woman said.

"I think I shall ask for three bolts. Sam Tyree will cheat us if we let him."

"Speak not of him. Tell us of the time you and I and Mounts-His-Horse-Funny tried to skin the grandfather elk."

Iron Heart turned the tooth between his fingers. "Why must I speak of this thing? You were there."

"No one tells it as well as you, and Sees Water wishes to hear it." She prodded her daughter with her elbow.

"Yes, Father," said Sees Water, with a start. "Tell of the time you and Mother and Mounts-His-Horse-Funny tried to skin the grandfather elk."

"It is a long story. My belly is empty."

"Your bowl is still warm from your last meal, my husband. Tell the story."

He filled and emptied his lungs with great resignation. But his eyes glittered. He deposited the tooth in the medicine bag tied around his neck, forgetting in his eagerness that the tooth was his own and as such carried no medicine for him.

"It was in the Summer That Should Have Been Autumn," he said. "Mounts-His-Horse-Funny and I had been in the high country for eight suns, shooting birds and rabbits and looking for larger game to feed the camp."

Porcupine Woman touched his knee. "My husband, the Summer That Should Have Been Autumn was not the time. It was in the Spring That Stayed Dead, when the snow refused to melt."

"It was the hot autumn. Old Standing Hawk fell dead of the heat."

"No, you are thinking of the time his wife gave birth to a dead son. Standing Hawk died the next autumn."

After a moment he nodded. "You are right. The hunt was the first time I wore the robe you made from the white buffalo. The air was cold."

"Tell the story, my husband."

"I am telling it. The camp was starving because of the cold. The buffalo did not come that time and we were heading for the mountains to look for the long-legged kind. Porcupine Woman came along to hold the horses when we climbed. You were not born yet, Daughter."

"It was her first spring," Porcupine Woman corrected. "I left her with White Water Woman, the sister of your mother."

His glitter faded. "What is that to the story?"

"You have always spoken of the importance of telling these tales the same way every time if they are to be remembered as they happened."

"This is so." Nodding absently, he looked far off, past the broken peaks of the tall rocks the white long knives called the Tetons; for there, in the silvery mists beyond the edge of the world, resided the people and things he found and brought back for his listeners. With each winter he saw them more clearly than those he walked among on this side. The day would come, he knew, when he would decide to stay with them rather than return to this place of fading shadows.

"Mounts-His-Horse-Funny had a blue roan which he stole from a Crow chief. Only Mounts could ride it, for it stamped its forefeet and showed its teeth to anyone else who approached. It pulled up lame and Mounts got off to see what was the matter."

"It was a pinto, and everyone could ride it who wished to except Mounts, whom it threw off at every opportunity. That was why he was afoot to see the grandfather elk."

Sees Water glanced annoyedly at her mother, who seemed determined not to let Iron Heart continue the story which she said would pull him back from the land of mists. But Porcupine Woman had eyes only for her husband.

"It was a roan. Mounts traded it to Standing Hawk for his daughter Crab Woman and a breastplate made from the bones of one hundred and forty field mice. Hawk gave it back when he found he could not ride it."

"You are thinking of Black Bull. Mounts was married to Wool Woman, who came to him after the death of her husband Runs-in-the-Rain."

"I remember this unimportant thing. Mounts fell off the pinto and tore his legging. When he bent to look at it, he saw the elk's track at his feet. He thought it was buffalo and we began to follow it. Two suns and two sleeps we followed, high into the mountains where the air is hard to breathe. By then we had seen its droppings and knew they were not those of the buffalo, though its hoofprint was larger than any elk's known to us, or to our fathers, or to their fathers. A spread hand would not cover it.

"The third sun was barely clear of the earth when we broke camp and saw it against the sky. We thought at first it was a trick of the mist, which fools the eye and makes a thing seem larger than it is. Bigger than any buffalo it was, the points upon its antlers as many as the wild ponies that ran in the land before the first long knives came. Its hide was as red as blood."

"Brown," Porcupine Woman said. "Brown like hickory, and it was not so big as that, though it weighed as much as a buffalo cow."

Iron Heart's glare was black. "Does my wife prefer this story to come from her lips?"

"No one tells it as well as you, my husband."

"It is so. I was carrying the musket that cost me twelve plew and a blanket at Bent's Fort, and I fired at the same time Mounts released a shaft from his bow. I do not know even now which of us delivered the fatal injury. The elk ran the length of a lance thrust and fell. We removed the entrails and fashioned a travois from the boughs of the lodgepole pine to drag the carcass back to camp, for neither of our horses would bear its weight. Then came the difficult business of removing the hide.

"No knife would penetrate its thick skin," he continued. "No axe would part its fibers. I myself broke a clovis point fashioned by my great-grandfather in the time of the white king, trying to make the first notch. We had first to place the tools in a fire until they glowed as red as the lifting sun that they would burn through the hide and hair. Still it would not surrender its hold upon the flesh. At last we hitched both our horses to the burned edge and slapped their rumps, that they would bolt and tear it away from the carcass. The turtle that carries the sun upon its back crossed the sky in the time it took to skin the grandfather elk."

Porcupine Woman cleared her throat. The face Iron Heart turned upon her was a stone slab. Yet he said nothing, allowing her to speak.

"It was not a clovis point you broke, but a bone knife. You always did insist upon using a fleshing tool for cutting. And we hitched one horse to the hide, not two. The turtle that carries the sun had half its journey still ahead of it when we finished. You traded six plew, not twelve, for the musket you bought at Bent's Fort. Even then you were cheated. It misfired that day, and so it was Mounts-His-Horse-Funny's arrow that killed the elk, which fell where it stood and did not run. But for those small things you told the story perfectly."

"Bah!" He scrambled to his feet and strode in the direction of the horses.

"Where are you going, my husband?"

"To the tall rocks, who will listen to my stories without interruption."

Moments later the women heard the rataplan of hoofs fading from camp.

"I have not seen Father so angry in many moons," Sees Water declared. "Why did you upset him so?"

Rising, Porcupine Woman shook the dust from the hem of her doeskin. "The story of the time we skinned the grandfather elk is one of the few he never tells right. Whenever I correct him, the blood comes into his face and the fire into his eyes and he is as he was the day I gave him my heart. He will be like this for a long while."

"And when he is over it?"

"Then I shall ask him to tell us of the time he and Otter Belt swam across the Canadian to steal horses from the Kiowa. He never tells that one right either." She touched one of her daughter's braids. "Come, child. Your father will bring back game to prepare and we must have our work done."

Frontier Birds

LINDA SPARKS

ICY WIND SWIRLED around Cat Burnum and her cowhand as they forked hay off the beavertail stack in a rhythmic counterpoint. Below, cows jostled for position. At the jingle of sleigh bells, Cat paused. "Gotta go be a lady, Hank," she said, before spearing the fork into a snowdrift and dropping lightly from the stack. The angle of her Uncle Matt's brows reminded her that riding the train in worn Levi's and battered Stetson wasn't the image she should be striving to attain. She climbed into the cutter.

"Humph!" he snorted.

Poking him playfully with an elbow, she leaned close. "I'll hide in the trainyard and sneak in after dark."

"Not likely. That husband of yours may's well kiss any

hope of a political career good-bye the same time he kisses you hello."

Cat sighed. Raised amid cows and cowboys, she was secure in her role as managing partner of the Ax T ranch. Playing the lady in Cheyenne made her feel like a cow pony at one of those fancy Eastern fox hunts Matt storied about. But the thought of enduring an entire winter separated from Harry by the snow-choked Laramie Mountains created an aching hole in her center.

Harrison Burnum wiped excess ink from the nib and leaned across his mahogany desk, extending the pen to Crayton Winsley. "Sign here, and here," he said, pointing to a manicured finger.

Sliding the document to the second man, the lawyer caught a flicker of movement. Good Lord! he thought, seeing the slender Stetson-topped form lounging in his doorway.

"You fellas ain't buying land, is ya? This polecat sold me a piece was nothin' but scrub! Pisser of a crick was alkali."

"Never mind, gentlemen, this is a joke," Burnum said, rising and striding across the room. Looming over the denim-clad intruder, he glowered. "This is *not* the time or the place!"

"You fellas git any cows in the deal, best check 'em close. Prob'ly tick 'fested."

The two dandified businessmen sidled through the doorway, one sucking hard at his portly stomach to avoid brushing against the cow-stenched denim as he escaped.

"Catherine! You are outrageous!" Harry growled.

"They're just Britishers. Prob'ly don't know steer from bull," she said, laughing as she slid her arms around his neck.

"They're clients—" His words were cut off as her lips searched under his luxuriant mustaches.

"I'll reform," she promised, as her kisses traveled to his chin.

Remembering Winsley's face as he squeezed through the doorway, Harry stifled a chuckle and grumbled, "In a pig's eye!"

Cat's stilted, high-button-shoe walk swished fine wool over pyramided petticoats as she strolled the afternoon boardwalks. From a shop window the pheasant wing perched in her chestnut hair reflected back at her. Harry claimed it was a hat. Wriggling inside the prison of her stays, she giggled, remembering it had taken his help to get her rigged out in this getup. A whole month of being prim for her husband's la-di-da friends; images of formal dinners and the *the-a-ter* were daunting.

Cheyenne was interesting to visit, but she wondered how Harry endured living here. Wagon and carriage wheels churned dust and dung together, then gusts flung it in her eyes, nose, and mouth; even the snowbanks lurking in the shadows were brown-furred. Coal and wood smoke grayed the air. Restaurant kitchens belched, mingling their reeking breath with laundry steam. The thuds and creaks of the wagons, the clanging of metal on metal as cars shifted in the railyards, and the ground-shaking rumble of the one-thirty train pulling into the station two blocks away deafened Cat's ears. And people, people, people: So many, her every breath smelled used. Eleven years of ranch life had purged cities from Cat's blood.

Stepping into the doorway of Waugh's Laundry, she gave way to a broad-beamed woman, her cape and skirts flapping, dragging three stair-step children down the boardwalk. A frigate, sails unfurled, Cat thought, towing dinghies in her wake. She chuckled to herself. *Least I can talk like a book when I want to—all Matt's teaching isn't wasted.* These days her uncle was torn between pride and consternation at her proficiency in handling cowpunchers and stock. He was hoping Harry would ladify her.

Resuming her stroll, Cat was nearly knocked into the

street when a girl was forcibly ejected from the drugstore. She lay sniffling in the street, and Cat's temper flared.

"What happened? Didn't you have enough money?" Cat asked, brushing dust from the girl's satin skirt, its shimmery blue sure to blind men to the old stains and fraying hem.

"Throwed me out, but I got the cash. I need the medicine for my sister. She's bad sick." Tears eroded her store complexion as she smoothed a crumpled scrap of paper.

"My name's Cat. Give me your list and quit crying. My rig's five doors down. One with the gray horse. Get in. I'll get your list."

Cat strode into the drugstore, piercing the weedy-looking fellow behind the counter with her silver eyes. "Excuse me, but did you just refuse a young girl service?"

"We don't do business with soiled doves, ma'am."

"I assume you will do business with me?" She watched his eyes sweep over her expensive cedar green coat, dyed-to-match deerskin gloves, and fancy hat, knowing she looked the lady despite the fact she was barely twenty.

The druggist nodded.

"Then fill the child's list and be quick about it." Cat slapped the paper on the counter. The druggist's expression said he would like to have seen her flying out the door on the heels of the other one, but the command in her voice and the sparks in her steely eyes sent his pale hands scurrying among the bottles and jars.

Minutes later, still seething, Cat returned to her husband's spider phaeton. "Get in, girl."

"Oh, ma'am, I can't ride in your buggy. The townfolk, they'd stone you." The girl's whine became a wail as tears again coursed through paint and powder.

Cat stared at the round-faced child: her mousy hair thin, her pale eyes already haunted. *Uppity damn town!* At least in Baltimore Cat remembered the whores as being adults; or so they'd seemed to her ten-year-old eyes. She softened her voice and corralled the girl's slumped shoulders with an arm. "Would you please get in the buggy? And stop crying. You have to tell me where your sister is, and I can't understand you when you're crying." Cat hoped that sounded like Matt; that kind of treacle worked for him. "No one's going to stone *this* buggy!"

Sniffling, the girl gathered her skirt and scrambled in, pointing south. She scrubbed her drippy nose on a cuff, pulled the thin wrap tight around her shoulders, and said her name was Alice. With more encouragement, she admitted to thirteen and said her sister, Maude, was sixteen. By the time Cat had learned that much, they'd reached the shack south of the tracks where the girls lived and worked. The inside was swept and neat and so cold Cat's breath formed damp clouds. The hovel smelled of piss and men, and the metallic odor of blood.

Maude was crumpled in the only bed. On the floor below, a pool of blood increased, one splat at a time, as the soaked mattress yielded droplets. Cat knew the pharmaceuticals were useless.

"What happened, Alice? Tell me quickly!"

"She got knocked up."

"And she lost it?"

"Doc got rid a it."

"Christ! Goddamn butcher! All right, we're going to try to save your sister. No more crying, no more hand-wringing!"

Sniffing, the girl helped Cat wrap Maude in the skimpy blanket and carry her to Harry's gleaming buggy. Clutching her sister, Alice's fingers crept reverently across the button-tufted Morocco to touch a soft fold of Cat's coat as she stood spraddle-legged, reins in hand, easing the horse into the street.

"Where's there a decent doctor?"

"Eddy 'bove Eighteenth. But, ma'am, he won't see Maude."

"He most certainly will!" Cat said. Cheyenne citizenry's concern for appearances was one of Matt's frequent lectures, but to let a girl die out of snobbery . . .

"Oh, no, ma'am, he only sees the swells. The only doctor what'll see us girls is the one left Maudie like this." Cat set her teeth, imagining the legal havoc her lawyer-husband would wreak on the doctor for refusing a patient.

And Cat wasn't taking Maude back to the butcher. She pulled up in front of the doctor's office and dashed inside. Ruched and bustled women, some with children, crowded the waiting room. She strode to the inner door and pounded a gloved fist. The scrape of a chair sounded, then heavy heels on bare floor, before a man in a Prince Albert coat opened the door. Gray winged back from his temples and dirt-lined creases sprouted above his nose. "Yes, what is it?"

The smell of sweat, old blood, and pus wafted from him, and Cat found herself staring at filthy fingernails embedded in the ends of his stubby fingers. Bile rose in her throat. "I've got an emergency. I'm looking for the doctor, is he here?"

"I'm Dr. Moresby, miss. What's the problem?"

Cat recoiled. *My God, I wouldn't deliver a calf with hands that filthy. 'Wash the hands and the heifer's posterior areas thoroughly with chloride of lime'—that's what Robert Jennings' book said. Hell, the veterinary surgeons were twenty years more advanced than this doctor!* Matt's friendship with Ben Craddick, M.D. of Laramie, had exposed her to only one doctor—he washed. She fled, tottery in the unfamiliar shoes. In the buggy, her mind raced. "Think, Alice, there must be more than two doctors in this town!"

"Nope, 'ceptin' the Army doctor down at the fort. And that little fat fella. Folks says he's touched in the head."

"How? I mean, why do they say that?"

"Don't want folks usin' ditch water. Always sweepin' and boilin'."

Hopeful, Cat thought. She pried the location of the fat fella out of Alice and touched the gray gelding with the whip.

Minutes later, barging though the fat doctor's door, she found a spotless, empty waiting room and the door to the office ajar. Carbolic fumes tickled her nose. Peering through the door, she saw a moon-faced man reading a journal at the desk, his prematurely balding head shiny in a ray of winter sun. With little time left, Cat marched across the room and snatched a hand from the journal. The nails were short and clean.

"You the doc? Got an emergency in the buggy. Need help carrying her."

Apparently amazed to see this striking young woman bull into his office and examine his hand, the rotund little man trotted along like a hound on fresh trail.

After carrying Maude to his table, the doctor examined her while Cat shed her coat, rolled her sleeves, and scrubbed. "I'll help, just tell me what to do." The doctor gave instructions, and in less than ten minutes they had cleaned up the girl and packed her to stop the bleeding. After moving Maude to a bed and assigning Alice to watch her, Cat and the doctor washed again and walked into the waiting room.

Extending a work-roughened hand, she said, "Thanks, Doc. My name's Catherine Burnum." Catherine! she snickered to herself; she hated the name, but Harry called her nothing else. "My husband's Harrison Burnum."

"My pleasure, ma'am. Everyone's heard of your husband. I'm Wilhelm Abramson. My friends, when I used to have them, called me Wil. How did you come to bring me a . . . a girl with a botched abortion? It's incongruous. And why me? I've been here four months but nobody uses my services."

"Incongruous?" Cat mused, suddenly remembering it was anything but. "The why is easy. Of the sons-of-bitches that call themselves doctors, one did the butchery and the other one . . . well, he and his office smell like the hind end of a fresh cut and branded calf!" *Whoops, not very ladified.*

"Doctor Moresby's very popular. And my dirt fanaticism has scared off the rest of the town," Wil said. "But how—"

The ticking grandfather clock, its moon at half-phase,

drew a gasp from Cat. "Damn! If that clock's right, I gotta go. My husband's expecting me." *Oh hell, I did it again.* She reached into her reticule and plucked out several scrunched bills, pressing them into the doctor's hand.

"Mrs. Burnum, this is too much money!"

"Depends on your point of view, Doc. S'long."

She hurried across the narrow walkway connecting the little house with the street, imagining Mrs. Frobisher, or whoever, smiling over her sherry and simpering: "What did you do on your first day in town, dear? Did you enjoy yourself?" "Yes, thanks. A stinking hovel, a revolting doctor, and a bleeding whore. A perfect afternoon." She giggled. Then she remembered her promise to behave.

Just before alighting on the buggy seat, her hand slid on the bloody smears. *Shit! Harry will have a conniption.* She drove off standing up.

When Burnum led his horse into the carriage shed, Catherine was scrubbing the phaeton's seat. All the signs said she was in a cougar mood, but something was missing. Putting up his horse, he studied her, remembering her bravado in his office. That was it, he thought, the cockiness is missing.

He removed overcoat and suit coat, rolled up his shirt sleeves, and picking up a rag, walked to the other side of the buggy. The first wipe identified the offending substance. "This is blood!" Scrutinizing her, he discovered a large blotch, rusty against the mint of her skirt. His heart thudded. "And there's blood on your skirt! Catherine, are you all right?"

"I wouldn't be scrubbing this seat if I weren't."

Harry didn't mind the growling, but he was a dismal failure at mind reading. Stepping over the shafts, he took the rag from her. "Tell me why you're angry, Catherine. I can't help if I don't know what the problem is."

"The problem is getting the damn blood off the seat!" She groaned, then leaned her forehead against his shoulder in apology. "I'm sorry. You didn't deserve that. After this mess is cleaned up, I . . . I have something to tell you."

A slave to Southern propriety from babyhood, he secretly envied his wife's devil-take-the-hindmost audacity. Now, suddenly it was gone, replaced by a hunted look. That look, that loss, didn't go with her brusque tone and he wondered if she knew she was frightened. He doubted it; he thought fear was as foreign to her as a parasol. Its familiar cold fingers crept around his throat.

In the parlor, Cat paced from his rolltop to the window and back while Harry waited, silent between the arms of his wing chair. When she began, her voice rang with anger as she told him about Maude.

"May I ask some questions?" he said when she'd finished. At her nod, he began. "I know about your penchant for rescues, but what set off this one? Cheyenne ladies give the, uh, *filles de joie* a wide berth."

"They're whores, Harry. My cowhands call 'em whores. I'm not lace and ruffles, I don't faint." She turned, stalking to the window. It was dark outside and the ebony panes reflected the lamp-lit interior of his cozy parlor: the fire burning cheerily, the bentwood rocker, the books stacked on the table. They evoked in her memories from a childhood spent peering into the windows of real homes back in Baltimore. The illusion rubbed the same scar that had itched when she saw Alice pitched into the street.

The glass was cool against her forehead. *My God, how will I tell him? Why didn't I tell him before?* That answer was easy: She'd been afraid it would scare him off. Maybe if he understood—if she could bring herself to tell him—her behavior wouldn't be so reprehensible.

Prowling the parlor, she fought back the prickle of tears. When she was sure her voice was steady, she said, "I hardly ever see them. Even on my occasional trips to Laramie, I just visit my friends. The few days I'm ever in Cheyenne, we see your friends."

"Catherine," Harry's Texas drawl reached out, caressing her, "no one can hurt you here. Tell me what's frightened you."

She gulped a breath. "When that girl came flying out of that store, when I saw her lying in the dust . . . she was me."

When nothing more followed, Harry prodded, "Go on, dear."

"You don't know. You had parents."

"And you have me. Tell me."

She fixed her eyes, now stone gray, on his blue ones. "I lived in a bawdy house in Baltimore with my mama. If she hadn't shipped me off to her brother before she died, if Uncle Matt hadn't been . . . Uncle Matt . . . I'd be a whore." Tears gathered but she refused to let them spill.

"Good Lord, girl," Harry said, crossing the room in four long strides, "it's me you're afraid of!" He pulled her rigid body into his arms, laying his cheek atop her head. "You don't think I care about that? You were only ten."

"Your mother would! Your Cheyenne friends will," she said, pushing away. "I'm no better than Alice and Maude, or any of the rest of them south of the tracks, just luckier."

Harry had already come to grips with her history; Matt had shared that confidence before the wedding. It was Harry's deal and he knew Catherine needed a winning hand.

"That's ancient history. Catherine, you and Wyoming busted some of the puffery out of me. I was a jackass when you married me. Too much Southern upbringing and too much Harvard. I'm still not sure why you bothered with me." He chuckled, recalling why, two years earlier, he'd bothered with her: She'd had the sinewy grace and beauty of a panther on the dance floor at the Stock Growers' social. And one kiss had scorched him to a cinder. He also recalled his mental anguish when he discovered he'd fallen in love with a whiskey-drinking, pants-wearing cattle rancher. Marrying her had taken all the courage he could muster. But ah, the rewards he'd reaped for that mustering, he thought, feeling his desire for her stir. Harry cupped her chin in his palm and grinned. "Pa'd call you a cactus wren. Know why?"

Cat shook her head.

"Because the cactus wren is a tough bit of feathers that carves a hole in a big, spiny cactus and tucks her nest in it. She's a survivor. From all that thorny armor, she darts into the world to take what she wants." He kissed the tip of his wife's nose. "Do you know what else?"

"What?" she asked, her eyes slowly returning to silver.

"You need to spend more time with me. Get to know the man you married."

The hall clock bonged and Catherine's eyes widened. "Your dinner plans! I rushed home and now—"

"The toffs at the Cheyenne Club will have to do without you on the dance floor tonight. We're righting wrongs!" he said, pulling on his lawyer face and injecting his voice with a brisk, efficient tone. A hawk in Cheyenne's business and legal community, Harry was a swift and agile wheeler-dealer. "What do you want to do about the, uh, soiled doves and the doctors?"

Cat's lips thinned at his euphemism. "I can't do anything about them. I can't get that doctor arrested. I'm not that naive."

"Darlin', there's always something that can be done about an unjust situation. It just takes studying on." Lord, he thought, Matt had taught her the principles of business, ranching and political maneuvering, but he'd failed to teach her how to manipulate the real world. Harry pulled her down on his lap. "Now then, since your Dr. Abramson doesn't have any patients anyway, see if he'll treat the . . . the whores. We should be able to find some place decent on the other side of the tracks for him to set up an office." That, he thought, might even pay future dividends—handled correctly it could draw votes from both sides of the tracks.

"Do you mean that?"

"Of course I mean it."

Cat kissed him soundly. "Do you think he'd do it?"

"Probably."

"He would if you asked him. Oh Harry, it's perfect."

Then Harry actually felt her elation trickle away.

"Everybody saw Alice and Maude in your buggy. I ruined your reputation!"

"There'll be talk. Nothing I can't handle." Especially, he thought, after I make you out as another Florence Nightingale. "I do wish you'd learn to tell me when you have a problem. We could work on it together. That's what marriage is about, and you aren't getting any practice living out there in the wilderness. Move to town. Let your foreman run the ranch."

Lightning in her eyes flashed a denial before she nestled down, rubbing her cheek invitingly against his silk-clad shoulder.

The next morning the Burnums visited Wil Abramson. Despite his relative youth, Harry radiated self-assurance, but he deliberately kept his manner easy. "I hear Catherine recruited you in one of her rescues. We have a proposition for you. Interested in the particulars?"

"I'm always willing to listen. Please come into the parlor. Good morning, Mrs. Burnum. I've coffee hot, can I get you a cup?"

"If you'll call me Catherine. How's Maude? Do you mind if I see her?"

"Maude's weak, but she'll recover, Mrs. . . . Catherine. They were asleep when I checked on her earlier, but you're welcome to look in."

She did. When she returned, Harry and Wil were chatting like old friends.

"Did you ask him, Harry? Will you do it, Doctor?"

Questions bloomed in the doctor's eyes.

Harry chuckled. "This is your project. I'm just providing guidance and moral support. You ask him."

She bit her lip, a wordless appeal shining in her eyes.

"Just tell him what you have in mind, dear," Harry said gently. He knew she'd spent a rare sleepless night worrying over it; this went beyond cows and cowboys, but the enterprise might involve her deeply enough to keep her in the city. He wanted her with him, wanted her scent in his nostrils while he slept.

Cat perched on the edge of the horsehair settee and outlined the plan. She hadn't gotten very far into the explanation before delight shone on the doctor's rosy face. "You'll do it, won't you?" she said. "Oh, I'm so glad. I'll help with everything. We have to find a place, and get your supplies, and don't worry about the money. There's so much to do. We'll have to get started right away. Maybe we can find a place today."

Catching her hand, Harry halted the tumbling words. "Catherine, the man's still trying to catch his breath. Drop me at my office and you can have the buggy. By the time you return, the doctor will have had time to collect his thoughts."

Harry rose, smiling at Abramson. "Lord help you, Doctor. Don't let her stampede you into doing something you don't want to do. She's like the Wyoming wind."

Wil Abramson walked out with them. As he drove off, Burnum saw bewilderment still decorating the round boyish face.

Cat and the doctor had found a likely building and the following day Harry met them at noon to look over their choice. Located several blocks south of the railroad roundhouse, it had been a carriage repair shop. From the leather scraps scattered about, the three good-sized rooms in the front had been used for harness-working. The large, floored room in the rear, where carriage parts had been milled, would serve as a ward. And Wil planned to live upstairs. Harry poked at walls, corners, and into the underside of the roof with his silver-headed cane, pleased to find that the building was in good condition and appeared to be weatherproof throughout.

Much of Harry's legal work was in real estate investment and leasing. The richest city of its size, Cheyenne teemed with offices and businesses. Harry bought, renovated, managed, and sold buildings, and agented for other investors. Less subject to the vagaries of Wyoming weather than the cattle barons' stock, Harry's properties were making him a rich man.

"Looks like you two made an excellent choice. I'll have my clerk find the owner and get you a good lease." Harry slid a hand under the tendrils of hair curling over his wife's collar. "Once that's done, I'll send my crew to fix up this place. And," he said to his wife, his hand firm on her neck, "they don't need a ramrod. They're quite professional."

Outside, Harry surveyed the neighborhood. On the way down, he'd ridden by a strip of bawdy houses, cheap saloons, billiard parlors, and one place—less than two blocks away—that leaked the sweet odor of opium. The building they'd selected stood among seedy businesses that catered to the laborers, railroad men, and independent whores living south of the tracks. While it was a good spot for the clinic, he didn't relish the thought of Catherine passing daily through these streets. She might not always think of herself as womanly, but no man made that mistake.

"You may as well order your equipment and supplies, Doc," Harry said. "By the time they get here, this place should be ready to go. You'll need to come to the bank while we open an account for the clinic. Know what you're going to call it?"

Doctor Abramson shook his head, his moon face shining. "I can't convince myself this is real. You two are overwhelming! Two days ago, I didn't know where next month's rent was coming from and now you're telling me I have a whole building, can order whatever I want, and not worry about money. I can't begin to thank you."

Harry laughed. "If you're as good at doctoring as Catherine says, you'll be doing the whole town a service. And you're right, Catherine and I are pushy. I suppose that's because she's the finest ranch manager in Wyoming, and I'm the best business lawyer in the Territories. We're used to doing things our way."

By month's end, the clinic building had been renovated and stocked with medical equipment, supplies, and furniture. Its two paid assistants, also scrubbed-up and clad in shirtwaists and skirts, looked quite proper. Maude, who could read and write, would help with the books and patients. Alice was going back to school, but she would help with laundry and cleaning. These two had spread the word that the clinic would be open the first of the following month. Folks could stop in for medical care or just to say hello and look around.

Maude would never be pretty, but health, regular hours, and good food had given her hair shine and bounce, and her smile put points of light in hazel eyes. She'd appointed herself Wil's cook and housekeeper, and Catherine suspected the girls ate with the doctor.

Harry had purchased an ivory-handled derringer and insisted Catherine carry it. The piece was as elegant and refined as her husband, but to her a gun meant the .44 thumb-buster that fit snugly against her hip when she was riding line, doctoring cows, or working roundup. Catherine thought the toy gun silly, but Harry refused to debate with her. He'd simply said she was not, under any circumstance, to go to the clinic without the pocket pistol. Some mornings he checked, as if she were a recalcitrant child. A month of teas and champagne socials in Cheyenne's mansions, of soirees, concerts, and theater had conditioned Catherine to ladies' ways: Ladies didn't have guns dragging down the pockets of their day dresses. Nevertheless, with each step, the derringer thumped against her leg.

On opening day, Catherine arrived at the clinic at nine to find the doctor all aflutter. "No one will come, Cather-

ine, I know it. You'll have spent all this money and no one
will come."

"Oh pooh, Wil, the doves all sleep 'til past noon."

The first patient arrived at two, hovering by the door
until encouraged to enter. By four o'clock, laces, satins,
and rough woolens scented the waiting room with flowers,
musk, and tobacco. They weren't all patients; some came
to gawk and others to quiz the sick ones as they left. But
they came, and they would come back and bring others.

Harry stopped by after he closed the law office, his
black cashmere overcoat swinging open as he crossed to
where Catherine sat behind the waiting room desk. The
chairs and benches still overflowed with the ruffles of the
doves' shimmery plumage, while a few men leaned against
the walls. "It looks like your enterprise is a huge success,
darlin'," he whispered, propping his well-tailored rear on
the edge of the desk and leaning close. He wound a vagrant tendril of her chestnut hair around one finger. "Have
I lost you forever to social reform? Will you come home
with me?"

"It should be cleared out by eight o'clock. The girls
have to work." Laughter percolated through Catherine.
Old and young, the whores in the waiting room were whispering and poking each other, the men eyeing Harry with a
mixture of awe and distaste. In his charcoal suit, silver-
belly Stetson, and gleaming black boots, her handsome
husband was quite the swell.

"I'll come back for you. Wait inside."

"That's not necessary," she hissed. As if Harry had to
protect her! she thought. He never even carried a gun.

"I won't have you on these streets alone at night. Would
you rather I wait here?"

"No!" she whispered, standing. "You're out of place.
They all think you're my first client for the evening."

Harry glanced around the room, where expressions
confirmed her words. Slipping a hand behind her neck, he
pulled her into a searing kiss. When he released her, he
ordered, "Eight o'clock, woman. I won't wait a minute

past." Rising from the desk, he sauntered out, swinging his silver-headed ebony cane and touching his hat to the ladies. Catherine's face flamed, and giggles ate through her composure, threatening to erupt. *So much for the Harvard blue-nose with his oh-so-proper airs! His mother would expire!* And even if north of the tracks Harry's Victorian propriety remained impeccable, she was tickled he'd loosened up a little. In private, he wasn't the least bit stuffy.

Several days later, Catherine was manning the waiting room desk when a man in a rusty-black Prince Albert coat stomped through the front door. Veins spider-webbed his nose and ruddy cheeks. A scraggly beard bushed around his mouth, trapping fragments from some recent meal. He exuded alcohol with each breath, but the underlying stench was worse. His wild eyes started nervous clawings in Catherine's innards. "Sir, if you'll have a seat, the doctor will be with you shortly. Or was there something—" she asked.

"Yeah, I want to see the doctor. I want to see the sneaky little bastard who's stealin' my patients. Get out here, Jew-boy!" the man bellowed, his words slurring. The disturbance brought Wil from the back room, allowing Catherine to move from behind the desk and sidle out of the man's line of vision. The last two women in the waiting room bolted.

Catherine's stomach knotted; her hands sought her pockets and the reassuring solidity of the little Colt with its two-and-a-half-inch barrel. It suddenly didn't seem silly; the .41 slug would stop anything on two legs at under twelve feet. This had to be the doctor who'd botched the abortion on Maude, and he sounded completely swacked. When he pulled a Colt Navy revolver from under his coat and pointed it at Wil, time snailed.

Catherine's brain registered two facts: that the piece was still uncocked; and if he cocked it, she would kill him.

The gun waved and danced in drunken hands, but continued to point in Wil's direction. Catherine dared not take her eyes from the weapon, but she was sure all the blood had drained from Wil's face and he was quaking; violence terrified the little man. Catherine began talking—a continuous, calm, low-pitched monotone. "Put the gun down, mister. You don't want to hurt anyone. If you're a doctor, you're sworn to save lives, not take them. Please, put the gun down. You kill him, you'll hang for sure. What will your wife and family do if you're dead?"

The muzzle of his gun wandered sideways toward her as the drunken doctor's eyes shifted. "Shut up, bitch! Wife died years ago."

Staring into the barrel of the Navy dried the spit in Catherine's mouth. Her eyes burned—she dared not blink. She must not miss the cocking of the hammer; only then could the gun be fired. She pulled the derringer from her pocket, then stuffed it back; the drunk would never take it seriously. Anger burned in Catherine, reverting her to ranch boss and ramrod. Command rang in her voice. "Doctor, put it down! If you don't, you'll force me to kill you. I won't let you hurt my friends. Goddammit, man, put the gun down!"

The drunk's left hand groped the air, searching for the hand already holding the revolver. When his left hand found the pistol grip, both thumbs pulled at the hammer.

She never heard the crack of her derringer, nor felt the powder burn her thigh. The big slug bore into the man's right side beneath his raised arm.

The Navy's report thundered in the closed room. Its bullet splintered the door frame next to Wil, and the rotund little doctor sank to his knees, sobbing. Wide-eyed in the doorway, Maude and Alice clung to one another.

Crossing the room through a haze of eye-burning gunsmoke, Catherine raised the doctor to his feet and turned him toward the amazed sisters. "Here," she ordered. "Take him back in the office. Get him a drink."

Catherine squared her shoulders and returned to the man on the floor. Bright froth pumped from his nose and mouth. Blood pooled under his arm. "You stupid son-of-a-bitch, it was your fault we started this clinic. If you hadn't nearly killed Maude, none of this would have happened." *Lord, at home killing you'd just be varmit extermination. Here, they'll try me for murder.*

Pushing open the front door, Catherine found a half-dozen overall- and denim-clad men and boys clumped in the street. "Will someone please get the sheriff?" she asked, hearing her own voice coming from far away. "I also need a boy who can run fast. It's worth fifty cents."

A little tow-headed fellow of about ten scurried up the steps. Catherine returned to the desk and wrote two notes. The first she asked the boy to read aloud.

He read: "Burnum and Thorndike, Eighteenth Street and Ferguson."

"Good boy. Keep that, that's where you're going. Do you know where it is?" He nodded. Catherine continued, "Please take this second note to Mr. Burnum, it's very important, so make sure he gets it. Here's two bits, and tell him he's to give you another quarter. And please, run as fast as you can."

The boy raced off. Although his legs seemed to move in long leisurely bounds, something inside her told Catherine he only looked slow. Sinking to the sagging step, she shut out the world. *Oh God, Harry, I'm sorry. I'll never be civilized. I should never have stayed in town.*

Harry heard his name and rose. Through mullion-paned windows he saw his clerk waving gartered, paper-cuffed arms, trying to hush and shoo a youngster, but the boy ducked, rushing past. Harry hurried from his glass-enclosed office.

"You Mr. Burnum? She said to give it just to Mr. Burnum. She said you'd give me two bits."

Harry unfolded the crumpled note. The fingers of one hand searched a pocket, finding a silver dollar and pressing it absently into the boy's palm. There were only two lines on the slip of paper:

> I needed the derringer.
> Now I need you. C.

"Damnation!" Harry exclaimed, whirling to race out the back to his horse. He reached the clinic within fifteen minutes of the shooting to find his wife still sitting—coatless—on the front step, stiff with cold. Pulling off his suit coat and wrapping it around her, Harry lifted her to her feet and turned her toward the door.

She balked, her foot braced against the step, resisting the hands propelling her. "No. I don't want to go in there."

"Darlin', you're chilled to the bone. I'm right here, everything will be all right. You need to be inside where it's warm. Come dear, let's go inside."

Still she resisted. "I ruined everything," she mumbled dispiritedly.

"Catherine!" he said sharply, turning her toward him. "Look at me! Do you know who I am?"

Lead gray eyes blinked, focusing on his face, and she nodded. "I'll go back to the ranch. I won't embarrass you anymore. I promise I won't."

"Nonsense," Harry said. "We're going inside. Whatever happened, it's over." He could fix it, he knew. Whatever it was. Whatever it cost.

She sagged against him as he guided her around the body of the doctor and into Wil's office. Harry took a quick look to see if anyone else had been hurt and found the girls still trying to stop Wil's blubbering. "Sit here, Catherine," he said, helping her to a chair.

He went to Wil and stood the little man up, shaking him. "Get a grip on yourself, man! This is no time to fall apart." When the doctor continued to cry, Harry slapped him twice, hard across the face. Wil gasped and stopped, sobering.

Harry heard a halloo from the outer office and stepped

through the door. One of Sheriff Potter's deputies was prodding the body with a boot toe. "Wanna tell me what happened here?" The officious voice worked its way around the cud of chaw in the deputy's cheek.

"My wife apparently shot this man. Why, I don't know. Maybe the girls who work here can tell you what happened. When I got here—not more than three, four minutes ago—Doc Abramson was hysterical. My wife's in shock. Everybody is back here, Deputy." Harry led the way into the office.

The deputy took one look at the sisters and turned to Harry. "These girls is hoores, counselor, what makes ya think they work here?" The back of his hand wiped at a bit of brown drool and he glanced around for a place to spit.

"Because, Deputy, the doctor hired them. I would appreciate your addressing them accordingly. I'm sure you can handle things here. I'm taking my wife home."

The deputy swallowed his spit with a grimace and an audible gulp. "Hold on there, Mr. Burnum. Ain't nobody leavin' here tills I question 'em. Then I decide who leaves."

"I'll talk to him, Harry. I'm fine," Catherine said, rising and starting toward her husband. Her knees buckled on the second step and Harry snaked an arm around her waist as she went down. Cradling his wife on the floor, Harry ground his teeth, betraying an urge to rip the deputy limb from limb.

Catherine's collapse was enough to restore Wil's professional manner. He hurried to her, a bottle of smelling salts in hand. "Leave her alone, Officer, she saved our lives," Wil snapped. "It's no wonder she fainted. She tried to talk that madman out of shooting us, but he wouldn't listen." Wil passed the smelling salts under Catherine's nostrils. She coughed, twisting away from him, but he caught her chin firmly, waving the bottle under her nose again.

Her eyes flew open. "Damn, get that stuff away from me! Why are we on the floor?" Then the smelling salts and her position made the circumstances clear. Color flooded her cheeks and she struggled against Harry's arms.

Abramson said, "Lie still, Catherine. You've had a severe shock and fainting's only normal."

"Sheriff knows my house, Deputy," Harry said, smoothing back the tendrils of hair that had escaped Catherine's chignon. "He can speak with her tomorrow. She's in no condition now."

Rising and pressing the salts on Harry, the doctor said, "Absolutely right! Take these with you, in case she has more spells. She should be in bed."

Alice hurried to retrieve Catherine's coat and help her on with it, as Harry steadied her. Then he pulled on his own coat and swept her up in his arms. She struggled and Harry's arms tightened. "Shhh . . . be still, darlin', I'll have you home in a few minutes." Carrying her out to his horse, he set her sidesaddle, swinging up behind her and turning the horse toward home.

Not the least surprised by her action, Harry was concerned about her reactions. Most of all, he was mystified over why she thought he'd be embarrassed. When the word got around, he'd be married to a heroine.

"Spells, indeed! I don't have spells! I was just dizzy. I don't faint! Dammit, Harry, let me go back there and tell that man what happened." *Good Lord, a month in skirts and fripperies, surrounded by ladies, and I've taken to having the vapors! It's contagious!* She shivered in disgust.

"Take it easy, girl, you're all right now, but you were *non compos mentis* when I arrived. And you make no statements to the law until we talk." When the horse walked into the carriage house, Harry stepped down, lifting Catherine off. "Can you walk, darlin'?"

"Of course I can walk!" *By God if I'll let him treat me like some hanky-waver.*

In the parlor, he poured a whiskey and held it for her to sip.

"Stop treating me like an invalid," she growled, taking the bourbon.

"Now, now, killing a man at close range is hard on anyone. I'm told it gives many a strong man the shakes, and sleepless nights as well." He sat next to her, taking her hand. "When you're able, start at the beginning and tell me everything, exactly the way it happened."

She drank the bourbon in four swallows and started at the beginning. When she finished, Harry nodded. "You're all right; there probably won't even be a trial. Now let's get you a nice hot bath and into bed. The sheriff will need the dress and the gun." Catherine no longer protested as he shepherded her up the stairs.

When she was in bed, he pulled up a chair, prepared to sit with her until she fell asleep.

"He didn't give me a choice, Harry."

"I know, darlin'. Close your eyes. I'll be right here."

Her hand gripped Harry's, but behind closed lids her mind replayed the events. *I unloaded the whole problem on Harry! And he took over. Like I was a Miss Pitapat. And fainting! Good grief! That's the price of skirts, silly high-button shoes, and refined ladyism. All those buttons, stays, and laces must keep blood from getting to the brain. I'm going back to the ranch.* In boots, pants, and a Stetson, she knew who she was and trusted her instincts. The clinic didn't need her anymore and Harry . . . well . . . Harry's reputation and aspirations would be better off without her suddenness. She sighed, slipping toward sleep. Dear Harry, he surely must wish he'd married a refined lady—a gentlewoman, she thought, as her grip on his hand softened.

He felt her let go, saw the tension melt from the line of her lips. She'd have no sleepless nights! He wondered how it felt to know what was right. Not to weigh the politics, profitability, or social correctness of an action—to just know it was right. And have the courage to act. By God, he admired courage!

Long Ride Back

ED GORMAN

Soon as I snuck into his campsite, and kicked him in the leg so he'd jerk up from his blanket, I brought down the stock of my single-shot .40-90 Sharps and did some real damage to his teeth.

He was swearing and crying all the time I got him in handcuffs, spraying blood that looked black in the dawn flames of the fading campfire.

In the dewy grass, in the hard frosty cold of the September morning, the white birches just now starting to gleam in the early sunlight, I got the Kid's roan saddled and then went back for the Kid himself.

"I ain't scared of you," he said, talking around his busted teeth and bloody tongue.

"Well, that makes us even. I ain't scared of you, either."

I dragged him over to the horse, got him in the saddle, then took a two-foot piece of rawhide and lashed him to the horn.

"You sonofabitch," the Kid said. He said that a lot.

Then I was up in my own saddle and we headed back to town. It was a long day's ride.

"They'll be braggin' about ya, I suppose, over to the saloon, I mean," the Kid said a little later, as we moved steadily along the stage road.

"I don't pay attention to stuff like that."

"How the big brave sheriff went out and captured the Kid all by his lonesome."

"Why don't you be quiet for a while?"

"Yessir. All by his lonesome. And you know how many murder counts are on the Kid's head? Why, three of them in Nebraska alone. And two more right here in Kansas. Why, even the James Boys walked wide of the Kid—and then here's this hick sheriff capturin' him all by hisself. What a hero."

This time I didn't ask him.

I leaned over and backhanded him so hard, he started to slide off his saddle. Through his pain and blood, he started calling me names again.

It went like that most of the morning, him starting up with his ugly tongue and me quieting him down with the back of my hand.

At least the countryside was pretty, autumn blazing in the hills surrounding this dusty valley, chickenhawks arcing against the soft blue sky.

Then he said, "You goin' to be there when they hang me?"

I shrugged.

"When they put the rope around my neck and the hood over my face and give the nod to the hangman?"

I said nothing. I rode. Nice and steady. Nice and easy.

"Oh, you're a fine one, you are," the Kid said. "A fine one."

Around noon, the sun very high and hot, I stopped at a fast blue creek and gave the horses water and me and the Kid some jerky.

I ate mine. The Kid spit his out. Right in my face.

Then we were up and riding again.

"You sonofabitch," the Kid said. There was so much anger in him, it never seemed to wane at all.

I sighed. "There's nothing to say, Kid."

"There's plenty to say and you know it."

"In three years you killed six people, two of them women, and all so you could get yourself some easy money from banks. There's not one goddamned thing to add to that. Not one goddamned thing." Now it was me who was angry.

"You sonofabitch," he said, "I'm your son. Don't that mean anything?"

"Yeah, Karl, it means plenty. It means I had to watch your mother die a slow death of shame and heartbreak. And it means you put me in a position I didn't ask for—you shot a man in cold blood in my jurisdiction. So I had to come after you. I didn't want to—I prayed you'd be smart enough to get out of my territory before I found you. But you weren't smart at all. You figured I'd let you go." I looked down at the silver star on my leather vest. "But I couldn't, Karl. I just couldn't."

He started crying, then, and I wanted to say something or do something to comfort him but I didn't know what.

I just listened to the owls in the woods, and rode on, with my own son next to me in handcuffs, toward the town that a hanging judge named Coughlin visited seven times a year, a town where the citizens turned hangings into civic events, complete with parades and picnics after.

"You really gonna let 'em hang me, Pa?" Karl said after a while, still crying, and sounding young and scared now. "You really gonna let 'em hang me?"

I didn't say anything. There was just the soughing wind.

"Ma woulda let me go if she was here. You know she would."

I just rode on, closer, ever closer to town. Three more hours. To make my mind up. To be sure.

"Pa, you can't let 'em hang me, you can't." He was crying again.

And then I realized that I was crying, too, as we rode on closer and closer and closer to where men with singing saws and blunt hard hammers and silver shining nails waited for another life to place on the altar of the scaffold.

"You gotta let me go, Pa, you just gotta," Karl said.

Three more hours and one way or another, it would all be over. Maybe I would change my mind, maybe not.

We rode on toward the dusty autumn hills.

Making History

SALLY ZANJANI

INSIDE THE BLACK TAPE RECORDER, tiny wheels turned busily. Satisfied that the tape was still running, the interviewer leaned toward Henry once more, fixed her intent gray-green eyes on his face, and asked, "Why did you go?"

Henry shifted uncomfortably on the plaid couch. The boy he was more than seventy years ago would have squirmed and ducked his head. The young man who had left for Goldfield in 1906 might have averted his eyes and turned sullen. The eighty-two-year-old that Henry had become in 1969, his blue eyes faded, his hair a white shock falling over the brow of a leonine head, his once powerful body a big shell, gave little sign that the question had struck home, except that his gnarled fingers gripped the cane more tightly.

"Went to make my fortune," he said. "Same as every-body else." That was the usual answer, the one that nobody questioned.

The interviewer sensed that there was more to be said. She was good that way. A little too good. "It must have been a big change for a nineteen-year-old boy who'd been clerking in a dry goods store in Iowa to go dashing off to Goldfield," she said helpfully, trying to bring him along with her.

"It was," said Henry, clamping his wide mouth shut. He did not want to be brought. In fact, just now he was sorry he had agreed to be interviewed. She'd started asking questions he didn't want to answer.

"What did your parents say when you told them you were joining a gold rush?" she asked, coming toward him from another angle.

Henry coughed and looked away from the intent gray-green eyes. There was something hypnotic about those eyes. They could draw the words right out of you if you weren't careful. You'd find yourself saying things you never meant to say. And there they would stay, in the little machine with the turning wheels, where you couldn't get them back.

"Said I was a young fool. They were right." There was more, of course. The sign ALTMAN & SON, DRY GOODS & SUNDRIES painted only a year earlier and hung proudly over the store. His father's anger and hurt, his mother's sobs, almost as though she had known, in spite of all his promises, that she would never see his face again.

"Did you ever go back to Iowa?"

"No, I never did. My parents came down with pneumonia that winter—the winter of 1906—while I was in Gold-field. By the time I heard they were sick, they were dead and buried. My uncle took over the dry goods business. There wasn't much to go back for after my folks were gone."

The guilt still wrenched him after more than sixty years. Not taking the time to stand for an hour or two in the mail line at the post office. Not even hiring a boy to do it for him because he'd been spending all his money at Jake's. Allowing the letter that told him of his parents' illness to wait there uncollected for weeks. Not being with them when they needed him.

She seemed to sense his pain and decently turned away. Henry liked her for that. Sometimes he had a feeling that she'd been working him over pretty smart, asking the ordinary questions she knew would start an old gaffer talking and then sliding in with the ones that cut to the bone. All the same, she'd taken the trouble to read up on Goldfield in the old newspapers, which was more than you could say for most of the young folks with tape recorders and notepads who came down to Tonopah to poke and prod at the last of the old gold rushers left alive. Nowadays that came down to Henry and his friend Chester, who lived next door in the tumble-down shack beside Henry's neat cabin.

"By the way, you said you went to make a fortune. Did you make one?"

"Guess not. Wouldn't be here if I did." Henry smiled grimly. It was a damn silly question, in his opinion. If he'd made a fortune, he wouldn't be sitting in a tiny cabin on a hillside in Tonopah. He'd be taking his ease in a mansion by the sea in Long Beach or San Francisco, where the nabobs went after they'd made a killing in the mines. Maybe she knew that and just kept circling back, by different ways, to the thing he didn't want to talk about. Couldn't talk about. It would have felt like taking his clothes off on Main Street.

"Did many people make fortunes in those gold rushes?"

"Very few. And even those who made money—well, mostly it went back into the ground."

She liked this phrase. "Went back into the ground," she repeated, cocking her head, with the straight brown hair clipped almost as short as a boy's. "Now what does that mean?"

"Means you couldn't stay satisfied. Kept thinking you'd

strike it rich again. Sank all the money you made into worthless mines."

She nodded. "Before I leave, I'd like to ask you a few follow-up questions about Goldfield in the boom days around 1906. You mentioned a dance hall called Jake's. What was it like in there?"

Henry relaxed. Now she was moving into safer territory.

"Jake's was noisy," he said. "People drinking and talking and laughing. Little band sawing away. And crowded. They had a fine maple wood floor down at Jake's, but we were squeezed in so tight we couldn't hardly get around. Of course, there were the girls, lots of pretty girls. That's what we came for."

He smiled at her and knew he didn't have the words to make her understand the way it was, the eerie desert stillness of the Malapai outside, with the ghostly shapes of joshua trees in the dim starlight, and the glowing warmth, the gay music, and the laughing voices that tugged you into Jake's. Tugged like a magnet to the iron nail that was you. You might have thought you'd be going somewhere else after coming in from the mines, having a wash, and starting out from your tent cabin of an evening, but you always ended up at Jake's. He remembered it still, the burn of whiskey in his throat, the stubbled faces of the miners and prospectors around him, the sweet curved body of a girl nestling in his arms for a dance. Gus in a green silk dress.

"About how often would you go to Jake's?"

"Pretty often." Actually, it was damn near every night.

"What kind of names did the girls have? I'm assuming they didn't use their real names."

Henry nodded. "None of them used their real names. Men's names were the fashion in those days—and boxers. Names like Jimmie Britt and Bat Nelson and Gus and Ray and Fighting Bill. Others too, Klondike Kitty and Maizie and Swivel Hips Sue."

He watched carefully to see if she would react to Gus's name. He had noticed during their interviews over the last three days that when she was hot on the trail of something she'd lean a fraction closer toward him, as though listening with her whole body, not just her ears, and the large gray-green eyes would widen and then narrow just a little. But she showed none of these signs. Maybe she wasn't on to Gus.

"How long did a dance last?" the interviewer continued.

"Not near long enough if you had one of the dance hall queens in your arms," said Henry, still remembering Gus. Some of the girls had their glasses filled with colored water when you bought them drinks, but not Gus. She could drink you under the table with the real stuff, dance all night, and then, if you were lucky, lead you by the hand to her cabin out back and love you till noon. "Jake kept the dances pretty short to make more money," he added.

"How much did those dance hall queens make? I've heard they made as much as five hundred dollars a night."

"I believe that's an exaggeration. But they did pretty well."

How well would *you* have done back in Jake's, thought Henry to himself, letting his eyes skate skeptically over the interviewer. First you'd have to grow you some hair, enough so it takes a good ten minutes to take all the hairpins out and a man can bury his face in it like a hog in a wallow, hair like Gus's long dark brown mane. And you'd have to put some meat on, so you'd be more than an armful of bones. You'd have to move altogether different. He thought of the smooth kind of wiggle, like a fish twitching its tail in a stream, that was Gus moving toward him across the crowded dance floor and the way her body seemed to flow around a man.

"How did the girls dress?"

"Bright colors. Pretty skimpy. They didn't wear overly much."

That's another thing you'd have to change, he thought, eyeing the woman's jeans with disapproval. You'd have had to dress like a female, in something like the green silk outfit that had clung to Gus's waist and switched from her hips. Henry hadn't minded when he woke up in the twenties to find a lot of female knees staring him in the face, as Will Rogers put it, and again in the sixties. Skirts could go up or down for all he cared, and best of all over a woman's head, but pants did nothing for the female form.

"Did any romances develop?"

"Might have. Can't rightly say." Henry knew himself for a barefaced liar.

"I've wondered if some of these girls might have had an appeal that a respectable woman, say a schoolteacher, didn't have?"

"They were pretty, some of them," said Henry, dodging the question.

"Do you know what happened to the girls after Goldfield went into decline and Jake's closed down?"

She was leaning forward now, eyes a little narrowed.

"I really can't say," said Henry, on guard.

"I've been told that some of the dance hall queens, as you call them, made good marriages and moved away and turned into pillars of society. Can you tell me any more about that?"

"I don't believe I can," said Henry, looking vague.

Somebody must have told her something. Maybe that fool Chester, who didn't know when to stop talking. But not Gus's married name, not where she lived, if she was still living, and Henry didn't want to imagine Gus any other way. He'd learned to live with how Goldfield was now, since the big fire of '23 left the better part of it a blackened smoking ruin, but he liked to picture Gus as the toast of high society, as once she'd been the toast of Jake's. Necessarily an older Gus, with a few streaks of gray in the dark brown mass of her hair, but still very much the same. He'd seen her photograph a few times in the society pages of a big-city newspaper, and that was how he wanted to think of her, laden with jewels at a charity ball, skimming over sunny seas in a yacht, sashaying down the aisle at the opera with just a touch of the old fish-tail wiggle. When she married the tycoon who carried her off on the same kind of sudden whim that made her throw everything she had on the roulette wheel when she felt lucky or spur her horse to a thundering gallop when she fancied a ride at dawn, Henry had wished her well. He knew she'd favored him, but Gus was never just his girl. Only the best he ever had.

"I could turn off the tape recorder if there's anything you'd like to tell me in confidence, Mr. Altman," coaxed the interviewer.

"Think I've told you just about everything I know." Just about. Never Gus. And not the other, which was kind of mixed up with Gus, in a way.

"I guess I haven't asked you if you found what you were looking for in Goldfield?"

She had asked him, several different ways, and they both knew it. He wondered briefly if she had figured out the answer and only wanted him to say she was right. The intent eyes had softened. Henry sensed that she would press him no further.

"Told you I never made much," he muttered, sticking to his story.

"I guess that about wraps it up then," she said. She snapped off the tape recorder and put it carefully in her carrying bag. Noticing that Henry was working to gather his strength, she added, "Please don't bother to get up."

She stepped quickly over to him, gripped his hand, and said shyly, in a sudden rush, "Thank you so much for talking with me, Mr. Altman. You know, you guys were making history down there in Goldfield, and you've helped me understand how it was. I'll let you know when the book comes out."

Henry shook her hand, feeling subtly rebuked. Making history. That was why he talked to these people who came down from the University up north in Reno. When he read some of the fool nonsense they were writing these days about the great rush to Goldfield, it made him so mad he'd cracked his cane on the doorpost. So when these writers came around wanting to see him, he tried to set them right about how the union got busted and how Goldfield was in the wild days before the mine owners turned it into a company town.

But if he was trying to set them right, why had he pointed her wrong with that easy answer about making his fortune? She hadn't believed it either. He wondered if he should have tried to explain. Looking out the window, he watched her dark green car making its way slowly down the hill toward Main Street and wondered if he should ask her to come back. Maybe phone her at the motel. She would doubtless be gone, though, speeding along the highway north to Reno. That was the trouble with these writers. They never stayed long enough to find out what it was really like in Tonopah, or thirty miles down the highway in Goldfield. And if you lived here long enough to learn how the mirages shimmered across the white sands of the Clayton Playa, how the wind blew when a storm was coming in, or how the hills turned into melting strawberry ice cream in the late afternoon light, then you probably didn't know how to write books.

With more effort than it had once taken him to demolish a hard rock ledge in the mines with his drill, Henry hoisted himself to his feet, leaning heavily on his cane. Every movement seemed like such an effort today that Henry was inclined to think he might not be around to see this latest book come out. Sometimes these writers took years to squeeze out a skimpy little book you could read in less time than it took to play a decent game of poker. Other times no book showed up at all. Maybe somebody ought to interview them and make them explain why this writing business took so long. Slowly, with faltering steps, he made his way to the door. It was almost three o'clock, the time of day when he always sat outside for a while with Chester, and Henry did not like to have his routine interrupted.

After he had negotiated the door, Henry saw Chester already waiting for him in an old kitchen chair on the porch in front of the cabin next door. The well-nailed tightly set boards and trim railing of Henry's porch, kept in good repair by the young man down the street, were decidedly better than the cracked uneven boards with widening gaps, set just a foot or so above the ground, that Chester called a porch, but Chester liked to sit on his own porch because two years ago he had seen a rattler slither under the boards. Ever since, he had been waiting to decapitate it with his shovel. Lean and wizened, his thin chest caved in like an old barrel, his bald head mottled, and his shapeless nose reddened by years of hard drinking, Chester sat out on the porch, coughing, smoking the cigarettes long forbidden to him by the doctor, stubbing them out in an empty can, and tapping on the boards now and then with the shovel he kept by his side. "I can hear him. He's still rustling around under there," he would say to Henry, and Henry humored him. Waiting for the snake lent a certain excitement to their afternoons.

Henry lowered himself with difficulty into the sagging seat of the dilapidated rocking chair beside Chester and sat looking silently over the rooftops and the abandoned mines of Tonopah below them. New places had gone up here and there, but some of the old buildings like the Mizpah Hotel still stood on Main Street. To Henry's way of thinking, that meant that Tonopah had grown old in the right way, like a person losing his hair and wrinkling up but still recognizably himself. Not like Reno and Las Vegas, so changed now that a man could walk down the street and feel he'd never been there before.

Henry turned his glance to Chester, seeing in the mottled ancient beside him a shade of the wild and wiry youngster, dark hair pasted to his skull like shoe polish and cigarette pasted to his lip, who used to pour drinks at Jake's over sixty years ago. "She been to see you?" he inquired.

"Came and went this morning," said Chester. "Told her all about me and Wyatt Earp. I even drew her a picture. Said I was standing here"—he tapped with the shovel—

"and old Wyatt was over there, cool as you please, and them claim jumpers busted into the mine right there with guns a-blazin'. You got to draw 'em a picture, Henry. It gets 'em every time."

"She was just too polite to tell you what an old liar you are," said Henry. "She probably knows Wyatt Earp was long gone for California before you ever got here."

Chester chuckled. "I'm tellin' you, Henry, I had her goin'. And the fella with the big concha belt and the little bitty mustache that come by last year—he swallered it whole. All you got to do is draw 'em a picture. Now here's ole Wyatt . . ." His chuckles hoarsened into a prolonged fit of coughing.

"Did she ask about Gus?" asked Henry when the coughs had subsided.

"She asked about them dance hall queens. Told her some of 'em married nabobs and moved away and turned into society queens. A course I didn't point to no places, and I didn't name no names." He looked at Henry with a teasing twinkle in his bleary eyes.

"You sure you didn't let that mouth of yours run away with you?" demanded Henry, eyeing him severely.

"I wouldn't tell on your girlfriend, Henry. Don't I know you'd split my head wide open with that cane of yours if I did?"

Henry leaned back in the rocking chair, feeling easier in his mind. Gus was safe from the black tape recorders and the prying eyes of history. None of the old crowd who used to watch her shimmy across the floor at Jake's was left to tell but him and Chester. She'd go to her grave a fine lady, with no one any the wiser.

He watched the shadows move down the slope over Tonopah, washing over the pale hillocks of tailings across the highway. Down below a rancher's pickup rattled noisily up the street, loaded with supplies. That was part of what had drawn Henry back to Tonopah, after he'd finally "played his string out," as the old Comstockers used to say in Goldfield. If Tonopah wasn't clotted with burros and

prospectors and freight wagons the way he'd first seen it, at
least it was still a real place, not fancied up for tourists like
Virginia City. No strangers with maps and cameras cluttering up the sidewalks and pointing at things. Most everybody you met on Main Street had business there, which
was the way Henry liked it to be. Tonopah was still a working town, done with silver mining maybe, but a supply
center for ranches and mines in the country all around and
a main stop on the highway south from Reno. The kind of
place where Henry could keep his bearings, without feeling as if he was turning into the display in a lighted glass
case in a museum.

"She ask why you went to Goldfield?" he said to Chester after a while. It was a question he had never put to
Chester in all these years. To Henry's way of thinking, your
reasons—your real reasons—were as much a part of you as
your arm. Maybe that was why he didn't like this writer
probing at him any better than he liked the doctor pressing
and testing the hurtful places in his naked flesh. And why
he never thought about his reasons any more than he
thought about his other parts until something started aching. Like now.

"She asked why we come right enough," said Chester.
"Told her Pap said we was goin', so we just up'n went."

"Did your dad figure on striking it rich there?"

"Don't know if he thought so big as all that. Don't
b'lieve he hardly gave no thought to it at all. It come on
him more like an itch. Everybody in Cripple Creek was
goin' to Goldfield, and so was we. We was like geese flyin'
south, or grasshoppers, or them ratty little creeturs that
runs into the sea all in a bunch. We was just goin'. When
folks was movin', Pap couldn't stay put."

A sudden thought struck him. "I should've thought
quicker," he said, chuckling. "When she asked why we
come, I should've said it was Wyatt. Now Wyatt wrote me
this letter, see. He says, 'Chester, I'm in a tight spot, and I
need your help real bad . . .'"

Henry wasn't listening. He was thinking about going to

the gold rushes to make your fortune. That had made sense to people, when he told them the stories he'd read about the nabobs who made millions in the mining booms. John Mackay, who was nothing but a poor Irish miner when he started and came out of the Comstock with money to burn. Or Al Myers, so poor he had to hock his trunk before Goldfield turned him into a millionaire.

Mining booms were risky, of course. He'd admitted that, sitting at the kitchen table back in Iowa with the newspaper stories about Goldfield spread out in front of him. His father had listened, hurt darkening his eyes, while his mother sat with her handkerchief to her face. But when he explained how with no capital and a lot of hard work you stood a good chance of making a fortune in a gold rush, it sounded like a dollars-and-cents decision. A way to make money that they could understand, if not approve. Almost logical.

What he couldn't tell his father, or the interviewer, or anyone else, was the yearning that had curled in the heart of a young man and left him wide-awake at night, staring at the forked shadows cast on his bedroom window by the old elm tree and thinking of the world out beyond the elm tree that he would never see. Not unless he cut himself loose from Altman & Son and all that was safe and familiar in the little town where he had grown up. He had spoken to his father of mining millionaires and dollars and cents because he couldn't talk about the truth, the secret wishes and the pictures in his head that couldn't come out in words. Pacing in his room at night, he had imagined himself riding through vast deserts and pitching his tent on the empty plain like the first explorers. The sun glittered on the icy peaks of the far Sierra. Hawks wheeled overhead. Herds of mustangs, sorrel, black, and white galloped through the canyons of purple mountain ranges. The spicy smell of sagebrush filled the air. The moon rose over silver sands by night as coyotes howled eerily in the distance, and mirages of impossible castles and gardens trembled over the horizon by day.

He would pause in his pacing to read the newspaper clippings he already knew by heart and look at the books about the West that stood stacked in the same spot on his bedside table where his mother had kept the Bible. The dream grew stronger by the day. He saw himself with his pants tucked into his boot tops in the miner's way striding into the saloons of an evening. He would listen to the stories the grizzled prospectors told, drink raw whiskey that smoldered like live coals in his belly, and throw his dice at a green table with adventurers from all the four corners of the world. He wouldn't care if he won or lost, and neither would anyone else. No trickle of whispers running through the neighborhood about what he did and what time he came home. No watchful eyes peeping out from behind the curtains. No more evenings spent in a parlor on a stiff little chair not half his size trying to make small talk and wondering if later on he might have the chance to hold a woman's hand.

The women in that saloon flickered through his daydreams, a bevy of beauties dressed in brilliant colors. They'd never worry about what was nice and proper or what folks might say, not if they had the grit to follow a gold rush. These would be the wild and wanton ones he could never meet at a church social in Iowa. He saw their gleaming naked shoulders. They had a way of moving to make a man stare and met the stares with bold eyes. Women whose touch could make a man's blood sing.

Gus, long before he knew her name.

Manitow and Ironhand

A Tale of the Stony Mountains

JOHN JAKES

Dedicated to the memory of Karl May.

THE FREE TRAPPER, a strapping shaggy white man of inde-
terminate age, waded into his secret stream about a quarter mile above the wide beaver dam. His darting glance
revealed no dangers; nor did he truly expect any, this far
into the wilderness.

His buckskin shirt was wet, and soiled by many hasty
meals. His buckskin leggings were stagged at the knees,
where he'd sewn on pieces of fine English blanket, which
wouldn't shrink. Leggings and his wool-lined moccasins
were last year's tipi of a Crow chief of his acquaintance.

Shadows of quaking aspens and bending willows were
growing longer. It was nearing the twilight hour, the ideal
time for setting out traps. He would set this one, his fifth

of the afternoon, then one more before returning to his campsite, there to rest until he rose before daybreak to clear the traps. He shifted his campsite nightly; a professional precaution of those who worked alone. Also, he now had eighty plews to protect—a valuable mixed bale of beaver, marten, and otter, weighing nearly a hundred pounds. So far the spring trapping season had been bountiful.

The late afternoon air was light and warm, but the water was still icy from the melted snows. The soft-burbling stream froze his bones and set his hands to aching, the good right one and the mangled left one he concealed with a filthy mitten except when he was at his trade, as now. He went by the name "Old Ironhand," though he really wasn't old, except in spirit. The snowy white streaks in his long hair were premature. There was a bitter cynicism in his eyes, the oldest part of him.

Once his name had been Ewing. Ewing Something. It was a name he no longer used, and struggled to remember. Ever since he'd split with the Four Flags outfit, and Mr. Alexander Jaggers—ever since they'd crippled his left hand, causing him to compensate with exercises that strengthened the other one, welding five digits into a weapon—to the free trappers and those who still gave allegiance to the large outfits, he was Old Ironhand.

He waded along, carrying the seven-pound trap and chain in his left hand, the pin pole in his right. He moved carefully, the small sounds of his passage undetectable because of the water's purl. This was a fine stream; he'd been working it for a year. It yielded fat mature beaver, fifty to sixty pounds each, with choice tails he charred, skinned, then boiled as a mealtime delicacy. Hip deep in his secret stream, he felt good as he approached a natural beaver slide worn into the bank at the water's edge. The shadowed air was sweet. The trees were a-bud, the mountain peaks pristine as a new wedding dress, the sky a pale pink, like a scene from a book about fairyland. He saw a mockingbird singing alertly on a bush. It was 1833, in the Stony Mountains, far from the civilized perfidy of other white men.

He laid the pin pole on the bank. He crouched in the water and lowered the trap to the bottom, drawing out the chain with its ring at the end. By now he was bent like a bow, half his beard immersed. The water smelled icy and clean.

He pushed the pin pole through the ring on the chain. Then he grasped the pole with both hands and began to twist it into the marly bottom. He leaned and pushed and twisted with his great right hand bloodless-white around the pole. If the trapped beaver didn't gnaw his paw off and escape—if he died as he should, by drowning—the pole would site his carcass.

In order to leave as little man-scent as possible, Ironhand worked obliquely backward toward the bank, to a willowy branch he'd already selected for its pronounced droop. He unstoppered his horn of medicine, which he compounded from secret ingredients added to the musky secretions of beaver glands, and with this he coated the end of the drooping branch. The strongly scented end of the branch hung near the pin pole.

Hands on his hips, he inspected his work. Though by now his teeth were chattering—the spring warmth was leaching from the plum-colored shadows—he was satisfied. Felt better than he had in a long spell. One more trap to place, then he'd have his supper, and a pipe.

He was turning to move on to the next location when the rifle shot rang out. The bullet hit him high in the back. Toppling, he thought not of the awful hot pain but instead of his failure to hear the rifleman stealing up for the cowardly ambush. *Careless damn fool! Should of kept your eyes skinned!* He was reasonably sure of his attacker's identity, but that wasn't much damn satisfaction as the muddy bank hurled up to strike him.

And that was all there was.

Someone had dragged him to level ground.
Someone had rolled him on his back.

Someone had built a fire whose comforting heat played along the left side of his seamed face, and the back of his ruined hand. The fire was vivid, shooting off sparks as brilliant as the mountain stars. A curtain of smoke blew away on a puff of breeze.

He elbowed himself to a raised position, clenching his teeth against the pain. The Samaritan was squatting on the other side of the fire. A young Indian, with a well-sculpted nose, firm mouth, light brown skin that shimmered bronze in the firelight. His glowing dark eyes were not unfriendly, only carefully, unemotionally observant.

Bluish-black hair hung like a veil down his back, to his waist. His costume consisted of moccasins ornamented with porcupine quills and bright trade beads, fringed leggings, a hunting coat of elk leather. Around his neck hung a small medicine bag that nestled inside his coat against his bare chest. Outside the coat, ornamentation was a three-strand necklace of bear claws. A double-barrel rifle rested within his reach.

"I put medicine on you. The ball is still there. It must come out. Do you understand?"

"Delaware," Ironhand grunted, not as a question. He understood perfectly.

"Yes." The Indian nodded. "I am Manitow."

"My pardner, the one they killed at the rendezvous two year ago, he was Delaware. Named after the great old chief Tammany. Fine man." So were most of the members of the tribe who roved the Stony Mountains. The Delaware had been driven from Eastern hunting grounds eighty to ninety years ago; had migrated over the Mississippi and successfully taken up farming on the plains. A few, more restless and independent, had pushed farther on to the mountains. Enemies of the Delaware, including ignorant whites, sneered at them as Petticoat Indians. That was not only stupid but dangerous. Ironhand knew the Delaware to be keen shots, excellent horsemen, superb trackers and readers of sign. They were honest; quick to learn; resourceful in the wilderness. You could depend on them unless for some reason they hated you.

The Delaware could find the remotest beaver streams as handily as a magnet snapped bits of iron to itself. Thus they were prized pardners of the free trappers, or prized employees of the outfits such as Four Flags.

The white man licked his dry lips, then said, "I'm called Old Ironhand."

"I have heard of you. Who shot you?"

"I think it was the Frenchman, *Petit Josep. Petit Josep Clair de Lune.* Little Joe Moonlight."

"Works for Jaggers."

"I worked for Jaggers . . ."

"I know that. Don't talk anymore. The ball must come out." In a calm, almost stately way, Manitow rose from his crouch. His hair shimmered, black as the seepage of one of the oil springs that produced the tar trappers like Ironhand rubbed on their arthritic joints.

Without being told, Ironhand rolled over to his belly. It hurt hellishly. In the firelight a long rustfree knife sparkled in Manitow's hand; an authentic Green River—Ironhand glimpsed the GR, *George Rex,* stamped into the blade in England. It was a knife as good as Ironhand's own, which he'd left with his possibles bag, his bale of plews, and his carbine, in what he'd presumed was a safe clearing upstream.

Manitow laid the knife on the ground. From a pocket in his coat he took the all-purpose awl most Delaware carried. He placed this beside the knife. One or the other, or maybe both, would mine for lead in Ironhand's back. The trapper stared at the implements with bleary eyes and made a heavy swallowing sound.

Manitow knelt beside him. With a gentle touch he lifted Ironhand's bloody shirt high enough to expose the wound glistening with smelly salve. With the fingers of his left hand Manitow spread the dark brown edges of the wound. A swift, sharp inhale from Ironhand was the only sound.

"Be sure you get it out," he said. "I don't want to go down with the sun. That bastard Jaggers has to pay. Little Joe Moonlight will pay. Go ahead, dig."

"I don't have whiskey," Manitow said.

"I don't need any whiskey," Ironhand said. "Dig."

A night bird trilled in the darkness. Old Ironhand listened drowsily. He was coming awake; hadn't died under Manitow's ministrations, which had hurt infernally. He had, however, fainted at the moment the Indian worked the rifle ball out of the wound with bloody fingers, ending the ordeal.

Ironhand's eyes fluttered open. Against a morning sky the color of lemons, Manitow crouched by the fire as he had the night before; a small dented pot, blue enamelware, sat in the embers.

A white mist floated on the high peaks. The air nipped; Manitow had found a colorful trade blanket as a coverlet for the trapper. Ironhand heard a nickering; tried to rise up.

"Your horses are safe, with mine," Manitow said. "Your gun and plews also." Small comfort, now that Ironhand realized the outfit was still after him.

Manitow stretched out his hand, offering a strip of *charqui*, the smoked buffalo meat that was a staple of frontiersmen. The trapper caught the meat between his teeth. He lay back, gazing at the sky, and chewed.

The enamel pot lid clinked when Manitow lifted it. "Coffee is boiling. Ready soon."

Ironhand grunted and kept chewing. A hawk sailed in heaven, then plunged and vanished in the mists. The cold ground smelled of damp and made him think of death, not springtime. On his back under his shirt, where the Indian had prospected for lead, a thick pad of some kind told him Manitow had improvised a dressing.

"You have been a trapper for many years," the Indian said in a reflective way.

Old Ironhand pushed the jerky into his cheek, like a cud, while he answered. "Twenty years next summer."

"All that time. And a man stalks you and you don't see any sign?"

"I wasn't looking for none."

"You didn't hear him?"

His anger was sudden, overriding his pain. "I was in the stream. It makes noise. I was thinking about my traps. I thought the outfit was done with me. Christ, they did me enough damage—why not?"

Manitow's grunt seemed to scorn that naive conclusion. The damn Indian made Ironhand uneasy with his quiet, unruffled manner. His air of wisdom annoyed and puzzled the trapper, because of Manitow's relative youth.

"Done with you?" Manitow repeated. "Not when the fur trade is sickly and you steal profits from the company by working for yourself and selling to others."

"You sure"—a gasp of pain punctuated the sentence—"seem to know a devil of a lot about me. How come?"

Ironhand's head was rolled to the side now; his old reddened eyes stared. Almost shyly, Manitow dropped his own gaze to the smoldering fire, from which he pulled the dented pot. He poured steaming coffee into Ironhand's own drinking cup.

"Help me sit up. Then answer my damn question."

There followed a slow and elaborate ritual of raising him, Manitow gently pulling on his forearms rather than pushing at his back. Resting on his elbows worsened Ironhand's pain again, but his position enabled him to suck some of the bitter hot coffee out of the cup Manitow held to his lips. At length the Indian said:

"The people in the Stony Mountains know Old Ironhand. They know the evil ways of Four Flags, too. For five winters and summers I have been north, Canada, hunting and trapping. Even so far away, we heard of the crimes of Four Flags. No more talk. Rest awhile now."

"I've got to go," the trapper protested, wriggling on his elbows and accidentally falling back, a terrific jolt that made him cry out. "Got to go," he repeated in a hoarse voice. "Catch that Little Joe . . ."

"In a day or two. No sooner."

The Indian's flat declaration angered the trapper again. Then a bolt of guilt struck him; he was being an ungrateful bastard. After licking a drop of coffee from his droopy mustache, he said, "I didn't thank you proper yet. For taking care of my wound and all. For coming along when you did. That was a piece of luck."

Manitow silently watched the ethereal mist drifting over the hidden peaks.

"Anyway—it's a debt I owe."

Manitow's eyes, black and opaque, met his again. "I am sorry I did not come in time to stop the assassin. Fortunately he was a bad shot."

"Little Joe has a big opinion of himself. I 'spect he thought he couldn't miss."

"And I was coming close, so he couldn't wait to find out. I was not far behind him, though approaching from a different direction. That's why I didn't see his sign, only heard his rifle. Until then I did not know there were two hunting you."

Confusion was followed by a stab of fear. "Two? Who else . . . ?"

Manitow stared.

"You? Why?"

"To see what kind of man you were. Are. I hold you responsible."

"For what?"

"The death of my brother. The one who was your partner."

Ah, Christ, Christ, Ironhand cried silently, stunned harder than he was when the rifle ball struck him. *He's no friend. He saved me for the pleasure of killing me himself.*

But there was no apparent hostility in the Indian's speech or demeanor. He merely asked the trapper to give him a brief history of the quarrel that had led to his brother's death, and the cowardly attack by the lackey of Four Flags.

"I'd have to go back a few years," Old Ironhand said. "The summer rendezvous of 'twenty-eight, I had quit as a brigade leader for the outfit a year before, but on good terms with Jaggers—we had an agreement that Four Flags would take all my plews and I'd work for no other." Four Flags was a fur company as big and powerful as Astor's. English, French, Russian, and American interests had pooled money to establish it. The boss west of St. Louis was Alexander Jaggers, who headquartered at Kirk's Fort.

The annual summer rendezvous was a combination trade mart and revel; a great gathering where spring plews were sold, and trappers bought new equipment pack-trained out from St. Louis, all in the midst of much drinking and horse racing and woman swapping and other familiar entertainments of the frontier. Manitow said that before he went to Canada he had come down from the Wind Rivers several times, to the barren and unlovely Upper Valley of the Green, there to take part in the rendezvous himself. Ironhand didn't remember meeting him, or hearing his name.

Speaking slowly, taking occasional sips of the cooling coffee, the trapper explained that it was at the summer rendezvous of 'twenty-eight that he saw his first black silk topper. A disreputable German merchant of traps, cutlery, and other metalware was wearing it. The hat was already hard-used, soiled by filthy stains and pierced by a bullet front and back. Ironhand had quickly understood it was the enemy when the peddler said:

"These they are wearing on the Continent now. Gents in the East are taking up the fashion. It's the modern style, beaver hats will go out, you mark me. Also my cousin in Köln writes me to say inventors are perfecting machines to manufacture fine felting cheaply from all kinds of materials, even paper. This trade will die. Is dying now."

The following two years confirmed it. In the great days, the high days of the trade, when Ironhand was still a brigade leader, the company paid as much as $9 a plew to certain free trappers to keep them working exclusively for Four Flags. By 1830 all was changed; average plews selling for $4 at St. Louis slipped to $3.75, no matter who trapped the animals. Then buyers at the summer rendezvous refused to go above $3.50. Ironhand was haunted by memories of the silk topper.

Alexander Jaggers was a short, prim Scot; a Glaswegian. A bachelor, his two passions were Four Flags and his religion. When he first came out to Kirk's Fort in 1822, he had transported a compact gleaming Philadelphia-made pump organ on which he played and sang Christian hymns in a stentorian voice.

In 1831 Jaggers spoke to Ironhand about the price of plews. They were still dropping. Every free trapper working for Four Flags would have to accept $3, St. Louis, or further business was impossible. Ironhand refused.

Alexander Jaggers showed no visible anger, merely turned his back, swished up his coattails, sat at the organ, and began to play and sing "Saviour, Like a Shepherd Lead Us." But to bring Ironhand in line, discipline him, show him his error, Jaggers's henchman, Little Joe Moonlight, set on Ironhand's pardner at the summer rendezvous.

Little Joe, a mustachioed weasel-chinned fellow, turned up with a couple of the bravos who frequently backed his most brutal plays. They cornered Ironhand's pardner while the trapper was occupied with a comely Snake woman, the Snake women being universally conceded as the most attractive, and the most generous with their favors, of all the women of the many tribes.

Little Joe and his cronies pretended they were merely sporting with Tammany, hazing him, before the accident happened. As Ironhand learned afterward, Little Joe and his bravos seized the Indian's wrist and swung him round and round in circles, cracking his arm like a whip. Tammany tried to fight them but the odds were wrong; he was soon reeling.

One of the bravos knocked the bung from a small whiskey keg and poured the contents over the Delaware. The bravos and Little Joe roared. But they swore ever afterward that the dousing was supposed to be the end of it. How the stray ember from a nearby cook fire accidentally fell on Tammany, igniting the spirits, was a mystery. Damn shame, but a mystery. Little Joe and his bravos fled the rendezvous before Ironhand could catch up to them. Ironhand's pardner lived a day and a night, in broiled black agony, before the mercy of death.

Ironhand, who at the time still went by his old name, left the encampment at once. He rode night and day for Kirk's Fort, there to confront Alexander Jaggers, who never personally went to the rendezvous. Little Joe Moonlight had beaten Ironhand to the fort and was hovering in Jaggers's quarters when Ironhand, full of drink, kicked the door down and leaped on the Scot to strangle him.

"Little Joe whistled up his bravos," Ironhand said to Manitow. "They swarmed on me. Looking pious as a deacon, Mr. Jaggers said that in a spirit of Christian forgiveness, Little Joe would only break the hand I used least."

He held up the twisted crooked fingers; Manitow had removed the dirty mitten while he slept.

The misshapen claw was sufficient to suggest the scene: Little Joe's helpers knocking Ironhand to the floor, stomping him into a stupor. Little Joe slapping Ironhand's outstretched arm over a table while the bravos held fast to the groggy trapper's shoulders; the bravos had flung him to a kneeling position.

Gleefully, Little Joe raised a trade hatchet and smashed the blunt end of the blade on the outstretched hand. At the organ, his back turned to the mayhem, Mr. Jaggers pumped and sang.

> "We've a story to tell to the nations
> That shall turn their hearts to the right!

A story of truth and mercy!
A story of peace and light!"

Little Joe Moonlight grasped Ironhand's index finger, bent it and broke it. Then he broke the middle finger. Next the ring finger. After a few more blows with the now-bloody hatchet, he broke the little finger. To Ironhand's everlasting disgust, when Little Joe bent the thumb backward and that snapped, he screamed. More than once. Sweaty-cheeked, Mr. Jaggers pumped faster, and sang to drown the noise:

> *"We've a song to be sung to the nations*
> *That shall lift their hearts to the Lord!*
> *A song that shall conquer evil*
> *And shatter the spear and sword!*
> *For the darkness shall turn to dawning . . ."*

He remembered his hand lying on the table like a bloody red piece of buffalo hump. He remembered starting to swoon.

> *"And the dawning to noonday bright!*
> *And Christ's great kingdom shall come on earth,*
> *The kingdom of Love and Light!"*

Then Ironhand heard Little Joe, his voice very distant, as though he were shouting in a windy cave. "You don't need to play no more, Mr. Jaggers, he's all done screaming."

Little Joe lifted Ironhand's head by the hair and let it fall, thump . . .

Out of some perverse piety that governed him, Mr. Jaggers rushed Ironhand to a comfortable bunk in the fort barracks, and saw to it that he was given excellent treatment until he recovered his senses.

His hand, of course, was permanently maimed. This Mr. Jaggers totally ignored when he and Ironhand parted. Jaggers shook the trapper's right hand—the left was already concealed by the first of many mittens. "The account book is closed, laddie." It was not, but Ironhand was too enraged to do anything except glare. "We part as competitors, but eternal friends. Christ counsels forgiveness above all."

"Forgiveness," Ironhand muttered, waving his mitten in an obvious way. Mr. Jaggers merely beamed and pumped the other hand . . .

"That was two years back," Ironhand explained to Manitow in a weary voice. "After a while I came to believe his crazy cant about forgiving and forgetting. I wanted to mend my life, so I didn't take after him as I could have. I sold my plews to Astor, though they say he's tired of falling prices too and will get out . . . what a fool I was, wouldn't you say? Trying to get on with keeping alive, forgetting Jaggers?"

The spring sun had burned off the spectral mist; the snow peaks were brilliant against hazy lavender sky. Ironhand was exhausted from speaking. Manitow chewed on a strip of *charqui* and considered what he'd heard. At last he said:

"Many traps are set in this wilderness. You were caught in the cruelest of all. Trust."

And do I dare trust you, you ring-tailed savage? Not so far's as I could throw you. I daren't turn my back.

Still, there were necessities:

"Will you help me up? I have to pee."

"Clasp my arm with both hands."

Ironhand braced his boot heels and was slowly, painfully raised to standing position. His eyes were close to Manitow's a moment but he could read nothing there, except what he imagined was there—an intent to murder. The trap of trust, was it? Well, not a second time . . .

As he hobbled toward a grove of white birch trees, he bit out, "This time I won't turn my cheek. I'm going after that pissant who does the dirty work for Jaggers."

"I will go with you."

Ironhand twisted around, causing a hell-hot pain in his bandaged back. "Why? So's you can pass judgment?"

His face a smooth bronze mask, Manitow said, "It may be so."

I won't turn my back, you red devil . . .

But he hobbled on, grasping Manitow's arm for support; for the present he was at the mercy of the unavoidable necessities.

They rode southeast, the direction of Kirk's Fort. The fort stood sixty miles beyond the foothills of the Stony Mountains, at the confluence of two shallow muddy streams. It was the jumping-off place for St. Louis. Ironhand presumed it was also the destination of the quarry whose sign they were following. He was in constant pain, but it was bearable. Hate was a stronger painkiller than opium.

He trailed his three pack mules behind his old roan. Manitow could have sped ahead because he had a better horse, which he rode with only a scrap of blanket and his moccasined heels. The Indian's horse was small, with spots like swollen inkblots on his white rump. The trapper enviously compared his faithful but sorry saddle animal, Brownie, with the other horse, which the Cayuse tribe had bred and sold to the Indian. Cayuse and Nez Perce horses were the best a man could find. Ironhand had evidence of it the first morning. He woke in his odorous blankets to find Manitow gone. A distant drumming stilled his sudden alarm. Somewhere in the foothills Manitow was galloping his spotted horse.

Another thing bred envy, in the same dark inner place as Ironhand's suspicion of murder being planned: Manitow's skill with sign. The second noon, examining horse dung, Ironhand said, "He's near a day in front of us."

Manitow shook his head. "Less than half a day. Moving slowly. Not fearful he will be caught."

Ironhand's cheeks turned red above his beard that still

held crumbs of ship's biscuit from breakfast. "Why'n hell not? He knows he didn't put me down for good."

"That may be so, it may not. I will show you why he doesn't worry." Manitow led him to a clump of stunted shrubbery, stepped around it, pointed. Ironhand saw more droppings. "There are three now. Your assassin and two more."

"Since when in hell—?"

"Sunset, yesterday."

"You damn well should of told me."

Manitow smiled. "It would have spoiled our supper. If I had told you then, would you have stopped this chase?"

"Not likely."

The Indian bobbed his head, vindicated.

They talked intermittently as they tracked Little Joe Moonlight and his companions moving southeast ahead of them. Manitow expressed no surprise at the treatment the trapper had received from Four Flags. "Theft, ambush, murder—it is the way of the strong companies against the single weak rebel. It is the way of those white men who are evil."

Which should have soothed Ironhand's suspicion a little, since it was clear from Manitow's voice and expression which side he favored. But Ironhand wasn't soothed. He continued to insist that Manitow ride ahead of him; they had sorted that out before they started. Ironhand still believed Manitow would try to murder him at the first opportunity.

They exchanged stories of their trials in the wilderness. Manitow pushed up the sleeve of his hunting coat to reveal a snakelike scar on his left forearm. Ironhand, who had seen plenty of horrors in his time, was nevertheless a little sick at the sight of the healed tissue, because of what had made it. Manitow had survived the bites of a rabid wolf, in the land of the Apaches, far south. He didn't explain why he had been in the land of the Apaches.

Ironhand told of nearly starving to death several times during his career. "I slew my mules and drank their blood once. I ate my moccasins twice. Another time, all I could find to feed on after five days was ants from an anthill." Manitow seemed to find these exploits unremarkable; almost to be expected.

He did express admiration for Ironhand's carbine. The trapper explained that it was a custom creation from the armory of the legendary Wyatt Henry of St. Louis. The revolving magazine, Henry's unique design, held five rounds.

Manitow asked to handle the piece. Ironhand said no. Manitow looked at him, and seemed to sneer just before he trotted his spotted horse ahead again.

As the mountains fell behind, the twisted gullies straightened; the shale ridges sank; the spring prairie rose up to greet them. They saw a migratory herd of buffalo passing southward in a dust cloud that boiled nearly to the apex of the sky. "Thousands upon thousands of shaggy brothers," Manitow said. Ironhand growled something under his breath; he already knew the herd was huge, they had been watching it the best part of an hour. The upstart savage was beginning to anger as well as worry him.

Or was it the sign they'd read—two unknown bravos and a third smug killer lolling their way toward Kirk's Fort without concern? Manitow insisted the trio was only a couple of hours ahead now.

A sunlit dust seemed to float above the silent plain surrounding them. The sky was tawny, like the earth, only a few cottonwoods with twisted shapes breaking the horizon. The vista had the serene quality of a landscape painting, but the diffuse light and dust gave it a touch of the unreal, like a picture from one of those fables of old Greek gods Ironhand dimly remembered reading from a hornbook when he was a child, in a civilized place somewhere.

At sunset they stopped to camp and eat. The trapper took some kindling from a parfleche strapped to a mule. Manitow watched him build a small pyramid of sticks, then said, "If you cook they will see the smoke."

"Hardly matters, does it? We'll find each other one way or another. That's the idea."

Late next day they approached a wide turgid stream Ironhand identified as Paint River, though the only artist's color represented in its flow was dirty brown. Natural features surrounding Kirk's Fort had been named by the fur men passing through.

While they watered and rested their animals, Ironhand advised the Indian that one more day would bring them to the headquarters of Four Flags. "I have to speed up. Leave the mules. Catch them before they're safe inside the fort."

"Even with three against you?"

Ironhand answered with a nod.

Manitow sighted ahead. "I will go on a little way."

He didn't ask permission, hitting his spotted horse with his heels and splashing on across Paint River. Ironhand hunkered down on the long narrow hump of an island in the middle of the water, where they'd pulled up. What the hell was the upstart savage about?

Manitow galloped away till he was a speck, then galloped back. He threw himself off his spotted horse, looking unhappy.

"One has gone on ahead, leaving two. Their tracks turn north. I think they saw the smoke and are circling back."

Ironhand's gaze crawled to stunted trees on the northern horizon. Nothing moved there, nor anyplace. Manitow said, "We should camp. I do not think you need to chase your enemy anymore. He will find you. He knows you are hurt. But he will think you are alone."

Ironhand scowled, gripping his Henry rifle with his powerful right hand. "I am. Isn't your fight."

"I am here, so it will be. There is no reason not to cook again. Have you any sticks left in the saddlebag?"

Ironhand slept badly, rolling around with his carbine clutched against his middle, the way he'd slept with it nightly since he met the prowling Indian. A new moon shed pale light on the plain, which was flat for miles in every direction save north, where a pronounced tilt raised the horizon. Along that horizon the crooked trees stood out. If there were a fight on this barren hump of island, would he have to look out for Manitow and Little Joe Moonlight at the same time? A threat of death from two directions . . . ?

He wished he could sleep but it was impossible. Manitow lay to his left, hands crossed on his shirt bosom, profile sharp in the pale moonshine. The Indian breathed softly, steadily, like a small boy sleeping without care.

He must have dozed. He woke to Manitow barking his name. Ironhand floundered to his knees, saw Manitow standing beyond the mules and pointing to the stunted trees. Two riders were pounding down the inclined plain, riding with their knees and reins in their teeth. Each held a brace of revolvers. Four guns against his one.

"Protect yourself," Manitow cried, diving under the belly of a snorting bucking mule. Seizing Ironhand, he tried to throw him to the ground. Little Joe Moonlight and his burly pardner were riding hell-bent for the hump island, but Ironhand refused to cower. He shook off the Indian and took his fighting stance with his carbine at his shoulder. His blood was up; he didn't care that he presented a perfect target.

The riders were closer. He distinctly saw Little Joe's mean white triangular face, his long Chinese-style mustaches, his leering smirk. Still short of the riverbank, Little Joe and his pardner opened up with all four barrels. Ironhand stood his ground and squeezed his trigger. Manitow tackled him. Yelling, Ironhand toppled. Only the fall prevented one of the flying bullets from finding him.

He didn't realize this; all his anger was directed against the damned Indian. He screamed oaths, trying to get up as Little Joe Moonlight galloped into the stream, closely followed by his henchman. Manitow snatched his double-barrel rifle from its saddle loop. The blued metal flashed. The charging horses tossed up fans of moonlit water.

Little Joe passed to the left of Ironhand and the Indian, the henchman to the right. They were firing continuously. One of their bullets hit Manitow's rifle, a lucky shot that blew apart the breech. Manitow leaped back, momentarily blinded. A bullet hit Ironhand's left thigh just as he stood up. With a cry he fell a second time. The back of his head struck the earth. Stars danced.

The mules bucked and bellowed. Two of them tore their picket pins out and ran into the stream, braying. Ironhand heard the attackers splash to the bank of Paint River behind him and there wheel for another charge. His back wound, cruelly bruised by his fall, hurt nearly as much as the thigh wound bleeding into the leg of his hide trousers. He had to get up . . . *had* to. Tried it and, with a howl of despair and fury, fell back again. He heard the attacking horses coming on, in the river.

Standing over the wounded trapper, Manitow said, "Give me the rifle."

He'll use it to kill me . . .

"The rifle!"

Don't dare, I can't trust . . .

"White man, if you don't, we'll die."

There was a halo of hoof-driven dust around Manitow's head. He looked like some ghost of one of his primitive ancestors. His outstretched brown hand opened, demanding. "White man—*obey me!*"

The hoofs were thunderous. Risking all, the supreme act of trust, Ironhand flung the carbine upward and Manitow snatched it and put it to his shoulder. Bullets were flying again but Manitow stood firm and fired and kept firing. As the horse of Little Joe's henchman passed within Ironhand's field of vision, the trapper saw the nameless bravo lift in his saddle as if being jerked to heaven. The bravo's horse ran out from under him and he crashed and rolled into the brown water, staining it with blood from his open belly.

Ironhand was shouting without realizing it. "Stop firing, there are only five—"

Too late; some part of his brain had already counted five shots. Manitow had exhausted the magazine in one volley.

And Little Joe Moonlight, his long, thin mustaches whipping against his cheeks, was unhurt.

He wheeled his horse in the water, making him dance to the island, then stand still while Little Joe raised his revolver with his shooting hand, clasped it with his other hand and pointed it at Manitow's head at close range.

It all happened quickly. Ironhand acted from instinct, coming upright, dizzy and tortured by pain but willing it not to matter. He leaped at Little Joe Moonlight and his prancing horse. Little Joe was angrily heeling the animal while trying to steady himself for the shot. Manitow crouched and pulled his knife to throw it but Little Joe would fire first. There was no cover to keep the Indian from death.

The horse sidestepped again; Little Joe screamed a filthy oath. He realized too late that his mount had sidestepped *toward* Ironhand . . .

Ironhand's face contorted into a bestial parody of a grin. His filthy mitten closed on Little Joe's right arm. Little Joe understood his peril and shrieked girlishly. Ironhand brought his huge right hand upward from his hip at great speed while pulling his enemy out of the saddle. The angle was right; the edge of the trapper's hand struck Little Joe's windpipe with speed and force.

Paralyzed, Little Joe dropped his revolver. Two streams of blood spurted from his nostrils. Ironhand threw Little Joe on the sere ground and knelt on his chest with one knee. He snatched his knife from the thong at his waist. Poised to cut Little Joe's throat, Ironhand started at a touch on his shoulder.

"Wait. Look at him. His spirit is gone. It flew before he touched the earth."

Ironhand changed position so that he could press an ear to his enemy's chest. He hunched that way for a long space, then raised his head, starting to shake from shock.

Manitow was right again. The heart of Little Joe Moonlight had stopped.

Ironhand lurched up. His wounded leg would barely support him. His back was screaming with pain. He poked his knife at the thong loop on his belt and missed. He missed a second time. Manitow took the knife from him and put it in place, giving the thong an extra twist to secure the hilt.

Ironhand raked a trembling hand through his dirty beard. "I—didn't want to give you the rifle."

"Why?"

"I knew you'd kill me after you saved yourself."

"Why?"

"Your brother—"

"The white man's mind," Manitow said with enormous disgust. "Don't you think I had a hundred opportunities to kill you before this?"

"But you said I was responsible—"

"That was before I met you. I wanted to learn what sort you are. I learned. You learned nothing, you were full of the poison bile of fear. You're like all the rest of the whites, even though not as bad as some. It's lucky you broke down and gave me the rifle or the story would end differently."

He stepped forward suddenly—it seemed menacing until Ironhand realized the true import. Then he felt a fool. Manitow supported his back and forearm gently. "Now you had better lie down before you fall down, white man." He no longer sounded scornful.

Stiff and sore in heavy bandages, Ironhand rode alone up the dirt track to the gate of Kirk's Fort. Draped in a U over the neck of his horse Brownie was the smelly corpse of Little Joe Moonlight.

Kirk's Fort was old and famous on the plains. It was a large rectangular stockade with a blockhouse at every corner. Cabins and warehouse buildings formed two of its walls. Ironhand passed through the palisade by the main gate, which opened on a long dirt corridor of sheds and shops. A second inner gate led to the quadrangle, where Indians were never admitted; all trading was done in the corridor, though even here there were precautions. Bars on the shop windows; iron shutters on the windows of the storehouse that held trade goods.

A toothless fort Indian sat against the wall, looking sadly displaced in a white man's knitted cap and a white soldier's discarded blouse. He popped his eyes at Iron-hand, whom he recognized. The trapper rode on through the second gate and straight across the trampled soil of the quadrangle to the Four Flags headquarters building. Company employees appeared around corners or from doorways of the accounting office, the strongbox room, the powder house, staring at Ironhand in a bewildered way. Someone called a greeting he didn't acknowledge. No one stopped him as he kicked the office door open and lumbered through, Little Joe's stiffening body folded over his shoulder, his Henry carbine tucked under his arm.

Alexander Jaggers was occupied with familiar things: his quill, his account books. Seeing the looming figure, he exclaimed, "Ewing! Laddie—what's this? Ye dinna hae the courtesy to knock or announce yersel—"

He was stopped by Ironhand slipping the Henry onto the seat of a chair, then laying the body of Little Joe Moonlight on top of the wide wooden desk. It disarranged the account books and overturned the ink pot, which dripped its contents on the old floor.

"He met with an accident. It happens often in the mountains," Ironhand said with a meaningful look at the master of Four Flags.

Jaggers reddened, puffing out his cheeks. He darted a hand to a drawer of the desk but Ironhand was quicker. He leaped on the desk, over Little Joe's corpse, and pushed Jaggers, toppling him and his chair at the same time. Jaggers flailed, kicking his legs in the air and yelling decidedly un-Christian oaths.

Ironhand jumped down and retrieved his Henry rifle

from the chair. He took aim and emptied the revolving
magazine, five rounds, into Mr. Jaggers's pump organ in
the corner. After the roar of the volley, the organ exhaled
once, loudly, like a man with pierced lungs gasping his last.

The trapper stepped to the pump organ and attacked
its wood cabinet with his right hand. The hand beat and
smashed like a hammer; a mace; a sledge. Thin veneers
cracked and snapped. Jaggers was screaming and vainly
trying to rise, but his fall had sprung some leg muscle, and
each attempt was more futile than the last; he continued
to wail on his back, heels in the air.

Ironhand locked his two hands together, the good with
the ruined, and brought this huge hammerhead of flesh
and bone down on the frame of the organ, breaking it in
two as if it were a man's spine.

Jaggers screamed misery and rage.

Ironhand picked up his Henry and walked out without
a backward look.

The daylight was waning too soon. Sunset was many hours
away. But the sky and the prairie were dark, and the air
was damp. Away in the north, thunder was bumping.

The dew and damp produced a ground mist that con-
gealed and spread rapidly. As Ironhand rode to the cottonwood grove two miles west of the fort, he craned around in
his saddle—at no small cost in pain—and saw the corner
blockhouses floating above murky gray mist-clouds, like
ogres' castles in the sky in a fairytale.

When he reached the grove, Manitow woke up,
scratched his back, stood, asked:

"Where for you now?"

"Back to the mountains. Back to the beaver. It's the
only trade I know. They aren't all wearing silk toppers in
New York town yet, I wager."

Manitow paused before saying, "I know secret streams,
Old Ironhand. Three or four, locked so far in the Stony
Mountains you would never find them alone."

"Hmm. Well. Let's see. I'd like a pardner again. A free trapper needs a pardner. But I never paid your brother any sort of fee, like many do. We split what the plews brought in."

"That would be agreeable."

"If you think you can trust me not to cost you your life?" Ironhand asked, a sudden flash of sourness.

Manitow took it calmly; seriously. "The old Scot will trouble you no more, I think. But can you trust me?"

Ironhand's wreck of a face seemed to relax. "We crossed that river a while back."

Slowly, with graceful ceremonious moves, Manitow the Delaware drew from his waist his splendid long Green River knife. He held it out, handle first.

With equal ceremony, Ironhand took his equally fine knife from its thong. He held it out the same way. Among the men of the mountains, white and red, there was no more significant gesture of trust.

"Pardner."

"Pardner."

They exchanged knives. Manitow kissed the fingers of his right hand and raised them over his head in a mystical gesture. Ironhand laughed, deep and rumbling. They mounted up and rode away together into the storm.

Afterword

The western writer Karl May probably did more to promote the splendor and excitement of the West to non-Americans than anyone except Buffalo Bill Cody, king of the scouts, the arena show and the dime novel. Yet not many fans of the genre, perhaps excluding specialist scholars, know of him.

Surely this is because Karl May was born in Saxony in 1842, wrote only in German, and visited America just once—four years before his death in 1912. By that time he had written seventy-four volumes, forty of them set in "the American Wild West."

May was decidedly an odd bird for this sort of missionary work. He knew about the West only through reading—some of which was done in prison. May was jailed four times in his early life, for assorted thefts and swindles. During his longest sentence, four years, he ran a prison library.

May's youth was hard. He was afflicted with spells of near-blindness. He came from what we would call a dysfunctional family. Of thirteen brothers and sisters, nine died.

When old enough, he entered a preparatory school for teachers. He was expelled for stealing. It didn't seem to teach him a lesson; other crimes—other incarcerations—followed.

But reading somehow turned him around, much as it turns around quite a few convict-writers. In 1875 Karl May published the first of his westerns.

His white hero had different names in different stories: Old Surehand; Old Firehand; Old Shatterhand. He was a *Westmänn* (Westman)—not a native frontiersman but a strong, suave, cultured European who quickly adapted to the rigors and perils of the West by means of intelligence and physical strength. Old Shatterhand possessed a "mighty fist" useful for dispatch of villains. But he also carried firepower, in the form of a fantastic repeating rifle custom-crafted by the "legendary" gunsmith, Mr. Henry of St. Louis. This *Henrystutzen* (Henry carbine) with its revolving chamber holding twenty-five rounds is not to be confused with the more familiar Henrys; there is no connection beyond the name.

Partnered with May's Surehand/Shatterhand character was a young Indian, first introduced to readers around 1892. Winnetou is a consistently brave and brainy Apache chief educated by a Christian tutor, hence receptive to the "civilized" ways of Europe, and the white man with whom he adventures.

The two heroes wandered all over the map of the West, meeting again and again by remarkable coincidence, and removing an untold number of malefactors. In one historical quarterly, a scholar did a body count of four representative May novels totaling 2,300 pages. The number of persons going to their rewards was 2,012. They were dispatched by shooting, scalping, knifing, drowning, poisoning—and sixty-one were put down by the "mighty fist" previously cited.

May had a fair grasp of Western geography, except in one respect. In addition to familiar settings of mountains and deserts, he repeatedly used "an impenetrable cactus forest"—exact location unspecified.

May's works have been translated into many languages but seldom, if at all, into English. Yet they've sold upwards of fifty million copies, and continue to sell. You find long shelves of May in almost every bookshop in Germany, just as you find long shelves of L'Amour throughout the United States.

At least thirty films have been made from May's novels. An entire publishing house devoted to them was founded in 1913. At summer encampments similar to those of American Civil War reenactors, mild-mannered fans gather in costume to act out the exploits of their two heroes. Now doctoral dissertations are being written about Karl May.

So it seemed fitting, and an enjoyable challenge, to pay respects to him with a story about a couple of Westerners who battle a decidedly rotten crew from a fur trust. The story takes place in what May sometimes called the Stony Mountains.

I have used variations of the names of his two leading characters, and kept the marvelous repeating Henry (reduced to an arbitrary five shots). Those are the only resemblances. Ironhand is not a "blond Teutonic superman who speaks a dozen languages fluently and lards his conversations with little sermons about God and Christianity."

Manitow is neither a chief nor an Apache. My intent was to create *un hommage* to an important figure in the literature of the West, not to write a pastiche of May's work, which I can't translate very well anyway with my rudimentary German. I wanted a story bathed in a diffuse pastel-colored mist, like a legend. A story not overly realistic. In short, the kind of western story someone might have written from afar.

One other note: The hymn Mr. Jaggers sings is reverse anachronism; it was composed years after the period of the story. But in context, the lyrics proved irresistible.

—J.J.

About the Authors

Presently Director of Texas Christian University Press, JUDY ALTER is the author of several novels, including *Libbie,* based on the life of Mrs. George Armstrong Custer, and the recently published *Jessie. Luke and the Van Zandt County War* (TCU Press) won the 1984 prize for juvenile literature from the Texas Institute of Letters, and *Mattie* (Doubleday, 1988) was named Best Western Novel of the Year by Western Writers of America, Inc. Her short story "Fool Girl" won a Western Heritage (Wrangler) Award from the National Cowboy Hall of Fame in 1993. She is a past president of Western Writers of America and currently secretary-treasurer of the Texas Institute of Letters. A native of Chicago, she holds an undergraduate degree from the University of Chicago and a Ph.D. in English, with a special interest in the literature of the American West, from Texas Christian University. A single parent of four now-grown children, she lists reading and cooking among her hobbies and likes to travel throughout the American West.

WIN BLEVINS brings authentic western flavor and style to his books and tales of America's last century. There's a laconic quality to his best work that reflects the times he writes about. Blevins has the same feel for his characters, who are always real, always individual, and always compelling. In the past few years, he has begun to build himself a real following among critics and readers alike. His books include *Give Your Heart to the Hawks* and *The High Missouri*.

ALBERT BUTLER has been a newspaper reporter, radio and TV copywriter, and has written two books for teenagers and five western/historical novels. He and his wife, Joan, live in Boise, Idaho, where he is presently at work on a long historical novel, *No Lion in the Path*. His books include *Get Judge Parker, Lockhart's Trail,* and *Three Rivers to Run*.

LENORE CARROLL's fiction is painted in many colors, some gentle, some not gentle at all. She has a particularly good sense of how people get along—or don't get along—in stressful moments, when the truth of them tends to come out. Her stories show us that there are many ways to re-create the old West—and the contemporary West, too. Lenore's is a provocative and singular literary voice.

LOREN D. ESTLEMAN may well be the best western novelist of his generation. Whether it is his masterpiece *Bloody Season* or his hardboiled and evocative Page Murdock series, Estleman is a formidable writer and stylist who accomplished more by age thirty-five than most writers accomplish in a lifetime. His growing number of fans will be happy to learn that after an absence of nearly ten years Page Murdock is returning to action. And Estleman hints that even larger historical western novels are also in the works.

JIM MARION ETTER, now of Oklahoma City, grew up during the 1930s and 1940s in the small eastern Oklahoma community of Oktaha, and since boyhood has loved storytelling flavored with the Old West and regional folklore. As a rural feature writer, he has roamed Oklahoma, mainly as a staff member of *The Oklahoman* newspaper, and some of Texas, where he has also lived. Books he has authored or co-authored include *Between Me & You & the Gatepost—Rural Expressions of Oklahoma, Daughters of the Land, The Salt of the Earth,* and *Oktaha, a Track in the Sand.* His articles have appeared in such magazines as *Persimmon Hill, Western Horseman, Cowboy, The Ketch Pen, Frontier Times, True West,* and *Oklahoma Today.* He rides his own horse regularly, and claims to have done "a little amateur rodeoin'."

RILEY FROH was born in Luling, Texas, where he grew up in the 1950s around ranch people very similar to the characters in his short story. He is descended from original settlers of the town. His great-grandfather drove cattle up the trails and his great-great-grandfather was a noted Texas Ranger. He holds a Bachelor's and a Master's degree from Southwest Texas State University and a Ph.D. from Texas A&M University, and presently teaches Texas history at San Jacinto College. He is the author of *Wildcatter Extraordinary, Edgar B. Davis and Sequences in Business Capitalism,* and several scholarly articles on Texas themes. He is married to Mary Binz of San Antonio, Texas, whose father was well known in the Alamo City as a horse trainer and trick rider. Their son, Noble King Froh, continues the cowboy tradition of both families.

ROBERT GLEASON is a consulting editor at Tor/Forge Books in New York. He is also an important writer of serious fiction both in and out of the western genre, as his current major novel, *The Wrath of God,* amply demonstrates. In western fiction, Gleason created the Jackson Cain cycle of novels, which take a balladic approach to the Old West of both myth and fact. Hopefully, these novels will be reissued soon. They fall on the ear like music, and are damned good reads besides. There is nothing else like them in all of western fiction.

Bill Pronzini said of ED GORMAN's Leo Guild westerns, "[They] have a haunting, almost mystical quality that lifts them to the brink of allegory." In addition to the five novels about bounty hunter Guild, Gorman has also written four other westerns, notably *Wolf Moon*, about which *Reflections* said, "If Jim Thompson had ever written a pure western, this would have been it." When Gorman submitted this story, he noted that he'd always wanted to write something for the 1940s pulp *Dime Western* and that this story would have been perfect for them.

MARTIN H. GREENBERG is a veteran anthologist who has edited or coedited over five hundred books—more than fifty of them in the western field, including *The Western Hall of Fame*, *The Arbor House Treasury of Great Western Stories*, and *In the Big Country*. He resides in Green Bay, Wisconsin.

After forty-five years in journalism, mostly as corporate communications specialist with such firms as Ford Motor Company in Ohio and Michigan and the NASA/Caltech Jet Propulsion Lab (JPL) in Pasadena, California, R. C. HOUSE "retired" at sixty-five to write westerns full-time. He has eleven novels and an Old West collectibles book published or in production, as well as an estimated two hundred magazine credits in short western fiction, book reviews, essays, columns, and articles on western history, collecting, and shooting muzzleloaders, and the hobby of "buckskinning." A member of Western Writers of America since 1976, he has been WWA president and editor of the association magazine, *Roundup*. An asteroid has been named for him, the tribute of its discoverer, a JPL astronomer and close friend, for his JPL contributions. The House family makes its home on acreage in rural Fallbrook, North San Diego County, California.

Americans love success stories, and few success stories—rags to riches, as it were—match that of JOHN JAKES. Following a long career in advertising, during which he wrote innumerable novels and short stories, in the mid-1970s Jakes was commissioned to write The American Bicentennial Series and very quickly became one of the world's bestselling authors. Jakes has written virtually every kind of fiction, and excelled at all of them, but the western seems to bring out his best work and most passionate feelings. He is particularly good with the characters common to the American frontier. "Manitow and Ironhand," which was written for this anthology, received the Western Heritage Award from the National Cowboy Hall of Fame for best western short story of 1994.

The transition may or may not have been inevitable, but TEDDY KELLER, who was born and raised in Kansas and lived for years in Colorado and New Mexico, gravitated naturally to the lives and legends of the West. His stories have appeared in many publications and have been anthologized and reprinted from Australia to Germany. He still feuds with editors who are certain that the Old West was unrelentingly earnest.

ELMER KELTON has brought realism, scope, depth, and almost operatic feeling to the serious novel of the West. He has chronicled the vagaries of his beloved Texas with a passion and fondness that imbue his work with humor, heart, and hard prairie wisdom. Among his many succesful novels are The Time It Never Rained, The Day the Cowboys Quit, The Good Old Boys, The Man Who Rode Midnight, Slaughter, and 1994's Spur Award-winning The Far Canyon. He is a seminal figure in western fiction.

ARTHUR WINFIELD KNIGHT has worked in a number of genres, veins, and styles, doing especially notable work with his reminiscences of significant people in the Beat literary movement of the late fifties and early sixties. He has a true sense of the Old West, and is able to convey it in prose that is always a pleasure to read.

RUTH WILLETT LANZA, born and raised in Oklahoma, has lived with her husband in Colorado since 1947. She attended Lindenwood College and Oklahoma University, and began writing seriously after raising six children. Specializing in southwestern history, her articles have appeared in regional and national magazines. Her short fiction placed first in a recent NLAPW State Contest and has been published in *American Humane Magazine* and *The Rampant Guinea Pig*. She's now at work on a novel, *A Vision in the Wind*, about the Ute Indians of Colorado. "The Leave-taking" was inspired by her maternal grandmother, who was an Oklahoma 89'er.

ELMORE LEONARD spent many years writing books that only a small audience was aware of. From his beginning in the pulps of the early 1950s, it was clear that Leonard had his own literary voice, and planned on doing things his own way. While he has become a worldwide bestseller known for his blackly comedic hardboiled crime stories, a number of critics feel that his best work has been done in the western genre—and such novels as *Hombre, Valdez Is Coming*, and *Gunsights* make it hard to dispute. The majority of readers seem to think he's a master of both genres, and that's probably a truer assessment.

JOHN D. NESBITT lives in the plains country of Wyoming. He teaches English and Spanish at Eastern Wyoming College in Torrington. His western stories have appeared in *Far West, Just Pulp*, and others; his modern West stories have appeared in *West Wind Review, American Literary Review*, and others. His fiction, nonfiction, poetry, and literary articles have appeared in numerous literary magazines. He has won many prizes and awards for his work, including a Wyoming Arts Council literary fellowship for his fiction writing. A western novel, *One-Eyed Cowboy Wild*, was published in 1994 by Walker and Company.

JOYCE ROACH is a three-time Spur Award Winner from Western Writers of America: nonfiction book, *The Cowgirls*; short nonfiction, "A High Toned Woman;" and short fiction, "Just As I Am," and was the recipient of the Texas Institute of Letters $5000 nonfiction book prize for *Eats: A Folk History of Texas Foods*. She has served as chairman of both the WWA Spur Awards and the Owen Wister Award.

GORDON D. SHIRREFFS is one of the grand old names of traditional (and not-so-traditional) western fiction. A particular favorite of paperback original readers, Shirreffs has spent many decades bringing resolute historical truth to the novel of the West, and doing so with high and colorful style. His many novels include *The Untamed Breed*, considered by many to be his masterpiece—and one of the true masterpieces of mountain man literature—*Showdown in Sonora, Gunswift* (as Stewart Gordon), and *Rio Desperado*.

"Frontier Birds" marks LINDA SPARKS's debut into the realm of fiction. After twenty-five years of service with the federal government, she followed her heart to the West. More than a hundred of her articles about dogs have appeared in specialized magazines, and in 1991 she was published in *Western Horseman*. That same year she decided to try her hand at fiction. Linda currently lives with her husband and five dogs in a log house in the Rockies. Her current project is a four-volume fictional history of the Ax T ranch and the four generations of Thorndikes and Burnums, who look back fondly on Cat and Harry Burnum.

DALE L. WALKER has distinguished himself both as a critic and a creator of serious and innovative western fiction. When the dust settles on our particular era of western stories, the reviews and criticism of Dale Walker will be among the work passed on to succeeding generations. His fiction will likely accompany his reviews because he applies his rigid critical standards to his own stories as well, as his story here demonstrates.

Bestselling author and lecturer MARIANNE WILLMAN has won both popular and critical acclaim for her work. She has published both fiction and nonfiction, including guest columns and book reviews for the *Detroit Free Press*, and her twelve historical novels have been sold in twenty-six countries around the globe. Her first western novel, *Pieces of Sky*, received the Reviewer's Choice Award and was named as one of the ten all-time best western historical romances by *Rave Reviews*. *Yesterday's Shadows* was also honored by the Reviewer's Choice Award, and Marianne was a contributor to the WWA anthology, *The West That Was*. She co-authored three screenplays currently in preproduction, and her newest novel, *The Court of Three Sisters*, was published by HarperCollins in April 1994.

An adjunct professor of political science at the University of Nevada in Reno, SALLY ZANJANI has published numerous articles on Nevada history and four nonfiction books. *The Ignoble Conspiracy: Radicalism on Trial in Nevada*, with Guy L. Rocha (1986), was largely responsible for posthumous pardons granted to Goldfield union radicals Morrie Preston and Joseph Smith in 1987, eighty years after their conviction. Her most recent book, *Goldfield: The Last Gold Rush on the Western Frontier* (1992), won the Westerners International Award.

Acknowledgments

INTRODUCTION COPYRIGHT © 1994 by John Jakes; "Hurrah for Capt. Early" copyright © 1994 by Elmore Leonard; "To Challenge a Legend" copyright © 1994 by Albert Butler; "Wildfire" copyright © 1994 by Marianne Willman; "The Death(s) of Billy the Kid" copyright © 1994 by Arthur Winfield Knight; "The Burial of Lettie Strayhorn" copyright © 1994 by Elmer Kelton; "The Day of the Rain" copyright © 1994 by Teddy Keller; "Sweet Revenge" copyright by Judy Alter; "Yearlings" copyright © 1994 by Jim Marion Etter; "Bloody Badge, Bloody Gun" copyright © 1994 by Robert Gleason; "Half a Day from Water" copyright © 1994 by Gordon D. Shirreffs; "We'll Kill the Old Red Rooster When She Comes" copyright © 1994 by R. C. House; "From Our Special Correspondent" copyright © 1994 by Dale L. Walker; "The Wedding Dress" copyright © 1994 by Win Blevins; "More Silent than the Male" copyright © 1994 by Riley Froh; "The Leave-taking" copyright © 1994 by Ruth Willett Lanza; "A Two-Gun Man" copyright © 1994 by Joyce Roach; "Reunion" copyright © 1994 by Lenore Carroll; "Spring Comes to the Widow" copyright © 1994 by John D. Nesbitt; "Iron Heart's Story" copyright © 1994 by Loren D. Estleman; "Frontier Birds" copyright © 1994 by Linda Sparks; "Long Ride Back" copyright © 1994 by Ed Gorman; "Making History" copyright © 1994 by Sally Zanjani; "Manitow and Ironhand" copyright © 1994 by John Jakes.